REDISCOVERY
Volume 2

Science Fiction by Women

(1953 – 1957)

Journey Press
journeypress.com

D1082548

Vista, California
Journey Press

Journey Press
P.O. Box 1932
Vista, CA 92085

Managing Editor: Gideon Marcus

Foreword © Janice L. Newman
Afterword essays © Lisa Yaszek, Andi Dukleth, Erica L. Frank, Jessica Dickinson
Goodman, Christine Sandquist, Marie Vibbert, Cat Rambo, Gwyn Conaway, Robin
Rose Graves, Janice L. Newman, Ntalie Devitt, Kerrie Dougherty, Laura Brodian
Freas Beraha, Erica Friedman, Kathryn Heffner, Cora Buhlert, Lorelei Esther, Alyssa
Winans, T. D. Cloud

"The Piece Thing" appears by permission of the Carol Emshwiller estate. "Change the
Sky" and "The Wines of Earth" appear by permission of the Margaret St. Clair estate.
"Moonshine" appears by permission of the Ruth M. Goldsmith estate.

According to U.S. copyright law, works published from 1923 through 1963 receive
95 years of protection if renewed during their 28th year. Extensive research did not
reveal the remaining selections included in this anthology to hold a renewed U.S.
copyright. They are believed to be in the public domain in the United States.

ART CREDITS
Cover art: Frank Kelly Freas — Cover of *The Magazine of Fantasy and Science
Fiction*, September 1956, used by permission
Cover design: Christine Sandquist

First Printing January 2022

ISBN: 978-1-951320-18-8

Published in the United States of America

To Dr. Lisa Yaszek, who is keeping the light of discovery alive!

Acknowledgments

This second volume in the Rediscovery series would not have been possible without the help of our reader team, who read virtually every woman-penned science fiction/fantasy story from the mid-'50s. Thank you Kris Vyas-Myall, Jason Sacks, Erica Frank, Katie Heffner, and Cora Buhlert for your tremendous work finding the very best stories.

Special thanks go to Christine Sandquist for her lovely cover design and to Dr. Laura Brodian Freas Beraha for licensing Kelly Freas' art.

Note:
Pursuant to feedback on the last volume, we have put the introductions after the stories. Which really makes them afterwords instead of introductions, but we like our tagline, "Yesterday's luminaries introduced by today's rising stars" too much to change it!

Contents

Foreword

When did women start writing science fiction?

If you ask some people this question, they'll tell you that women started to break into science fiction around the time of Ursula K. LeGuin or Octavia Butler. If you ask others, they'll claim that the dearth of women writing in science fiction in the past is exaggerated, that plenty of women were publishing stories, and that they've always been equal "partners in wonder".

Many modern readers ignore science fiction entirely if it was published before, say, 1980 or 1990, or some other arbitrary year after which science fiction supposedly suddenly became more diverse and less of a straight white men's club.

The truth is, as always, more complicated than any simple reduction. The number of women writing and publishing science fiction has both waxed and waned ever since the genre became a recognized genre, and even before—as any SF historian will be quick to tell you, Mary Shelley's "Frankenstein" is now widely recognized as the 'first' science fiction novel.

So many factors contributed, and still contribute, to the waning of women publishing science fiction at any given time that it's impossible to point to a single one. Was it for cultural reasons? Political? Economic? Personal? All of these together? None of them? Every woman had her own reasons for writing or not writing, for sharing or not sharing that work with a publisher. Every publisher had his—or her—reasons for accepting or not accepting any given piece.

But even if we can't say *why* particular trends occur, we can say with certainty that such trends exist. The proportion of women to men published in science fiction magazines in the mid fifties tended to be about 1 in 10 on average.

These stories often stood out from the other 90% in interesting ways. While some women wrote space opera adventures or technical science fiction in the same vein as their masculine counterparts (e.g. Leigh Brackett, Andre Norton), many women wrote about things that they experienced in their day to day lives.

Stories by women envisioned other kinds of realities, and not always happy ones. Though they share some of the same fears with the male writers of the time, fears like nuclear annihilation, their 'if this goes on' extrapolations also include ideas like ubiquitous and unavoidable advertising, door to door salesmen who have to be fought off by increasingly violent means, and worlds where children encounter beauty or horror far beyond their understanding. Whereas stories by men often projected a future that was both an extension of the present and a power fantasy: a world where men populated positions of power even on spaceships and women existed as helpmates, cooks, and, in the more unpleasant stories, as the mens' sexual relief.

Male authors rarely included children in their stories—unless it was a story written for and about children: the 'juveniles' which almost invariably focused on a brilliant (white) boy's adventures on earth and into space. Stories by women of the time are a sharp contrast. Over half of the stories in this volume include children, and this sample is representative. Sometimes the children are only tangentially involved, family members who are simply caught up in the situation. Sometimes the children are more important, yet still background characters. And sometimes the stories center around a child's experiences, but not at all the way the juveniles did. These are not stories *for* children. They are stories *about* children, meant to be viewed with adult eyes and interpreted through an adult's understanding of the world. Even stories about aliens often explore the inner lives of children and their relationship to the world around them.

Another prominent theme is the idea of relationships between men and women. Far from the simplified version so often seen in the male-penned stories of the day, where the sole female character is both goal and reward in one but never actually *refuses* the protagonist's advances, the relationships in women-penned stories are often fraught. Fascinatingly, they are as likely to be written from a male point of view as a female one, touching on vulnerabilities and doubts that men of the fifties couldn't, or didn't dare express, even in fiction. Whether the main character is male or female, the traditional 'happy-ending', with the main-character male and his woman marrying and living 'happily ever after', isn't inevitable in these works. Even when the story does end in a happy relationship, there is often an element of parody or satire woven into the fabric of the piece, with the reader left to wonder, a little uncomfortably, if the characters really are happy, or if they are simply accepting the best option available or doing their best in a world over which they have very little control—conditions that would have been familiar to women of the time.

The fact that women's stories had a different, often domestic focus was derided by some. SF that concentrated on themes normally ignored by the magazines and book publishers of the time, domestic themes that reflected the day to day life and societal expectations placed on women, was given the derogatory nickname of 'diaper fiction'. Yet this so-called diaper fiction was and is refreshing and exciting to read precisely because it *is* different. In a plethora of stories about spaceships crewed by ten white men and one woman, speculative stories with a contrasting focus are a breath of fresh air.

Women have always been a part of science fiction's history, and while science fiction stories by women were neither as common as some would have you believe, neither were they so rare as some claim. As the stories collected herein prove, Joanna Russ and Anne McCaffrey were not born in a vacuum, and good, diverse, interesting science fiction did not suddenly begin in 1980, 1990, or at the beginning of the new millennium. Join us in Rediscovering these stories and you'll be surprised at how many of them resonate with the world of today.

—Janice L. Newman
December 2021

Games

by Katherine MacLean

(Originally appeared in the March 1953 issue of *Galaxy*. It has not been available in print since 2011.)

Ronny was playing by himself, which meant he was two tribes of Indians having a war.

"Bang," he muttered, firing an imaginary rifle. He decided that it was a time in history before the white people had sold the Indians any guns, and changed the rifle into a bow. "Wizz*thunk*," he substituted, mimicking from an Indian film on TV the graphic sound of an arrow striking flesh.

"Oof." He folded down onto the grass, moaning, "Uhhhooh…" and relaxing into defeat and death.

"Want some chocolate milk, Ronny?" asked his mother's voice from the kitchen.

"No, thanks," he called back, climbing to his feet to be another man. "Wizzthunk, wizzthunk," he added to the flights of arrows as the best archer in the tribe. "Last arrow. Wizzzz," he said, missing one enemy for realism. He addressed another battling brave. "Who has more arrows? They are coming too close. No time—I'll have to use my knife." He drew the imaginary knife, ducking an arrow as it shot close.

Then he was the tribal chief standing somewhere else, and he saw that the warriors left alive were outnumbered.

"We must retreat. We cannot leave our tribe without warriors to protect the women."

Ronny decided that the chief was heroically wounded, his voice wavering from weakness. He had been propping himself against a tree to appear unharmed, but now he moved so that his braves could see he was pinned to the trunk by an arrow and could not walk. They cried out.

He said, "Leave me and escape. But remember…" No words came, just the feeling of being what he was, a dying old eagle, a chief of warriors, speaking to young warriors who would need advice of seasoned humor and moderation to carry them through their young battles. He had to finish the sentence, tell them something wise.

Ronny tried harder, pulling the feeling around him like a cloak of resignation and pride, leaning indifferently against the tree where the arrow had pinned him, hearing dimly in anticipation the sound of his aged voice conquering weakness to speak wisely of what they needed to be told. They had many battles ahead of them, and the battles would be against odds, with so many dead already.

They must watch and wait, be flexible and tenacious, determined and persistent — but not too rash, subtle and indirect — not cowardly, and above all be patient with the triumph of the enemy and not maddened into suicidal direct attack.

His stomach hurt with the arrow wound, and his braves waited to hear his words. He had to sum a part of his life's experience in words. Ronny tried harder to build the scene realistically. Then suddenly it was real. He was the man.

He was an old man, guide and adviser in an oblique battle against great odds. He was dying of something and his stomach hurt with a knotted ache, like hunger, and he was thirsty. He had refused to let the young men make the sacrifice of trying to rescue him. He was hostage in the jail and dying, because he would not surrender to the enemy nor cease to fight them. He smiled and said, "Remember to live like other men, but — remember to remember."

And then he was saying things that could not be put into words, complex feelings that were ways of taking bad situations that made them easier to smile at, and then sentences that were not sentences, but single alphabet letters pushing each other with signs, with a feeling of being connected like two halves of a swing, one side moving up when the other moved down, or like swings or like cogs and pendulums inside a clock, only without the cogs, just with the push.

It wasn't adding or multiplication, and it used letters instead of numbers, but Ronny knew it was some kind of arithmetic.

And he wasn't Ronny.

He was an old man, teaching young men, and the old man did not know about Ronny. He thought sadly how little he would be able to convey to the young men, and he remembered more, trying to sum long memories and much living into a few direct thoughts. And Ronny was the old man and himself, both at once.

It was too intense. Part of Ronny wanted to escape and be alone, and that part withdrew and wanted to play something. Ronny sat in the grass and played with his toes like a much younger child.

Part of Ronny that was Doctor Revert Purcell sat on the edge of a prison cot, concentrating on secret unpublished equations of biogenic stability which he wanted to pass on to the responsible hands of young researchers in the concealed-research chain. He was using the way of thinking which they had told him was the telepathic sending of ideas to anyone ready to receive. It was odd that he himself could never tell when he was sending. Probably a matter of age. They had started trying to teach him when he was already too old for anything so different.

The water tap, four feet away, was dripping steadily, and it was hard for Purcell to concentrate, so intense was his thirst. He wondered if he could gather strength to walk that far. He was sitting up and that was good, but the struggle to raise himself that far had left him dizzy and trembling. If he tried to stand, the effort would surely interrupt his transmitting of equations and all the data he had not sent yet.

Would the man with the keys who looked in the door twice a day care whether Purcell died with dignity? He was the only audience, and his expression never changed when Purcell asked him to point out to the authorities that he was not being given anything to eat. It was funny to Purcell to find that he wanted the respect of any audience to his dying, even of a man without response who treated him as if he were already a corpse.

Perhaps the man would respond if Purcell said, "I have changed my mind. I will tell."

But if he said that, he would lose his own respect.

At the biochemists' and bio-physicists' convention, the reporter had asked him if any of his researches could be applied to warfare.

He had answered with no feeling of danger, knowing that what he did was common practice among research men, sure that it was an unchallengeable right.

"Some of them can, but those I keep to myself."

The reporter remained dead-pan. "For instance?"

"Well, I have to choose something that won't reveal how it's done now, but—ah—for example, a way of cheaply mass-producing specific antitoxins against any germ. It sounds harmless if you don't think about it, but actually it would make germ warfare the most deadly and inexpensive weapon yet developed, for it would make it possible to prevent the backspread of contagion into a country's own troops, without much expense. There would be hell to pay if anyone ever let that out." Then he had added, trying to get the reporter

3

to understand enough to change his cynical unimpressed expression, "You understand, germs are cheap — there would be a new plague to spread every time some pipsqueak biologist mutated a new germ. It isn't even expensive or difficult, as atom bombs are."

The headline was: "Scientist Refuses to Give Secret of Weapon to Government."

Government men came and asked him if this was correct, and on having it confirmed pointed out that he had an obligation. The research foundations where he had worked were subsidized by government money. He had been deferred from military service during his early years of study and work so he could become a scientist, instead of having to fight or die on the battlefield.

"This might be so," he had said. "I am making an attempt to serve mankind by doing as much good and as little damage as possible. If you don't mind, I'd rather use my own judgment about what constitutes service."

The statement seemed too blunt the minute he had said it, and he recognized that it had implications that his judgment was superior to that of the government. It probably was the most antagonizing thing that could have been said, but he could see no other possible statement, for it represented precisely what he thought.

There were bigger headlines about that interview, and when he stepped outside his building for lunch the next day, several small gangs of patriots arrived with the proclaimed purpose of persuading him to tell. They fought each other for the privilege.

The police had rescued him after he had lost several front teeth and had one eye badly gouged. They then left him to the care of the prison doctor in protective custody. Two days later, after having been questioned several times on his attitude toward revealing the parts of his research he had kept secret, he was transferred to a place that looked like a military jail, and left alone. He was not told what his status was.

When someone came and asked him questions about his attitude, Purcell felt quite sure that what they were doing to him was illegal. He stated that he was going on a hunger strike until he was allowed to have visitors and see a lawyer.

The next time the dinner hour arrived, they gave him nothing to eat. There had been no food in the cell since, and that was probably two weeks ago. He was not sure just how long, for during part of the second week his memory had become garbled. He dimly remembered something that might have been delirium, which could have lasted more than one day.

Perhaps the military who wanted the antitoxins for germ warfare were waiting quietly for him either to talk or die.

Ronny got up from the grass and went into the kitchen, stumbling in his walk like a beginning toddler.

"Choc-mil?" he said to his mother.

She poured him some and teased gently, "What's the matter, Ronny—back to baby-talk?"

He looked at her with big solemn eyes and drank slowly, not answering.

In the cell somewhere distant, Dr. Purcell, famous biochemist, began waveringly trying to rise to his feet, unable to remember hunger as anything separate from him that could ever be ended, but weakly wanting a glass of water. Ronny could not feed him with the chocolate milk. Even though this was another himself, the body that was drinking was not the one that was thirsty.

He wandered out into the backyard again, carrying the glass.

"Bang," he said deceptively, pointing with his hand in case his mother was looking. "Bang." Everything had to seem usual; he was sure of that. This was too big a thing, and too private, to tell a grownup.

On the way back from the sink, Dr. Purcell slipped and fell and hit his head against the edge of the iron cot. Ronny felt the edge gashing through skin and into bone, and then a relaxing blankness inside his head, like falling asleep suddenly when they are telling you a fairy story while you want to stay awake to find out what happened next.

"Bang," said Ronny vaguely, pointing at a tree. "Bang." He was ashamed because he had fallen down in the cell and hurt his head and become just Ronny again before he had finished sending out his equations. He tried to make believe he was alive again, but it didn't work.

You could never make-believe anything to a real good finish. They never ended neatly—there was always something unfinished, and something that would go right on after the end.

It would have been nice if the jailers had come in and he had been able to say something noble to them before dying, to show that he was brave.

"Bang," he said randomly, pointing his finger at his head, and then jerked his hand away as if it had burned him. He had become the wrong person that time. The feel of a bullet jolting the side of his head was startling and unpleasant, even if not real, and the flash of someone's vindictive anger and self-pity while pulling a trigger… *My wife will be sorry she ever…* He didn't like that kind of make-believe. It felt unsafe to do it without making up a story first.

Ronny decided to be Indian braves again. They weren't very real, and when they were, they had simple straightforward emotions about courage and skill and pride and friendship that he would like.

A man was leaning his arms on the fence, watching him. "Nice day." *What's the matter, kid, are you an esper?*

"Hul-lo." Ronny stood on one foot and watched him. *Just making believe. I only want to play. They make it too serious, having all these troubles.*

"Good countryside." The man gestured at the back yards, all opened in together with tangled bushes here and there to crouch behind, when other kids were there to play hide and seek, and with trees to climb. *It can be the Universe if you pick and choose who to be, and don't let wrong choices make you shut off from it. You can make yourself learn from this if you are strong enough. Who have you been?*

Ronny stood on the other foot and scratched the back of his leg with his toes. He didn't want to remember. He always forgot right away, but this grownup was confident and young and strong-looking, and meant something when he talked, not like most grownups.

"I was playing Indian." *I was an old chief, captured by enemies, trying to pass on to other warriors the wisdom of my life before I died.* He made believe he was the chief a little to show the young man what he was talking about.

"Purcell!" The man drew in his breath between his teeth, and his face paled. He pulled back from reaching Ronny with his feelings, like holding his breath in. "Good game." *You can learn from him. Don't leave him shut off, I beg you. You can let him influence you without being pulled off your own course. He was a good man. You were honored, and I envy the man you will be if you contacted him on resonant similarities.*

The grownup looked frightened. *But you are too young. You'll block him out and lose him. Kids have to grow and learn at their own speed.*

Then he looked less afraid, but uncertain, and his thoughts struggled against each other. *Their own speed. But there should be someone alive with Purcell's pattern and memories. We loved him. Kids should grow at their own speed, but… How strong are you, Ronny? Can you move ahead of the normal growth pattern?*

Grownups always want you to do something. Ronny stared back, clenching his hands and moving his feet uneasily.

The thoughts were open to him. *Do you want to be the old chief again, Ronny? Be him often, so you can learn to know what he knew? (And feel as he felt. It would be a stiff dose for a kid.) It will be rich and exciting, full of memories and skills. (But hard to chew. I'm doing this for Purcell, Ronny, not for you. You have to make up your own mind.)*

"That was a good game. Are you going to play it any more?"

His mother would not like it. She would feel the difference in him, as much as if he had read one of the books she kept away from him, books that were supposed to be for adults only. The difference would hurt her. He was being bad, like eating between meals. But to know what grownups knew…

He tightened his fists and looked down at the grass. "I'll play it some more."

The young man smiled, still pale and holding half his feelings back behind a dam. *Then mesh with me a moment. Let me in.*

He was in with the thought, feeling Ronny's confused consent, reassuring him by not thinking or looking around inside while sending out a single call, *Purcell, Doc,* that found the combination key to Ronny's guarded yesterdays and last nights and ten minutes agos. *Ronny, I'll set that door, Purcell's memories, open for you. You can't close it, but feel like this about it* — and he planted in a strong set, *questioning, cool, open, a feeling of absorbing without words…it will give information when you need it, like a dictionary.*

The grownup straightened away from the fence, preparing to walk off. Behind a dam pressed grief and anger for the death of the man he called Purcell.

"And any time you want to *be* the old chief, at any age he lived, just make believe you are him."

Grief and anger pressed more strongly against the dam, and the man turned and left rapidly, letting his thoughts flicker and scatter through private memories that Ronny did not share, that no one shared, breaking thought contact with everyone so that the man could be alone in his own mind to have his feelings in private.

Ronny picked up the empty glass that had held his chocolate milk from the back steps where he had left it and went inside. As he stepped into the kitchen, he knew what another kitchen had looked like for a five-year-old child who had been Purcell ninety years ago. There had been an iron sink, and a brown-and-green-spotted faucet, and the glass had been heavier and transparent, like real glass.

Ronny reached up and put the colored plastic tumbler down.

"That was a nice young man, dear. What did he say to you?"

Ronny looked up at his mamma, comparing her with the remembered mamma of fifty years ago. He loved the other one, too.

"He tol' me he's glad I play Indian."

Afterword by Lisa Yaszek

"Games" first appeared in the March 1953 issue of *Galaxy* magazine, a popular midcentury science fiction periodical known for publishing social satire. And indeed, MacLean's tale is very much in line with the new subgenre of mutant or "slan" stories introduced by A.E. Van Vogt in his eponymous 1949 novel and popularized by women writers including Zenna Henderson and Wilmar Shiras. Like her counterparts, MacLean uses her story of gifted but persecuted mutants to critique the Cold War rage for conformity. However, while Henderson and Shiras tempered their critiques by telling their stories from the perspective of "normal" adult teachers who heroically protect their young proteges from the hostile forces around them, MacLean writes from the perspective of the mutant child himself, using her tale to directly illuminate the cost of American manifest destiny. What begins seemingly as suburban idyll, in which a young boy whiles away his afternoon playing games of pretend, turns out to be a horror story. Our young hero's natural ability to feel the pain and anger of indigenous people brutally removed from their lands by white colonists triggers a psychic connection to a modern-day scientist, who is tortured and killed by the American government for refusing to share knowledge that might be weaponized. Ever the social scientist, MacLean is careful to depict the physical and psychic toll this experience takes upon her little hero in the kind of heart-rending detail that would not be replicated until Orson Scott Card's *Ender's Game* over two decades later. As such, MacLean's "Games" reminds us that imaginative play is a kind of serious fun that shapes the future just as decisively as any science or technology.

Katherine Anne MacLean was born on January 22, 1925 in Glen Ridge, New Jersey. She was the daughter of chemical engineer Gordon MacLean and homemaker Ruth (Crawford) MacLean, who raised her along with two older brothers in Flushing, New York. MacLean studied math and science in high school while working a range of jobs including "nurse's aide, store detective, pollster, econ graph-analyst, antibiotic lab researcher, food factory quality controller, office manager, payroll bookkeeper, college teacher, reporter." As an economics undergraduate at Barnard in the late 1940s, she worked as a technician in a food laboratory, an experience which helped cultivate her interest in technology and science fiction.

MacLean published her first short story, "Defense Mechanism," in the October 1949 issue of *Astounding Science Fiction* while still at Barnard. After a brief marriage to Charles Dye (1951–53), she married David Mason, with whom she had a son in 1957. MacLean published her first novel, *Unclean Sacrifice*, in 1958, followed by *Cosmic Checkmate* in 1962 (co-authored with Charles V. De Vet). She released her first collection of short stories, *The Diploids*, that same year. In the late 1960s, MacLean moved to Maine to care for her invalid mother. She continued to write novels through the mid 1970s, including *Trouble with Treaties* (1972) and *The Missing Man* (1975), based on her 1972 Nebula Award-winning novella of the same name. In 1979 she published a second collection, *The Trouble with You Earth People*, and married fellow science fiction author Carl P. West, with whom she co-authored *Dark Wing* (1979). During this period, she taught literature and creative writing at the University of Maine, the University of Connecticut, and the Free University of Portland. MacLean died on September 1, 2019, at the age of 94.

The quality of MacLean's work has long been recognized by the science fiction community. Influenced by her undergraduate study of economics and her post-graduate work in psychology, MacLean helped pioneer a new mode of science fiction that used the soft sciences to understand the impact of hard sciences on society and individuals alike, thus anticipating one of the central techniques of New Wave science fiction. In 1962, fellow author and editor Damon Knight noted that "as a science fiction writer, [MacLean] has few peers". She was the professional Guest of Honor at the first feminist science fiction convention, WisCon, in 1977, and in 2003 she was honored by the Science Fiction Writers of America as Author Emeritus. In 2011, MacLean received the Cordwainer Smith Rediscovery Award.

And, in a lovely coincidence, MacLean has headed both this and the first books in the *Rediscovery* series. It is a fitting tribute to one of science fiction's more noteworthy creators.

Captive Audience
by Ann Warren Griffith

(Originally appeared in the August 1953 issue of *The Magazine of Fantasy and Science Fiction*. It has not been in print in English since 1977.)

Mavis Bascom read the letter hastily and passed it across the breakfast table to her husband, Fred, who read the first paragraph and exclaimed, "She'll be here this afternoon!" but neither Mavis nor the two children heard him because the cereal box was going "Boom! Boom!" so loudly. Presently it stopped and the bread said urgently, "One good slice deserves another! How about another slice all round, eh, Mother?" Mavis put four slices into the toaster, and then there was a brief silence. Fred wanted to discuss the impending visit, but his daughter Kitty got in ahead of him, saying,

"Mom, it's my turn to choose the next cereal, and this shot-from-a-cannon stuff is almost gone. Will you take me to the store this afternoon?"

"Yes, dear, of course. I must admit I'll be glad when this box is gone. 'Boom, boom, boom,' that's all it ever says. And some of the others have such nice songs and jingles. I don't see whyever you picked it, Billy."

Billy was about to answer when his father's cigarette package interrupted, "Yessir, time to light up a Chesterfield! Time to enjoy that first mild, satisfying smoke of the day."

Fred lit a cigarette and said angrily, "Mavis, you know I don't like you to say such things in front of the children. It's a perfectly good commercial, and when you cast reflections on one, you're undermining all of them. I won't have you confusing these kids!"

"I'm sorry, Fred," was all Mavis had time to answer, because the salt box began a long and technically very interesting talk on iodization.

Since Fred had to leave for the office before the talk was over, he telephoned back to Mavis about her grandmother's visit. "Mavis," he said, "she can't stay with us! You'll have to get her out just as soon as possible."

"All right, Fred. I don't think she'll stay very long anyway. You know she doesn't like visiting us anymore than you like having her."

"Well, the quicker she goes the better. If anybody down here finds out about her I'll be washed up with MV the same day!"

"Yes, Fred, I know. I'll do the best I can."

Fred had been with the Master Ventriloquism Corporation of America for fifteen years. His work had been exceptional in every respect and, unless word leaked out about Mavis' grandmother, he could expect to remain with it for the rest of his life. He had enjoyed every step of the way from office boy to his present position as Assistant Vice-President in Charge of Sales, though he sometimes wished he could have gone into the technical end of it. Fascinating, those huge batteries of machines pouring out their messages to the American people. It seemed to him almost miraculous, the way the commercials were broadcast into thin air and picked up by the tiny discs embedded in the bottle or can or box or whatever wrapping contained the product, but he knew it involved some sort of electronic process that he couldn't understand. Such an incredibly complex process, yet unfailingly accurate! He had never heard of the machines making a mistake; never, for instance, had they thrown a shoe polish commercial so that it came out of a hair tonic bottle. Intrigued though he was by the mechanical intricacies of Master Ventriloquism, however, he had no head for that sort of thing, and was content to make his contribution in the sales end.

And quite a contribution it was. Already in the two short years since his promotion to Assistant Vice-President he had signed up two of the toughest clients that had ever been brought into the MV camp. First had been the telephone company, now one of the fattest accounts on the Corporation's books. They had held out against MV for years, until he, Fred, hit upon the idea that sold them — a simple message to come from every telephone, at fifteen-minute intervals throughout the MV broadcasting day, reminding people to look in the directory before dialing information. After the telephone company coup, Fred became known around the Corporation as a man to watch. He hadn't rested on his laurels. He had, if anything, topped his telephone performance. MV had pretty much given up hope of selling its services to the dignified, the conservative New York *Times*.

But Fred went ahead and did it. He'd kept the details a secret from Mavis. She'd see it for the first time tomorrow morning. Tomorrow morning! Damn! Grandmother would be here. You could bet she'd make some crack and spoil the whole thing.

Fred honestly didn't know if he would have gone ahead and married Mavis if he'd known about her grandmother.

For the sad fact of the matter was that Grandmother had never adjusted to MV. She was the only person he and Mavis knew who still longed for the "good old days," as she called them, the days before MV, and she yapped about them *ad nauseam*. She and her "A man's home is his castle" — if he'd heard her say it once he'd heard her say it 500 times. Unfortunately, it wasn't just that Grandmother was a boring old fool who refused to keep up with the times. The sadder fact of the matter was that she had broken the law, and today was finishing a five-year prison term. Did any other man here at MV have such a cross to bear?

Again and again he and Mavis had warned Grandmother that her advanced years would not keep her from being clapped into jail, and they hadn't. She'd gone absolutely wild on the day the Supreme Court had handed down the Earplug Decision. It was the climax of a long and terribly costly fight by the MV Corporation. The sale of earplugs had grown rapidly during the years MV was expanding, and just at a peak period, when MV had over 3,000 accounts, National Earplug Associates, Inc. had boldly staged a country-wide campaign advertising earplugs as the last defense against MV. The success of the campaign was such that the Master Ventriloquism Corporation found itself losing hundreds of accounts. MV sued immediately and the case dragged through the courts for years. Judges had a hard time making up their minds. Some sections of the press twaddled about "captive audiences." The MV Corporation felt reasonably certain that the Supreme Court justices were sensible men, but with its very existence at stake there was nerve-wracking suspense until the decision was made. National Earplug Associates, Inc. was found guilty of Restraint of Advertising, and earplugs were declared unconstitutional.

Grandmother, who was visiting Fred and Mavis at the time, hit the ceiling. She exhausted herself and them with her tirades, and swore that never never never would she give up her earplugs.

MV's representatives in Washington soon were able to get Congress to put teeth into the Supreme Court's decision, and eventually, just as Fred and Mavis predicted, Grandmother joined the ridiculous band who went to jail for violating the law prohibiting the use or possession of earplugs.

That was some skeleton for anybody, let alone an executive of MV, to have in his closet! Luckily, it had, up to now, remained in the closet, for at no time during her trial or afterwards did Grandmother mention having a relative who worked for the Corporation. But they had been lulled into a false sense of security. They assumed that Grandmother would die before finishing her prison term and that the problem of Grandmother was, therefore, solved. Now they were faced with it all over again. How were they going to keep her from shooting off her mouth before their friends and neighbors? How persuade her to go away and live in some distant spot?

Fred's secretary broke in on these worrisome thoughts, bringing him an unusually large batch of morning mail. "Seems there's kind of an unfavorable reaction to the new Pratt's Airotsac campaign. Forty-seven letters of protest already — read 'em and weep," she said saucily, and returned to her own office.

Fred picked a letter out of the pile and read:

> Dear Sirs,
>
> Like most mothers, I give my baby Pratt's Airotsac every time she cries for it. For the past few days, however, it has seemed to me that she has cried for it much more often than usual. Then I heard about the new Pratt's Airotsac commercial, and caught on that part of the time it wasn't my baby but the MV baby crying. I think it's a very cute idea, but am wondering if you could possibly use another baby because the one you have now sounds so much like mine and I cannot tell them apart so that I do not know when my baby is actually crying for Pratt's Airotsac and when it's the MV baby.
>
> Thanking you in advance for anything you can do about this, and with all good wishes for your continued success, I am,
>
> Mrs. Mona P. Hayes.

Fred groaned and flipped through some of the other letters. The story was the same — mothers not knowing whether it was their own baby or the MV baby and consequently confused as to when to administer the medicine. Dopes! Why didn't they have sense enough to put the Airotsac bottle at the other end of the house from the baby, and then they could tell by the direction the sound came from whether it was a bona fide baby or an advertising baby! Well, he'd have to figure out some way to change it, since many of the letters reported babies getting sick from overdoses. The Master Ventriloquism Corporation certainly didn't want to be responsible for that sort of thing.

Underneath the 47 complaints was a memo from the Vice-President in Charge of Sales, congratulating Fred on his brilliant handling of the New York *Times*. Ordinarily, this would have made it a red-letter day, but what with Grandmother and Pratt's, Fred's day was already ruined.

Mavis' day was not going well, either.

She felt uneasy, out-of-sorts, and in the lull between the Breakfast Commercials and the Cleaning Commercials she tried to analyze her feelings. It must be Grandmother. Perhaps it was true, as Fred said, that Grandmother was a bad influence. It wasn't that she was *right*. Mavis believed in Fred, because he was her husband, and believed in the MV Corporation, because it was the largest corporation in the entire United States. Nevertheless, it upset her when Fred and Grandmother argued, as they almost always did when they were together.

Anyway, maybe this time Grandmother wouldn't be so troublesome. Maybe jail had taught her how wrong it was to try to stand in the way of progress. On this hopeful note her thinking ended, for the soap powder box cried out, "Good morning, Mother! What say we go after those breakfast dishes and give our hands a beauty treatment at the same time? You know, Mother, no other soap gives you a beauty treatment *while* you wash your dishes. Only So-Glow, So-Glow, right here on your shelf, waiting to help *you*. So let's begin, shall we?"

While washing the dishes, Mavis was deciding what dessert to prepare. She'd bought several new ones the day before, and now they all sounded so good she couldn't make up her mind which to use first. The commercial for the canned apple pie ingredients was a little playlet, about a husband coming home at the end of a long hard day, smelling the apple pie, rushing out to the kitchen, sweeping his wife off her feet, kissing her and saying, "That's my girl!" It sounded promising to Mavis, especially when the announcer said any housewife who got to work right this minute and prepared that apple pie could be almost certain of getting that reaction from her husband.

Then there was a cute jingle from the devil's-food cake mix, sung by a trio of girls' voices with a good swing band in the background. If she'd made the mistake of buying only one box, it said, she ought to go out and buy another before she started baking because one of these luscious devil's-food cakes would not be enough for her hungry family. It was peppy and made Mavis feel better. She checked her shelves and, finding she had only one box, jotted it down on her shopping list.

Next, from the gingerbread mix box, came a homey type commercial that hit Mavis all wrong with its: "MMMMMMMMM, yes! Just like Grandmother used to make!"

After listening to several more, she finally decided to use a can of crushed pineapple. "It's quick! It's easy! Yes, Mother, all you do is chill and serve." That was what she needed, feeling the way she did.

She finished the dishes and was just leaving the kitchen when the floor wax bottle called out, "Ladies, look at your floors! You know that others judge you by your floors. Are you proud of yours? Are they ready—spotless and gleaming for the most discerning friend who might drop in?" Mavis looked at her floors. Definitely, they needed attention. She gave them a hasty going over with the quick-drying wax, grateful, as she so often was, to MV for reminding her.

In rapid succession, then, MV announced that now it was possible to polish her silverware to a higher, brighter polish than ever before; wondered if she weren't perhaps guilty of "H.O. — Hair Odor," and shouldn't perhaps wash her hair before her husband came home; told her at three different times to relax with a glass of cola; suggested that she had been neglecting her nails and might profit from a new coat of enamel; asked her to give a thought to her windows; and reminded her that her home permanent neutralizer would lose its wonderful effectiveness the longer it was kept. By early afternoon she had done the silver and the windows, given herself a shampoo and a manicure, determined to give Kitty a home permanent that very afternoon, and was full of cola. But she was exhausted.

It *was* a responsibility to be the wife of an MV executive. You had to be sort of an example to the rest of the community. Only sometimes she got so tired! Passing the bathroom, she was attracted by a new bottle of pills that Fred had purchased. It was saying, "You know, folks, this is the time of day when you need a lift. Yessir, if you're feeling listless, tired, run down, put some iron back in your backbone! All you do is take off my top, take out one tablet, swallow it, and feel your strength return!" Mavis was about to do so when an aspirin bottle called out, "I go to work instantly!" and then another aspirin bottle (Why *did* Fred keep buying new ones before they'd finished up the old ones? It made things so confusing!) said, "I go to work twice as fast!" Aspirin, Mavis suddenly realized, was what she needed. She had a splitting headache, but heavens, how did one know which to take? One of each seemed the only fair solution.

When the children came home from school, Kitty refused to have her hair permanented until her mother took her to the store, as promised. Mavis felt almost unable to face it. What was it Grandmother used to call their supermarket? Hell on earth, hell on wheels, something like that. Mavis, of course, understood that simultaneous MV messages were necessary in the stores in order to give every product a chance at its share of the consumer dollar, but just this afternoon she did wish she could skip it.

Having promised, though, there was nothing to do but get it over with. Billy had to come along too, naturally — both the children loved visiting the supermarket more than most anything else. They made their way down the aisles through a chorus of "Try me... Try me... Here is the newer, creamier... Mother, your children will... Kiddies, ask Mom to pick the bright green and red package... Here I am, right here, the shortening all your friends have been telling you about...

Billy listened to as many as he could while they were passing by, and for the thousandth time wished that he could hear the store-type commercials at home. Why, some of them were just as good as the home-type! He always tried to talk the supermarket checkers out of tearing off the Buy-Me-Discs, but they always grumbled that them was their orders and they didn't have no time to bother with him. That was one of the reasons Billy had long since decided to be a supermarket checker himself when he grew up. Think of it! Not only would you hear the swell home-type commercials all day while you worked, and be hep to the very latest ones, but you'd get to hear all the store commercials too. And what with the thousands of Buy-Me-Discs he'd be tearing off, as a Checker, he bet he could slip some into his pockets from time to time, and then wouldn't his friends envy him, being able to receive store-type commercials at home!

They reached the cereal area, and as always the children were entranced. Their faces shone with excitement as they picked up one box after another, to hear the commercials more clearly. There were sounds of gunfire; all kinds of snapping, crackling, and popping; there were loud shouts of "CRISPIER! NUTTIER! YUMMIER!" There were more modulated appeals, addressed to Mother, about increased nourishment and energy-building; there were the voices of athletes, urging the kids to come on and be one of the gang; there were whinnies of horses and explosive sounds of jets and rockets; there were cowboy songs and hillbilly songs and rhymes and jingles and bands and quartets and trios! Poor Kitty! How could she ever choose?

Mavis waited patiently for twenty minutes, enjoying the children's pleasure even though her headache was growing worse, and then told Kitty that she really must make up her mind.

"OK, Mom, I'll take this one this time," said Kitty. She held the box close to her mother's ear. "Listen to it, Mom, isn't it swell?" Mavis heard a shattering command, "FORWARD, MARCH!" and then what sounded like a thousand marching men. "Crunch, crunch, crunch, crunch," they were shouting in unison, above the noise of their marching feet, and a male chorus was singing something about Crunchies were marching to your breakfast table, right into your cereal bowl. Suddenly, inexplicably, Mavis felt she couldn't stand this every morning. "No, Kitty," she said, rather harshly, "you can't have that one. I won't have all that marching and shouting at breakfast!" Kitty's pretty face turned to a thundercloud, and tears sprang into her eyes. "I'll tell Daddy what you said! I'll tell Daddy if you don't let me have it!" Mavis came to her senses as quickly as she had taken leave of them. "I'm sorry, dear, I don't know what came over me. Of course you can have it. It's a very nice one. Now let's hurry on home so we can give you your permanent before Grandmother comes."

Grandmother arrived just in time for dinner. She kissed the children warmly, though they didn't remember her, and seemed glad to see Mavis and Fred. But it soon became clear that she was the same old Grandmother. She tried, at table, to shout above the dinner commercials, until Mavis had to shush her or the family would have missed them, and she nearly succeeded in spoiling their pleasure in the new Tummy's campaign, which they had been eagerly looking forward to for several days.

Fred knew the kids were going to like it. He had a brand new roll of Tummys in his pocket, all ready to receive it. It was nicely timed—just as Fred was finishing his pineapple came a loud and unmistakable belch. The children looked startled and then burst into laughter. Mavis looked shocked, and then joined the laughter as a man's voice said, "Embarrassing, isn't it? Supposing that had been *you!* But what's worse is the distress of suppressing stomach gases. Why risk either the embarrassment or the discomfort? Take a Tummy after each meal and avoid the risk of (the belch was repeated, sending the children into fresh gales of laughter). Yes, folks, be sure it doesn't happen to YOU."

Fred handed Tummys to all of them amidst exclamations from the children, "Gee, Daddy, that's the best yet," and "I can't wait for tomorrow night to hear it again!" Mavis thought it was "very good, very effective." Grandmother, however, took her Tummy tablet, dropped it on the floor, and ground it to powder with her foot. Fred and Mavis exchanged despairing glances.

That evening the children were allowed to sit up late so they could talk to their great-grandmother after the MV went off at 11. They had been told she'd just returned from a "trip," and when they asked her about it now she made up stories of far away places where she'd been, where there wasn't any MV. Then she went on, while they grew bored, to tell them stories of her girlhood, before MV was invented, long before, as she said, "that fatal day when the Supreme Court opened the door to MV by deciding that defenseless passengers on busses had to listen to commercials whether they wanted to or not."

"But didn't they *like* to hear the commercials?" Billy asked.

Fred smiled to himself. Sound kid. Sound as a dollar. Grandmother could talk herself cross-eyed but Billy wouldn't fall for that stuff.

"No," Grandmother said, and she seemed very sad, "they didn't like them." She made a visible effort to pull herself together. "You know, Fred, the liquor business is missing a big opportunity. Why, if there were a bottle of Old Overholt here right now, saying, 'Drink me, drink me,' I'd do it!"

Fred took the hint and mixed three nightcaps.

"As a matter of fact," Mavis said, looking proudly at her husband, "Fred can claim a lot of the credit for that. All those liquor companies begged and pleaded with him for time, offered piles of money and everything, but Fred didn't think it would be a good influence in the home, having bottles around

17

telling you to drink them, and I think he's right. He turned down a whole lot of money!"

"That was indeed splendid of Fred. I congratulate him." Grandmother drank her drink thirstily and looked at her watch. "We'd all better get to bed. You look tired, Mavis, and one must, I assume, especially in this household, be up with the MV in the morning."

"Oh yes, we usually are, and tomorrow," Mavis said excitedly, "Fred has a wonderful surprise for us. Some big new account he's gotten and he won't tell us what it is, but it's going to start tomorrow."

Next morning as the Bascoms and Grandmother were sitting down to breakfast there was a loud knock at the door.

"That's it!" shouted Fred. "Come on, everybody!"

They all ran to the door and Fred threw it open. Nobody was there, but a copy of the New York *Times* was lying on the doorstep, saying,

"Good morning, this is your New York *Times*! Wouldn't you like to have me delivered to your door *every* morning? Think of the added convenience, the added..." Mavis pulled Fred out onto the lawn where he could hear her. "Fred!" she cried, "the New York *Times* — you sold the New York *Times*! However did you do it?"

The children crowded around, congratulating him. "Gosh, Dad, that's really something. Did that knocking come right with the message?"

"Yep," said Fred with justifiable pride, "it's part of the message. Look, Mavis," he waved his hand up and down the street. In both directions, as far as they could see, families were clustered around their front doors, listening to New York *Timeses*.

When it was over, the nearer neighbors shouted, "That your idea, Fred?"

"'Fraid I'll have to admit it is," Fred called back, laughing.

From all sides came cries of "Great work, Fred," and "Swell stuff, Fred," and "Say, you sure are on the ball, Fred." Probably only he and Mavis, though, fully realized what it was going to mean in terms of promotion.

Unnoticed, Grandmother had gone into the house, into her room, and extracted a small box from one of her suitcases. Now she came out of the house again and crossed to the family group on the lawn.

"While you're out here where we can talk, I've something to tell you. It might be better if you sent the children into the house."

Mavis asked Kitty if she weren't afraid of missing her new Crunchies commercial, and the children raced inside.

"I can't stand another day of it," Grandmother said. "I'm sorry, but I've got to leave right now."

"Why Grandmother, you can't — you don't even know where you're going!"

"Oh, I do know where I'm going. I'm going back to jail. It's really the only sensible place for me. I have friends there, and it's the quietest place I know."

"But you can't..." Fred began.

"But I can," Grandmother replied. She opened her hand and showed them the little box.

"Earplugs! Grandmother! Put them out of sight, quickly. Wherever did you get them?"

Grandmother ignored Mavis' question. "I'm going to telephone the police and ask them to come and get me." She turned and started into the house.

"She can't do that," Fred said wildly.

"Let her go, Fred. She's right, and besides it solves the whole problem."

"But Mavis, if she calls the police here it'll be all over town. I'll be ruined! Stop her and tell her we'll drive her to some other police station!"

Mavis reached her grandmother before Grandmother reached the police, and explained Fred's predicament. A wicked gleam appeared in Grandmother's eye, but it was gone in a second. She looked at Mavis with some tenderness and said all right, just as long as she got back to the penitentiary as quickly as possible.

They all had breakfast. The children, humming the new Crunchies song, marched off to school—they would be told at night that Grandmother had suddenly gone on another "trip"—and Mavis and Fred drove to a town 50 miles away, with Grandmother and her luggage in the back seat. Grandmother was happy and at peace, thinking, as she listened to the gas tanks yelling to be filled up, the spark plugs crying to be cleaned, and all the other parts asking to be checked, or repaired, or replaced, that she was hearing MV for the last time.

But as the Bascoms were driving back home, after depositing Grandmother, it hit Fred all of a sudden. He fairly shouted in his excitement. "Mavis! We've all been blind as bats!"

"How do you mean, dear?"

"Blind, I tell you, blind! I've been thinking about Grandmother in prison, and all the thousands of people in jail and prison, *without MV*. They don't buy any products, so they don't get any MV. Can you imagine what that does to their buying habits?"

"Yes, you're right, Fred—five or ten or twenty years without it, they probably wouldn't *have* any buying habits after all that time." She laughed. "But I don't see what you can do about it."

"Plenty, Mavis, and not just about prisons. This is going to revolutionize the Corporation! Do you realize that ever since MV was invented we've just assumed that the discs had to be right with the products? Why? In the name of heaven, why? Take a prison, for instance. Why couldn't we, say, have a little box in each cell where the discs could be kept and that way the prisoners could still hear the MV and it would sort of preserve their buying habits and then when they got out they wouldn't be floundering around?"

"I wonder, Fred, about the prison authorities. You'd have to get their co-operation, I mean they'd have to distribute the discs, wouldn't they?"

Fred was way ahead of her. "We make it a public service, Mavis. Besides the regular MV, we get a few sponsors with vision, some of those big utilities people that like to do good, and they'll be satisfied with just a short plug for their product and then the rest of the message can be for the benefit of the prisoners, like little talks on honesty is the best policy and how we expect them to behave when they get out of jail—things that'll really help prepare them for life on the outside again."

Impulsively, Mavis put her hand on his arm and squeezed it. No wonder she was so proud of her Fred! Who but Fred—Mavis blinked to keep back the tears—who but Fred would think right off, first thing, not just of the money-making side, but of the welfare and betterment of all those poor prisoners!

(Editor's note: After the initial publication of "Captive Audience", Ann Warren Griffith sent this letter to the magazine's editor:

"I have just returned from a trip to my local supermarket where I discovered that a reasonably exact facsimile of MV has been installed! There was a big stack of jars of prunes, and coming out of its midst, via tape-recording, one of those ghastly cheerful women's voices saying try the new delicious ready-cooked prunes, why don't you pick up a jar right now, etc., etc., etc., over and over and over...

God help us all!")

Afterword by Andi Dukleth

Many of us born pre-1990 can remember the pop-up nightmare that marred the mid 2000s internet. Logging on to check one's email, read the news, or send a virtual birthday card, we were pelted with ad after ad, each more obnoxious than the last. And that was just a taste of things to come.

Ann Warren Griffith takes this concept — decades before the internet was even born — and runs with it in *Captive Audience*. Originally published in 1953, the story satirizes what American life looks like when dominated by a bombardment of inescapable advertisements. The story was an exaggeration (at least at the time!) of the lengths marketing firms will go to reach new audiences, and the lengths consumers will go to escape them altogether. With decades of hindsight, which now includes a social media landscape constantly vying for your attention, one can see that the world of *Captive Audience* wasn't too far off in the end.

Ann Warren Griffith was born in Newton, Massachusetts, sometime between 1911 and 1918. She went on to become a member in the Women's Army Service Pilots and later worked for an Array Red Cross club in Wildflecken, Germany. After experiencing hostility from the locals, she was inspired to write about the experience for the *New Yorker*, and her "Babes in the Wildflecken Woods" was published in 1950. Warren Griffith continued to write for the *New Yorker*, as well as in *The American Mercury*, *The Atlantic*, and the aviation magazine *Pegasus*. As she developed her style, she became known for her humorous essays, one Chicago Tribune review describing her as "the wackiest of writers ever to set a salty witticism down on paper."

But despite the number of publications she appeared in, she published only two science fiction stories. *Captive Audience*, which was originally published in *The Magazine of Fantasy and Science Fiction*, is the better-known work. Prior to that, she published *Zeritsky's Law* in *Galaxy Science Fiction* in 1951.

Not much else is known about Warren Griffith's life. She married her husband after World War II (a man who hated flying, despite Warren Griffith's aviation background) and eventually passed away in 1983.

Although Warren Griffith is not well known in the literary world, *Cap-

tive Audience has fared unusually well, being reissued periodically over the decades, most often in French (most recently in 1989). *Rediscovery* marks the first time it has appeared in English since 1977. Given how normalized targeted advertising via influencer culture has become, it's safe to say that Warren Griffith's work is as relevant in 2021 as it was in 1953.

Gallie's House

by Thelma D. Hamm

"Gallie's House" by Thelma D. Hamm was first published in *The Magazine of Fantasy and Science Fiction* in September of 1953. It has only been republished once, in 1954.

"Eeny, meeny, miney, mo—" Nelda's eight-year-old voice rang out happily, her small finger pointing in rhythmic alternation at a slender birch and some unseen companion.

"There, Gallie!" she squealed ecstatically. "I thought for a minute the tree would be *out* and you'd be *in!*" Her laughter bubbled like water. "Oh dear, there's mother calling—see you after lunch!"

She bounced into the house, dashed into the bathroom and out again leaving a wake of soiled towels and soap spatters. Julia Smithers sighed in resignation, decided to ignore the problem once more and queried brightly, "Having fun, dear?"

Nelda spooned up her soup and nodded. "Yes, and Gallie says the *funniest* things." She giggled reminiscently. "She said if the birch tree was *it*, imagine it running after us on its roots!"

Her mother laughed. "Who *is* Gallie, dear?"

"She's a little girl...can I have another piece of bread?"

"*May* I," Julia corrected automatically. "But where does she live?"

"Here," Nelda returned vaguely. "Oh, there she is! Excuse-me-please," and galvanized into sudden activity, she was gone in a whirl of flying skirts and banging doors.

A few days later Julia, busy at the ironer, tried vainly to quell a growing sense of uneasiness. Surely this country isolation was better for a child than the atomic bogey-man terror of the city? She raised her head. The sudden cessation of noise outside was as audible to the ear as a clap of thunder. Assailed with a panic she was at a loss to understand, she flung open the door and called sharply, "Nelda! *Nelda!*"

The yard was empty, the high old wall unclimbable, the house behind her silent—

"Yes, Mama?" said an innocent voice behind her.

"Nelda! Where *were* you!"

"In Gallie's house," Nelda explained matter-of-factly. "And she has a train—a real 'lectric train. Can I have one for Christmas, mama? Can I?"

Julia pushed her hair back. "Nelda! You nearly scared me out of my wits. And how did you get in anyway? The front door was locked."

"Gallie's door wasn't."

"Nelda, stop this nonsense and show me how you got in."

"O.K.," said Nelda obediently, walked to the dining room door, made a sharp turn and disappeared.

As she clung to the edge of the sink, Julia's mind ranged dizzily over the probabilities of (1) amnesia, (2) need of glasses and (3) plain insanity.

"Nelda," she quavered.

Nelda instantly reappeared, looking innocent inquiry.

"You look funny, Mama. Are you sick?"

"I don't know," said Julia in all honesty. "But Nelda, will you, just for a while, play in the *yard*? Please?"

"O.K." Nelda headed for the door.

"And Nelda—"

"Yes, Mama?"

"We must remember how important it is to—to understand things and—well, keep them straight. Now we know that Gallie isn't a real little girl. She's just an imaginary little girl in an imaginary house." Julia found her hands gripping the sink as her mind clutched at this needed reassurance. "Isn't she?"

"That's funny," said Nelda. "That's what *her* mother says about *me*."

The door slammed, the familiar, comforting shrieks resumed and normality settled down on the Smithers household.

A few evenings later, an unwontedly subdued Nelda looked up from her plate and said hesitantly, "Daddy, what does '*at*-omic' mean?"

"A-*tom*-ic," he corrected absently; then with a start, "Where did you hear that?" Blast people anyway, this was what they had been trying to shield her from—

"Gallie heard her father and mother talking about it. What *is* it, Daddy? They were scared..." Her voice trailed off unhappily. In her world grownups were loving, snappy and liable to fits of incomprehensible laughter...but not *scared*.

"That's silly," her father said briskly. "Atomic power makes electricity and runs ships and airplanes, but it's nothing to be scared of...please God," he added silently.

Nelda looked up at him with admiration, her faith restored.

"Goody, I'll tell Gallie tomorrow. She was scared too, but I wasn't."

"That's my girl," Julia grinned. "Come on now...bedtime."

The nightly ritual over, silence settled, broken only by the click of Julia's knitting needles, the rustle of Nelson's paper...

Without conscious volition they found themselves jostling on the staircase, the appalling scream from Nelda's room still echoing in their ears. They reached the landing together as Nelda burst from her room, running blindly toward the back stairs.

"Baby!" Julia screamed.

The gray eyes turned towards them unseeing, occupied with some distant terror. "Gallie's hurt!" she wailed, turned sharply and disappeared.

Toward dawn they simply gave up the search and sat waiting. In the back of Nelson's mind ran like a refrain, "What's 'at-omic'... Gallie's father and mother are scared... Gallie's scared, too..."

The darkness had just given way to the first weary grayness of dawn, when they heard the tired, stumbling footsteps coming up the walk, onto the porch...

They reached the door together. Nelda stood looking at them, shocked gray eyes enormous in the dirt-and-tear-stained face. Unmoved by their embraces and their cries of pity and love, she stood stiffly, submitting to being felt all over for nonexistent injuries, moving like a little automaton to their demands.

It was Julia, desperate in the face of that shocked silence, who broke the spell.

"Why didn't you come back..." her voice stumbled over the phrase, "... through the...'door'?"

Nelda looked past her with that set, frightening stare. Her lips moved stiffly.

"The house all fell down. All the doors were gone. But after awhile I found a piece of wall and came over...and it fell down, too. I can't ever get back."

There was a pause. Julia whispered, "And...Gallie?"

Nelda's chin quivered. "She's back there of course. Under the bricks. I heard her crying, but I couldn't... And then she stopped crying and I came away."

She looked at her father with that terrible clarity which marks the final disillusionment. "'Airplanes'...!" she said. "'Lectricity'...!" She ran past them into the house.

Afterword by Erica L. Frank

Thelma D. Hamm's stories remind me of Hans Christian Andersen's works. They carry a thread of wonder; the characters exist in a world that is both brighter and and starker than our own. Like Andersen's, Hamm's tragedies linger in my mind, leave me wanting to howl, "Why did you make me care about these people if you were just going to crush them?"

Thelma D. Hamm wrote professionally as T.D. Hamm from 1952 to 1961. She was active in science fiction fandom, attending conventions throughout the 50s. Her husband, fellow author E. Everett Evans, was one of the founding members of the National Fantasy Fan Federation (known as N3F), and she was often mentioned alongside him in fannish newsletters and zines. They were, from several accounts, a fannish *couple*, sharing both authorial careers and social lives: they published stories, attended conventions together, and hosted fannish gatherings at their home in southern California.

They married late: in 1953, he was 60; she was 48. There are faint rumours he may have been gay, but those were put to rest at the time by their marriage; in the 50s, nobody imagined a happy couple with an actively shared social life could be anything but straight. He died five years later in 1958; a few years after that, she stopped publishing, and she did not remarry or publish again before her death in 1994. Her presence in fandom was strong enough that, even decades after her last work was published, *Locus* magazine ran a short obituary about her.

She published fewer than a dozen stories over the span of less than a decade. None reached any great acclaim or were nominated for awards. They are all *dark*, in some way or another: stories of failure and anguish and despair that can't be fought with courage alone.

"Gallie's House" may be the least bleak story Thelma Hamm ever published. Like most of her works, it's short and ruthlessly sharp. Hamm wrote several stories about families and children, almost all of which had themes of parental neglect or benign ignorance, all of which had traumatic endings, usually for the children themselves. This is one of the few where the protagonist's story doesn't end with her own tragic death.

However, although Nelda survives, her faith in her parents has been shaken, and she carries the invisible trauma of standing helpless while her best friend dies. Moreover, nobody but her parents will ever believe that best friend existed—and they are likely to encourage her to forget, to pretend it wasn't real, to "focus on the future" instead of a bizarre incident from one summer in her childhood. She may have years of therapy ahead of her, as doctor after doctor fights to convince her that her friend was all in her mind, just a face to put on her fears of atomic power.

At eight years old in 1953, Nelda would have been born in 1945, the year of the Hiroshima and Nagasaki bombings. I don't know if Hamm had that detail in mind when she wrote "Gallie's House," but it fits the era of extensive atomic testing—and worries about its effects. Many stories of the 50s and 60s featured characters who had strange abilities from exposure to radiation. Perhaps Nelda will find another "door" in the future; perhaps not.

Hamm's stories—even the ones that end in death for everyone involved—carry a tiny, subtle thread of hope. Not for the characters: they are mired in their misfortunes, stuck in an unforgiving world that failed to provide help when they needed it most. But for us, who read the stories, there are warnings: Pay attention to your loved ones; not all "irrational" fears are harmless; neither love nor skill is enough to keep you safe. And on the other side of the warnings, a lesson:

Cherish life and the people in it, because both may be gone too soon. Technological wonders will not bring us happiness and security. Only trust, compassion, and acceptance—the kind that none of Hamm's protagonists receive—will make the future better than the present.

The First Day of Spring
by **Mari Wolf**

(Originally appeared in the June 1954 issue of *If*. It was republished in print once, in 2011.)

The First Day of spring, the man at the weather tower had said, and certainly it felt like spring, with the cool breeze blowing lightly about her and a faint new clover smell borne in from the east. Spring — that meant they would make the days longer now, and the nights shorter, and they would warm the whole world until it was summer again.

Trina laughed aloud at the thought of summer, with its picnics and languid swims in the refilled lakes, with its music and the heavy scent of flowers and the visitors in from space for the festival. She laughed, and urged her horse faster, out of its ambling walk into a trot, a canter, until the wind streamed about her, blowing back her hair, bringing tears to her eyes as she rode homeward toward the eastern horizon — the horizon that looked so far away but wasn't really.

"Trina!"

His voice was very close. And it was familiar, though for a moment she couldn't imagine who it might be.

"Where are you?" She had reined the horse in abruptly and now looked around her, in all directions, toward the north and south and east and west, toward the farm houses of the neighboring village, toward the light tower and the sun tower. She saw no one. No one else rode this early in the day in the pasture part of the world.

"I'm up here, Trina."

She looked up then and saw him, hovering some thirty feet off the ground in the ridiculous windmill-like craft he and his people used when they visited the world.

"Oh, hello, Max." No wonder she had known the voice. Max Cramer, down from space, down to the world, to see her. She knew, even before he dropped his craft onto the grass beside her, that he had come to see her. He couldn't have been on the world for more than the hour she'd been riding.

"You're visiting us early this year, Max. It's not festival time for three months yet."

"I know." He cut the power to the windmill blades, and they slowed, becoming sharply visible. The horse snorted and backed away. Max smiled. "This world is very — attractive."

His eyes caught hers, held them. She smiled back, wishing for the hundredth time since last summer's festival that he were one of her people, or at least a worldling, and not a man with the too white skin of space.

"It may be attractive," she said. "But you always leave it soon enough."

He nodded. "It's too confining. It's all right, for a little while, but then..."

"How can you say that?" She shook her head sadly. Already they were arguing the same old unresolvable argument, and they had scarcely greeted each other. After all his months in space they met with the same words as they had parted. She looked past him, up and out, toward the horizon that seemed so many miles away, toward the morning sun that seemed to hang far, far off in the vaulted blue dome of the sky.

"How can you even think it? About this?"

His lips tightened. "About *this*," he repeated. "A horizon you could ride to in five minutes. A world you could ride around in two hours. A sun — you really call it a sun — that you could almost reach up and pluck out of that sky of yours." He laughed. "Illusions. World of illusions."

"Well, what do you have? A ship — a tiny ship you can't get out of, with walls you can see, all around you."

"Yes, Trina, with walls we can see."

He was still smiling, watching her, and she knew that he desired her. And she desired him. But not the stars.

"You have nothing like this," she said, knowing it wouldn't do any good. She looked past him at the light tower, one of the many that formed the protective screen about her world, that made it seem great and convex, a huge flattened sphere with the sun high above, and not the swift curving steel ball that it actually was.

This was her world. It was like Earth, like the old Earth of the legends of the time before the radiation wars. And even though her mind might know the truth about the screens that refracted light and the atomic pile that was her sun, her heart knew a more human truth. This was a world. As it had been in the beginning. As it must be till the end — or until they found a new Earth, somewhere, sometime... Max sighed. "Yes, you have your world, Trina. And it's a good one—the best of its kind I've ever visited."

"Why don't you stay here then?"

A spaceman, she thought. With all the dozens of men in my world, why did it have to be a spaceman? With all the visitors from New France and New Chile and New Australia last festival, why did it have to be him?

"I have the stars, Trina."

"We do too!" Last festival, and the warm June night, heavy, druggedly heavy with honeysuckle and magnolia, and the hidden music from the pavilions. And Max Cramer, tall and strong boned and alien, holding her in his arms, dancing her away from her people, out onto the terrace above the little stream, beneath the full festival moon and the summer stars, the safe, sane, well ordered constellations that their ancestors had looked upon from Earth.

"My stars are real, Trina."

She shook her head, unable to argue with him. World-woman and spaceman, and always different, with nothing in common between them, really, except a brief forgetfulness at festival time.

"Come with me, Trina."

"No." She gathered up the reins and chucked at the horse and turned, slowly, for the village.

"You wouldn't come—for me?"

"You wouldn't stay, would you?"

She heard the windmill blades whir again, and a rustling of wind, and then he was beside her, skimming slowly along, barely off the ground, making her horse snort nervously away.

"Trina, I shouldn't tell you this, not until we've met with your councilmen. But I—I've got to."

He wasn't smiling now. There was a wild look about his face. She didn't like it.

"Captain Bernard's with the council now, giving them the news. But I wanted to see you first, to be the one who told you." He broke off, shook his head. "Yet when I found you I couldn't say anything. I guess I was afraid of what you'd answer..."

"What are you talking about?" She didn't want to look at him. It embarrassed her somehow, seeing him so eager. "What do you want to tell me?"

"About our last trip, Trina. We've found a world!"

She stared at him blankly, and his hand made a cutting gesture of impatience. "Oh, not a world like this one! A planet, Trina. And it's Earth type!"

She wheeled the horse about and stared at him. For a moment she felt excitement rise inside of her too, and then she remembered the generations of searching, and the false alarms, and the dozens of barren, unfit planets that the spacemen colonized, planets like ground-bound ships.

"Oh, Trina," Max cried, "This isn't like the others. It's a new Earth. And there are already people there. From not long after the Exodus..."

"A new Earth?" she said. "I don't believe it."

The council wouldn't either, she thought. Not after all the other new Earths, freezing cold or methane atmosphered or at best completely waterless. This would be like the others. A spaceman's dream.

"You've got to believe me, Trina," Max said. "And you've got to help make the others believe. Don't you see? You wouldn't live in space. I wouldn't live here—on this. But there, on a real planet, on a real Earth..."

Then suddenly she felt his excitement and it was a part of her, until against all reason she wanted to believe in his mad dream of a world. She laughed aloud as she caught up the reins and raced her horse homeward, toward the long vista of the horizon and the capital village beyond it, ten minutes gallop away.

Max and Trina came together into the council hall and saw the two groups, the roomful of worldmen and the half dozen spacemen, apart from each other, arguing. The spacemen's eyes were angry.

"A world," Captain Bernard said bitterly, "there for your taking, and you don't even want to look at it."

"How do we know what kind of world it is?" Councilman Elias leaned forward on the divan. His voice was gentle, almost pitying. "You brought no samples. No vegetation, no minerals..."

"Not even air samples," Aaron Gomez said softly. "Why?"

Bernard sighed. "We didn't want to wait," he said. "We wanted to get back here, to tell you."

"It may be a paradise world to *you*," Elias said. "But to us..."

Max Cramer tightened his grip on Trina's hand. "The fools," he said. "Talking and talking, and all the time this world drifts farther and farther away."

"It takes so much power to change course," Trina said. "And besides, you feel it. It makes you heavy."

She remembered the stories her father used to tell, about his own youth, when he and Curt Elias had turned the world to go to a planet the spaceman found. A planet with people—people who lived under glass domes, or deep below the formaldehyde poisoned surface.

"You could be there in two weeks, easily, even at your world's speed," Captain Bernard said.

"And then we'd have to go out," Elias said. "Into space."

31

The worldmen nodded. The women looked at each other and nodded too. One of the spacemen swore, graphically, and there was an embarrassed silence as Trina's people pretended not to have heard.

"Oh, let's get out of here." The spaceman who had sworn swore again, just as descriptively, and then grinned at the councilmen and their aloof, blank faces. "They don't want our planet. All right. Maybe New Chile..."

"Wait!" Trina said it without thinking, without intending to. She stood speechless when the others turned to face her. All the others. Her people and Max's. Curt Elias, leaning forward again, smiling at her.

"Yes, Trina?" the councilman said.

"Why don't we at least look at it? Maybe it is — what they say."

Expression came back to their faces then. They nodded at each other and looked from her to Max Cramer and back again at her, and they smiled. Festival time, their eyes said. Summer evenings, summer foolishness.

And festival time long behind them, but soon to come again.

"Your father went to space," Elias said. "We saw one of those worlds the spacemen talk of."

"I know."

"He didn't like it."

"I know that too," she said, remembering his bitter words and the nightmare times when her mother had had so much trouble comforting him, and the winter evenings when he didn't want even to go outside and see the familiar, Earth encircling stars.

He was dead now. Her mother was dead now. They were not here, to disapprove, to join with Elias and the others.

They would have hated for her to go out there.

She faltered, the excitement Max had aroused in her dying away, and then she thought of their argument, as old as their desire. She knew that if she wanted him it would have to be away from the worlds.

"At least we could look," she said. "And the spacemen could bring up samples. And maybe even some of the people for us to talk to."

Elias nodded. "It would be interesting," he said slowly, "to talk to some new people. It's been so long."

"And we wouldn't even have to land," Aaron Gomez said, "if it didn't look right."

The people turned to each other again and smiled happily. She knew that they were thinking of the men and women they would see, and all the new things to talk about.

"We might even invite some of them up for the festival," Elias said slowly. "Providing they're — courteous." He frowned at the young spaceman who had done the swearing, and then he looked back at Captain Bernard. "And providing, of course, that we're not too far away by then."

"I don't think you will be," Bernard said. "I think you'll stay."

"I think so too," Max Cramer said, moving closer to Trina. "I hope so."

Elias stood up slowly and signalled that the council was dismissed. The other people stood up also and moved toward the doors.

"We'd better see about changing the world's course," Aaron Gomez said.

No one objected. It was going to be done. Trina looked up at Max Cramer and knew that she loved him. And wondered why she was afraid.

It was ten days later that the world, New America, came into the gravitational influence of the planet's solar system. The automatic deflectors swung into functioning position, ready to change course, slowly and imperceptibly, but enough to take the world around the system and out into the freedom of space where it could wander on its random course. But this time men shunted aside the automatic controls. Men guided their homeland in, slowly now, toward the second planet from the sun, the one that the spacemen had said was so like Earth.

"We'll see it tomorrow," Trina said. "They'll shut off part of the light tower system then."

"Why don't they now?" Max Cramer asked her. It was just past sunset, and the stars of a dozen generations ago were just beginning to wink into view. He saw Venus, low on the horizon, and his lips tightened, and then he looked up to where he knew the new sun must be.

There was only the crescent of Earth's moon.

"Now?" Trina said. "Why should they turn the screens off now? We're still so far away. We wouldn't see anything."

"You'd see the sun," Max said. "It's quite bright, even from here. And from close up, from where the planet is, it looks just about like Earth's."

Trina nodded. "That's good," she said, looking over at the rose tints of the afterglow. "It wouldn't seem right if it didn't."

A cow lowed in the distance, and nearer, the laughing voices of children rode the evening breeze. Somewhere a dog barked. Somewhere else a woman called her family home to supper. Old sounds. Older, literally, than this world.

"What are the people like, out there?"

He looked at her face, eager and worried at the same time, and he smiled. "You'll like them, Trina," he said. "They're like—well, they're more like *this* than anything else."

He gestured, vaguely, at the farmhouse lights ahead of them, at the slow walking figures of the young couples out enjoying the warm spring evening, at the old farmer leading his plow horse home along the path.

"They live in villages, not too different, from yours. And in cities. And on farms."

"And yet, you like it there, don't you?" she said.

He nodded. "Yes, I like it there."

"But you don't like it here. Why?"

"If you don't understand by now, Trina, I can't explain."

They walked on. Night came swiftly, crowding the rose and purple tints out of the western sky, closing in dark and cool and sweet smelling about them. Ahead, a footbridge loomed up out of the shadows. There was the sound of running water, and, on the bank not far from the bridge, the low murmuring of a couple of late lingering fishermen.

"The people live out in the open, like this?" Trina said.

"Yes."

"Not underground? Not under a dome?"

"I've told you before that it's like Earth, Trina. About the same size, even."

"*This* is about the same size, too."

"Not really. It only looks that way."

The fishermen glanced up as they passed, and then bent down over their lines again. Lucas Crossman, from Trina's town, and Jake Krakorian from the southern hemisphere, up to visit his sister Lucienne, who had just had twins…

Trina said hello to them as she passed, and found out that the twins looked just like their mother, except for Grandfather Mueller's eyes, and then she turned back to Max.

"Do people live all over the planet?"

"On most of it. The land sections, that is. Of course, up by the poles it's too cold."

"But how do they know each other?"

He stopped walking and stared at her, not understanding for a minute. Girl's laughter came from the bushes, and the soft urging voice of one of the village boys. Max looked back at the fishermen and then down at Trina and shook his head.

"They don't all know each other," he said. "They couldn't."

She thought of New Chile, where her cousin Isobelle was married last year, and New India, which would follow them soon to the planet, because Captain Bernard had been able to contact them by radio. She thought of her people, her friends, and then she remembered the spacemen's far flung ships and the homes they burrowed deep in the rock of inhospitable worlds. She knew that he would never understand why she pitied the people of this system.

"I suppose we'll see them soon," she said. "You're going to bring some of them back up in your ship tomorrow, aren't you?"

He stood quietly, looking down at her. His face was shadowed in the gathering night and his whole body was in shadow, tall and somehow alien seeming there before her.

"Why wait for them to come here, Trina?" he said. "Come down with us, in the ship, tomorrow. Come down and see for yourself what it's like."

She trembled. "No," she said.

And she thought of the ship, out away from the sky, not down on the planet yet but hanging above it, with no atmosphere to break the blackness, to soften the glare of the planet's sun, to shut out the emptiness.

"You'd hardly know you weren't here, Trina. The air smells the same. And the weight's almost the same too. Maybe a little lighter."

She nodded. "I know. If we land the world, I'll go out there. But not in the ship."

"All right." He sighed and let go his grip on her shoulders and turned to start walking back the way they had come, toward the town.

She thought suddenly of what he had just said, that she would hardly be able to tell the difference.

"It can't be so much like this," she said. "Or you couldn't like it. No matter what you say."

"Trina." His voice was harsh. "You've never been out in space, so you couldn't understand. You just don't know what your world is like, from outside, when you're coming in."

But she could picture it. A tiny planetoid, shining perhaps behind its own screens, a small, drifting, lonely sphere of rock. She trembled again. "I don't want to know," she said.

Somewhere in the meadows beyond the road there was laughter, a boy and a girl laughing together, happy in the night. Trina's fingers tightened on Max's hand and she pulled him around to face her and then clung to him, trembling, feeling the nearness of him as she held up her face to be kissed.

He held her to him. And slowly, the outside world of space faded, and her world seemed big and solid and sure, and in his arms it was almost like festival time again.

At noon the next day the world slowed again and changed course, going into an orbit around the planet, becoming a third moon, nearer to the surface than the others.

The people, all of those who had followed their normal day-to-day life even after New America came into the system, abandoned it at last. They crowded near the television towers, waiting for the signal which would open up some of the sky and show them the planet they circled, a great green disk, twice the apparent diameter of the legendary Moon of Earth.

Max stood beside Trina in the crowd that pressed close about his ship. He wore his spaceman's suit, and the helmet was in his hand. Soon he too would be aboard with the others, going down to the planet.

"You're sure you won't come, Trina? We'll be down in a couple of hours."

"I'll wait until we land there. If we do."

Curt Elias came toward them through the crowd. When he saw Trina he smiled and walked faster, almost briskly. It was strange to see him move like a young and active man.

"If I were younger," he said, "I'd go down there." He smiled again and pointed up at the zenith, where the blue was beginning to waver and fade as the sky screens slipped away. "This brings back memories."

"You didn't like that other world," Trina said. "Not any more than Father did."

"The air was bad there," Elias said.

The signal buzzer sounded again. The center screens came down. Above them, outlined by the fuzzy halo of the still remaining sky, the black of space stood forth, and the stars, and the great disk of the planet, with its seas and continents and cloud masses and the shadow of night creeping across it from the east.

"You see, Trina?" Max said softly.

The voices of the people rose, some alive with interest and others anxious, fighting back the planet and the unfamiliar, too bright stars. Trina clutched Max Cramer's hand, feeling again the eagerness of that first day, when he had come to tell her of this world.

"You're right," she whispered. "It *is* like Earth."

It was so much like the pictures, though of course the continents were different, and the seas, and instead of one moon there were two. Earth. A new Earth, there above them in the sky.

Elias let out his breath slowly. "Yes," he said. "It is. It's not a bit like that world we visited. Not a bit."

"When you're down there it's even more like Earth," Max said. "And all the way down you could watch it grow larger. It wouldn't be at all like open space."

At the poles of the planet snow gleamed, and cloud masses drifted across the equator. And the people looked, and pointed, their voices growing loud with eagerness.

"Why don't we land the world now?" Trina cried. "Why wait for the ship to bring people up here?"

"Landing the world would take a lot of power," Elias said. "It would be foolish to do it unless we planned on staying for quite a while." He sighed. "Though I would like to go down there. I'd like to see a really Earth type planet."

He looked at Max, and Max smiled. "Well, why not?" he said.

Elias smiled too. "After all, I've been in space once. I'll go again." He turned and pushed his way through the people.

Trina watched him go. Somehow he seemed a symbol to her. Old and stable, he had been head of the council since she was a child. And he had gone into space with her father...

"Please come, Trina," Max said. "There's nothing to be afraid of."

With both Max and Elias along, certainly it couldn't be too bad. Max was right. There was nothing, really, to be afraid of: She smiled up at him.

"All right," she said. "I'll go."

And then she was walking with Max Cramer toward the ship and trying not to remember her father crying in his sleep.

The ship rose, and Trina cried out as she felt the heaviness wrench her back against the cushions. Max reached over to her. She felt the needle go into her arm again, and then sank back into the half sleep that he had promised would last until they were ready to land.

When she awoke the planet was a disk no longer, but a great curving mass beneath the ship, with the mountains and valleys and towns of its people plainly visible. But the planet's sky still lay below, and around them, in every direction except down, space stretched out, blacker than any night on the world. The world. Trina moaned and closed her eyes, glad she hadn't seen it, somewhere tiny and insignificant behind them.

Max heard her moan and reached toward her. She slept again, and woke only when they were down and he was tugging the straps loose from around her. She sat up, still numbed by the drug, still half asleep and unreal feeling, and looked out about her at the planet's surface.

They were in a field of some sort of grain. Beyond the scorched land where they had come down the tall cereal grasses rippled in the soft wind, a great undulating sea of green, reaching out toward the far off hills and the horizon. Cloud shadows drifted across the fields, and the shadow of the ship reached out to meet them.

Trina rubbed her eyes in wonder.

"It *is* like the world," she said. "Just like it."

For a moment she was sure that they were back on the world again, in some momentarily unrecognized pasture, or perhaps on one of the sister worlds. Then, looking along the row of hills to where they dropped away into an extension of the plain, she saw that the horizon was a little too far, and that the light shimmered differently, somehow, than on her home. But it was such a little difference.

"Come on outside," Max Cramer said. "You'll be all right now."

She stood up and followed him. Elias was already at the airlock, moving unsteadily and a little blankly, also still partly under the influence of the narcotic.

The lock opened. Captain Bernard stepped out and went down the ladder to the ground. The others followed him. Within a few minutes the ship stood empty.

Trina breathed the open air of the planet and felt the warmth on her face and smelled the scent of grass and the elusive fragrance of alien flowers. She heard the song of some strange, infinitely sweet throated bird.

"It's — it's Earth," she whispered.

Voices, eager, calling voices, sang out in the distance. Then, little cars rolled toward them through the field, mowing down the grass, cutting themselves a path to the ship. People, men and women and children, were calling greetings.

"This is where we landed before," Max said. "We told them we'd be back."

They were sunbronzed, country people, and except for their strange clothing they might have been from any of the worlds. Even their language was the same, though accented differently, with some of the old, unused words, like those in the legends.

"You've brought your people?" the tall man who stood in the forefront said to Captain Bernard.

"They're up there." Bernard pointed up at the sky, and the people looked up. Trina looked up too. One of the planet's moons was almost full overhead. But the world was invisible, shut off by the sky and the clouds and the light of the earthlike sun.

"They'd like some of you to come visit their world," Bernard said. "If any of you are willing."

The tall man nodded. "Everyone will want to go," he said. "Very few ships ever land here. Until you came, it had been years."

"You'd go out in space?" Trina said incredulously.

Again the man nodded. "I was a spaceman once," he said. "All of us Mac-Gregors were." Then he sighed. "Sometimes even now I want to go out again. But there've been no ships here, not for years."

Trina looked past him, at the women and the children, at the lush fields and the little houses far in the distance. "You'd leave this?"

MacGregor shook his head. "No, of course not. Not to live in space permanently. I'd always come back."

"It's a fine world to come back to," Max said, and he and the tall man smiled at each other, as if they shared something that Trina couldn't possibly understand.

"We might as well go into town," MacGregor said.

They walked over to the cars. MacGregor stopped beside one of them, his hand on the door button.

"Here, let me drive." The girl stepped forward out of the crowd as she spoke. She was tall, almost as tall as MacGregor, and she had the same high cheekbones and the same laughter lines about her eyes.

"Not this time, Saari," MacGregor said. "This time you can entertain our guests." He turned to Max and Trina and smiled. "My daughter." His face was proud.

They climbed in, Trina wedging herself into the middle of the back seat between Max and the planet girl. The car throbbed into motion, then picked up speed, jolting a bit on the rough country road. The ground rushed past and the fields rushed past and Trina leaned against Max and shut her eyes against the dizzying speed. Here, close to the ground, so close that they could feel every unevenness of its surface, it was far worse than in the windmill like craft the spacemen used on the worlds.

"Don't you have cars?" Saari asked.

"No," Trina said. "We don't need them."

A car like this would rush all the way around the world in half an hour. In a car like this one even the horizons wouldn't look right, rushing to meet them. Here, though the horizons stayed the same, unmoving while the fence posts and the farmhouses and the people flashed past.

"What do you use for transportation then?"

"We walk," Trina said, opening her eyes to look at the girl and then closing them again. "Or we ride horses."

"Oh."

A few minutes later the car slowed, and Trina opened her eyes again.

"We're coming into town," Saari said.

They had climbed up over the brow of a small hill and were now dropping down. At the bottom of the hill the houses clumped together, sparsely at first, then more and more of them, so that the whole valley was filled with buildings, and more buildings hugged the far slopes.

"There are so many of them," Trina whispered.

"Oh, no, Trina. This is just a small town."

"But the people—all those people…"

They crowded the streets, watching the cars come in, looking with open curiosity at their alien visitors. Faces, a thousand faces, all different and yet somehow all alike, blended together into a great anonymous mass.

"There aren't half that many people on the whole world," Trina said.

Saari smiled. "Just wait till you see the city."

Trina shook her head and looked up at Max. He was smiling out at the town, nodding to some men he apparently knew, with nothing but eagerness in his face. He seemed a stranger. She looked around for Curt Elias, but he was in one of the other cars cut off from them by the crowd. She couldn't see him at all.

"Don't you like it?" Saari said.

"I liked it better where we landed."

Max turned and glanced down at her briefly, but his hand found hers and held it, tightly, until her own relaxed. "If you want to, Trina, we can live out there, in those fields."

For a moment she forgot the crowd and the endless faces as she looked up at him. "Do you mean that, Max? We could really live out there?"

Where it was quiet, and the sun was the same, and the birds sang sweetly just before harvest time, where she would have room to ride and plenty of pasture for her favorite horse. Where she would have Max, there with her, not out somewhere beyond the stars.

"Certainly we could live there," he said. "That's what I've been saying all along."

"You could settle down here?"

He laughed. "Oh, I suppose I'd be out in space a good deal of the time," he said. "The ships will come here now, you know. But I'll always come home, Trina. To this world. To you."

And suddenly it didn't matter that the girl beside her chuckled, nor that there were too many people crowding around them, all talking at once in their strangely accented voices. All that mattered was Max, and this world, which was real after all, and a life that seemed like an endless festival time before her.

Evening came quickly, too quickly, with the sun dropping in an unnatural plunge toward the horizon. Shadows crept out from the houses of the town, reached across the narrow street and blended with the walls of the houses opposite. The birds sang louder in the twilight, the notes of their song drifting in from the nearby fields. And there was another sound, that of the wind, not loud now but rising, swirling fingers of dust in the street.

Trina sat in front of the town cafe with the planet girl, Saari. Max Cramer was only a few feet away, but he paid no attention to her, and little to Elias. He was too busy telling the planet people about space.

"Your man?" Saari asked.

"Yes," Trina said. "I guess so."

"You're lucky." Saari looked over at Max and sighed, and then she turned back to Trina. "My father was a spaceman. He used to take my mother up, when they were first married, when the ships were still running." She sighed. "I remember the ships, a little. But it was such a long time ago."

"I can't understand you people." Trina shook her head. "Leaving all of this, just to go out in space."

The room was crowded, oppressively crowded. Outside, too many people walked the shadowed streets. Too many voices babbled together. The people of this planet must be a little mad, Trina thought, to live cooped together as the spacemen lived, with all their world around them.

Saari sat watching her, and nodded. "You're different, aren't you? From us, and from them too." She looked over at Max and Bernard and the others, and then she looked at Curt Elias, who sat clenching and unclenching his hands, saying nothing.

"Yes, we're different," Trina said.

Max Cramer's voice broke incisively into the silence that lay between them then. "I don't see why," he said, "we didn't all know about this world. Especially if more than one ship came here."

Saari's father laughed softly. "It's not so strange. The ships all belonged to one clan. The MacGregors. And eventually all of them either were lost in space somewhere or else grew tired of roaming around and settled down. Here." He smiled again, and his high cheekboned face leaned forward into the light. "Like me..."

Night. Cloudless, black, but hazed over with atmosphere and thus familiar, not like the night of space. The two small moons, the stars in unfamiliar places, and somewhere, a star that was her world. And Trina sat and listened to the planet men talk, and to the spacemen among them who could no longer be distinguished from the native born. Outside, in the narrow street, wind murmured, skudding papers and brush before it, vague shadows against the light houses. Wind, rising and moaning, the sound coming in over the voices and the music from the cafe singers.

It was a stronger wind than ever blew on the world, even during the winter, when the people had to stay inside and wish that Earth tradition might be broken and good weather be had the year around.

"We'd better get back to the ship," Elias said.

They stopped talking and looked at him, and he looked down at his hands, embarrassed. "They'll be worried about us at home."

"No, they won't," Max said. Then he saw the thin, blue-veined hands trembling and the quiver not quite controlled in the wrinkled neck. "Though perhaps we should start back…"

Trina let out her breath in relief. To be back in the ship, she thought, with the needle and its forgetfulness, away from the noise and the crowd and the nervousness brought on by the rising wind.

It would be better, of course, when they had their place in the country. There it would be warm and homelike and quiet, with the farm animals near by, and the weather shut out, boarded out and forgotten, the way it was in winter on the world.

"You're coming with us?" Captain Bernard was saying.

"Yes, we're coming." Half a dozen of the men stood up and began pulling on their long, awkward coats.

"It'll be good to get back in space again," MacGregor said. "For a while." He smiled. "But I'm too old for a spaceman's life now."

"And I'm too old even for this," Elias said apologetically. "If we'd found this planet the other time…" He sighed and shook his head and looked out the window at the shadows that were people, bent forward, walking into the wind. He sighed again. "I don't know. I just don't know."

Saari got up and pulled on her wrap too. Then she walked over to one of the other women, spoke to her a minute, and came back carrying a quilted, rough fabricked coat. "Here, Trina, you'd better put this on. It'll be cold out."

"Are you going with us?"

"Sure. Why not? Dad's talked enough about space. I might as well see what it's like for myself."

Trina shook her head. But before she could speak, someone opened the door and the cold breeze came in, hitting her in the face.

"Come on," Saari said. "It'll be warm in the car."

Somehow she was outside, following the others. The wind whipped her hair, stung her eyes, tore at her legs. The coat kept it from her body, but she couldn't protect her face, nor shut out the low moaning wail of it through the trees and the housetops.

She groped her way into the car. The door slammed shut, and the wind retreated, a little.

"Is it — is it often like that?"

Saari MacGregor looked at her. Max Cramer turned and looked at her, and so did the others in the car. For a long moment no one said anything. And then Saari said, "Why, this is *summer*, Trina."

"Summer?" She thought of the cereal grasses, rippling in the warm day. They'd be whipping in the wind now, of course. The wind that was so much stronger than any the world's machines ever made.

"You ought to be here in winter," Saari was saying. "It really blows then. And there are the rainstorms, and snow…"

"Snow?" Trina said blankly.

"Certainly. A couple of feet of it, usually." Saari stopped talking and looked at Trina, and surprise crept even farther into her face. "You mean you don't have snow on your world?"

"Why, yes, we have snow. We have everything Earth had." But snow two feet deep… Trina shivered, thinking of winter on the world, and the soft dusting of white on winter mornings, the beautiful powdery flakes cool in the sunlight.

"They have about a sixteenth of an inch of it," Max said. "And even that's more than some of the worlds have. It hardly ever even rains in New California."

Saari turned away finally, and the others did too. The car started, the sound of its motors shutting out the wind a little, and then they were moving. Yet it was even more frightening, rushing over the roads in the darkness, with the houses flashing past and the trees thrashing in the wind and the people briefly seen and then left behind in the night.

The ship was ahead. The ship. Now even it seemed a safe, familiar place.

"This isn't like Earth after all," Trina said bitterly. "And it seemed so beautiful at first."

Then she saw that Saari MacGregor was looking at her again, but this time more in pity than in surprise.

"Not like Earth, Trina? You're wrong. We have a better climate than Earth's. We never have blizzards, nor hurricanes, and it's never too cold nor too hot, really."

"How can you say that?" Trina cried. "We've kept *our* world like Earth. Oh, maybe we've shortened winter a little, but still…"

Saari's voice was sad and gentle, as if she were explaining something to a bewildered child. "My mother's ancestors came here only a few years out from Earth," she said. "And do you know what they called this planet? A paradise. A garden world."

43

"That's why they named it Eden," Max Cramer said.

Then they were at the ship, out of the car, running to the airlock, with the grass lashing at their legs and the wind lashing at their faces and the cold night air aflame suddenly in their lungs. And Trina couldn't protest any longer, not with the world mad about her, not with Saari's words ringing in her ears like the wind.

She saw them carry Curt Elias in, and then Max was helping her aboard, and a moment later, finally, the airlock doors slipped shut and it was quiet.

She held out her arm for the needle.

When she awoke again it was morning. Morning on the world. They had carried her to one of the divans in the council hall, one near a window so that she could see the familiar fields of her homeland as soon as she awoke. She rubbed her eyes and straightened and looked up at the others. At Elias, still resting on another divan. At Captain Bernard. At Saari and her father, and another man from the planet. At Max.

He looked at her, and then sighed and turned away, shaking his head.

"Are we—are we going back there?" Trina asked.

"No," Elias said. "The people are against it."

There was silence for a moment, and then Elias went on. "I'm against it. I suppose that even if I'd been young I wouldn't have wanted to stay." His eyes met Trina's, and there was pity in them.

"No," Max said. "You wouldn't have wanted to."

"And yet," Elias said, "I went down there. Trina went down there. Her father and I both went out into space." He sighed. "The others wouldn't even do that."

"You're not quite as bad, that's all," Max said bluntly. "But I don't understand any of you. None of us ever has understood you. None of us ever will."

Trina looked across at him. Her fingers knew every line of his face, but now he was withdrawn, a stranger. "You're going back there, aren't you?" she said. And when he nodded, she sighed. "We'll never understand you either, I guess."

She remembered Saari's question of the night before, "Is he your man?" and she realized that her answer had not been the truth. She knew now that he had never been hers, not really, nor she his, that the woman who would be his would be like Saari, eager and unafraid and laughing in the wind, or looking out the ports at friendly stars.

Elias leaned forward on the divan and gestured toward the master weather panel for their part of the village, the indicators that told what it was like today and what it would be like tomorrow all over the world. "I think I understand," he said. "I think I know what we did to our environment, through the generations. But it doesn't do much good, just knowing something."

"You'll never change," Max said.

"No, I don't think we will."

Captain Bernard got up, and MacGregor got up too. They looked at Max. Slowly he turned his head and smiled at Trina, and then he too stood up. "Want to come outside and talk, Trina?"

But there was nothing to say. Nothing she could do except break down and cry in his arms and beg him not to leave her, beg him to spend the rest of his life on a world she could never leave again.

"No," she said. "I guess not." And then, the memories rushed back, and the music, and the little lane down by the stream where the magnolias spread their web of fragrance. "It's—it's almost festival time, Max. Will you be here for it?"

"I don't know, Trina."

It meant no; she knew that.

The weeks slipped by, until it was summer on the world, until the festival music sang through the villages and the festival flowers bloomed and the festival lovers slipped off from the dances to walk among them. There was a breeze, just enough to carry the mingled fragrances and the mingled songs, just enough to touch the throat and ruffle the hair and lie lightly between the lips of lovers.

Trina danced with Aaron Gomez, and remembered. And the wind seemed too soft somehow, almost lifeless, with the air too sweet and cloying.

She wondered what a festival on the planet would be like.

Max, with Saari MacGregor, perhaps, laughing in the wind, running in the chill of evening along some riverbank.

I could have gone with him, she thought. I could have gone…

But then the music swirled faster about them, the pulse of it pounding in her ears, and Aaron swept her closer as they danced, spinning among the people and the laughter, out toward the terrace, toward the trees with leaves unstirring in the evening air. All was color and sound and scent, all blended, hypnotically perfect, something infinitely precious that she could never, never leave.

For it was summer on the world, and festival time again.

Afterword by Jessica Dickinson Goodman

Mari Wolf is often credited with being the first writer to use the term "droid" in print, 25 years before George Lucas managed to noose a trademark around the phrase. In her first published short story, "Robots of the World! Arise!" (*If*, 1952), one of her characters narrates a robot uprising, describing androids "stopping robots in the streets—household Robs, commercial Droids, all of them." She wrote those words while working at the Jet Propulsion Laboratory in the 1950s, in the rocket testing lab's wind tunnel section.

There are no robot uprings in "The First Day of Spring." It is a soft story that reveals the violence in compelled softness. Tina rides her horse on a tiny, human-created world whose horizons can be reached within minutes, where snow never falls deeper than a 16th of an inch and the breezes are mild. Tina loves Max, her itinerant spaceman, and agrees to visit an earthlike world he's found. The distant horizon, the crowds, the crisp wind, and the "elusive fragrance of alien flowers" all delight her at first. But by the end of her day-trip to the surface, she is freezing and overwhelmed. She returns home, knowing she will lose Max to someone less afraid.

For all Tina's world is as cute as that of the home of Antoine de Saint-Exupéry's *Little Prince* (1943), Wolf's descriptions can't help but bring to mind the fuzzy pink handcuffs of traditional femininity. In this regard, it echoes Charlotte Perkins Gilman's "If I Were A Man," written a half-century earlier (1914). In that more didactic story, "pretty little Mollie Matthewson" yearns to be stronger, less subject to the whims of men and femininity. Her wish is granted and she becomes her husband, a man with pockets, money, shoes he can run in.

Wolf's Tina and Perkins Gilman's Mollie Mathewson are expected to live in small, soft worlds; to be what their husbands and fathers demand them to be; to never brave failure or discomfort. Their stories end differently: Mollie rides alongside her husband's consciousness, spies on powerful men, and steers his views towards feminism, while Tina returns to her gentle festivals and quiet breezes. But in the final scene, as she dances, Tina thinks that "the wind seemed too soft somehow, almost lifeless, with the air too sweet and cloying." Perhaps, in time, she will learn to brave cold winds and make her own way into the stars.

The Agony of the Leaves
by Evelyn E. Smith

(Originally appeared in the July 1954 issue of *Beyond Fantasy Fiction*. It has never been republished before now.)

The chimes over the door sounded. Ernest didn't want to answer, but he knew there was no use struggling any more—the outcome was inevitable. He walked to the foyer as slowly as he could, wondering which one of them it was this time. Whichever it was, she apparently thought he was taking too long to answer, for, when he was within a few yards of the door, his feet picked themselves up of their own volition and began to run.

He saved himself from a headlong crash into the door by thrusting his palm out flat before him. Instead of meeting inflexible wood, however, his hand was sucked into a spongy substance that became more glutinous the more it yielded. Damn the woman! She was melting down the door again. He was sure it was Mrs. Greenhut—Miss Levesque would never do anything as subtle as all that.

He pulled his hand free and the door subsided in a puddle on the sill. Mrs. Greenhut stood in the corridor, a smile on her round, freshly washed face, a plate of cookies in her plump hand. Anybody seeing her for the first time—the bosomy, tightly corseted figure, the ruffled pink apron over the be-flowered green housedress, the plainly combed brown hair sprinkled with gray—would have taken her for just a pleasant, middle-aged matron. That was how Ernest had placed her when he'd moved into the apartment…had it been only two months before? It seemed like several eternities.

And to think he'd been fool enough to smile at this motherly looking fiend, just in the hope of getting invited to a home-cooked meal! She could cook adequately, but she couldn't even brew a good pot of tea!

"I've brought you some cookies, Ernest dear," Mrs. Greenhut purred. "I baked them this morning, 'specially for you. They're real nice too, if I do say so myself."

"They look very good," he said, without extending a hand. "But, as a matter of fact, I do have a touch of indigestion, and the doctor said—"

"Take them, Ernest," Mrs. Greenhut said. "You'll love them."

His right arm moved out stiffly, almost dislocating his shoulder, and took the plate.

"You will eat every one of them, Ernest. Do you understand?"

"Yes, Mrs. Greenhut," Ernest mumbled.

"I've told you a thousand times, if I've told you once, to call me Gertrude."

"Yes, Gertrude. I'll eat every one of them—I swear it."

"Good boy," she approved, patting his cheek with a soft, floury hand. "Maybe they'll help to put a little flesh on your bones. Lately, you've been looking mighty peaked, seems to me."

"I like my physique exactly the way it is," Ernest protested. After all, if she didn't like his appearance, why was she pursuing him with her attentions? "I don't want to get fat."

"I like a man to eat hearty," Mrs. Greenhut said with finality. "And I like him to *look* hearty, too."

"Yes, Mrs. Greenhut—Gertrude."

"I have no use for thin people," she went on contemplatively. "'Specially thin women. Take that girl on the ground floor, for instance. Some people might call her attractive, but I personally think she's just a bag of bones. Probably starves herself too."

"Disgustingly skinny," Ernest agreed hastily. "Completely repulsive! Not at all womanly, like—" he gulped "—like you, Gertrude."

"You have *such* good taste, Ernest. That's one of the reasons why I...like you. Of course—" she pinched his cheek affectionately—"there are other reasons too." Ernest turned red and looked away. How he could hate her, if she would only let him!

"Well," she said briskly, "I must be running along. I have a roast in the oven."

"Good-by, Gertrude. Thank you for the delicious cookies."

"Good-by, Ernest. And remember, don't break the plate this time. It made me very, very unhappy when you smashed that other one, after I'd gone and brought you such a lovely devil's food cake."

"I didn't break the plate last time," he defended himself. "It was Miss Levesque. She dropped a piece of the ceiling on it."

"Oh, she did, did she?" Mrs. Greenhut said darkly. "I'll fix *her*! She did it purposely—she knows I set a lot of store on my Rockingham. It was my grandmother's." She resettled one of the combs in her hair and changed the subject with a simper. "Wouldn't you like to maybe kiss me before I go, Ernest?"

He bent over stiffly and gave her a peck on the cheek. Satisfied—fortunately, she did not make the demands on him that Miss Levesque did—she started away.

"Wait a minute!" he called down the corridor after her. "How about my door?"

She turned with a giggle. "I do declare, that was a plumb silly thing for me to do, wasn't it? But I've always been such a giddy creature—I just can't control my mad impulses. That's what Mr. Greenhut always used to say. 'Land's sakes, Gertie, I guess you'll just never grow up,' he used to say."

Ernest wondered vaguely, as he had wondered many times since signing his ill-fated lease, what had happened to the apparently deceased Mr. Greenhut. He wouldn't have been a bit surprised to hear that the woman had authored his departure.

Aloud, he complained. "But I really do need my door, Gertrude. There's a draft coming in from outside. You know, if anything happened to my nasal passages, it could ruin my future." She sniffed, and he added, "Or I might catch pneumonia and die." It would serve her right too… if only his death wouldn't involve himself so drastically.

"I'll solidify your door right away, dear boy," she said, apparently moved by this horrible prospect. "I wouldn't for the world," she went on archly, "want to lose you."

He groaned in an undertone.

She restored the door and Ernest trudged back into his living room, munching a cookie as he went. It tasted good. If only he could forget what was in it!

The gaunt, brightly painted features of Miss Levesque glared at him from the huge Venetian mirror over the mantelpiece. "Stop eating those cookies this very instant, Ernest. I *command* you!"

"I can't, Désirée," he said, fretfully. "You know that as well as I do. I'm under a spell. You remember what happened when you made me drink that champagne you made yourself?" In addition to being spiked, her wine had tasted as if she hadn't bothered to remove her shoes before trampling the grapes.

Miss Levesque emerged from the mirror, catching the train of her long red satin evening gown in the glass. She freed it with a jerk. "I *order* you to stop," she said, fixing him with her hot black eyes and gasping for breath, as she clambered down from the mantelpiece. Ernest held his breath until he could be sure that his *shu-dei* and *haku-dei* teapots were undamaged. She—both of them—were so careless with other people's property, as well as with other people themselves.

"Can't stop," he mumbled through a full mouth. "Besides, they're pretty good cookies at that. Why don't you try one? I don't suppose it would have any effect on you. Go ahead," he urged.

Miss Levesque bit a cookie critically. "Wouldn't you know she'd skimp on the shortening? And she shouldn't have used the love potion *instead* of the vanilla."

"I'd offer you a cup of tea to go with 'em, but I can't stop eating long enough to go make it."

"Ernest Fitch!" She stamped her foot. "*Stop* eating the rest of those cookies. Do you hear me?" A heavy paperweight whizzed off the French provincial desk and shattered plate and cookies into bits.

Ernest mechanically got down on his hands and knees and began to pick fragments of the cookies out of the shards on the rug, dust them off and eat them. "*Now* see what you've done," he complained, chewing. "You've only given me more trouble, because I've got to eat them, every one. She put her spell on me first. And you've broken one of her good plates again too..."

"Hussy, *painted* hussy!" said Mrs. Greenhut's voice from thin air, for she was much too proper to materialize inside a man's apartment, even chaperoned by Miss Levesque. "Spoil my Rockingham set, will you? Two can play at that game, dear."

To his horror, Ernest found himself rising jerkily to his feet, walking— only it was actually more like dancing—over to the desk and picking up a bottle of ink. This he poured methodically over Miss Levesque's head, down her decolletage. Although the act was against his volition, it was not against his inclination. "*Désirée!*" he yelped, fearing she could tell from his expression that he was not altogether unhappy. "I didn't mean to do it, honestly! She's *making* me!"

Miss Levesque forgot she was a lady. "Bless the heavenly woman!" she yelled. "Bless her, *bless her*!...just you wait and see, Gertrude! Will I put a spell on *you* later!" She tossed her head.

Ernest winced, as ink spattered on the beautiful new turquoise rug. Miss Levesque had selected it to match the color of his eyes, but he had paid for it, and a free-lance tea-taster's earnings—even if he were permitted to work steadily—wouldn't allow him to buy new rugs every day.

"I know it's not your fault, hon," she murmured in a tender bass, advancing upon him as he still scrabbled for crumbs on the floor. "Come here and give me a nice gooey kiss."

He backed away on all fours. She frowned ominously. "So you find me repulsive, do you?"

"No, no!" Ernest's voice rose to a squeak, as unseen, icy fingers used his spine for a xylophone. "You're fascinating, really *fascinating*, Désirée, I assure you." His voice cracked. "But you've ink all over yourself. You wouldn't want me to get ink on my suit, would you? It's a Brooks Brothers' suit," he added lamely.

"I suppose not," she sighed, halting her advance. "I wouldn't want to do a single, solitary thing to make you less handsome than you are, sweetie."

He hid his eyes in embarrassment and started again to eat crumbs hurriedly from the rug. It wouldn't even occur to her to offer to make him a cup of tea. Not that she could—without a tea bag, she'd be lost. Mrs. Greenhut and Miss Levesque being coffee drinkers were, like the rest of that vast, insensitive tribe, prone to foist their own vulgar tastes upon others.

"Lover," she went on huskily, "why don't you marry me? Then that Greenhut woman would never bother you again. She has old-fashioned ideas of morality and would never dream of coming between a husband and wife… as, of course, is only right and proper."

"I can't marry you, Désirée," he said through a mouthful of crumbs, "because I love Gertrude. And I can't marry Gertrude because I love you. Both of you have been feeding me so many love potions that I suspect you've ruined my digestion entirely."

"I'll bet, if you were left to yourself, you wouldn't marry either of us," Miss Levesque said darkly. Ernest chewed cookie crumbs and swallowed them without commenting.

"I've seen you giving the eye to that little blonde trollop who moved in the other week," she went on. "Nasty little foreigner. If there's one thing I can't stand, it's foreigners. If you ask me, a lot of these so-called refugees didn't escape from their countries—more likely, they were *asked* to leave." Miss Levesque glared at him disapprovingly. "*Refugee!*"

The idea of calling that angelic creature a trollop! To think that there was any country, any place or any one that did not find her desirable! But he must conceal his interest, or poor Nadia might find herself the innocent victim of some particularly unpleasant spell. It was for this praiseworthy reason that he had been avoiding her. Several times, in fact, he had actually lifted his hand to knock on her door and ask her to share a dish of tea with him, and each time he'd stifled the impulse.

"I only know her to say hello to," he protested, licking the last crumb off his mouth. That was almost true, but there are hellos and hellos. "Besides, I'm getting sick of all women. If I ever can get away from you two, I think I ought to join a monastery." He looked up at her anxiously, to make sure she recognized a joke.

Miss Levesque smiled slyly. "And what makes you think we can't get into a monastery? Oh, Gertrude and I have had some jolly times together before you came between us."

"I certainly never *wanted* to come between you," Ernest muttered. Blast the day he'd accepted this woman's offer to help him decorate his apartment. Simply because she looked an artistic type! He should have known that it's usually the artistic types who are the most passionate and besides, she had proved to have terrible taste. He'd even been lucky that she'd let him put his Hokasais away in the closet instead of in the wastepaper basket.

"I'll gladly step aside!" he went on eagerly. "I realize that true friendship is far more important than—"

"Don't be ridiculous. It isn't. Nothing in the world is more important than the love of a man for a woman. And vice versa." She flung her arms wide. "Come, embrace me, Ernest, with ardor tempered by tenderness."

"I already told you why not," he repeated, annoyed. "You're dripping with ink."

"Of course," she agreed, sounding regretful. "I quite forgot—I always get carried away by the intoxication of your presence, sweetie." Ernest repressed a shudder, remembering times when this had actually happened. On one such occasion, he hadn't been able to distinguish between Foochow and Faggot for days afterward.

She blew him a kiss. "I'll just float upstairs and change. Then, maybe, I'll put a spell on that Greenhut creature, if I can think of something really horrid. See you later, lover."

"Good-by," Ernest said. "Nice of you to drop in," he added perfunctorily. It was safest to be especially polite to these—women. They became provoked so easily. That's how he'd lost his best Chinese hoccarro teapot.

As soon as she'd disappeared, he grabbed his hat, adjusted his muffler—for the early spring day could be treacherous—and made for the door. He had been abstinent far too long—he must have his *tea*! Although he made an infinitely better cup himself, at least he'd be relatively safe from all undesired attentions in Schrafft's. Neither of the ladies liked to make a public spectacle of herself if it could be avoided.

Besides, they couldn't really object to his taking a quiet drink alone—although he remembered the time well, when he had tried to go downtown to taste a break of fully fine Oolong that had just arrived from Formosa, on an afternoon that Désirée had intended to spend with him! It had been a long time since he'd been allowed to have so much as a thought, let alone an action, of his own contriving. He might as well be dead. After all, didn't the old myth say tea-tasters always died young? His time had come, and it was probably none too soon.

He flung himself down the stairs in a burst of energy that, he hoped, would provide enough momentum to carry him past any unseen impediments at the door. As he bounded off the bottom step, he collided with something warm and soft and sweetly scented, like extra high-grade Pouchong. "I'm terribly sorry," he apologized, reluctantly releasing the girl from the embrace in which he somehow found himself holding her. "I hope I didn't hurt you, Miss Koldunya."

"You did not hurt me by the runnings into me," she smiled, adjusting the small fur hat on her smooth, shining ash-blonde hair. "And I am very happy to see you, even if you are seeing me only to be knocking me down. Almost knocking me down," she added—for she was apparently a stickler for accuracy.

"Yes…well," Ernest said, gazing apprehensively over his shoulder at what seemed to be a shadow in the upstairs hall, "I must be running off. Awfully nice seeing you, Miss Koldunya…"

"Are you making an avoidance of me, Mr. Fitch?" she asked, looking directly into his eyes. "You seemed so friendly when first we encountered. I thought you were interesting in me. Since then you have performed so coldly, so strangely. Have I done anythings—said anythings?"

In her earnestness, she placed a small, suède-gloved hand upon his arm. The glow he derived from the contact was very different from any of the sensations the ladies upstairs could evoke in him at their pleasure, although it was undoubtedly the kind they would have liked to be able to arouse. This was, he feared, the *real thing*.

But it was not to be. It was too late. He was doomed.

"Have I? Yes? No?" she persisted.

"Eh? Oh, yes—er—no. I really must be going," he said desperately. "Not a moment to lose. A matter of life and death."

"Where are you going?" she asked with disarming directness. Her large, luminous eyes looked at him intently.

How could he lie to *her*? "I'm going to Schrafft's for a cup of tea," he blurted.

"Good, *good!*" she said gaily. "I am absolutely attenuated from thirstiness. I will go along with you, and you will buying me also a drink, if you will be so kindly." He couldn't refuse a request like that. But would *they* — he glanced fearfully upstairs — understand? They would not.

"Miss Koldunya — Nadia!" he declared, taking both her vibrant hands in his. "You mustn't come with me. You'll be in terrible danger if you do."

She freed her hands, and he felt a deep, physical sense of loss. "Why, Ernest, how melodramatically you are sounding. Like the cinema almost. You excite my inquiry."

"You don't understand — danger!" he babbled.

She moved away slightly and looked at him with a sad little smile. "I — I am not understanding what danger is? *Ha!*" She laughed and, at last, he understood what a mirthless laugh was. "Haplessly, you do not know where I am coming from. I am a refugee — what is the euphemism? — a dispersed people. I have no country any more, no families, nothing. I am escaping from Eastern Europe underneath rather displeasing conditions."

She shuddered and he shivered in sympathy. Poor little creature — she needed a man to protect her after all she'd been through. He flexed the muscles that lay dormant beneath the Brooks Brothers' suit.

"I am assuring you, Ernest, danger is an elderly acquaintance of mine." She shrugged her shoulders. "However, if you are not wishful to buy me a beverage, it is completely all right. I understand. I have been too forward. It is not the costum here for the womens to make the askings." She turned her face away.

"No, you *don't* understand!" Ernest protested, in spite of himself. "I *do* want to buy you a beverage. More than anything else in the world. Only — oh, what's the use? Please *do* come," he said recklessly.

Immediately, Nadia was as gay again as if she had suffered no rebuff. He swung open the heavy door of the old brownstone. Outside, spring lay bright over the shabby, nondescript street, but the sun's rays halted sharply at the gloomy entry, almost as if there were some barrier there. He felt that he too would be unable to cross that threshold, that he could not go out to meet the sun. And he felt very sorry for poor Ernest Fitch, doomed to stay forever in this gloomy brownstone, unable to taste the delights of Uji Yamashiro and Nadia's smile.

Then Nadia gave him her hand and they were out of the house, clattering down the steps...and actually on the sidewalk at last.

The very matter-of-factness of the street was enormously appealing to him, enhanced as it was by the sun's yellow rays, which illuminated each homely garbage can with loving solicitude and left shimmering highlights in Nadia's long, pale hair—the exact color of Moyune Gunpowder—which the gentle breeze left undisturbed.

Feeling the warm sunlight on his face, listening to the girl's pleasantly innocuous prattle, he could hardly believe that, for the last two months, he had actually been undergoing such improbable experiences. For a moment, he felt relaxed and free and was moved to lift his voice in a Japanese teaplunkers' song. "*Natsu mo,*" he caroled, "*chikazuku Hachi-Ju-Hachi-Ya…*"

And then he stopped short. Why was it that, although there was no one near them in the street, he could hear footsteps following them very distinctly?

The girl continued her cheerful chattering all the way, not seeming to notice the glances he kept throwing over his shoulder. But then, of course, if she came from behind the Iron Curtain, she would accept this as perfectly conventional behavior.

She told him how lucky she had been, as a foreigner of suspect nationality, to get a job as a school 'p-sychologist.' "Do you not think it fascinating to work with childrens, Ernest? To assist shaping their little minds as they make development? It is a wonderful privilege and a tremense responsibility."

"Er—ah—yes, children," Ernest agreed, wondering perhaps whether he'd only imagined the sound of footsteps behind them. Mrs. Greenhut and Miss Levesque couldn't be watching him *all* the time. It was hard to distinguish between imagination and reality, when the latter was so much the more fantastic of the two. Yet, if he reasoned the matter out, he would know that Mrs. Greenhut and Miss Levesque undoubtedly had far more efficient methods of transportation than mere walking. What was that flash in the air over his head?

"Children," he repeated, comprehending that he was not making any notable contribution to the conversation. "Nice—er—children. Here's Schrafft's." And he plunged into its comfortingly murky interior, leaving Nadia to make her own way after him.

A swanlike hostess swam up to them, greeted Ernest with approval, regarded Nadia with hauteur and turned them both over to a waitress with the cryptic command, "Two."

"We'd like a table in a corner, where I can keep my back to the wall." Ernest turned on a charming smile. "I—I'm susceptible to chills in my back," he explained.

"*Ha!*" Nadia observed enigmatically.

"Two teas, please," he said to the waitress, when she had seated them in the darkest comer, "and two orders of tea sandwiches."

"Please to serving me in a glass, accompanied by two slices of lemming,"

Nadia demanded, stripping off her gloves with great deliberation. "Recollect that the water must be at the absolutely bubbly boil — and *no* little bandages around the tea!"

"But we *always* serve tea in bags, madam," the waitress protested, aghast, looking to Ernest for moral support.

"Not to me you are serving bandaged tea," Nadia said, looking the girl firmly in the eye. "And I am wanting a dish of preserves on the side. Any flavoring," she added graciously, "except quincy."

"But — yes, madam," the waitress said, a glazed look in her eyes. "Right away, madam."

"Er — I'll have my tea without a tea bag too," Ernest said feebly, marveling at Nadia's boldness in daring to beard Schrafft's. "But in a pot, not a glass. And with milk!"

Nadia snorted, as the waitress moved off. "*Milk*! An illegitimate innovation. Did you not know that milk is not being pushed into tea until 1680 A.D.? And it was some womans from West Europe who is doing this terrible thing — of course."

"There have been improvements in many things since 1680," retorted Ernest, pleased to find himself still capable of argument. "The tea industry is continually progressing. After all, we don't flavor tea with ginger, onion or orange any more, do we?"

"You are never knowing in plenty restaurants," Nadia said. "Anybodies who is strangling their tea through bandagings have ability of anythings."

"Milk not only mellows the taste," Ernest explained, "but it prevents the tannin in tea from injuring the digestive organs."

Nadia drew out a long, gold-tipped cigarette and handed Ernest a lighter. "You are knowing considerable about the tea, Ernest." Her skin, he thought, was like the petals of a tea blossom which is, of course, of the same genus as the camellia.

"Well, I'm in the tea business," he explained.

"So, that is how you earn your existence? What are you doing particularly?"

"I'm a tea-taster," he said. "I can blend too —" He jumped up as a shadow fell upon him.

It was only the waitress, bearing a tray which contained a glass of tea and a pot of tea and a jug of hot water and a dish of lemon slices and a dish of strawberry jam and a jug of milk and two large dishes containing immense quantities of sandwiches. Schrafft's had never done him so proud before. He could see Nadia knew her way around tearooms.

The waitress went away, and Nadia put a warm hand on his. He could feel tangible reassurance rising from it. She was a nice kind of girl to have around. Soothing.

"What is the matter, Ernest?" she asked. "You are trembling like an aspic. Is it that the secret police are trailing after you, yes?"

He was momentarily shocked out of his apprehension. "The police! Certainly *not*—I've never done anything wrong in my life."

"You certainly do look as if somebodies were haunting you," she said, sipping her tea and making a face. "Why you are not disclosing to me about it, if only for the therapeutic value of confession?"

Why shouldn't he? Perhaps he would feel better if he could confide in someone—and who would be better for him to unbosom himself to than this lovely, sympathetic, altogether understanding girl? Besides, moral duty required him to warn her of the terrible danger she was exposing herself to by associating with him.

He looked around furtively to make sure they were not overheard. "As a matter of fact, there is somebody after me. But it's not the police—it's witches."

Nadia's expression was so well trained that the sudden gleam of clinical interest in her eyes was barely perceptible. "My poor Ernest," she said, patting his hand. "My poor, paranoid Ernest."

He pulled his hand away. "You don't *believe* me!" It had simply not occurred to him that she would not believe him. Previously, of course, he himself had not believed in witches, but, now that he knew them to be factual entities, he expected her to accept his word. Couldn't she tell he was sincere? But it probably wasn't his sincerity she doubted, he realized—it was more likely his sanity.

"You don't believe there are witches?" he questioned with less assurance.

"For sure, there are witches," she said, eating a sandwich. "The middle-aged stereotype of the witch is only an unconscious symbolization of one's own guilt-feelings, a projectioning of them upon other peoples. You were saying before that never you had doing anythings wrong in your life. To the trained p-sychologist, such a statement is fraught with significantness. It—"

"But these aren't medieval witches," he interrupted. "They're modern, contemporary witches. They live upstairs from me. From you, too," he added, to drive the matter home. "Mrs. Greenhut owns the house."

"Regressioning to the fantasty world of your childhoodness," she added kindly. "Not an uncommon dynamism, for sure, but potentially dangerous."

Nadia didn't seem to understand at all what he meant. He tried again. "You know Mrs. Greenhut and Miss Levesque? They're witches, I tell you."

"If they are witches, pigeon, why is it that they are seeming to me simplicitly just a coupling of nice, dull, medieval-aged womens?"

Ernest thought he heard a hiss in the air and fervently hoped he was wrong. "Because the higher type witch doesn't advertise herself—that's why," he explained triumphantly. "Both of them told me so. Separately, of course, because they haven't spoken to each other—politely, anyhow—since I moved into the house. They don't want anything out of you, so why should they let you in on their secret?"

"Well, then, what is it so especially they are wanting out of *you*, Ernest?"

"They are wanting…they want to marry me," he said sulkily, wishing she would stop chewing when he spoke to her.

"Oh, Ernest!" she said, with her mouth full. "That is to project, indeed. You probably are imagining every womans you meet is wanting to marry you or somethings, that you are an irresistible fellow. Wish-fulfillmenting to almost pathological degree, as a resulting of thwartled developments of ego neediness." She gestured with an oversized tea sandwich. "I am loathsome to say this, Ernest, but I am fearful you are showing evidence of deep emotional maladjustment."

"I do *not* think every woman wants to marry me," Ernest protested, casting an involuntary glance at himself in the mirror set in the wooden paneling over the table. Catching her eye, he flushed.

"Tea must be brewed by now," he muttered, lifting the lid and peering into the pot. "One of the worst things about tea bags," he added absently, "is that they keep you from seeing the agony of the leaves."

"The *which*, Ernest?"

He smiled. "No, I'm not betraying any more interesting symptoms. That's a tea-tasting term—means the unfolding of the leaves when boiling water's poured on them."

She leaned over and looked curiously into the pot. The odor of jasmine that arose from her was almost overpowering. He would have enjoyed taking her in his arms. "It is looking to me as if somebodies put those leaves out of their agony much time ago," she observed.

She sat back and let Ernest light another cigarette for her. "Better imbibe it, pigeon. Even torpid tea is stimulizing and will have a favorable p-sychological affection upon you."

"You're quite right about that, you know," he agreed. "There was an article on the subject in the London *Lancet* sometime in the eighteen-sixties.

Something about tea having a strange influence over mood, a strange power of changing the look of things, and changing it for the better, so that we can believe and hope and do, under the influence of tea, what we should otherwise give up in discouragement and despair."

He poured the amber fluid into his cup and sipped. "Not too good a blend for hard water," he commented. And then, "I don't suppose you could expect much of a nose."

She blew a cloud of smoke and smiled at him. "Well, pigeon, have the lookings of things changed strangely for the betterment?"

He looked at her calmly. "You know, Nadia, Mrs. Greenhut and Miss Levesque are real witches. They cast spells on me and force me to do whatever they want. You psychologists are too much inclined to consider everything outside the range of your own textbooks as either nonexistent or unimportant. I tell you those were genuine spells."

"Compulsions, Ernest," she corrected him, eating a spoonful of jam, "not spells. And it is you who are casting them upon yourself." She daintily licked the spoon clean.

"But they do all sorts of odd and inexplicable things," he protested. "I've seen them with my own eyes."

"You cannot always be trustful of your own eyes," she observed, wavering between two equally attractive sandwiches. "Obviously, you are demonstrative of typical phobic reactings. Some traumatic experiencing in your childhoodness is undoubtedless responsive for your presently maladjustative behaviorism."

"Maloo mixture!" Ernest snapped. He drank more tea. "They feed me love potions all the time," he said, flatly irritated at her narrow-mindedness. "I am madly in love with both of them."

She smiled, for a moment the woman, rather than the 'p-sychologist.' "If these so-said love potations are officious, pigeon," she said coyly, "how is it you are imbibing here with me and not with your witch friends, eh?" She glanced at the mirror and nodded her head, apparently feeling that what she saw there answered her question completely.

"Now," she went on briskly, once more the scientist, "you must not be evasive, Ernest. You must facing around your problems squarely and apply the intelligentness and rationable analysizing to them. Why should two respectful medieval womens be using witchcraftiness to making you marry them?"

"And who do you think you're calling an elderly woman, slut?" shrieked Miss Levesque disrespectfully, as her cavernous head rose out of a crust on the table before them. "I'll give you just one second to clear out of here, baby, and leave my Ernest alone, before I let you have it!"

"*Your* Ernest!" stated a voice from the air, for Mrs. Greenhut wouldn't have dreamed of materializing in Schrafft's wearing a housedress. "You have some nerve! *Your* Ernest, indeed!"

And Miss Levesque's long, lank, black hair stood tautly on end, as if some invisible hand were tugging at it. She gave vent to prolonged and uninhibited ululation.

"*There!*" Ernest said triumphantly. "Who's having hallucinations now?"

Nadia raised bland blue eyes to his. "What are you intending to tell me, Ernest?" she asked, nibbling a piece of date-nut bread.

He pointed with a trembling finger. "D-don't you see Miss Levesque's head in the middle of the table?"

"A head in the middle of the ta—Oh, Ernest, this hallucinating is of uttermost seriousness. You are betraying prominent schizophrenic tendencies."

Miss Levesque's hair suddenly subsided in limp streaks over her bony face, as the invisible power holding it relaxed its grip. "She's a liar," she declared angrily, blowing the hair out of her way. "Just pretending not to see me out of spite, the little trollop!"

"Maybe there's something wrong with her eyes," Ernest put in anxiously. "Nadia, have you ever tried sleeping on a pillow stuffed with tea leaves? It's an old Chinese remedy for eye trouble."

"*Ha!*" Nadia smiled seductively at him. "If you are really desiring to know what my pillows are being stuffed with, why don't you—"

"Listen here, you little..." Miss Levesque began, in a voice choked with wrath.

The waitress approached the table apprehensively. "Anything else, sir?" she asked, keeping her eyes on her apron. "M-madam?"

Ernest greeted her arrival with enthusiasm. "Miss, what do you see on top of this cruet?"

The girl knitted her brows and bent herself to the problem. "I see oil, vinegar and mustard," she replied conscientiously. "Did you want ketchup? For tea?"

"In Bokhara," Nadia pointed out, pensively ladling jam into her tea, "they are flavoring tea with mutton fat. After they have drunken it, then they are eating the leaves. Very economomical, those Bokharans."

"Ugh," observed Mrs. Greenhut's voice.

"I imagine ketchup in tea would be more like *letpet*," Ernest commented. "Did you know they pickle tea in Burma?" he asked the waitress.

"N-no, sir," the girl said, clutching her tray to her bosom.

"They make a salad out of it, with garlic, oil and, occasionally, dried fish. It's a great treat—they eat it only on holidays and special occasions."

"I don't believe a word of it," stated Miss Levesque's head flatly.

"You don't?" Ernest was angry. "I suppose you don't believe that in Siam they chew tea mixed with salt and garlic or hog fat?"

Nadia opened her beautiful eyes wide. "Why, I *do* believe you, Ernest."

"*I* don't!" snapped Miss Levesque. "He's making it all up."

"I would like a large further quantity of little sandywitches," Nadia interrupted, licking jam from her full pink mouth, "and another glass of what I am very politely calling tea, if you will be so pleasing."

The waitress looked at her coldly. "Those little sandwiches have an awful lot of calories."

"I don't have to worrying about my outline," Nadia confided with a complacent smile. "I can eating all I want and it keeps staying just as nicely. I am a lucky girl, no?"

"Something to do with your glands, prob'ly," the waitress sniffed.

"I wouldn't be a bit surprised," Mrs. Greenhut's voice agreed.

"*Miss*," Ernest insisted. "Don't you see a head on the table?"

The waitress's eyes widened and she backed away. "Schrafft's don't like for you to spike your tea," she protested, all gentility lost.

"He has not put any spokes in the tea," Nadia explained, blowing smoke in the girl's face. "He is just thinking he is funny."

"Oh," the girl said feebly. "Ha, ha! Heads on the table," she repeated, laughing more conscientiously as she thought of her tip. "Ha, ha! That's a good one—I must tell the cashier."

"You can *perfectly* well see me!" put in Miss Levesque angrily. "You're lying too. It's all part of a plot."

"Your spells aren't strong enough, dear," another smug voice said from the air. "But it isn't your fault. You just can't do any better. You can hear *me* all right, can't you, young woman?"

"Another pot of tea for you, sir?"

Ernest nodded. "Better make it a double one," he said weakly.

"Young woman!" the voice from the air spoke again. "Will you kindly answer me when I address you? I declare, I don't know what the younger generation is coming to these days!"

The girl picked up her tray and walked away, looking over her shoulder and giggling every time she caught Nadia's eye.

"Why are you looking so funnily, Ernest?" Nadia asked, spooning up the remainder of the jam greedily.

"She—she didn't see her," Ernest quavered. "She didn't hear either of them."

"Oh, dear!" Nadia sighed. "Auditorium *and* visual hallucinations both. Now, listening to me, Ernest. She is not seeing or hearing them because they are existing only inside your mind."

"Now, that's silly!" he said indignantly. "How can Mrs. Greenhut and Miss Levesque possibly exist only inside my mind? You must have seen both of them. They have their names over the mailboxes and everything." He tried to gulp some tea, but it was cold and tasted of dead fish.

"For sure they have real existence," Nadia said impatiently, "but they are not witches. They are simplicity a coupling of harmless old womens whom you are fancifuling to be witches. The reality-irreality continuum is—"

"Harmless old woman!" Mrs. Greenhut's voice shrilled. "I'll show the little hussy who's old—and harmless," she added ominously. "Hit her, Ernest. Hit her right in that pasty painted face of hers."

Ernest's right arm swung out ahead of him. He struggled to gain control, even though he knew it would be impossible. Mrs. Greenhut had taken charge. Disregarding the wishes of its owner, the arm reached toward Nadia's lovely face. He watched with detached horror as his hand hovered in the air before her dainty nose. Then the stiff fingers relaxed and stroked her cheek clumsily.

"Why, Ernest!" Nadia giggled, patting his hand. "Already we are establishing rapport!"

"*Ernest!*" Mrs. Greenhut's voice emitted visible sparks. "I said *hit* her!"

"I can't," he replied, rolling his eyes up toward the point from which her voice seemed to originate. "I didn't want to, but I tried, and I couldn't!"

Nadia gripped his hand tensely. She was surprisingly strong. "Ernest, you are talking with much incoherentness. I am worrying intensively over you. You are now being demonstrative of hebephrenic symptomatology." Her eyes were intent on his.

"I don't understand it!" Mrs. Greenhut wailed. "It's downright uncanny—*that's* what it is."

"Leggo his hand, you little tart," Miss Levesque snarled, "or you'll be plenty sorry!"

The waitress arrived with fresh tea and sandwiches. "I brought you some more jam, miss," she said defiantly. "But don't blame me if it sticks to your hips."

She departed. "There will be no jamb on my hips, pigeon," Nadia assured

Ernest. "You will see."

"Watch me, Gertrude!" Miss Levesque commanded desperately. "This time, I'll show the heavenly little wench she can't ignore *me*!"

The glass of tea zoomed up from the table and hung upside down over Nadia's gleaming head. It descended a fraction of an inch in a vacillating sort of way. Then it halted and remained immobile in mid-air, not a drop of the tawny liquid emerging to dampen the chic little mink cap.

"Nadia!" Ernest screeched. "Look *out*!"

"Look out for what, pigeon?" she asked, removing the top from a sandwich and peering inside to see whether she approved of the filling.

"Your tea! It's hanging over your head. And I wish you'd stop eating all the time I'm talking to you!"

"Please do not being ridiculous, Ernest. My tea — if you are calling it tea — is right here in my hand. What is more, you are much uncourtly."

She sipped her tea. Ernest looked to see whether there might be two glasses, but the air above her head was empty.

Nadia leaned forward, frowning anxiously. "Ernest, cannot you envision for yourself that there is something very wrongly amiss with you? Normal running-with-the-mill peoples are not believing in witches any more — you know that."

She gestured toward the roomful of stout matrons contentedly and obliviously having their afternoon tea. "None of them is envisioning anything exceptionable. You are manifestating p-sychotic divergencies from the group thinking. Ergo, you are suffering from the deludings. You see?"

"I wonder whether I've been drinking too much tea," he mused. "An excess of any stimulant may very well prove deleterious to the nervous system."

"Good tea," Nadia said, "never hurt any bodies. You must coming to my apartment, and I will show you some good tea from my samovar. I will also show you other things."

"*Delusions!*" wailed Miss Levesque's head. "But I happen to know for a fact that we aren't delusions! We're real. I simply cannot understand why you don't see me, or hear either of us. I don't know why everything is going wrong unless…"

"…unless," Mrs. Greenhut's voice took up the sentence grimly, "she's a more powerful witch than either one of us. Let's face it, Désirée, that's just about the only logical explanation. There's a lot of talent for this sort of thing in Eastern Europe."

A brief baffled silence ensued. Ernest cleared his throat. "Now, look here!"

he said firmly. Nadia and Miss Levesque looked at him, and he could sense Mrs. Greenhut's steady stare. Under their combined gazes, he felt like a tea leaf uncurling underneath the onslaught of the boiling water. "Er—ah—yes," he said.

"Have some more tea, Ernest," Nadia said softly.

"Gertrude," Miss Levesque said, with plaintive determination, "we were once friends. For old times' sake..."

"...we must unite against the common enemy," Mrs. Greenhut finished for her. "Just what I was thinking myself. Now, Désirée, we must act together. One—two—three—*Go!*"

And Ernest found his legs propelling him past the other tables, past the cashier at a great rate, and out of Schrafft's at an even faster pace.

Then he was swooping into a postcard blue sky.

Ernest zoomed up the street, but he had none of the delicious sense of flying that one has in dreams. He felt simply as if he were being pushed and pulled and hauled and mauled, but he knew enough not to struggle. They were perfectly capable of dropping him, inadvertently of course, but motives never count for much in the ultimate run. He closed his eyes and hoped he was not going to be seasick. An experience like this could damage his palate permanently.

The little aerial cortege finally halted outside the windows of his apartment. Few second-floor tenants are given the privilege of viewing their dwellings from this angle, but Ernest, fluttering wildly in the air, failed to appreciate his position.

"Heavens to Betsy!" he heard Mrs. Greenhut's exasperated voice exclaim. "I should have remembered that these foolish windows have to be opened from the inside! Can you hold him all by yourself, Dési, while I dissolve them?"

"All right, Gertie," Miss Levesque said almost amiably, "but hurry." Ernest felt himself shifted into an even more precarious balance and repressed a faint moan. "He's no lightweight, especially after all those cookies and things you kept on feeding him—and all that tea he's been swilling."

"I'm going as fast as I can," Mrs. Greenhut retorted, "and please don't chatter. How can anybody work a good spell if you fuss, fuss, fuss? Be *careful!*" she shrieked, as Ernest started to slip from the invisible grasp in which he was insecurely held.

He gave a yelp as he plummeted downward.

"*I've* got him," Miss Levesque yelled triumphantly. Ernest could feel a bony hand twisting his jacket all out of shape. "But do hurry. We may not be able to put him together again if he gets smashed. At least, not in the same way. And I happen to like this particular arrangement."

Slowly — too slowly — the window liquefied and Ernest was inserted in the resultant aperture, one invisible lady pushing him, the other pulling. They dumped him on the rug, where he lay panting, unable to get up and not particularly wanting to anyway.

"Well, Ernest!" Nadia said, putting *Vogue* back on the marble top of the coffee table. "It's approximately the time for you to revert." She was sitting comfortably before the fireplace, her legs crossed to reveal a pair of handsomely filled nylons. "I do not think it was very couth of you to arise and digress in such a fashion, leaving me to settle for the account, including the teacup you sequestered."

"Teacup?" Ernest said vaguely. He looked at his hand and there, sure enough, was a teacup with tea surprisingly in it. He'd never be able to show his face in Schrafft's again.

"Still," she added more gently, "I had fear you might perhaps be troubled, so I came to make an investigation."

"I — I *didn't* — I didn't get up and walk out! How can you say such a thing? I was being forced out. You must have seen me."

She shook her head slowly and sadly. There was a feeling of intense loneliness at the pit of his stomach.

Underneath the smart hat, the face of the model on the cover of the magazine looked strangely like Miss Levesque's. "Go on, ask her how she got in the door?" she demanded. "Or have you been giving out duplicate keys, Ernest?"

"Certainly not!" he said firmly. "I wouldn't dream of — well, I wouldn't *do* it anyway. Nadia," he asked obediently, "how did you get into my apartment?"

She helped herself to some cashews from a T'ang bowl on the table and raised her eyebrows. "Why, you are leaving the door unjarred, so I am ingesting. I did not think you would be objectioning."

"I'm not — no — of course — I — oh, hell, I don't know what's happening to me," he declared miserably, shifting to a more comfortable position on the rug. "What's more, I'm beginning not to care. This is all just too much. I'm glad tea-tasters never live to grow old. I'm glad, I'm *glad*!"

There was a look of concern on Nadia's face. "But you are sickly, pigeon," she murmured, getting up. "You do look rather pallorous. Haplessly I am running you amuck, with too much analysis all in concert. I am undermining you, forcing you into apatheticity." She went over to him and stroked his head with cool, comforting fingers. "I am so sorrowful, pigeon," she cooed. "I would not for all the hemisphere want to hurting you. All I am wishful to infect is a restoration of the integratation of your personality resourcefulness. In other words—" and she gave him a long, lingering look out of her cobalt eyes—"I am just wanting to make you happy. Come down and see my samovar."

"I can't," he said wretchedly. The old spells were on him again. "They won't let me. You know they won't let me."

"I will boil some waters and make you a tea right here then," she announced. "In a cup," she concluded magnanimously.

"I have tea already," he said, and took a slug from the Schrafft brew, which strangely seemed to have retained its heat although it was flat and stale. "Nadia," he asked, looking bleakly up at the girl, "tell me—are *you* a witch also?"

She sat down, cross-legged, beside him on the rug. "So you are one of those peoples who are terminating analysis as witch-doctors, yes?"

He shook his head. "Not a witch-*doctor*—only *witch*."

She shrugged. "If there are being witches," she said gaily, "then I dare to say that you could name a p-sychologist or a p-sychoanalyst one, as much as any other scientific population. But, Ernest, we *know* there are being no such creations existing today. This is a hard-hitted, rationalizing society."

There was a knock at the door. "Excuse me," Ernest said politely, scrambling to his feet. "I'd better open it, or else."

"Good afternoon, Ernest dear," smiled Mrs. Greenhut. For the occasion, she had changed her housedress to a snug black crêpe, ornamented by a rope of pearls. "May I come in?"

He stood aside silently, knowing that, if she wanted in, she would come in. He had fought her—both of them—at first, and it had been painful and humiliating and useless.

"Why, if it isn't Miss Koldunya from downstairs," Mrs. Greenhut said graciously, "How do you do, my dear?"

Nadia got up from the rug and brushed the well-shaped back of her skirt painstakingly. "How are you doing?" she replied, after a pause just long enough to be insolent.

"Ha, so you *do* see me!" Mrs. Greenhut snapped, abruptly shedding her company manners. "You admit it!"

Nadia looked with meaning at Mrs. Greenhut's portly form. "How could anybodies be not seeing you?" she asked pleasantly.

Mrs. Greenhut turned a mottled red and began to swell like a balloon. Ernest watched, fascinated, as the seams of the black crêpe visibly stretched further than any normal seam ever could.

Then Mrs. Greenhut controlled herself with a visible effort and bared her teeth in a vicious social smile. "Since you seem to be trying to *delude* this poor, dear boy into believing that there are no such beings as witches, Miss Koldunya, how do you explain the fact that I, an ordinary, harmless woman, came into the room through the *closet*?" she demanded triumphantly. "You have the apartment on the ground floor, where the layout is slightly different," she continued, "so of course you didn't know his front door was on the other side of the foyer."

"Closet!" Nadia raised her eyebrows. "You are coming in through the closet? But, admissibly, that is a common thing to be doing. Nice people are not injecting themselves via closets."

She crossed over to the door through which Mrs. Greenhut had entered and flung it open. The outside hall was clearly visible beyond.

Nadia smiled. "I am fearful you must have mistaken yourself, Mrs. Greenhut. This—" she opened what Ernest had always thought to be his front door—"is the closet." And so it was. Ernest gulped a draught of tea. Pushing him around was bad enough, but he did not like having his closet displaced. Was nothing sacred to these women?

"What pretty depictions!" he heard Nadia exclaim. "All about Japanese peoples imbibing teas. Why are you not dangling them from the walls, Ernest, instead of hoodwinking them in a closet?"

"I'll bet you think you're pretty smart!" Miss Levesque growled, oozing out of the coffee table in a purple velvet gown. "Still claim you can't see me, baby?"

"Oh, I am seeing you very much indeed," Nadia replied, taking a mint from a Satsuma *gusuri chawan* on the piano. "You ingressed with this other womans. It is always nice for womans of a certain age to have friendshipmates of their own sex—it makes compensation for their not abling to distract other sex."

"Don't pull that on us, you—you *witch*!" Miss Levesque snarled.

"Ah, she is wielding the word in a colloquiational sense, no?" Nadia observed to Ernest, with an air of enlightenment. "Mayhaps she is not as I diagnosized. She is signifying only that—"

"She is using the word quite literally," Mrs. Greenhut corrected. "*I* am a witch—*you* are a witch—*she* is a witch."

"My English is truly very bad," Nadia admitted. "I am so full of gratitudeness for this lesson."

"We are *so* witches!" Miss Levesque shrieked, bursting into angry tears. She stamped her foot on the rug. "We are so—we *are*—we are so!"

"Désirée!" Mrs. Greenhut commanded. "Control yourself!"

Breathing hard, Miss Levesque fanned herself with *Some Chinese Ghosts*.

"*Ha!*" Nadia said, comprehension appearing to dawn in her lovely eyes. "My poor Ernest," she apologized, "I have made a great fallacy about you. I admit it happily. It is not you who are frustrating – it is these two old witches. Sex-starved old haggises, who will use any means to acquisitioning themselves a mans, even if they are having to hypnotize him and themselves, into fancifulling they are using witchcraftiness to secure him."

"*Sex-starved!*" Mrs. Greenhut gasped indignantly. "A decent young woman wouldn't *dream* of using language like that!"

"Who said she was a decent young woman?" sobbed Miss Levesque. "It's my belief she's nothing better than a –"

Ernest tossed off the rest of his tea and got to his feet. "Look here," he said firmly. "I won't have you talking about Nadia like that. And take your paws off that book, you! It's a valuable first edition."

Lafcadio Hearn fell to the carpet with a dull thunk. All three women turned to him with startled expressions on their faces. "Whether all this witchcraft is imaginary or not," he continued, pleased to see that Nadia looked as incredulous as the others, "you ought to be ashamed of yourselves – all three of you."

"Me as well?" Nadia asked in a small voice. "Not *me*, Ernest?"

"You too – you haven't been behaving one bit better than the others. And you should know better, too, because you've had the advantage of a better education." He scratched his head. "I guess I just happen to like you, although heaven knows why, because you've been treating me like an idiot also."

"It's not *heaven* that knows why you like her," Mrs. Greenhut commented.

"If she is a witch," Ernest said, whirling upon her, "at least she had the grace not to *tell* me that she was feeding me love potions or practicing her wiles upon me. So, if I'm in love with her, there's a fighting chance that it was my own idea as well as hers. What's more, she shares my interests – or, at least, she's taken the trouble to bone up on them. She's very sound on tea – and she wouldn't dream of trying to make me drink *coffee!*" He spat out the word contemptuously.

"Well, we're at least frank," Miss Levesque pouted. "Don't you believe in the virtue of candor?"

"I happen," Ernest said spiritedly, testing the return of his independence, "to be a perfectly normal and conventional member of society, in spite of both of you – and you, *pigeon*." He bowed toward Nadia. "And, as a perfectly normal and conventional member of society, I *like* hypocrisy – it is the basis of all civilized behavior."

"Bourgeois mentality," sniffed Nadia.

"Witchcraft," said Mrs. Greenhut.

Ernest grinned. "I'm not so sure it's all witchcraft," he said, giving Nadia a head-to-foot glance that should have made her blush, but didn't. "Look at her face and figure — *those* aren't witchcraft."

"Oh, *no*?" Mrs. Greenhut said meaningly.

"All right then, if it's witchcraft, why didn't you use some of it? At least she's got better taste than either of you two. And uses more up-to-date methods. I'm all in favor of such progress."

"*Ernest*!" Miss Levesque howled. "How can you *say* things like that about us? After all you and I have been to one another!"

Ernest prudently affected not to hear this. "Either Nadia's just an ordinary girl. I mean," he added hastily, catching her eye, "an extraordinary girl, but without any supernormal powers. Or else she's a more capable witch than the two of you put together. If she's just a — girl — and it's the power of true love that's made me able to resist you two, then that's fine. And if she's a witch, why, it seems I like her blend of tricks better than yours."

"*Ernest*!" Nadia exclaimed, overcome by emotion. "Those are the nicest things anybodies is ever saying to me without compulsiveness."

"What's more," Ernest concluded, taking her hand, "whatever she is, I'm going to marry her, so the two of you might just as well leave now." He lifted her hand to his lips. "Momikiri," he murmured. "That's the name of a high-grade Japanese blend of tea. It also means 'pretty fingers.'" Nadia giggled coyly.

"*Pipsqueak*!" Mrs. Greenhut commented rancorously. "There're a thousand boys better looking, better everything than you. You were just convenient — that's all."

"Living in the same house and all," Miss Levesque explained, still sniffling. "It just saved time and b-b-bother, really."

The phone rang. Ernest picked it up. "Yes, Mr. Van Linschooten," he said crisply. "I'll be down without fail, first thing in the morning, to taste the Dimbula. Right you are. See you at the hong." He hung up.

"Is *she* going to let you go?" Miss Levesque sneered.

Ernest looked at Nadia. "She is going to let me do whatever I want to do, aren't you, pigeon?"

"With precision," Nadia agreed, smiling up at him.

"You'll do whatever *she* wants you to do," Mrs. Greenhut commented cynically.

"Whatever *he* is wanting to do," Nadia murmured, gazing adoringly at him, "is what I am wanting him to do."

The shrill sound of a whistle screamed through the apartment. "The annunciation of the bubbly boil!" Nadia cried, hurtling toward the kitchenette. "I will concoct the tea."

"No," Ernest said firmly. "Let them make their own tea. I have quite a decent little Terai they may use," he said graciously. "It's not the best, but they won't know any better."

"Tea!" said Miss Levesque. "I want coffee!"

"Not in *my* apartment," Ernest told her, quietly but firmly. "From now on no one is going to be permitted to so much as pass the door who has even a trace of mocha on his or her breath."

Nadia looked at him and again he felt like a tea leaf—uncurling sensually as the steaming water permeated his receptive tissues. But the sensation was pleasurable, not agonizing at all. He didn't even care if the water in his kitchenette had boiled without anyone's having put the kettle on the stove. A little witchcraft might come in very handy in coping with domestic routine.

"You and I, Nadia," he said, "will go down to your apartment and you will show me how you make tea on your samovar."

"She not only makes him do what she wants," Mrs. Greenhut said, with grudging admiration, "but she makes him *think* it's what he wants. Let's face it—we're licked, Dési."

"Maybe," Miss Levesque said wistfully, "since she's taking Ernest away from us, the least she can do is teach us some of her modern methods. What with us being neighbors and all."

Nadia turned to look back over her shoulder. "In truth, ladies," she said, "I would be willing to teaching you my methodology. If only," she added pensively, "I myself can resolving just how it was I am doing it."

Afterword by Christine Sandquist

Born in New York City, it is perhaps no surprise that Evelyn E. Smith (25 July 1922 – 4 July 2000) was engaged in pushing boundaries and challenging traditional notions of propriety, her tools consisting of cutting wit and satirical humor. She was intensely interested in witchcraft, gender, and power. Under the pen name Delphine C. Lyons, she wrote romance and nonfiction on those same subjects. In "The Agony of the Leaves," Smith pulls all of her interests together into a single work. Layers of social and gendered commentary lurk beneath the tongue-in-cheek exterior, deceptively subversive.

Ernest, a young man whose demeanor matches his name, finds himself beset by the attentions of two middle-aged matrons, Mrs. Greenhut and Miss Levesque, who happen to be witches. In their pursuit of his hand, they flip the script on who is expected to be the hunter vs the prey in a romantic relationship. They use every tool at their disposal to turn Ernest's heart towards them: love potion-laced cookies, magical compulsions, and more.

On a surface level read, Mrs. Greenhut's and Miss Levesque's antics are ridiculous and silly. They follow him about, sabotage his attempts to see other women by manifesting on tea tables, and even fly him spinning through the air when he's been out longer than they deem fit. The tone remains lighthearted and jocular. Yet, there is an undercurrent of horror and dread present on closer inspection. Ernest is not a willing participant in this hunt. He is afraid and fearful, unable to live his life as he pleases for fear of arousing their wrath.

Smith's understanding of power dynamics and control comes through clearly in every scene. In a relationship with traditional gender roles, the man would be the one exerting power over the woman, setting rules about where she can go, who she can see, and what type of activities are appropriate for her to engage in. With witchcraft in play, that power balance is reversed. By taking away power from the man and placing it in the hands of women, Smith cleverly shines a light on the horror inherent in such controlling relationships. In modern times, Mrs. Greenhut and Miss Levesque would be labeled stalkers and emotional abusers.

With the introduction of Nadia, a young refugee and psychiatrist, Smith provides a glimpse into what healthy relationships and power dynamics look like. Nadia, too, is a witch...and yet, she uses her power to support Ernest and give him freedom. She is portrayed as rational, educated, and intelligent, even if she may struggle with English as a second language. In every way, she is a break from tradition—in fact, it is she who demands Ernest take her out for tea! She appears to use her power unconsciously and her only intent is apparently to help those who she cares for. It seems to spring forth from her as naturally as breathing. Under her attentions and protection, Ernest is able to bloom into a better version of himself.

However, in a perfectly satirical little twist, Ernest notes that even if Nadia *is* subtly manipulating him with her power, at least she's giving him an illusion of choice: "If she is a witch...at least she had the grace not to *tell* me that she was feeding me love potions or practicing her wiles on me. So, if I'm in love with her, there's a fighting chance that it was my own idea as well as hers." If he must be in a cage, at least let it be a pleasant one, for as he notes, brutally and incisively, "...as a perfectly normal and conventional member of society, I *like* hypocrisy—it is the basis of all civilized behavior."

We all have different degrees of power conferred onto us by our own efforts or through circumstance. Often, this is directly linked to gender. In "Agony," where women hold power, it becomes clear to a reader that maliciously weaponizing it for personal gain is both harmful and amoral. This, however, is the reality most women face in a patriarchal society, unless they manage to find their own Nadia amongst the flocking Greenhuts and Levesques: someone who will give them a choice—or at the very least the illusion of choice. The question left unanswered, of course, is what might have happened to Ernest without Nadia as a savior. To where does unchecked power over others lead us when used for selfish ends?

Perhaps Smith was successful in getting men to ponder this question. One can but hope...

Two-Bit Oracle
by Doris Pitkin Buck

(Originally appeared in the August 1954 issue of *The Magazine of Fantasy and Science Fiction*. It has only been republished once, in 1955.)

Life is hard in this Thracian temple. If you think that as a soothsayer you would be better fed than in the village, that under our roof you would be dryer than under thatch, you are right. But that is only part of the story.

My last assistant left for Delphi after I had done all an oracle-priest could do to train him. I would not want you to leave after I have worked with you for about a year. Better to understand the disadvantages now. They are many, my young friend, many. The head priestess, Amasara, and I are the only professionals in this oracle. For the rest, we work with villagers.

Do you know what that means? It means you will have to be quick to cover up the inevitable mistakes. You will need the patience that built the Pyramids. Above all, you will need a heart that won't break from discouragement if you deal with a girl like Rhodis.

I had had no trouble getting her — a wretched little orphan — to come here. She must be about fifteen, though she does not know exactly. At first I thought she was glad to change her rags for embroidery — but it was more than that.

She would grind up colored stones and smear them on herself, looking old as a sibyl or rosy-fingered as dawn. She put on purple, bound sandals on her feet — and in her mind became Queen Hecuba. Sometimes she was a terrified sacrifice, dragged to the altar. Or Eurydice, down in hell, wailing for Orpheus. I could not have stopped Rhodis from this play if I had wanted to. And of course I encouraged her.

Most village girls deliver an oracle as if they had just learned it by heart — which of course they have. Rhodis had more possibilities. Give her an idea and she would put it into her own words. With a girl like that, I decided to take a risk. The first day that she ever sat on the tripod-throne, I gave her one

74

of the biggest cases we ever handled — a king. He had made journeys to Delphi and Dodona. I could not expect him to listen to a wooden-faced amateur. So that morning I coached Rhodis in what, as the voice of the god, she would be expected to say. It was a great honor, as you can see. She disappointed me by becoming almost hysterical.

I rather pride myself on the way I manage hysteria. There is a good deal of it here, even with our most stolid girls. I ignored everything Rhodis said, and when she found no one noticed her, of course she became a great deal calmer. Then I told her that she was to handle a couple of other cases after the king. I made up my mind about those on the spur of the moment. You see I knew, from considerable experience, that one can capitalize on hysteria. The girl's excitement, her tension, carry over to the people who hear her.

But when I stood in the darkness of the temple chamber with a young assistant, I had a bad moment. I knew the king was kneeling before the steps of the throne, and in the darkness I thought of everything that could go wrong, from Rhodis's forgetting completely what she must say to her laughing instead of groaning when thunder rumbled. I was taking a great chance.

I heard our cymbals clash. Then three notes sounded from the deep-toned gong. A shaft of cold white light fell upon Rhodis, who was pale as the light itself. Her hand went to her throat as if she were afraid the muscles in it would not work. I stood there in the darkness beside the young priest, hoping — hoping —

Rhodis found her tongue suddenly. She intoned: "I am the voice of the God, the God-who-dwells-in-darkness. I am his voice. You may question."

She was wonderful. Even I could almost believe in a god, the way she said it.

The shaft of light grew wider till I could see the king too, in his purple and gold. Most of the girls here would have gawked at him, but Rhodis looked quietly over his head. We heard him tell her that barbarians had fallen upon his people, overwhelming his archers by sheer numbers. Now they were beneath the walls of his city. Though his voice was deep and clear, I knew he was afraid. Rhodis's tense white face had done that.

"Will the God be merciful?" he asked. "Will he turn back the invaders before the city gates?"

Rhodis only said, "The God is angry."

"Angry?" he questioned, while I gave the signal for a low rumble of thunder. He began to tell what a good king he had been, how justly he had ruled, how he opened the royal granary in famines and gave his people wheat and barley.

Rhodis repeated, "The God is angry." The king started to speak, but she

75

interrupted. "I see a ruler of the people. He lies bleeding in a little room. A secret room. I see—"

Her voice broke, and I wondered if after that splendid beginning she would not be able to finish. I helped her with a clap of thunder that sounded like the end of the world. Then there was stillness. It seemed unending. It became something a man could hardly stand. Certainly the king could not stand it. He mumbled that his brother had died after one single stab; he had not given him a slow painful death.

Rhodis came in quickly. She had not lost her voice at all; she had been building up her effect. "But the stench of blood is in the God's nostrils. Therefore the God punishes with war. In his time he will send pestilence." She paused. Though her eyes were apparently not on the king, I could tell that she noticed a big blue vein throb by his temple. She watched him rest his hand on the ground, where no one could tell whether or not it trembled. She said in a voice that was almost kind, "Perhaps, perhaps even now the God might be merciful."

I let thunder rumble again, faintly.

The king muttered, "What would the God ask of me?"

She told him simply, as I had suggested, "The God-who-dwells-in-darkness has looked upon his temple. Rains pour in where the roof has fallen. But if he saw a roof of Cyprian bronze above his image, enduring bronze where the shingles rot—"

"Not bronze." The king was practical. "Cedar."

Beyond him in the darkness I chanted with my assistant, "A roof of bronze, of Cyprian bronze."

"Perhaps," Rhodis whispered, "the God might be merciful. Perhaps—" She let the whisper die. Her head sank on her breast. Her hands hung lax. She hardly moved her lips when she said, "The God has spoken."

Nobody heard the two light taps I gave—nobody but the worker I had hidden. It seemed a miracle when the hall began to fill with light. We drew aside the curtains. The king paced out.

I waited a full minute. Then did we bustle! My assistant rolled up the carpet on which royalty knelt; underneath was a simple rush mat for the next poor fool. I quickly readjusted the curtains; if we had more metal rings for them, I would not have to work so hard at these times. Rhodis stayed in her place, of course. But she opened one eye and whispered, "Did I do it right?"

I nodded.

"Oh," she gasped, "I was so frightened."

I should have remembered her hysteria earlier in the day. I ought to have concentrated on the girl, not on details like curtains. But I was in a hurry.

When she asked, "Suppose the king hadn't believed me?" I said, "People believe anything," and went on with my work.

"And," my assistant added, "we have the dirt in our files; who killed who and all the scandals."

That lad was always dropping into waterfront slang, taking away the dignity of the oracle. He came here—like me—from an Ionian seaport he had left in something of a hurry.

Rhodis ignored his crude expression. She asked, "What will happen to the king?"

"Depends on what Amasara can get from him," said my young priest. "If it's enough, our revered High Priestess will have you scare the living daylights out of those barbarians and send them home. Their chieftains are in the court now. The king knows. He'll be reasonable about the roof. But while he and Amasara haggle, you might as well do something for a farmer's wife who's been waiting two hours."

"You know the one," I explained. "The mother of a crippled boy. Tell her he'll be all right."

Rhodis drooped at that. "Could I—Could I skip the next one?"

I shook my head. "Now, now, now, suppose we all wanted to handle only big cases—a king, a delegation of barbarians. How'd we keep the pot boiling?" I gave her knee a fatherly pat. "Remember," I slipped into waterfront argot myself, "we're a little two-bit oracle trying to keep out of the red. A king doesn't consult us every day. We can't pass up a thing."

My assistant snorted that she must think she was good, holding out for a bigger cut. And her first day too!

"No!" she cried. "No! It's not that."

Naturally we looked puzzled.

Rhodis said in a shaky voice, "The boy won't ever walk, will he?"

We admitted he would not, but pointed out an important fact she overlooked: We got a drachma every so often for keeping up the mother's spirits.

She planted her little sandaled feet and shut her lips firmly.

Now was the moment to give her a glimpse of my philosophy. "See here, aren't you doing that farmer's wife a favor, making her happier? People think they love truth. They really love a comforting pack of lies. Tell them what they want to hear."

"I can't lie to her," said Rhodis.

"And you can't go temperamental, not on a day like this." My assistant was sharp.

Rhodis looked at her gold-shod feet. She avoided our eyes. "I can't," she whispered.

"Why not?"

She pleated the silk of her robe and hung her head.

"Because I'm—"

"You're what?"

"Afraid." We could hardly hear her.

My man exploded. In fact he made quite a speech about girls with stage fright.

"That isn't what I'm—afraid of."

We were so surprised we stood stock still and looked at her. "No? Then what is it?"

She had gone white again. She hugged herself in her thin silk and looked hardly bigger than a child as she whispered, "The God."

We roared with laughter.

"Who makes the thunder?" I asked.

"You do. You do."

"And the darkness?" I even added. "You know about the cymbals and the gongs and the light effects?"

"Yes," she admitted.

"Look," I said reasonably, sensing the next attack of hysterics on its way, "nobody who works here has believed in a god for over a hundred years. Besides, if a god could kill, I would have died long ago."

"It's different for you," she insisted. "You never believed. But I did—in my village. I shall be punished as a priestess was once—with visions too terrible for a mortal to bear. I shall die mad."

"Can't argue with that type." My assistant (Birdbrain I called him) caught her wrist to twist it. I stopped that.

"She's tired," I explained. "She has a right to be. Look at the way she played up to the king. No false starts. No backtracking. Dearie," I even forgot to talk like a soothsayer, "you've got that certain something. If we'd had you when Alexander came here, we'd be on the map now. Just you forget about that mad priestess. She was nutty to start with."

Birdbrain made some silly remarks about arm-twisting.

I ignored him. It was natural for her to be jumpy, I said, especially as it was her first time. Did she want a rest?

She nodded.

I advised her to lean back, breathe deeply, and take a few minutes to pull herself together. I almost had to push Birdbrain to get him out. He scowled but he went with me. At the curtains I paused. "Forget that farmer's wife till we go to the grove and back. But be yourself when we get in again—"

"—or else," said Birdbrain before he too slipped through the curtains.

I suspected what would happen while we were supposed to be in the grove. Of course we hadn't really gone; we both had our eyes at peepholes. I must say I've seldom enjoyed myself more.

At first the girl sat rigid. Then she ran across the hall, flung the drapery aside, and disappeared. In a couple of minutes she returned, pulling the waiting country woman into the room.

"They never did it like this before," the farmer's wife said. She frowned so hard at Rhodis there were deep lines between her eyes.

Rhodis did not notice. She laid a finger on her own lips. "Hush! We have only a minute."

"I had music the other time," the woman complained.

"Listen—"

The farmer's wife felt for a stray lock and tucked it under her new fillet of wool. "You're making me look a sight, yanking me in like this. You needn't think you can whisper the oracle to me because I'm a woman who sells eggs and honey. I paid my drachma, same as anybody else—"

"Yes. Yes. But hear me."

"—and I'm going to have my message with all the trimmings: music and a vision and everything. I've got rights same as other people."

"But my prophecies, they're all—"

"Look, young woman." The mother stood, arms akimbo, and let her voice rise. "I didn't come for no nonsense. I don't put up with no nonsense. I've been saving egg money close on two months. I know what Amasara gives for a drachma and I mean to have it. You start this oracle all over." She turned and stalked angrily away.

"Listen, only listen—" Rhodis caught her by the shoulder.

The farmer's wife squealed, "You keep your hands to yourself. Some folks say it makes a woman crazy if a priestess sets a finger on her. You keep away from me or I'll complain to Amasara, I will." She gave Rhodis a nasty look, then bolted like a rabbit.

The girl faced the three-legged seat. She shivered a little as we came in. I hadn't prevented my young assistant from returning with a whip in his hand. He gestured to her to sit down. She looked toward me, but I was busy picking bits of lint off my tunic. Birdbrain gestured again—with the whip. The girl went to her place slowly, but she went. Her shoulders sagged with discouragement.

My young priest hid his lash. I removed a brazier (no use wasting incense) and replaced it with jars of water and fresh herbs. I crushed a little sweet marjoram, and afterward I gestured. Flute music sounded faintly, then grew louder.

"Ready?" Birdbrain spoke to Rhodis out of the side of his mouth as he went toward the curtained wall. His eyes stopped where his whip was hidden. "Ready?" he muttered again. Rhodis and I nodded. Then with a slow, stately movement I drew the curtains aside.

The farmer's wife walked in, tossing her head a little. The priestess had risen; her eyes looked beyond the woman.

"I see a child, a man child, walking." Her tone was glad yet somehow solemn too. "I see a woman binding fennel and sweet herbs upon his ankles. He dances. He runs." She caught her breath. "Oh the swift runner! He races the boys in the meadow. Quick, child! Quick, or you will not beat them!" She moved her eyes as if they followed someone skimming past.

Then she looked down, noticing for the first time the woman at her feet. "But this—this is the woman of my vision." She raised her hands to her forehead. "The very woman," she murmured. "Do I wake? Do I sleep?"

"Your son will be cured of his affliction." I moved toward the farmer's wife. "Only bind sweet herbs and fennel upon his feet." I smiled like an old man looking at his favorite daughter. The flute music was loud as twenty birds.

The farmer's wife lumbered to her feet. "That's what I paid for," she announced. She sniffed, partly to enjoy the sweet marjoram, partly to express her opinion of Rhodis. She took her time walking out of the room while Birdbrain and I held back the heavy linens hanging between the columns.

"We shall rest a minute," I said to Rhodis after the curtains fell into place. "Then the barbarians. Then you're through for the day."

My assistant fixed his eyes on the girl. "And no monkey business about 'I can't. I won't. I'm scared.' You're good, but not good enough to get away with that."

She had not noticed my man moving toward the hidden whip, but it was in his hand.

"I won't—again. Not even—if you—" Rhodis gasped. She cried to me, "It's coming—closer. My terror."

Her hands caught at her throat. I have seen animals in traps. Her eyes had that look.

"Can you *act!* But when you feel this," Birdbrain raised his lash and she saw it was knotted, "the yell you let out won't be phony." I was afraid his language would completely upset a girl sensitive as Rhodis—perhaps even more than his whip.

As a matter of fact, the whip was all she noticed. She gaped silently, unable to move her lips. Then before anyone so much as touched her, she fainted.

That was something to handle carefully. When Rhodis came to herself,

Birdbrain was not there; only I, patting her hand, holding something under her nostrils. I told her gently not to worry, fondled her hand, and said over and over that another girl could be the god's voice for our important cases. I thought she would straighten up and object. But no, she only looked grateful. I kept on saying it.

At last she did speak. "Yes. Yes. Take anyone—anyone else. I'm running away. Back to my village."

Now I rather like acting myself. I sat on the step below her carved chair and looked sad. My voice got confidential. "And I thought I was helping you when I brought you here, when we fed you. How often does anyone in your village eat a full meal? Or leave anything over for you? No hut for you, was there? Dirtiest rags in the place." I fingered her robe. "Remember?"

She nodded.

"You liked it here at first," I went on. "And did you wolf your food!" I paused a long while. "Forgotten what it's like to be hungry?"

"No." Rhodis gave a faint miserable sigh.

"You know when you're well off. We'll hold the barbarians till you're ready. I was only joking when I talked about using a different girl. You're the best we have. Then tomorrow—"

"No!" She looked frightened. "No! I'll go—now."

"I suppose it doesn't matter if they beat me because of a runaway priest-ess."

"But you're important. Nobody'd—They couldn't hurt *you*."

"Couldn't they !" I laughed—hard, hollow laughter.

"But—But—You're Amasara's right hand. You know how everything's done."

"Yes, and showed everything to you." I watched her eyes get wide with horror. I stroked her again. "But don't think about me. If you want to go, go. You'll find a way; if not now then some dark night. And I'm an old man. I can face what comes my way. Even—death."

She shuddered.

"I'm not complaining." I wish you could have heard me quaver. "I thought—oh, never mind—" I held her shaking little hand against my cheek. "I had a daughter once. I saw you and—well—Remember how happy I was when those thin cheeks of yours got so pretty, when you began to smile as you woke up instead of thinking, 'Another day. Another day?' No, don't re-member that." I spoke quickly; timing meant a lot in this crisis. "I was nothing to you. I fooled myself. All you liked was a full plate." I laughed again in an ugly way. Her eyes grew moist. "Don't ever think of this place again—of me," I sniffed, "the old man who gave you real love."

I walked away from her, my head down. A big sob tore out of her throat. She ran to me, throwing her arms round my neck. How she cried, right on this shoulder! I knew I had won even before she breathed, "I'll stay. I'll stay."

I led her back to the seat with carved arms and settled her among the cushions.

"And all this while the god hasn't done a thing, not one thing. Come on," I slipped into waterfront talk again, "just one grade-A vision for those characters with a lingo like baa-baa-beh. Then you're through. Then there's wine, wine with honey, waiting. Why, you'll laugh yourself sick at the idea of being scared. *Who was scared? Scared of what?* you'll say. Come on, sweetheart. Give. First thing the old man ever asked. You're not letting him down. He knows that." I watched while she straightened herself. I adjusted the thongs of her sandal. "A few tears look good. Pretty, shiny eyes."

She only stared past me the way she had stared past the king, the farmer's wife. She hardly seemed to know what was happening around her.

My assistant slipped in again. He signaled for me to start, whispering, "All settled about the roof."

"What'd we get?" I whispered back. "Cedar? Bronze?"

"Tile. That split the difference. Now Amasara wants us to send the barbarians back where they came from—fast. They're lousing up the whole shrine." He gestured toward the priestess with his thumb. "She ready?"

She was ready. She was magnificent. Her face looked as if she were having a vision of all the horror that could be crowded into one mortal's life. That face by itself could start the barbarians running to their forests. You know they're even stupider than most of the people who come here.

Then I heard thunder come up with a low rumble and end crashing. Flames poured down like forked violet rivers. Between flashes I felt the darkness would smother me. I wanted to run out but I was so sick and dizzy I could only lean against a pillar.

Each time lightning blazed, I remembered my mother's stories about the gods and their revenges. I remembered people who turned to stone or became blind. I believed like a child. I heard the young soothsayer groan; he felt what I did.

By the flashes, we could see Rhodis groping—and even with the thunder, I sometimes caught what she said. "Shoes." I could see her lips make the word even when the crashes drowned her voice. Then she cursed war. She wept. She was crying, I think, over the dead bodies of her sisters, but even while she cried, she was saying, "I can't go barefoot." She tore something from the dead feet of the children in her vision.

"I've got to. I've got to," we heard her say. "The house is rubble. I haven't a pair." She sobbed and shook as she tried to force her feet into what they had worn. I thought she must have been a princess or a great lord's daughter, but in her vision all the children went about shod till the war came. It sounded strange, but I could make nothing else out of her babblings.

After she put the shoes on, she hunted through ruins, looking for food. I could tell by her gestures that she did not find it. She moaned, "I've had nothing since morning." All the while she spoke of this and that thing, for in the land of her vision they had many, many strange foods. She talked of chests, even rooms, piled full of meats and fruits that would not spoil. But after a long search she said wearily, "People will know real hunger now. I'll know it."

Then she began to shiver and cry again. I could not follow all she said; I caught the word *destruction*. The girl was wild with fear, and screamed about something that travelled faster than the sound it made. Frightened as I was, I knew nothing could do that. I looked at Birdbrain, who was shaking his head now.

Then what do you think she wailed? "I'm hurt—cut—badly. I didn't even know it—first." That sounded right. I've seen soldiers in battle, bleeding and not realizing they were wounded till afterward. I felt my flesh chill. At least I shivered until she sobbed, "I must have—have been cut by flying glass—when—the windows shattered."

Imagine: glass windows! We had one little glass vase here. You could look through the sides, almost like looking through air. One day a priestess broke it, and a smooth piece cut her as if it had been a knife. See how Rhodis's mind worked? That glass window made me realize I was dealing with a girl and her make-believe, not with any god. For minutes, though, I felt as if that war were something real, happening somewhere; as if Rhodis had been swept into it by a pure miracle.

Then suddenly darkness was gone. The last thunderclap rumbled and quiet came. (I never did find out how Rhodis learned the thunder signal. I'm supposed to be the only one who gives it.) I thought clearly for the first time in half an hour—and I saw that Rhodis had put on such a performance she'd made a hard-boiled professional like me accept it. Remember what I told you about hysteria and how it creeps into an audience? Birdbrain and I had been spellbound, spellbound by a girl we'd seen practicing a hundred times. Busy as I was that afternoon, my mind raced off into a golden future. I planned a new oracle, for Rhodis and me—

There's no need to go into that. For then came the strangest part of all. Rhodis acted as if she were still seeing her vision. She talked in a hopeless tone of a Second World War (whatever that might be), of food doled out to a people who had had plenty, and of the good life—the good life for everyone which their wise men had almost brought into their reach. She said, "We were mad to destroy this. Mad to let it be destroyed. Mad. Mad. Mad."

The child had worked herself into such a state that she believed—actually believed—in everything she'd made up, from all the food to glass windows. I can't blame anyone but myself for her state of mind. It came from my attending to those curtains after the king went out, instead of making Rhodis roll up the rug and do a dozen little active things that would have kept her steady, so that she wouldn't be wailing now, "Then God has punished me. I have been one with a future people who broke their world into pieces. I cannot forget it."

"Look," I said in my kindest voice, for I had to get her in shape for the barbarians, "I can prove that you never saw any kind of future. Then you won't go mad, not over—nothing!"

She only stared.

"I know something about fools, having spent my life around an oracle." My assistant broke in, "You know the saying: Fools, damn fools, and people who go to oracles."

I argued, "Even a god couldn't dream up the kind of fools you saw. If they had half the things you talked about, there'd be enough for everybody in the world." I did not mention the incredible, like windows; just simple things that could almost have been real. "Think again of shoes for everybody, not just the king. Why, fellows like Birdbrain here could get all your food dealt out and then everybody'd be happy. Even barbarians don't go to war unless they're hungry. Stop shuddering a minute. What you've been saying doesn't make any sense, does it?"

She kept crying, "It was a true vision, I tell you. I shall go mad."

I was stern at that. "A priestess would go mad much faster if she left us than if she stayed and worked here. Why did you think we let you talk to the farmer's wife? So you could see for yourself how people feel. Remember she wouldn't let you touch her? Suppose you ran away. Nobody in the village would give you water; nobody'd give you bread."

"There are other villages."

My young soothsayer licked his lips as he remarked, "We have influence right to the Thracian border."

"Let me go. I'll live in the forest."

"One girl tried that," I remarked.

My young friend added, "They found her bones later."

"Gnawed clean," I finished.

I let that sink in. Finally I said, very gently, "Ready to see those hairy fellows in wolf skins?"

"What else can I do?" She went back to her place. This time *I* gave the light signal.

The barbarians filed in. Rhodis scared them into going home, not that she was half as good as she had been when only Birdbrain and I saw her, but she was good enough.

After that, though, she lost her fire. You'd like to see her? Why, you did. That girl in the courtyard, staring with a faraway look at nothing. And I once believed she had possibilities!

Now to get back to business: If you can stand working under conditions like ours, I'll be glad to take you on as my assistant.

Afterword by Marie Vibbert

In 1954, Doris Pitkin Buck told Anthony Boucher of *F&SF* that she was just a housewife, "I take in writing as some women take in wash." Quite the modest claim for a prolific freelance author churning out nonfiction titles and regular appearances in *The New Yorker*, aside from radio scripts and trade papers. Not to mention her day job as a museum publicist and working public relations for the Department of the Interior! She seems about as housewifely as James Bond. One can hardly imagine a man with such publication credits brushing it off as "taking in writing."

Perhaps she was being modest, or deftly deflecting backlash before it even began. Or it was yet another excellent *bon mot* from a sharp mind always on the lookout for social commentary. You can certainly feel her snark in this story, which sees timeless patterns in human nature that make chicanery as integral to a Thracian oracle as it is to modern mega-churches preaching that if you just donate enough, Jesus will make you rich.

Buck invites us to join her in winking behind the back of the narrator, a pure fraud, not believing even a little bit in the god he pimps for donations; but she also shows us compassion for Rhodis, a young protagonist who balances belief with practical knowledge, and excels at her chosen profession. We view her through the sexist gaze of her handler, an emotionally manipulative old man who *knows* he's being emotionally manipulative, and there's no question that we're invited to take Rhodis' side in this. She's not only not "hysterical" as he calls her, she's right, proven right in a way the audience can see more than the characters.

It's interesting that Buck chose to have the god of this Oracle be male, despite using female oracles and a female "high priestess" (sadly off-camera but clearly well skilled in converting a prophecy into a new roof donation) who are more often linked with female deities in antiquity (though not always). There's a real sense of men reaping the benefit of women's work, which would have echoed familiar to Buck's fellow housewives of the 50s.

Yet Buck is a consummate professional, an actress of stage and screen herself, experienced at playing both charlatan and true believer, and she invites us to be both, too. Taking a step away from her usual science-fiction and fact-writing, Buck enters a high fantasy world, and uses it to turn a mirror back on the absurdity of her own post-war world.

Doris Pitkin was the daughter of a chemist who dreamed of leaving her the business before she decided to devote herself to letters instead. Still, her science background was always important to her. She recalled seeing an image of Saturn at the age of seven and becoming "wedded to space."

"Real science fiction is based on science," she told the Washington Post in 1963. Even in this fantasy, we see the science and artistry of the oracle, from crushing gems for jewelry to shaking metal for thunder, and the technology of the future in her vision.

While Rhodis' prophecy seems to have fallen on deaf ears, Doris Pitkin Buck never retired to the cloister, herself, but used her knowledge to help others in the genre. She taught English at Ohio State University and became a founding member of the Science Fiction Writers of America, influencing countless others to advance the genre. She continued to write all her life, with her last piece being published posthumously in 1981 in *The Magazine of Fantasy and Science Fiction*. She died in 1980, just shy of her 83rd birthday.

Change the Sky
by Margaret St. Clair

(Originally appeared in the March 1955 issue of *The Magazine of Fantasy and Science Fiction*. It was last reprinted in 1976.)

"It would be an expensive world to make," said the artist. He rolled a lump of play putty into a rope, coiled it up on itself, and whacked it down on his drawing board. "From what you say, you'd want lots of flowers…and women. That would come high."

"It isn't women I want," Pendleton said stiffly and a little wearily. "I've been to many worlds with beautiful, willing women. I'm not asking you make me some sort of lustful paradise. What I'm hunting is a place that's so beautiful, or so winning, or so *right*, that I'll feel, 'This is the place in the whole universe that I love best. This is home.'"

"Um." The artist bounced his putty on the floor a couple of times. "Tell me about yourself," he said without looking up. "I don't get many clients like you, you know. Most of them are people who aren't physically able to go starside and visit the worlds in person. It's unusual for somebody to come in here who's done much traveling."

A shadow crossed Pendleton's face. There was no use in telling the artist, but he himself wouldn't be physically able to go from world to world much longer, hunting the one right place. He'd had deceleration sickness badly in his last berth, when he was purser on the *Tyche*. Two more trips, and he'd be done for. If he hadn't found what he was looking for by then… It was that knowledge that had brought him into the artist's atelier.

"I've spent most of my life in space," he said unwillingly. "There isn't really much to tell."

The artist raised one eyebrow. "I doubt that. For example, I gather you're a traveled person. Which one, of the various worlds you've visited, has seemed to you the most beautiful? Or the most-appealing? Or interesting? And so on."

"Genlis is the most beautiful, by far," Pendleton answered. "It's a water world, with deep green, swelling, foam-laden seas, and a sky so intensely blue that it's almost purple. On the islands—there are a few islands—tall graceful trees like palms lean into the wind, and the perfume of the flowers is so sweet it makes you dizzy. There are flowers everywhere. They say that no matter how far you get from land on Genlis, you can always smell the flowers. The air is soft and yet fresh, and when the wind blows against your face or body, you feel your skin tingle with delight.

"Nothing could be more beautiful than Genlis. But there aren't many people on that world, and after I'd been there a few days I felt lonely. I was glad to get back to the ship."

"So perhaps it wasn't *your* kind of beauty," said the artist. He was punching crescents with his thumbnail in his putty lump. "Which of the worlds you visited seemed to you the most interesting?"

"Oh...Kruor, I think. It's a long way from its primary, and there's nothing on its surface but snow and ice. The snow is very soft, for some reason, and when the wind blows—there's a great deal of wind—it carves the snow into caves and grottoes and long pointed arches that collapse if you stamp your foot.

"The nights on Kruor are very bright. There's an ionizing layer in the atmosphere that gives the sky a constant glow like a night with a full moon on earth. When the snow arches and caves sparkle in the glow, like a million diamonds, it's a fine sight. Then the green sun comes up, and the surface of the snow caves melts a little and turns to ice. You should see the sparkle then! It almost blinds you. Usually it snows again before night. Kruor is a most interesting place."

"You say it was interesting, but you seem to have thought it was beautiful," the artist commented. He had shaped his lump of play putty into the torso of a tiny woman—round breasts, dimpled belly, long full thighs. "Now, which of the worlds you've visited seemed to you the most appealing? I mean, gave you most nearly the sensation that I gather you're looking for?"

There was a long pause. The body of the miniature woman the artist had shaped sank slowly back into the play putty as the resilient stuff resumed its natural globular shape. "I've liked a lot of places," Pendleton said at last. "There was a world called Phlegra that was nothing but volcanoes and geysers. The planet's magnetic field was funny, and sometimes an eruption from one of the geysers would just go on up. Hours later you might be hit in the back of the neck by an icy spray—but I suppose that's not what you meant."

"No," the artist said. His eyes swept Pendleton's face.

The older man's gray cheeks colored faintly. He rubbed his forehead with one hand. "Well, there was Asterope," he said. "I don't know what I liked about it, actually. It was quite an ordinary world. But there was a great deal of electrical activity on the planet, and there'd be a dozen thunder storms in twenty-four hours. Once I was out in one of them at night. I took cover in a sort of hollow in a cliff, and watched the lightning. There'd be a great flash, and the sky would turn blue-black—the sky of Asterope was very dark, with almost no stars—and the leaves of a funny little tree with white leaves would blaze out in the flash like the stars that were missing in the sky. Then it would be dark again until the next flash.

"Asterope wasn't an appealing world, like Phlegra. But during that storm I liked it. I almost felt at home there."

"Um-*hum*," said the artist. He had put down his lump of play putty and was drawing something on a piece of paper with a brush. When Pendleton tried to see what the picture was, the artist covered it quickly with one hand. "You said something about Earth. Have you spent much time here?"

"No, I was nearly thirty when I came here for the first time."

"That's unusual. Were you born on one of the colonial planets?"

"No, I was born in a space ship. And I'd never set foot on anything larger than an asteroid until I was nineteen."

"Go on, please. This is the sort of background stuff I've got to have."

"Um—well—my mother died when I was two. Of course I don't remember her. I suppose she must have been the sort of person my father was. I don't imagine she wanted a child very much."

The artist crumpled up the sketch he had made. "Go *on*, Mr. Pendleton. What was your father like?"

"He—well—I haven't thought about him in years—he was a sort of a fanatic. He wasn't unkind to me, actually, but he was a strict disciplinarian, and reserved and remote."

"What was he a fanatic *about*?"

Pendleton laughed. "As I said, I hadn't thought of him in years. Why, he had a theory that the culture of the whole solar system was derived from Xeres, the planet of Aldebaran, originally, and he went from asteroid to asteroid looking for evidence to prove it. I understand that historians consider the theory quite preposterous. But father had a private income large enough to let him indulge his whims. As I said, he spent his time searching asteroids."

"How did he die?" the artist asked softly.

Pendleton gave a sort of start. He glanced sharply at the artist, but the younger man was looking down at another sketch he had begun to brush.

"I can't imagine why you want to know that," he observed. "—It was on an asteroid. Father thought that the Xerian colonists had landed originally on the planet that later broke up to form the asteroid belt, and that by the time they got around to settling on Earth and Mars, their home culture had become too diluted to look much like that of Xeres any more. What he was hunting for on the asteroids was an artifact of unmistakable Xerian origin.

"This asteroid was less than a kilo across, and only very roughly round. I don't suppose it even has a number in the asteroid catalogue. Most of its surface was rough and irregular, but in the middle of all the bumps there was a very smooth, shallow pit—made, I suppose, by a fusing meteor impact.

"Father was looking over this pit with one of the hand lights, and I was inside the ship working an astrogational problem he'd set me. I was just seventeen.

"Suddenly, through the ship's speaker, I heard him give a great cry. 'Son! Son!' he called. 'I've found it! Come and see!' He only called me 'son' when he was pleased.

"I climbed into my suit and ran out. He was almost too excited to be able to talk. '"I've found it,' he kept saying over and over, while the hand light shook in his hand. 'I've found it. The proof. An adahn.'"

"What's an adahn?" asked the artist.

"It's an ellipse with a cross in the middle. But the long arm of the cross is another, very flattened, ellipse. It looks something like a drawing of a toy gyroscope. It's a characteristically Xerian element of design.

"I looked down where the hand light was bobbing. At first glance there did seem to be an ellipse in one side of the pit. But when you looked closer you saw that it was just a bunch of fortuitous cracks. The inner ellipse, in particular, was missing. There was nothing there but a collection of feathery lines. It was unmistakable once you noticed it.

"I hesitated. I didn't know how he'd take my doubting his discovery. 'Father, look again,' I said. 'Check it. You want to be absolutely sure.'

"'I am sure,' he answered. 'An adahn! Real proof! See, there's the outer ellipse—and there's the inner...' The confidence in his voice died away as he tried to trace out the shape.

"'I—' he said, 'I can't stand it—it's been so long—' He gave me a terrible look. The light fell out of his hand. Then he clutched at his chest and keeled over. He'd had a heart attack.

"I got him back in the ship and did what I could for him. I couldn't think of much to do. I held ammonia under his nose, and so on. But he died. He was dead within ten minutes after he keeled over outside. He was still glaring at me when he died."

"What happened after that?" asked the artist.

"I had a public guardian appointed for me. Most of father's income stopped with his death. I went to school for a year. Then I got a berth as third officer on a tramp freighter. Father had insisted that I learn astrogation thoroughly, and I didn't have any trouble getting it. I've been in space pretty much ever since.

"When father was alive and I was with him, I used to think that when I was grown up I'd go straight to the most beautiful spot in the universe and stay there—the place that was home. I hated the ship and the asteroids. I never thought I'd have trouble finding the place."

"No, you haven't found it," the artist agreed. He folded the sketch he had made and put it in the breast pocket of his tunic. "I've got an idea for a world for you," he said. "I'm not going to tell you what it is, because I'm pretty sure you'll say it won't work, and I'd like to try whether it will. One thing, it won't be an expensive world to make. Do you want me to try?"

"How much?" asked Pendleton.

The artist named a sum. It wasn't, Pendleton supposed, much according to his standards.

Pendleton hesitated. But after all, what else could he do? He wasn't a young man any more, and the world—the *real* world—he was hunting for might not exist. "All right," he said. "When will it be done?"

"Oh—today's Monday. Um…let's say a week from today, at about the same time? Right."

"It looks like an out-size egg," Pendleton said.

The artist laughed. "That's only the sheathing. And an ovoid is the most economical solid for it. After you're in you'll lose all sense of the shape. Have you ever been in an artificial world before?"

"No."

"Well, for it to be fully successful there has to be some cooperation from you. After you enter—pierce the shell of the egg—there's a period of preparation and acclimatization that's partly physical and partly psychological. There's a gas in the air, for example—but I don't want to give away trade secrets.

"Abandon yourself. Don't resist. And don't try to hurry things. It takes a little time. The preparation will come to an end eventually. And then you'll be in your world."

"Suppose I don't like it, or, after I've been in it a while, decide I've had enough. How do I get out? The same way I got in?"

"No." The artist handed him a metal circlet. "Put this on your wrist. After you've had enough of the world I've set up for you, press the stud in the middle of the wrist band. That will initiate the reverse acclimatization—a sort of decompression period. It's nothing abrupt, like going through a door."

"If I like the world, can I visit it again?"

"Of course. Sometimes I leave worlds set up for months, even for years. All you have to do is to pay me a small rental fee."

"Do people ever — live in them?"

The artist frowned. "Now you're getting into something..." He fished the lump of play putty out of his tunic pocket and began squeezing it. "You see, what we artists make are worlds that seem absolutely real. And yet, of course, they're artificial. They're artistic creations. And like other artistic creations, they seem at times to have a life of their own.

"In this trade of mine, you hear stories. Stories about people who've got into worlds and stayed there, somehow, after the power sources were cut and the world was dismantled. Permanent worlds, some people call them.

"They're just stories. I don't believe them myself, I don't know anyone who does believe them. And yet — it might be possible. I just don't know."

Pendleton had withdrawn his attention when he heard the note of negation in the artist's voice. He studied the enormous bulging golden bulk — the big end of the egg — that lay before him. "I hadn't realized it would be so big," he said. "Your worlds must take a great deal of room."

The artist laughed. "They do. That's why I have my workshop out here, miles and miles from anywhere. But — Mr. Pendleton, I think you're stalling. You're hopeful, but you're nervous about your world, too. Go ahead and enter it."

"How?"

"Just walk up and push on the sheathing. It's made to give at any accessible place. And remember what I said about not trying to hurry the acclimatization period."

Pendleton swallowed. He was more excited than he had thought he would be. His knees felt uncertain and weak. His mouth was very dry; he swallowed again. Then he walked resolutely toward the golden sheathing of his world.

It gave on a minimum of pressure. A puff of air — salty, and yet somehow smelling disagreeably of violets — went past his face. Pendleton had time to wonder irritably why the artist hadn't simply provided his world with a door, instead of electing this fantastic sort of ingress. Then he stepped inside.

It wasn't as absolutely dark as he had thought it would be, though he couldn't see any trace of the break in the sheathing through which he had come. There was a mist — salt-and-violet smelling but quite dry — around him, a dirty sepia mist that moved in eddies of black and charcoal, and he had the dim impression that somewhere to the right was a little hill.

He took a step forward uncertainly. There was a blaze of orange-colored light behind his eyeballs, and the tincture of light died away entirely, leaving him in a blackness that was hard to breathe. Ahead—behind?—a bell rang with a high, mocking note.

A train of rhomboids bobbled past him in the darkness at eye level. They were brightly colored, reds and yellows, and lit like paper lanterns from within. Pendleton was suddenly furiously angry. He put up one hand to stop the swimming rhomboids, and received a paralyzing shock in the palm of his hand for his pains.

He put his hand down, swearing. What was it the artist had told him? —to relax, to take it easy, to cooperate. But perhaps his getting angry had been a part of the cooperation. It was difficult to say.

Something hard, long, and thin slipped into his still tingling hand and was withdrawn again. He looked down. The rest of his body was invisible, but his two feet—such big feet—were to be seen dimly glowing with their own blue light.

He wanted to laugh. He wanted to sit down; he was tired. But his body was too stiff to bend, and besides his dim blue feet were too far off for him ever to be able to reach them.

A string of luminous blue and purple circles, much paler than the rhomboids had been, came down at him from above. He regarded them passively, and after a moment or two they hauled themselves up again. The darkness seemed blacker than ever after they had gone, and when he looked down at his feet they had disappeared into the general night.

An irritable impatience invaded him. How much longer was this foolishness going to continue? Nobody named Pendleton—and there was a man named that—ought to have to put up with it. Cooperation—relaxation—would mean sitting down and letting himself rest.

And all the time he wasn't walking, but his legs were carrying him on.

The darkness was withdrawn gradually, as if someone were pulling a curtain to one side. Pendleton drew a deep breath and rubbed one hand over his face. His sense of personal identity had come back to him, and with it the stirrings of curiosity. Where would he be? Would it be in his own world?

He stood on a plain—wide, bleak, sulphur-smelling—before a cliff with a dark opening. Far off to his left there was a liquid quaking, a dark stirring against the drab plain, and he knew the flicker of motion must be from a lava pool. It did not interest him greatly, but the dark opening drew him. He wanted to go in.

He had no light. Or—why, yes, there was a hand torch strapped to his belt. He hadn't noticed it before. He drew the torch from its fastening, flicked the switch, and for a moment sent the beam of light up and down the dun-colored surface of the low cliff. Nothing. He stepped inside the dark hole.

He almost cried out in surprise. He didn't know what he had expected, exactly — some grand cavern, perhaps, with sheeted stalactites and answering stalagmites, cascades of intricate frozen stone tracery in translucent amber and mauve, rivers, vaulted ceilings, and in the end an underground sea. What it actually was was that he was standing inside a hollow, perfectly polished and absolutely spherical, of black basalt. The jet surface reflected the light of his torch dizzily.

At the side of the bubble of stone was another opening. He went through it and stood in another basalt sphere, a little smaller than the one before. Down low in its side there was another hole.

The third bubble was larger, so large that the beam of the torch was remote over his head. The next bubble was smaller, and so was the one after that. Pendleton went from bubble to bubble, not bored, not unhappy, not thinking, in a relaxed mindlessness that was not quite a trance. Sometimes the exits were so low and narrow he had to crawl to get through them, sometimes they were ample and commodious. There was always another bubble to succeed the one in which he stood.

It came to him that the artist had spoken truly when he called this a world. It would be possible for Pendleton to go on from sphere to sphere throughout the rest of his life, and he would never come to the end of them. The artist had made him a world. Pendleton neither liked nor disliked the fact that the bubbles were alike. Large or small, they were alike. Polished and black and perfect and pierced by two openings. But in the sixtieth bubble, or it might have been the two hundredth, or the thousandth, the beam of his torch picked up an irregularity on the black, lens-smooth surface. He leaned forward to look, wholly incredulous. And it was, it was. There had been incised, in grayish lines against the polished blackness, an adahn.

An adahn. For a moment a deep emotion stirred in him. He drew back from it, afraid, unable to name it. It was as if a great depth of water parted, and showed him something undreamed of. He stood transfixed, leaning against the curving basalt, unable to move.

Then the emotion was gone, and though he sent the light of the torch over the symbol again and again, it didn't come back. After a little he sighed and went into the next sphere.

Its surface was unmarked, mirror-smooth, as that of all the others but one had been.

Pendleton couldn't have told how many bubbles later it was that he stopped, admitting finally that the coldness in his heart had grown into despair. He could, of course, go back through the bubbles to the one with the adahn, and beyond it to the hole in the dun-colored cliff where he had come in. He could walk over the plain to the lava pool. There might be other things on the plain, interesting things, besides the lava pool. He didn't want to. There was nothing here for him.

His fingers had already pressed the stud.

The decompression period was quite different from what that of acclimatization had been. The basalt bubble around him seemed to fracture into a thousand jagged pieces, each glinting with the reflection of the torch he held in his hand. The pieces began to recede from each other with increasing velocity, faster and faster, as if blown outward by some explosion of which he was the center. He felt that filaments of himself were being blown out with them.

When the pieces were very far away, they softened and melted into a grayish haze. Pendleton stood motionless in the haze for what seemed a very long time. Doubt as to who the man called Pendleton was assailed him. He did not recognize his thoughts.

The haze brightened to a silvery pearl gray, as if a light were shining behind it. Pendleton felt an instant of desperate giddiness. Then it passed and he was himself again. He was standing outside the egg.

The shell was intact. How he had got in—and out—without breaking it was no odder than anything else had been. But—Pendleton's mouth drew into angry lines as he realized what had happened—but what had made the artist shape such a world for him? How could he possibly have thought that an endless series of black basalt bubbles was what Pendleton was looking for?

He glanced around him. The artist was nowhere to be seen. Pendleton must have been in the world for a long time, for the sky over it had grown quite dark, and floodlights had been turned on down at the end.

No, the world had been a ridiculous failure. All that money...all that time...all that hope—wasted. A ridiculous fiasco. He'd find the artist and have it out with him.

With long, angry strides he started toward the shack where the studio was. The surface of his mind was seething with anger. But there was bitter, almost unendurable, disappointment in his heart.

The studio was empty. On one of the big drawing tables an envelope was propped up. Pendleton's name had been brushed in large flowing characters on it.

He tore the envelope open. The note read:

Dear Mr. Pendleton —

You have been in your world for so long that I am beginning to hope that I have succeeded in making what you want. (The cave element, of course, came from what you told me about the snow caves on

Kruor, and the adahn and the polished sides of the bubbles from the pit on the asteroid where your father met his death. I deliberately disregarded what you said about Asterope, except for the glitter in the lava pools. It seemed to me that it was too conscious to be of much help in constructing a suitable world for you. I hope my choice of construction elements was wise.)

If you read this before midnight, won't you please call me at ZEN dorf 0329? I am anxious to know how you came out.

Sincerely, Byrd.

Pendleton grimaced. It was an explanation; the artist had, he supposed, done his best. He was still angry. He called the number Byrd had given him.

A party was going on; he got Byrd after a little delay. The artist peered at him sharply in the viewing plate. He whistled. "It wasn't an unqualified success," he observed. "Judging from your face."

"It wasn't a success at all," Pendleton replied grimly.

"What kept you so long, then?" Byrd asked. "People usually come out right away when a world's not right."

Pendleton had been placed on the defensive. He didn't like it. "The succession of bubbles had a, um, hypnotic effect," he answered. "But it wasn't at all what I was looking for."

"No part of it?" the artist asked. He sounded rather deflated. "Not even the adahn, for example?"

Pendleton's lips set in a thin line. "None of it," he said.

"Oh." Byrd was frowning. "I'd thought I might be able to develop...but I guess not." He cleared his throat.

"Well, Mr. Pendleton, I don't think there's any point in our wasting any more of each other's time," he said. "I'd like you, though, to get in touch with another artist, a man named Selim Zweig. He doesn't do much constructing, and he's difficult to work with. But I think he can make what you want if anybody can. Have you got the name? Selim Zweig."

"Yes," answered Pendleton. He started to hang up.

Something in his face seemed to alarm Byrd. "Wait!" he cried. "Don't do anything foolish! Let me come and talk to you. I—" But Pendleton had already broken the connection.

No, he wasn't going to do anything foolish, he thought as he walked down the grassy lane toward his copter. He wasn't, for instance, going to get in touch with the Selim Zweig Byrd had suggested to him. There was a disgust that was as bitter as gall in his mouth. He was done with fantastic artificial worlds and the men who created them. Tomorrow he'd make arrangements to leave Earth. There were still plenty of real worlds, starside, that he hadn't visited. Tomorrow he was going to ship out.

They took his application at the hiring hall next day. His references, his experience, were splendid, they assured him. They sent him in to the doctor for the usual physical examination. And Pendleton didn't pass.

He was stunned. For half a day he couldn't believe it. Starside was gone, he'd never ship out again, he was stuck on earth. He'd never find the world he had been hunting for so long. It was too late.

He passed two days in misery so acute that it made him want to groan aloud. Then—it was inevitable—he called Selim Zweig.

Zweig was a little man, as ugly and restless as a monkey, and Pendleton disliked him on sight. Nonetheless, it was easier to talk to him than it had been to Byrd. He didn't like him, but he trusted him.

He told him much the same things he had told Byrd. The details were a little fuller, that was all. Zweig listened, cracking his knuckles and nodding peremptorily from time to time. When Pendleton had finished, Zweig scratched his head and grinned.

"Sure, I can make you a world," he said. "Won't cost much, won't take long to make. Sure."

Pendleton felt a thrill that was not all hope, though he didn't know what the second emotion in it was. "But—will it be right?" he asked anxiously. "Will it be what I've been looking for? A place where I'll feel at home?"

"Um-hum. You bet. Sure will."

Pendleton gave him a searching look, but the artist kept on grinning. There wasn't anything else Pendleton could do. "Go ahead and make it," he said.

Zweig called on the third day to say that the world was ready. His workshop was even more remote than Byrd's, and yet it seemed to Pendleton that he got there almost before he wanted to. He walked across the field to the workshop with long steps that were eager and yet a little hesitant. Now that the realization of his dream was so near, he was unsure.

"That's it," Zweig said, pointing. He indicated a big grayish sheet of something that looked like wrapping paper and was stretched across an arch in the area behind his studio.

"There's nothing behind it," Pendleton objected after a moment.

"Oh, yes there is."

"Byrd used an egg."

"Well, I don't," Zweig answered. He grimaced and scratched himself on the chest. "An egg's a purely mechanical limitation, and besides...that's it."

Still Pendleton hung back. "Oh, for God's sake," Zweig said irritably, "go on in. The acclimatization's all been taken care of. Go in!"

Pendleton walked forward and pushed against the sheet.

He fell through. That was the only way he could have described it: he fell through. He fell for quite some little time, and ended with a cushioned thump on what seemed to be a rubber pad.

The impact of his fall seemed, momentarily, to have shaken the wits out of him. He didn't know who he was—no, that was all right; he was Bruce Pendleton—or where, or why. He felt around on the rubber pad with his fingers blankly, as if he expected contact with it to resolve his difficulties. Then he got to his feet.

He was at one end of a long, tall, metal-lined corridor. It was lit at intervals by inset golden fluors, and the air in it seemed to vibrate to a low, constant hum, almost too deep to be heard.

The locale was hauntingly familiar, and after a second Pendleton realized what it was. He was on a ship, and the ship must be in space, since the low constant hum could come only from its anti-grav.

A ship, certainly, but a ship for giants. The proportions of the corridor— length, height, even the size of the fluors—were quite unlike what Pendleton was used to. Only people of enormous stature could pilot such a ship.

He pressed his hands over his eyes and tried to think. There was something about a man...a little, ugly man, like a monkey...who'd made something...

He couldn't capture the thought, and after a second he didn't think it mattered. But he understood about the ship. It wasn't that it was unusually large, it was just that he himself, Bruce, wasn't very tall.

Halfway down the corridor there was a direct-contact viewing plate set in the ship's wall. Bruce Pendleton stopped in front of it. He did that whenever he went along the corridor, because he loved to look out at the stars. It was like looking out of a cave into paradise.

How beautiful they were! Against the intense velvety darkness of space they burned, they seemed to glitter and flash with a blinding sparkle, more bravely than a billion diamonds would have done. He knew *that* was illusion, stars in space don't glitter, they burn with a steady light. But they did seem to blaze out at him.

And each one was a sun, an unimaginable furnace, and around each sun were its unimaginable worlds. One of them, Pendleton knew, was more beautiful than all the others, and that one was his own world. It would take time; he had to wait. But sooner or later he was going there.

At the end of the corridor a door was set flush in the metal sheathing. Bruce hesitated in front of it. His right hand ran over his left wrist uneasily. It seemed to him there ought to be something on his wrist...not the little chronometer, but something else...a metal circlet with a...with a... But he couldn't think what it was, and he'd better not spend any more time puzzling over it. He'd dawdled enough in the corridor.

He rapped on the door, as he'd been taught, and waited until he heard the deep voice saying, "Come in." Then he opened it.

The desk was piled high with books and papers, but the big man's face lay in shadow. There was a pool of shadow around him on the floor.

"Well, son," he said without turning, "have you memorized your astrogation tables thoroughly? I've just finished a most interesting book about the adahn in Mayan culture, and I can spare you a few minutes. Do you want to recite the tables to me now, or would you rather wait until tomorrow morning? I don't want to hear them unless you know them thoroughly."

The lines of anger and unhappiness had faded from around Pendleton's mouth. His face had become young and timid and hopeful, a forward-looking, eager face.

"Well, sir," he said doubtfully to the man who was his father, "I thought I knew them pretty well. But maybe I'd better wait until tomorrow before I try to say them for you, sir. Yes."

Afterword by Cat Rambo

Margaret St. Clair used the pseudonym Idris Seabright for less than two dozen stories, all published during the 50s. All but a few appeared in *The Magazine of Fantasy and Science Fiction*, under the editorship of Anthony Boucher. Critics have noted that the Seabright stories tend to be a bit more glossy and what *The Science Fiction Encyclopedia* calls "less confrontational," but they've also been called "weirder" than the St. Clair byline stories. The truth of the matter seems to me to be due in part to more pragmatic factors—St. Clair frequently had more than one story in an issue, and editors preferred not to run two stories with the same byline. Use of the alias may have contributed to St. Clair's later obscurity by diverting some of the fame Seabright's way, but she was an influential writer in her time under both names, with a collective total of over 150 short stories published and eight novels.

Like other stories from the period in *The Magazine of F&SF*, the Seabright stories often use classic tropes for their launch point. Nonetheless, the Seabright stories read differently from some of their fellows in the magazine, coming from an author aware of and interested in gender issues rather than blind to them. "Change the Sky" has some delicate nuances in the beginning as the artist listening to Pendleton shapes his protoclay into a woman's torso, and Pendleton rejects the idea that the ideal world is composed of ornamental flowers and women, saying he doesn't want "some sort of lustful paradise."

"What do women want?" Freud had mused a couple of decades earlier, and here St. Clair flips the question—what do men want? And the ending is surprisingly devoid of those flowers and women, as Pendleton finds himself in Selim Zweig's creation, becoming a boy again, until the end where he has finally re-found his lost father.

Freud would probably have a somewhat misguided field day with details in "Change the Sky", like the egg that Pendleton must enter or the series of bubbles he moves through, but St. Clair has a masterful hand with nuances at levels that slide past the reader. For example, we don't find out the name of the first artist until he signs his note, two thirds of the way into the story, and we don't know Pendleton's first name, Bruce, until the last page—choices that are informed by craft, rather than accident. And her descriptions of planets, the days on Genlis and the nights of Kruor, are full of the sense of wonder and intensity that thrills the speculative fiction reader of any era. St. Clair was one of the best of her time, and the complexities of "Change the Sky" show her in fine form.

Miss Quatro

by Alice Eleanor Jones

(Originally appeared in the June 1955 issue of *Fantastic Universe*. It has never been republished before now).

Edith Horton said into the telephone, "Oh, Myra, I'm so sorry you can't go... Yes, it ought to be fun. And no worry about Judy. Miss Quatro's taking care of her." She glanced across the room to where the housekeeper sat sewing, her head bent over the child's dress.

"What? ...Oh, she's wonderful! Marvelous with Judy, yes. We've had her nearly a month now. Just after you went to the cottage... Oh, of course a new dress! Blue..." She spoke kindly to the housekeeper. "The light's not good there, Miss Quatro. You'll hurt your eyes."

"The light is entirely adequate, madam," Miss Quatro said precisely. She looked at Edith. She was a small woman, slender and pale, very genteel, with no-color hair and no-color eyes. She wore a black dress with a white collar, and a flat milky brooch like a blind eye, and black stockings and shoes. "I can go into the other room if you prefer it," she added courteously, in her no-color voice.

Edith blushed. "Oh, no, Miss Quatro, I didn't mean—Yes, I'm still here, Myra. Stay where you are, Miss Quatro."

"Yes, madam." Miss Quatro's head bent again; her thin fingers skillfully mended the dress.

"I'll see you Friday, Myra, at Helen's? ...Good. And I do think it's a shame Mrs. Beck disappointed you."

"If you will excuse me, madam," Miss Quatro said. "I could not help over-hearing. Is there trouble finding a sitter for Mrs. Glenn's children?"

Surprised, Edith turned from the phone. "Just a minute, Myra... What did you say, Miss Quatro?"

"I beg your pardon, madam," said the housekeeper, inclining her head in

103

the merest sketch of a bow, "if I seem to intrude. I was about to suggest that if Mrs. Glenn were to bring her children here this evening I should be glad to look after them for her. They might even stay the night, madam."

Edith smiled delightedly. "Why, Miss Quatro, how kind of you! Mrs. Glenn will be very grateful. But won't it be too much for you?"

"No, madam, not at all."

"I'll tell her, then... Myra, Miss Quatro's offered to take the children... Yes, here. They could stay till morning... Yes, isn't it? Didn't I tell you?... Mrs. Glenn wants to talk to you, Miss Quatro."

The housekeeper put down her sewing and moved to the telephone. She had a strange silent walk, oddly stiff, as if her legs carried the rest of her about like a parcel. The conversation was brief, consisting mostly of "Yes, madam" and "Quite all right, madam" and "Thank you, madam."

"Shall I hang up now, madam?" asked Miss Quatro, turning to Edith.

"Yes, please... Miss Quatro, that was such a kind thing to do."

"Not at all, madam," said Miss Quatro.

"Yes, it was. Thank you. Thank you very much... Will you have dinner a little early tonight? About six? I'll have to dress."

"As you wish, madam. At six."

During the first intermission at the country club dance, the Hortons and the Glenns sat together on the wide porch, sipping drinks and talking.

"Edie, this is nice!" Myra Glenn said, leaning her dark head back with a gentle sigh. "Your Miss Quatro's very kind. But she's" — she hesitated, frowning — "don't you think there's something... That sounds ungrateful; forget it, Edie."

"She is rather odd," Edith agreed, and smiled. She was looking exceptionally pretty in a dark blue dress that set off her blonde coloring. "Very efficient, though, and so good with Judy."

"It was darned nice of her to take on three strange kids at such short notice," said Bob Glenn.

"Oh, she knows them," said Myra. "They came home from Judy's yesterday just full of the wonderful Miss Quatro."

"She likes kids," said George Horton in his solid comfortable voice. "Make it another round, waiter."

"We're lucky to have her," Edith said earnestly to Myra. "And I—like her."

"You can't mean you actually —" Myra stopped and began again.

"They say she tells them stories."

"Stories, dear?"

"Not stories, *the* story," said George. "The kids make a big point of that. She tells them *the* story. Sure you're not tired, Edie?"

She smiled at him affectionately. "No, George. I'm not an invalid any more."

"What kind of a story?" asked Bob idly. He was dark and slender like his wife; both the Hortons were fair.

Edith laughed. I've never heard it," she said. "It's a secret between her and the children. The music's started again; dance with me, Bob."

The four children sat up in their beds on the Hortons' sleeping porch where Judy slept in summer. Judy's bed was a double, and she was sharing it with Carla Glenn. They were both seven years old, one blonde and one dark, with big eyes, and long hair done in braids. Bobby and Jeff Glenn, the five-year-old twins, had cots dragged down from the attic. Their cropped heads bobbed up and down. They could not bear to be still, especially at bedtime.

Four pairs of eyes were fixed upon Miss Quatro, who was adjusting windows and blinds. She moved softly about the porch with her odd walk, her face pale and quiet.

her hands deft. When she had finished she sat down on the foot of Judy's bed.

"Now tell us the story, Miss Quatro," demanded Judy.

"Yes, Miss Quatro, tell us now!" cried Carla.

"Tell, tell!" chorused the twins, bouncing mightily.

"Very well, children," said Miss Quatro quietly. "Now I shall tell you the story. Robert, Jeffrey, come over here so that you can see."

"You're tired," Edith said gently to Miss Quatro, as the housekeeper sat at the kitchen table polishing the silver. "Don't do that now."

"It is nearly finished, madam," said Miss Quatro, busy with the cream pitcher. "I am not tired."

Edith took the pitcher out of her hands. "Yes, you are," she said. "You look exhausted. The silver doesn't matter. Go and rest."

Miss Quatro looked at her. Most surprisingly, faint color appeared in her checks. "Very well, madam, if you wish." She left the kitchen, going quickly, hurrying.

"And all I hear from my two," said Helen Talbot toward the end of an afternoon of Scrabble, "is Miss Quatro. What have you got at your house, Edie—a pied piper?"

Myra said, " —and one is eighteen," and drew two tiles. "She's certainly got *something*." Scrabble was a very exacting game, and Myra half-wished she had suggested bridge instead.

"She's got the perfect housekeeper and the perfect nursemaid," said Ruth Hallman a shade enviously. "Our plutocratic friend!"

"I had to," Edith said apologetically. People were always apologizing to red-headed, sharp-eyed, sharp-tongued Ruth. "Thirty, Helen... I had to, after I—after I lost the baby."

"Shut up, Ruth," said Helen calmly, writing "30" in Edith's column. Sturdy, blunt Helen—she never apologized to anybody. "Edith can have a housekeeper if she wants one—and can afford it! 'Lory,' Edie? I don't believe it."

Edith smiled. "It's a bird, Helen. Want to challenge?"

"Oh, no, I know you too well. Let it go. I must say, though, Edie, she's an odd-looking specimen, your Miss Quatro."

Myra shivered. "She gives me a chill. I'm sorry, but she does."

Ruth said, "Darn it, Edie, you spoiled my word. Full-time help that sleeps in wouldn't chill me! I heard she's come down in the world, Edie—used to work for Park Avenue. What's she doing here?"

"Not Park Avenue," Edith said diffidently, Ruth always made her nervous. "She did have a job in New York, though, with a Mrs. Beekman, It was too much for her—Miss Quatro. She needed a quieter place, smaller. The Beekmans gave her a wonderful reference."

Helen said, "You checked it, I hope."

"I meant to," said Edith, "but the others who answered the ad were awful, and she seemed so—so *respectable*, and I was feeling... Well, by the time she'd been with us two days I knew we couldn't do without her." She looked around the table almost defiantly. "And we can't."

"Well, it's your house," Myra said, "and your business. Are you going to do anything, Ruth?"

"Don't rush me, just don't rush me."

"I'm writing your check, Miss Quatro," George Horton said, looking up from the papers on his desk, "and I have to fill out these forms, too. What's your social security number? May I see the card?"

"I am sorry, sir," said Miss Quatro, "I must have lost it, and I do not recall the number."

"That's all right, Miss Quatro. Let me know when you get it replaced." He smiled at her, "I don't think we told you how much we like having you here."

Edith said, "How much we appreciate all you do." She added impulsively, "How much we like you!"

Miss Quatro looked at them, a strange expression in her no-color eyes, but she said only, "Thank you, sir. Thank you, madam. Now if you will excuse me—"

"And the way she talks," Myra said, as she and Edith drove home from the parent-teachers'. "No idioms, no contractions even! Is she a foreigner? Quatro—that sounds Italian, or Spanish,"

"I don't know," Edith said slowly. "I don't really know, Myra." Myra took her eyes off the road long enough to look earnestly at her friend. "Edie, she's living in your house. She takes care of your child. You ought to know something about her."

Edith smiled a little. "I know that she manages the house perfectly. I know that she's honest and courteous and intelligent. And I know that Judy loves her; I can't quite see why, her manner's so odd. But she does. Don't you think that's enough?"

"It wouldn't be for me," said Myra. "But you're always so trusting, Edie. And the way you treat that woman—like a member of the family. How can you? I'm—I'm almost afraid of her!"

Edith said quietly, "I'm not. Do you know, Myra, she acts sometimes as if she were—afraid of us."

Myra raised her eyebrows. "For heaven's sake, why?"

"I don't know," Edith said thoughtfully, "She works so hard—too hard. She does things that aren't necessary. Myra, my house is so clean it's ridiculous. But when we try to thank her, or tell her to take it easier, she just—shies away from us, effaces herself, goes out of the room. Why, Myra?"

"Because she's queer," the other said with conviction.

"You know," Edith went on, frowning a little, "she did something once, I even forget what—oh, I know, it was the table for Judy's birthday party—and it was beautiful, I remember I said, 'You can be proud of that,' and she gave me such a look... Maybe I sounded patronizing; I didn't mean to. I just don't understand her, Myra.

Myra braked sharply to avoid a cat crossing the road. "Darn fool thing!... All the same, Edie, if it were me I'd find out more about her. You're going shopping in the city next week, aren't you? Why don't you look up this Mrs. Beekman, Edie, and ask her."

Edith said quickly, "Oh, Myra, I wouldn't do that."

"Call her, then. Or write to her."

"Well—maybe I will. Just to prove you're wrong." Edith laughed suddenly. "Miss Quatro... Miss Four!"

On the Saturday when Edith went to New York Miss Quatro took the children on a picnic. She took every child in the neighborhood, and there were a great many. She led them off through the woods to Palmer's field, a wide pasture that had once been part of Palmer's farm, long abandoned and overgrown. The pasture was often used for picnics. It was a pleasant place in late summer, drowsy with sunshine, fragrant and still. Miss Quatro was a staid and spinsterish piper in her black clothes, with the children frolicking after her.

George met Edith at the station in the late afternoon. She looked upset, and her face was paler than it ought to have been.

"George," she said as she stepped into the car, "there isn't any Mrs. Grant Lester Beekman in New York."

George was having trouble getting the Dodge up the grade. He said absently, "I'm afraid she's had it, Edie. We're going to have to trade her in."

"George, listen to me!" Edith's voice was tense. "I said there isn't any Mrs. Grant Lester Beekman. There isn't any in the phone book. So I asked information for the phone number, and there isn't any."

George coaxed the car to the top of the hill. "Edie, you're not making sense."

"*Listen*, George! I couldn't believe it, so I got a taxi, and I asked the driver to go there, and there isn't any such place."

George looked at her and stopped the car. "Edie, start from the beginning and take it slow."

"All right. Give me a cigarette, George." She drew on it nervously. "I was checking on Miss Quatro.

I did it mostly to prove to Myra... Well, I thought I'd just check the reference, anyway. And it's phony, George—completely phony!"

George's face was serious. "You mean there isn't any Mrs. Beekman? And there isn't any address like the one in the letter?"

"No, George. Not in the entire city of New York."

George said slowly, "Let's not jump at anything, Edie."

"And the social security card," Edith said suddenly. "She never showed it to us. George, I'm scared!" She began to cry.

He put his arm around her. "The card wouldn't prove anything, one way or the other," he said soberly. "Anybody can get one, and anybody can lose one."

I should have checked," Edith sobbed. "If only I'd checked!"

"Don't get excited, Edie," George said, patting her shoulder. "Miss Quatro's a good housekeeper, isn't she? And Judy loves her, don't forget that—all the kids do. That's the main thing. There can't be much wrong with anybody the kids are so crazy about. There's probably some simple explanation for the whole business. Don't cry, Edie. We'll ask her. When she comes back from the picnic we'll just ask her."

The children sat in a close semicircle around Miss Quatro in Palmer's field — three deep, kneeling, squatting, crouching, their faces expectant. "Tell us the story, Miss Quatro...tell us now...tell us."

"Very well, children," said Miss Quatro quietly. "Now I shall tell you the story."

She looked all around the circle. The children were silent; their faces were eager and wild. Miss Quatro took off the brooch that looked like a blind eye and held it in her hands. "Look, children," she said softly, "look."

She began to speak, and her voice changed. It had color now, all the colors in the world. Her eyes changed, and they too had all the colors in the world.

"There is a place, children," said Miss Quatro, "like no other place you have ever seen. It is a city, a city of jewels, a city of light... Look, children, look at the city." She moved the brooch slowly in a half-circle, twice, once low and once high, so that even those in the back row could see it.

"Tell us about the towers, Miss Quatro, said Judy Horton dreamily, and the words echoed around the circle. "The towers...tell us again!"

"The towers are high and shining," said Miss Quatro. "The slaves built them for a thousand years, and many gave their lives in the building. The towers are made of onyx and amber and chalcedony. They are made of amethyst and opal and porphyry and jade." Her voice sang the lovely words they did not understand. "And the walls of the city are of ruby, red as fire, and the gates are chryselephantine...of ivory and gold."

She paused and moved the brooch again. "See it, children...do you see it?" Her voice compelled them. It was not so much the pictures, it was not so much the words, it was the voice. They sat in the drowsy meadow, and the voice enchanted them, as it had done so often before.

"We see...we see, Miss Quatro!"

"Parts of the walls are covered with pictures carved in the stone," said Miss Quatro. "Many slaves were blinded carving them." She smiled a little. "No one says to a slave — *You will hurt your eyes!*"

The children waited, patient, expectant.

"The sky is a color you have never seen," said Miss Quatro, "and the streets are full of music. The flowers are of crystal, and they glitter like a shower of rain. The slaves tend them."

"Tell us about the people, Miss Quatro. Tell us about the people!"

The brooch flashed again.

"The people are beautiful," said Miss Quatro, "with eyes like diamonds and hair like gold. They move to music from a thousand pipes and strings. The slaves make the music all night long."

"All night, Miss Quatro? Don't they get tired ?"

"Yes, they get tired. No one says to a slave – *Go and rest.*"

"But don't they sleep?"

"Yes, they sleep. They sleep to restore their bodies for the work they are commanded to do. That is the law. I have told you before, children."

"The people don't like the slaves." It was Judy, sounding troubled.

Miss Quatro said slowly, "No one says to a slave – *How much we like you.* The city belongs to the people, children, and the slaves belong to the people."

They were eager again; they forgot the slaves. "Tell us how happy the people are, Miss Quatro! Tell us what they do. Tell us again."

Miss Quatro paused for a long moment and covered the brooch with her hands, A sigh of disappointment went up from the circle. "Show us, Miss Quatro…show us!"

"Soon, children… Children, the story changes. This part of the story you have never heard. Listen, listen carefully."

The children sat like stone, the sun warm on their bodies, their faces tranced and seeking.

"The people are sad," said Miss Quatro, and her voice mourned like the deep notes of a bell. "The people weep in the towers. The people weep in the streets."

A moan, of frantic sorrow swept around the circle. "Why, Miss Quatro?"

"Because" – her voice shook and cried – "because there is no food. Because there is no – food – left."

"No food?"

"It is so little that is required…so little, that goes so far. And there is so little time to find it. There is no food in the city, children. There is none outside the gates. And the people starve. The – people – starve!"

The children wept.

"But there is hope." The voice hoped, and the children hoped. They raised their faces to the sunlight, their tears dried.

"The slaves are searching in other places, far from the city – far, children, far! – for the food, for the life, as they have been commanded to do. Commanded with…there is a thing that is done to slaves."

She stopped. The eyes of the children were on her, blind with wonder, and fear, and love. "They are searching everywhere for the food," said Miss Quatro at last. "And one of them has found it. Only one."

The children cried, "Show us, Miss Quatro! Show us!"

"Soon, children... The slave has found the food that is not bought in the shops, that is not taken in the hands, that is not taken in the bowl, that is not eaten with the mouth. It remains only to take it back to the city. Quickly, for the time has run out. Humbly and with dread, for no one says to a slave— *Thank you*... Look, children!"

Miss Quatro uncovered the brooch and held it high. The children looked. It was a blaze, it was a fire, it was all the colors in the world, it was all the colors they had never seen. It was suddenly Miss Quatro's eyes, it was a door.

Miss Quatro held the brooch and gazed at the children. The sun shone gently on them, the grass moved in the light wind, there was no sound.

Miss Quatro said suddenly, "I will not go back! Let the city die!" She said to the children, "Cover your faces!"

She turned and cast the brooch from her, far out and away. There was a sharp sound, not loud, like the shattering of glass, and a flare of light. Miss Quatro fell and lay quiet in the field.

For a minute the children were shocked and still. Then they began to move, to stand up, and some of the smaller ones began to cry. Miss Quatro did not stir.

"Oh, look—oh, look!" Carla said, and ran to her.

The children crowded around, sobbing. "Miss Quatro—Miss Quatro—"

Their treble voices broke as they clutched at her sleeve.

Miss Quatro briefly opened her no-color eyes and closed them again. She said quietly in her no-color voice, "Go home, children. They will be kind to you, as they were kind to me. I was not a slave here. A slave has no pride, and I am proud now."

Miss Quatro said quietly, as her life left her, "Children—go home."

Afterword by Gwyn Conaway

Alice Eleanor Jones was a brazen mind, determined to push the boundaries of storytelling through her speculative short stories, and to stimulate the minds of other writers. With a body of work that spans fiction and nonfiction, from *The Magazine of Fantasy and Science Fiction* to *Seventeen*, she had a lasting impact on female writers and our perception of the suburban woman. She was a tireless advocate for writing in itself. That is to say, she believed that writing, regardless of whether or not the story sells, is as important an exercise for the author as it is for the reader.

As a result, her published speculative fiction works are a powerful handful of poignant and observant forays into the duties and expectations of women in middle class America. Her speculative fiction is concentrated in the year 1955, including the tales of "Life, Incorporated"; "Miss Quatro"; "Recruiting Officer"; and "The Happy Clown". Her seminal work, "Created He Them" (also from 1955), has become a must-read classic, and finds echoes in *The Handmaid's Tale* by Margaret Atwood.

"Miss Quatro" is an excellent example of Jones' complex view of women. The housekeeper is unassuming, but has immense power over the neighborhood children through her Story. A Pied Piper that only shares her melody with children away from the eyes and ears of adults, Miss Quatro unnerves their parents while also impressing them. Other mothers tell Edith Horton, her employer, how lucky she is to have the housekeeper, but how strange the woman seems. Despite this, Edith is kind and inclusive. In the end, it's her acknowledgment of Miss Quatro's humanity that saves the children. Jones makes it abundantly clear that if any other mother in town had employed Miss Quatro, the ending would have been a tragedy.

Jones' interest in the ugly undercurrents of America's civil freedoms and women's lives are themes she returns to again and again with an eerie, mesmerizing command. Her work is a quiet horror, for she doesn't always speak directly to the reader through her words, but sometimes in the space between them. The suggestion of oppression and subservience in her writing is often accepted by readers, because it is accepted by her characters.

In the case of "Miss Quatro", it is only at the end of the story that we realize the subtle rebuke of these accepted practices woven into the tale. It is not the aliens' cruelty that we must grapple with, but our own. Would we, we are forced to ask ourselves, have treated Miss Quatro as kindly as Edith did?

The Princess and the Physicist
by Evelyn E. Smith

(Originally appeared in the June 1955 issue of *Galaxy*. It was recently published as a chapbook; before that, it had not been available since 1958.)

Zen the Terrible lay quiescent in the secret retreat which housed his corporeal being, all the aspects of his personality wallowing in the luxury of a day off. How glad he was that he'd had the forethought to stipulate a weekly holiday for himself when first this godhood had been thrust upon him, hundreds of centuries before. He'd accepted the perquisites of divinity with pleasure then. It was some little time before he discovered its drawbacks, and by then it was too late; he had become the established church.

All the aspects of his personality rested...save one, that is. And that one, stretching out an impalpable tendril of curiosity, brought back to his total consciousness the news that a spaceship from Earth had arrived when no ship from Earth was due.

So what? the total consciousness asked lazily of itself. *Probably they have a large out-of-season order for hajench. My hajench going to provide salad bowls for barbarians!*

When, twenty years previously, the Earthmen had come back to their colony on Uxen after a lapse of thousands of years, Zen had been hopeful that they would take some of the Divine Work off his hands. After all, since it was they who had originally established the colony, it should be their responsibility. But it seemed that all humans, not merely the Uxenach, were irresponsible. The Earthmen were interested only in trade and tribute. They even refused to believe in the existence of Zen, an attitude which he found extremely irritating to his ego.

True, Uxen prospered commercially to a mild extent after their return, for the local ceramics that had been developed in the long interval found wide acceptance throughout the Galaxy, particularly the low bowls which had hitherto been used only for burning incense before Zen the Formidable.

Now every two-bit planet offered hajench in its gift shops.

Culturally, though, Uxen had degenerated under the new Earth administration. No more criminals were thrown to the skwitch. Xwoosh lost its interest when new laws prohibited the ancient custom of executing the losing side after each game.

There was no tourist trade, for the planet was too far from the rest of the Galaxy. The commercial spaceships came only once every three months and left the same day. The two destroyers that "guarded" the planet arrived at rare intervals for fueling or repairs, but the crew never had anything to do with the Uxenach. Local ordinance forbade the maidens of Uxen to speak to the outlanders, and the outlanders were not interested in any of the other native products.

But the last commercial spaceship had departed less than three weeks before on its regular run, and this was not one of the guard ships.

Zen reluctantly conceded to himself that he would have to investigate this situation further, if he wanted to retain his reputation for omniscience. Sometimes, in an occasional moment of self-doubt, he wondered if he weren't too much of a perfectionist but then he rejected the thought as self-sacrilege.

Zen dutifully intensified the beam of awareness and returned it to the audience chamber where the two strange Earthmen who had come on the ship were being ushered into the presence of the king by none other than Guj, the venerable prime minister himself.

"Gentlemen," Guj beamed, his long white beard vibrating in an excess of hospitality, "His Gracious Majesty will be delighted to receive you at once."

And crossing his wrists in the secular xa, he led the way to where Uxlu the Fifteenth was seated in full regalia upon his imposing golden, gem-encrusted throne.

Uxlu himself, Zen admitted grudgingly, was an imposing sight to anyone who didn't know the old yio. The years—for he was a scant decade younger than Guj—had merely lent dignity to his handsome features, and he was still tall and upright.

"Welcome, Earthlings, to Uxen," King Uxlu said in the sonorous tones of the practiced public speaker. "If there is aught we can do to advance your comfort whilst you sojourn on our little planet, you have but to speak."

He did not, Zen noted with approval, rashly promise that requests would necessarily be granted. Which was fine, because the god well knew who the carrier out of requests would be—Zen the Almighty, the All-Powerful, the All-Put-Upon...

"Thank you, Your Majesty," the older of the two scientists said. "We merely seek a retired spot in which to conduct our researches."

"Researches, eh?" the king repeated with warm interest. "Are you perhaps scientists?"

"Yes, Your Majesty." Every one of Zen's perceptors quivered expectantly. Earth science was banned on Uxen, with the result that its acquisition had become the golden dream of every Uxena, including, of course, their god.

The older scientist gave a stiff bow. "I am an anthropologist. My name is Kendrick, Professor Alpheus Kendrick. My assistant, Dr. Peter Hammond—" he indicated the tall young man with him—"is a physicist."

The king and the prime minister conferred together in whispers. Zen wished he could join them, but he couldn't materialize on that plane without incense, and he preferred his subjects not to know that he could be invisibly present, especially on his day off. Of course, his Immaterial Omnipresence was a part of the accepted dogma, but there is a big difference between accepting a concept on a basis of faith or of proven fact.

"Curious researches," the king said, emerging from the conference, "that require both physics *and* anthropology."

"Yes," said Kendrick. "They are rather involved at that." Peter Hammond shuffled his feet.

"Perhaps some of our technicians might be of assistance to you," the king suggested. "They may not have your science, but they are very adept with their hands…"

"Our researches are rather limited in scope," Kendrick assured him. "We can do everything needful quite adequately ourselves. All we need is a place in which to do it."

"You shall have our own second-best palace," the king said graciously. "It has both hot and cold water laid on, as well as central heating."

"We've brought along our own collapsible laboratory-dwelling," Kendrick explained. "We just want a spot to set it up."

Uxlu sighed. "The royal parks are at your disposal. You will undoubtedly require servants?"

"We have a robot, thanks."

"A robot is a mechanical man who does all our housework," Hammond, more courteous than his superior, explained. Zen wondered how he could ever have felt a moment's uneasiness concerning these wonderful strangers.

"Zen will be interested to hear of this," the prime minister said cannily. He and the king nodded at one another.

"*Who* did you say?" Kendrick asked eagerly.

"Zen the Terrible," the king repeated, "Zen the All-Powerful, Zen the Encyclopedic. Surely you have heard of him?" he asked in some surprise. "He's Uxen's own particular, personal and private god, exclusive to our planet."

"Yes, yes, of course I've heard about him," Kendrick said, trembling with hardly repressed excitement.

What a correct attitude! Zen thought. *One rarely finds such religious respect among foreigners.*

"In fact, I've heard a great deal about him and I should like to know even more!" Kendrick spoke almost reverently.

"He *is* an extremely interesting divinity," the king replied complacently. "And if your robot cannot teleport or requires a hand with the heavy work, do not hesitate to call on Zen the Accommodating. We'll detail a priest to summon—"

"The robot manages very well all by itself, thank you," Kendrick said quickly.

In his hideaway, the material body of Zen breathed a vast multiple sigh of relief. He was getting to like these Earthmen more and more by the minute.

"Might I inquire," the king asked, "into the nature of your researches?"

"An investigation of the prevalent nuclear ritual beliefs on Uxen in relation to the over-all matrix of social culture, and we really must get along and see to the unloading of the ship. Good-by, Your Majesty... Your Excellency." And Kendrick dragged his protesting aide off.

"If only," said the king, "I were still an absolute monarch, I would teach these Earthlings some manners." His face grew wistful. "Well I remember how my father would have those who crossed him torn apart by wild skwitch."

"If you did have the Earthlings torn apart by wild skwitch, Sire," Guj pointed out, "then you would certainly never be able to obtain any information from them."

Uxlu sighed. "I would merely have them torn apart a little—just enough so that they would answer a few civil questions." He sighed again. "And, supposing they did happen to—er—pass on, in the process, think of the tremendous lift to my ego. But nobody thinks of the king's ego any more these days."

No, things were not what they had been since the time the planet had been retrieved by the Earthlings. They had not communicated with Uxen for so many hundreds of years, they had explained, because, after a more than ordinarily disastrous war, they had lost the secret of space travel for centuries.

Now, wanting to make amends for those long years of neglect, they immediately provided that the Earth language and the Earth income tax become mandatory upon Uxen. The language was taught by recordings. Since the Ux-enach were a highly intelligent people, they had all learned it quickly and for-gotten most of their native tongue except for a few untranslatable concepts.

"Must be a new secret atomic weapon they're working on," Uxlu decided. "Why else should they come to such a remote corner of the Galaxy? And you will recall that the older one — Kendrick — said something about nuclear be-liefs. If only we could discover what it is, secure it for ourselves, perhaps we could defeat the Earthmen, drive them away —" he sighed for the third time that morning — "and rule the planet ourselves."

Just then the crown princess Iximi entered the throne room. Iximi really lived up to her title of Most Fair and Exalted, for centuries of selective breeding under which the kings of Uxen had seized the loveliest women of the planet for their wives had resulted in an outstanding pulchritude. Her hair was as golden as the ripe fruit that bent the boughs of the iolo tree, and her eyes were bluer than the uriz stones on the belt girdling her slender waist. Reproduc-tions of the famous portrait of her which hung in the great hall of the palace were very popular on calendars.

"My father grieves," she observed, making the secular xa. "Pray tell your unworthy daughter what sorrow racks your noble bosom."

"Uxen is a backwash," her father mourned. "A planet forgotten, while the rest of the Galaxy goes by. Our ego has reached its nadir."

"Why did you let yourself be conquered?" the princess retorted scornful-ly. "Ah, had I been old enough to speak then, matters would be very different today!" Although she seemed too beautiful to be endowed with brains, Iximi had been graduated from the Royal University with high honors.

Zen the Erudite was particularly fond of her, for she had been his best stu-dent in Advanced Theology. She was, moreover, an ardent patriot and leader of the underground Moolai (free) Uxen movement, with which Zen was more or less in sympathy, since he felt Uxen belonged to him and not to the Earth-lings. After all, he had been there first.

"*Let* ourselves be conquered!" Her father's voice rose to a squeak. "*Let* ourselves! Nobody asked us — we *were* conquered."

"True, but we could at least have essayed our strength against the con-querors instead of capitulating like yioch. We could have fought to the last man!"

"A woman is always ready to fight to the last man," Guj commented.

"Did you hear that, ancient and revered parent! He called me, a princess of the blood, a — a woman!"

"We are all equal before Zen," Guj said sententiously, making the high xa.

"Praise Zen," Uxlu and Iximi chanted perfunctorily, bowing low.

Iximi, still angry, ordered Guj—who was also high priest—to start services. Kindling the incense in the hajen, he began the chant.

Of course it was his holiday, but Zen couldn't resist the appeal of the incense. Besides he was there anyway, so it was really no trouble, *no trouble*, he thought, greedily sniffing he delicious aroma, *at all*. He materialized a head with seven nostrils so that he was able to inhale the incense in one delectable gulp. Then, "No prayers answered on Thursday," he said, and disappeared. That would show them!

"Drat Zen and his days off!" The princess was in a fury. "Very well, we'll manage without Zen the Spiteful. Now, precisely what is troubling you, worthy and undeservedly Honored Parent?"

"Those two scientists who arrived from Earth. Didn't you meet them when you came in?"

"No, Respected Father," she said, sitting on the arm of the throne. "I must have just missed them. What are they like?"

He told her what they were like in terms not even a monarch should use before his daughter. "And these squuch," he concluded, "are undoubtedly working on a secret weapon. If we had it, we could free Uxen."

"Moolai Uxen!" the princess shouted, standing up. "My friends, must we continue to submit to the yoke of the tyrant? Arise. Smite the…"

"Anyone," said Guj, "can make a speech."

The princess sat on the steps of the throne and pondered. "Obviously we must introduce a spy into their household to learn their science and turn it to our advantage."

"They are very careful, those Earthlings," Guj informed her superciliously. "It is obvious that they do not intend to let any of us come near them."

The princess gave a knowing smile. "But they undoubtedly will need at least one menial to care for their dwelling. I shall be that menial. I, Iximi, will so demean myself for the sake of my planet! Moolai Uxen!"

"You cannot do it, Iximi," her father said, distressed. "You must not defile yourself so. I will not hear of it!"

"And besides," Guj interposed, "they will need no servants. All their housework is to be done by their robot—a mechanical man that performs all menial duties. And you, Your Royal Highness, could not plausibly disguise yourself as a machine."

"No-o-o-o, I expect not." The princess hugged the rosy knees revealed by her brief tunic and thought aloud, "But…just…supposing…something…went wrong with the robot… They do not possess another?"

"They referred only to one, Highness," Guj replied reluctantly. "But they may have the parts with which to construct another."

"Nonetheless, it is well worth the attempt," the princess declared. "You will cast a spell on the robot, Guj, so that it stops."

He sighed. "Very well, Your Highness; I suppose I could manage that!"

Making the secular xa, he left the royal pair. Outside, his voice could be heard bellowing in the anteroom, "Has any one of you squuch seen my pliers?"

"There is no need for worry, Venerated Ancestor," the princess assured the monarch. "All-Helpful Zen will aid me with my tasks."

Far away in his arcane retreat, the divinity groaned to himself.

Another aspect of Zen's personality followed the two Earthmen as they left the palace to supervise the erection of their prefab by the crew of the spaceship in one of the Royal Parks. A vast crowd of Uxenach gathered to watch the novelty, and among them there presently appeared a sinister-looking old man with a red beard, whom Zen the Pansophic had no difficulty in recognizing as the prime minister, heavily disguised. Of course it would have been no trouble for Zen to carry out Guj's mission for him, but he believed in self-help—especially on Thursdays.

"You certainly fixed us up fine!" Hammond muttered disrespectfully to the professor. "You should've told the king we were inventing a vacuum cleaner or something. Now they'll just be more curious than ever... And I still don't see why you refused the priest. Seems to me he'd be just what you needed."

"Yes, and the first to catch on to why we're here. We mustn't antagonize the natives; these closed groups are so apt to resent any investigation into their mythos."

"If it's all mythical, why do you need a scientist then?"

"A physical scientist, you mean," Kendrick said austerely. "For anthropology is a science, too, you know."

Peter snorted.

"Some Earthmen claim actually to have seen these alleged manifestations," Kendrick went on to explain, "in which case there must be some kind of mechanical trickery involved—which is where you come in. Of course I would have preferred an engineer to help me, but you were all I could get from the government."

"And you wouldn't have got me either, if the Minister of Science didn't have it in for me!" Peter said irately. "I'm far too good for this piddling little job, and you know it. If it weren't for envy in high places—"

"Better watch out," the professor warned, "or the Minister might decide you're too good for science altogether, and you'll be switched to a position more in keeping with your talents—say, as a Refuse Removal Agent."

And what is wrong with the honored art of Refuse Removal? Zen wondered. There were a lot of mystifying things about these Earthmen.

The scientists' quaint little edifice was finally set up, and the spaceship took its departure. It was only then that the Earthmen discovered that something they called cigarettes couldn't be found in the welter of packages, and that the robot wouldn't cook dinner or, in fact, do anything. *Good old Guj,* Zen thought.

"I can't figure out what's gone wrong," Peter complained, as he finished putting the mechanical man together again. "Everything seems to be all right, and yet the damned thing won't function."

"Looks as if we'll have to do the housework ourselves, confound it!"

"Uh-uh," Peter said. "You can, but not me. The Earth government put me under your orders so far as this project is concerned, sir, but I'm not supposed to do anything degrading, sir, and menial work is classified as just that, sir, so—"

"All right, all *right!*" Kendrick said. "Though it seems to me if I'*m* willing to do it, *you* should have no objection."

"It's your project, sir. I gathered from the king, though," Peter added more helpfully, "that some of the natives still do menial labor themselves."

"How disgusting that there should still be a planet so backward that human beings should be forced to do humiliating tasks," Kendrick said.

You don't know the half of it, either, Zen thought, shocked all the way back to his physical being. It had never occurred to him that the functions of gods on other planets might be different than on Uxen...unless the Earthlings failed to pay reverence to their own gods, which seemed unlikely in view of the respectful way with which Professor Kendrick had greeted the mention of Zen's Awe-Inspiring Name. Then Refuse Removal was not necessarily a divine prerogative.

Those first colonists were very clever, Zen thought bitterly, *sweet-talking me into becoming a god and doing all their dirty work. I was happy here as the Only Inhabitant; why did I ever let those interlopers involve me in Theolatry? But I can't quit now. The Uxenach need Me...and I need incense; I'm fettered by my own weakness. Still, I have the glimmerings of an idea...*

"Oh, how much could a half-witted menial find out?" Peter demanded. "Remember, it's either a native servant, sir, or you do the housework yourself."

"All right," Kendrick agreed gloomily. "Well try one of the natives."

So the next day, still attended by the Unseen Presence of Zen, they sought audience with the prime minister.

"Welcome, Earthmen, to the humble apartments of His Majesty's most unimportant subject," Guj greeted them, making a very small xa as he led them into the largest reception room.

Kendrick absently ran his finger over the undercarving of a small gold table. "Look, no dust," he whispered. "Must have excellent help here."

Zen couldn't help preening just a bit. At least he did his work well; no one could gainsay that.

"Your desire," Guj went on, apparently anxious to get to the point, "is my command. Would you like a rojh of dancing girls to perform before you or—?"

"The king said something yesterday about servants' being available," Kendrick interrupted. "And our robot seems to have broken down. Could you tell us where we could get someone to do our housework?"

An expression of vivid pleasure illuminated the prime minister's venerable countenance. "By fortunate chance, gentlemen, a small lot of maids is to be auctioned off at a village very near the Imperial City tomorrow. I should be delighted to escort you there personally."

"Auctioned?" Kendrick repeated. "You mean they *sell* servants here?"

Guj raised his snowy eyebrows. "Sold? Certainly not; they are leased for two years apiece. After all, if you have no lease, what guarantee do you have that your servants will stay after you have trained them? None whatsoever."

When the two scientists had gone, Iximi emerged from behind a bright-colored tapestry depicting Zen in seven hundred and fifty-three of his Attributes.

"The younger one is not at all bad-looking," she commented, patting her hair into place. "I do like big blond men. Perhaps my task will not be as unpleasant as I fancied."

Guj stroked his beard. "How do you know the Earthlings will select *you*, Your Highness? Many other maids will be auctioned off at the same time."

The princess stiffened angrily. "They'll pick me or they'll never leave Uxen alive and you, Your Excellency, would not outlive them."

Although it meant he had to overwork the other aspects of his multiple personality, Zen kept one free so that the next day he could join the Earthmen—in spirit, that was—on their excursion in search of a menial.

"If, as an anthropologist, you are interested in local folkways, Professor," Guj remarked graciously, as he and the scientists piled into a scarlet, boat-shaped vehicle, "you will find much to attract your attention in this quaint little planet of ours."

"Are the eyes painted on front of the car to ward off demons?" Kendrick asked.

"Car? Oh, you mean the yio!" Guj patted the forepart of the vehicle. It purred and fluttered long eyelashes. "We breed an especially bouncy strain with seats; they're so much more comfortable, you know."

"You mean this is a *live* animal?"

Guj nodded apologetically. "Of course it does not go very fast. Now if we had the atomic power drive, such as your spaceships have—"

"You'd shoot right off into space," Hammond assured him.

"Speed," said Kendrick, "is the curse of modern civilization. Be glad you still retain some of the old-fashioned graces here on Uxen. You see," he whispered to his assistant, "a clear case of magico-religious culture-freezing, resulting in a static society unable to advance itself, comes of its implicit reliance upon the powers of an omnipotent deity." Zen took some time to figure this out. *But that's right!* he concluded, in surprise.

"I thought your god teleported things?" Peter asked Guj. "How come he doesn't teleport you around, if you're in such a hurry to go places?"

Kendrick glared at him. "Please remember that I'm the anthropologist," he hissed. "You have got to know how to describe the Transcendental Personality with the proper respect."

"We don't have Zen teleport animate objects," the prime minister explained affably. "Or even inanimate ones if they are fragile. For He tends to lose His Temper sometimes when He feels that He is overworked—" *Feels, indeed! Zen* said to himself—"and throws things about. We cannot reprove Him for His misbehavior. After all, a god is a god."

"The apparent irreverence," Kendrick explained in an undertone, "undoubtedly signifies that he is dealing with ancillary or, perhaps, peripheral religious beliefs. I must make a note of them." He did so.

By the time the royal yio had arrived at the village where the planetary auctions for domestics were held, the maids were already arranged in a row on the platform. Most were depressingly plain creatures and dressed in thick sacklike tunics. Among them, the graceful form of Iximi was conspicuous, clad in a garment similar in cut but fashioned of translucent gauze almost as blue as her eyes.

Peter straightened his tie and assumed a much more cheerful expression. "Let's rent *that one!*" he exclaimed, pointing to the princess.

"Nonsense!" Kendrick told him. "In the first place, she is obviously the most expensive model. Secondly, she would be too distracting for you. And, finally, a pretty girl is never as good a worker as a plain... We'll take that one." The professor pointed to the dumpiest and oldest of the women. "How much should I offer to start, Your Excellency? No sense beginning the bidding too high. We Earthmen aren't made of money, in spite of what the rest of the Galaxy seems to think."

"A hundred credits is standard, Guj murmured. "However, sir, there is one problem — have you considered how you are going to communicate with your maid?"

"Communicate? Are they mutes?"

"No, but very few of these women speak Earth." A look of surprise flitted over the faces of the servants, vanishing as her royal highness glared at them.

Kendrick pursed thin lips. "I was under the impression that the Earth language was mandatory on Uxen."

"Oh, it is; it is, indeed!" Guj said hastily. "However, it is so hard to teach these backward peasants new ways." One of the backward peasants gave a loud sniff, which changed to a squeal as she was honored with a pinch from the hand of royalty. "But you will not betray us? We are making rapid advances and before long we hope to make Earth universal."

"Of course we won't," Peter put in, before Kendrick had a chance to reply. "What's more, I don't see why the Uxenians shouldn't be allowed to speak their own language."

The princess gave him a dazzling smile. "Moolai Uxen! We must not allow the beautiful Uxulk tongue to fall into desuetude. Bring back our lovely language!"

Guj gestured desperately. She tossed her head, but stopped.

"Please, Kendrick," Peter begged, "we've got to buy that one!"

"Certainly not. You can see she's a troublemaker. Do you speak Earth?" the professor demanded of the maid he had chosen.

"No speak," she replied.

Peter tugged at his superior's sleeve. "That one speaks Earth."

Kendrick shook him off. "Do you speak Earth?" he demanded of the second oldest and ugliest. She shook her head. The others went through the same procedure.

"It looks," Peter said, grinning, "as if we'll have to take mine."

"I suppose so," Kendrick agreed gloomily, "but somehow I feel no good will come of this."

Zen wondered whether Earthmen had powers of precognition.

No one bid against them, so they took a two-year lease on the crown princess for the very reasonable price of a hundred credits, and drove her home with them.

Iximi gazed at the little prefab with disfavor. "But why are we halting outside this gluu hutch, masters?"

Guj cleared his throat. "Sirs, I wish you joy." He made the secular xa. "Should you ever be in need again, do not hesitate to get in touch with me at the palace." And, climbing into the yio, he was off.

The others entered the small dwelling. "That little trip certainly gave me an appetite," Kendrick said, rubbing his hands together. "Iximi, you had better start lunch right away. This is the kitchen."

Iximi gazed around the cubicle with disfavor. "Truly it is not much," she observed. "However, masters, if you will leave me, I shall endeavor to do my poor best."

"Let me show you—" Peter began, but Kendrick interrupted.

"Leave the girl alone, Hammond. She must be able to cook, if she's a professional servant. We've wasted the whole morning as it is; maybe we can get something done before lunch."

Iximi closed the door, got out her portable altar—all members of the royal family were qualified members of the priesthood, though they seldom practiced—and in a low voice, for the door and walls were thin, summoned Zen the All-Capable.

The god sighed as he materialized his head. "I might have known you would require Me. What is your will, oh Most Fair?"

"I have been ordered to prepare the strangers' midday repast, oh Puissant One, and I know not what to do with all this ukh, which they assure me is their food." And she pointed scornfully to the cans and jars and packages.

"How should I know then?" Zen asked unguardedly.

The princess looked at him. "Surely Zen the All-Knowing jests?"

"Er—yes. Merely having My Bit of Fun, you know." He hastily inspected the exterior of the alleged foods. "There appear to be legends inscribed upon the containers. Perchance, were we to read them, they might give a clue as to their contents."

"Oh, Omniscient One," the princess exclaimed, "truly You are Wise and Sapient indeed, and it is I who was the fool to have doubted for so much as an instant."

"Oh you doubted, did you?" Terrible Zen frowned terribly. "Well, see that it doesn't happen again." He had no intention of losing his divine authority at this stage of the game.

"Your Will is mine, All-Wise One. And I think You had best materialize a few pair of arms as well as Your August and Awe-Inspiring Countenance, for there is much work to be done."

Since the partitions were thin, Zen and the princess could hear most of the conversation in the main room "...First thing to do," Kendrick's voice remarked, "is find out whether we're permitted to attend one of their religious ceremonies, where Zen is said to manifest himself actually and not, it is contended, just symbolically..."

"The stove is here, Almighty," the princess suggested, "not against the door where you are pressing Your Divine Ear."

"Shhh. What I hear is fraught with import for the future of the planet. Moolai Uxen."

"Moolai Uxen," the princess replied automatically.

"...I wonder how hard it'll be to crash the services," Kendrick went on. "Most primitives don't like outsiders present at their ritual activities."

"Especially if there *are* actual manifestations of their god," Hammond contributed. "That would mean the priests are up to some sort of trickery, and they wouldn't care to run the risk of having us see through—"

He was interrupted by a loud crash from the kitchen.

"Are you all right, Iximi!" he yelled. "Need any help?"

"All is well!" she called back. "But, I pray you, do not enter, masters. The reverberation was part of a rite designed to deflect evil spirits from the food. Were a heretic to be present or interrupt the ceremonies, the spell would be voided and the food contaminated."

"Okay!" Peter returned and, in a lower tone, which he probably thought she could not overhear, "Seems you were right."

"Naturally." There was complacency in the professor's voice. "And now let us consider the validating features of the social structure as related to the mythos—and, of course, the ethos, where the two are not coincident—of the Uxenians..."

"Imagine," Zen complained in the kitchen, "accusing *Me* of being a mere trick of the priesthood—Supreme Me!"

"Supreme Butterfingers!" the princess snapped, irritation driving her to the point of sacrilege. "You spilled that red stuff, the..." she bent over to read the legend on the container "...the ketchup all over the floor!"

"The floor is relatively clean," Zen murmured abstractedly. "We can scoop up the substance and incorporate it in whatever dainty dish we prepare for the Earthlings' repast. Now they'll think that I, Zen the Accessible, am difficult to have audience with," he mourned, "whereas I was particularly anxious to hold converse with them and discover what quest brings them to Uxen. That is," he added hastily, remembering he was omniscient, "just how they would justify its rationale."

"Shall we get on with our culinary activities, Almighty One?" Iximi asked

126

coldly.

If the Most Fair and Exalted had a flaw, Zen thought, it was a one-track mind.

"What in hell did you put in this, Iximi?" Kendrick demanded, after one taste of the steaming casserole of food which she had set proudly before the two Earthmen.

"Ketchup, that's for sure..." Peter murmured, rolling a mouthful around his tongue as he sought to separate its component flavors. "And rhubarb, I should say."

"Dried fish and garlic..." Kendrick made further identifications.

"And a comestible called marshmallow," Iximi beamed. "You like it? I am *so* glad!"

"I do *not*—" Kendrick began, but Peter intervened.

"It's very nice, Iximi," he said tactfully, "but I guess we're just used to old run-of-the-mill Earth cooking. It's all our fault; we should have given you a recipe."

"I had a recipe," Iximi returned. "It came to me by Divine Inspiration."

Kendrick compressed his lips. "Useful sort of divinity they have around here," Peter said. "Everything that goes wrong seems to take place in the name of religion. Are you sure you didn't happen to overhear us talking before, Iximi?"

"Don't be silly, Hammond!" Kendrick snapped. "These simple primitives do not have the sophistication to use their religious beliefs consciously as rationalization for their incompetence."

"Even had I wished to eavesdrop," Iximi said haughtily, "I would hardly have had the opportunity; I was too busy trying to prepare a palatable repast for you and—" her voice broke—"you didn't like it."

"Oh, I did like it, Iximi!" Peter protested. "It's just that I'm allergic to rhubarb."

"Wait!" she exclaimed, smiling again. "For dessert I have an especial surprise for you." She brought in a dish triumphantly. "Is this not just how you have it on Earth?"

"Stewed cigarettes with whipped cream," Kendrick muttered. "Stewed cigarettes! Where on Ear—on Uxen did you find them?"

"In a large box with the other puddings," she beamed. "Is it not highly succulent and flavorful?"

The two scientists sprang from their chairs and dashed into the kitchen. Iximi stared after them. When they returned, they looked much more cheerful. They seated themselves, and soon fragrant clouds of smoke began to curl toward the ceiling.

They are calling me at last, Zen thought happily, *and with such delightful incense! Who wants chants anyway?*

"But what are you *doing!*" the princess shrieked.

Zen hastened to manifest himself, complete with fourteen nostrils, before she could spoil everything. "The procedure is most unorthodox," he murmured aloud, "but truly this new incense has a most delicious aroma, extremely pleasing to My Ego. What is your will, oh, strangers?"

"All-Merciful Zen," the princess pleaded, "forgive them, for they knew not what they did. They did not mean to summon You."

"Then who," asked Zen in a terrible voice, "is this wonderful smoke for? Some foreign god whom they worship on My Territory?" And he wouldn't put it past them either.

Peter looked at the anthropologist, but Kendrick was obviously too paralyzed with fright to speak. "As a matter of fact, Your—er—Omnipotence," he physicist said haltingly, "this is not part of our religious ritual. We burn this particular type of incense which we call tobacco, for our own pleasure."

"In other words," Zen said coldly, "you worship yourselves. I work and slave My Godhood to the bone only to have egotists running all over My Planet."

"No, it's nothing like that at all," Kendrick quavered. "We smoke the tobacco to—well—gratify our appetites. Like—like eating, you know."

"Well, you will have to forego that pleasure," Zen said, frowning terribly. Even the tall one cowered, he noted with appreciation. It had been a long time since people had really cringed before his frown. The Uxenach had come to take him too much for granted; they would learn their mistake. "From now on," he said portentously, "the tobacco must be reserved for My Use alone. Smoke it only for purposes of worship. Once a day will be sufficient," he added graciously, "and perhaps twice on holy days."

"But we do not worship alien gods," Kendrick persisted in a shaky voice. "Even if you *were* a god..."

Zen frowned. "Would you care to step outside and test my divinity?"

"Well, no...but..."

"Then, as far as you're concerned, I am Divine, and let's have no more quibbling. Don't forget the tobacco once a day. About time I had a change from that low-grade incense."

He vanished. Too late he remembered that he'd planned to ask the Earthlings why they had come to Uxen, and to discuss a little business proposition with them. Oh, well, time for that at his next materialization for them. And, now that he considered the matter, the direct approach might very well be a mistake.

He hoped Iximi would make sure they burned him tobacco regularly—really good stuff; almost made godhood worthwhile. But then he'd felt that way about incense at first. No, he had other ideas for making divinity worthwhile, and Iximi was going to help him, even if she didn't know it. People had used him long enough; it was his turn to use them.

In the kitchen, Iximi recalled Zen and together they washed the dishes and listened to the scientists quarreling in the next room.

"You will note the use of incense as standard socio-religious parallelism, Hammond. Men have appetites that must be gratified and so they feel their supreme being must also eat...only, being a deity, he consumes aromas."

"Yes," Peter said. "You explained all that to Him much more succinctly, though."

"Hah! Well, have you any idea yet as to how the trick was worked?"

"Worked? What do you mean?"

"How they made that talking image appear? Clever device, I must say, although the Scoomps of Aldebaran III—"

"Didn't look like a trick to me."

"That's a fine young man," Zen said approvingly to Iximi. "I *like* him."

"You really do, Most High? I am *so* glad!"

"You don't mean you really believe this Zen is an actual living god?" Kendrick spluttered.

There was a silence. "No, not a god," Peter said finally, "but not a human, either. Perhaps another life-form with attributes different from ours. After all, do we know who or what was on Uxen, before it was colonized by Earth?"

"Tcha!" Kendrick said.

Iximi looked at Zen. Zen looked at Iximi. "The concept of godhood varies from society to society," the divinity told the princess. "Peter is not being sacrilegious, just manifesting a healthy skepticism."

"You're a credulous fool," Kendrick said hotly to his assistant. "I don't blame the Secretary for demoting you. When we return to Earth, I shall recommend your transfer to Refuse Removal. You have no business at all in Science!"

There was the sound of footsteps. "Leaving my noxious company?" Peter's voice asked tightly.

"I am going out to the nearest temple to have a chat with one of the priests. I can expect more sensible answers from him than from you!" The outside door slammed.

"Speaking of Refuse Removal, Almighty," Iximi said to Zen, "would you teleport the remains of this miserable repast to the Sacred Garbage Dump? And you need not return; I'll be able to handle the rest myself."

"Moolai Uxen," Zen reminded her and vanished with the garbage, but, although the refuse was duly teleported, the unseen, impalpable presence of the god remained.

The door to the kitchen opened, and Hammond walked in, his face grim. "Need any help, Iximi?" he asked, not very graciously. "Or should I say 'Your Royal Highness'?"

Iximi dropped a plate which, fortunately, was plastic. "How did you know who I was?"

He sat down on a stool. "Didn't you remember that your portrait hung in the great hall of the palace?"

"Of course," she said, chagrined. "A portrait of a servant would hardly be hung there."

"Not only that, but I asked whom it depicted. Do you think I wouldn't notice the picture of such a beautiful girl?"

"But if you knew, why then did you...?"

He grinned. "I realized you were up to no good, and I have no especial interest in the success of Kendrick's project."

Iximi carefully dried a dish. "And what is his project?"

"To investigate the mythos of the allegedly corporeal divinity in static primitive societies, with especial reference to the god-concept of Zen on Uxen."

"Is that *all*?"

All! Zen thought. *Sounds like an excellent subject for research to me. Unfortunate that I cannot possibly let the study be completed, as I am going to invalidate the available data very shortly.*

"That's all, Iximi."

"And how is it that Professor Kendrick did not recognize me from the picture?"

"Oh, he never notices girls' pictures. He's a complete idiot... You overheard us just now? When we get back to Earth, I'm going to be a garbage collector."

"Here on Uxen, Refuse Removal is a Divine Prerogative," Iximi remarked.

"Poor Zen, whatever he is," Peter said to himself. "But a god, being a god," he went on in a louder voice, "can raise himself above the more sordid aspects of the job. As a mere human, I cannot. Iximi, I wonder if..." He looked nervously at his watch. "I hope Kendrick takes his time."

"He will not return soon," Iximi told him, putting away the dish towel. "Not if he is determined to find a temple. Because there are no temples. Zen is a god of the Hearth and Home."

"Iximi," Peter said, getting up and coming closer to her, "isn't there some way I can stay here on Uxen, some job I can fill? You're the crown princess— you must have a drag with the civil service." He looked at her longingly. "Oh, if only you weren't so far above me in rank."

"Listen, Peter!" She caught his hands. "If you were the Royal Physicist, our ranks would not be so far disparate. My distinguished father would make you a duke. And princesses have often..." she blushed "...that is to say, dukes are considered quite eligible."

"Do you think I have a chance of becoming Royal Physicist?"

"I am certain of it." She came very close to him, "You could give us the atomic drive, design space ships...weapons...for us, couldn't you, darling?"

"I could." He looked troubled. "But it's one thing to become an extraterrestrial, another to betray my own world."

Iximi put her arms around him. "But Uxen will be your world, Peter. As prince consort, you would no longer be concerned with the welfare of the Earthlings."

"Yes, but..."

"And where is there betrayal? We do not seek to conquer Earth or its colonies. All we want is to regain our own freedom. We are entitled to freedom, aren't we, Peter?"

He nodded slowly. "I...suppose so."

"Moolai Uxen." She thrust a package of cigarettes into his hand. "Let us summon the Almighty One to bless our betrothal."

Peter obediently lit two cigarettes and gave one to her.

Zen materialized his head. "Blessings on you, my children," he said, sniffing ecstatically, "and welcome, Holy Chief Physicist, to My Service."

"*Royal* Chief Physicist," Iximi corrected.

"No, that is insufficient for his merits. Holy and Sacrosanct Chief Physicist is what he will be, with the rank of prince. You will have the honor of serving Terrible Zen Myself, Peter Hammond."

"Delighted," said the young man dubiously.

"You will construct robots that do housework, vehicles that carry refuse to the Sacred Garbage Dump, vans that transport household goods, machines that lave dishes..."

"Will do," Peter said with obvious relief. "And may I say, Your—er—Benignness, that it will be a pleasure to serve You?"

"But the atomic power drive...freedom?" Iximi stammered.

"These will point the surer, shorter way to the true freedom. My Omni-dynamism has stood in the way of your cultural advancement, as Professor Kendrick will undoubtedly be delighted to explain to you."

"But, Your Omnipotence..."

"Let us have no more discussion. I am your God and I know best."

"Yes, Supreme One," Iximi said sullenly.

"You Uxenach have kept Me so busy for thousands of years, I have had no time for My Divine Meditations. I shall now withdraw Myself from mundane affairs."

The princess forgot disappointment in anxiety. "You will not leave us, Zen?"

"No, My child, I shall be always present, watching over My People, guiding them, ready to help them in case of emergency. But make sure I am not summoned save in case of dire need. No more baby-sitting, mind you."

"Yes, Almighty One."

"The incense will continue to be offered to me daily by everyone who seeks My Sacred Ear, and make sure to import a large quantity of this tobacco from Earth for holy days...and other occasions," he added casually, "when you wish to be especially sure of incurring My Divine Favor. And I wish to be worshipped in temples like other gods." *Less chance of my being stuck with some unexpected household task.* "I shall manifest Myself on Thursdays only," he concluded gleefully, struck by the consummate idea. "Thursday will be My Day to work and your holy day. All other days you will work, and I will indulge in Divine Meditation. I have spoken."

And he withdrew all aspects of his personality to his retreat to wallow in the luxury of six days off per week. Naturally, to make sure the Uxenach kept the incense up to scratch, he would perform a small miracle now and again to show he was still Omnipresent.

Being a god, he thought as he made himself more comfortable, was not a bad thing at all. One merely needed to learn how to go about it in the right way.

Afterword by Robin Rose Graves

While Evelyn E. Smith would go on to write the Miss Melville Mysteries, the series for which she is perhaps best known today, Smith's first publications were all science fiction. Impressively, Smith published under her own name rather than a male pseudonym or initials, as women often did in the 1950s.

Perhaps it was because she was a frequent contributor to *Galaxy Science Fiction*, in which this story was first published in 1955. *Galaxy*, particularly in its early days, welcomed women. Less "hard" than its competitor, *Astounding*, and purposefully less pulpy than most of the other science fiction magazines of the time, *Galaxy* focused on social commentary rather than technology. "The Princess and the Physicist" perfectly exemplifies *Galaxy*'s taste in science fiction.

By far the most interesting character and concept in "Princess" is Zen, the god of Uxen. Although the story is a comedy, Zen's position is understandable and even poignant. So human is he that the reader may well begin the story thinking that he once *was* a human, and that he had divinity 'thrust upon him' by some arcane or technological marvel. It is only as the story nears its end that the reader begins to suspect that Zen isn't human — and never was. In fact, he is a native of Uxen, an alien being tricked into slavery by the colonizing humans in exchange for the title of god and occasional offerings of incense. Despite his powers, he is trapped in his role.

Ironically, and surely deliberately, the human characters' development remains shallow in comparison to that of the vibrant lead. They are almost stereotypes. Zen, in sharp contrast, is a fascinating mix of human and divine. Like a powerful god, he is self-important, all-knowing, with eyes on every happening of his domain — even during his designated "holy day off." Like a human, he is overworked by his occupation as god and easily manipulated. He gets bored as well as needs to sate hunger.

The cardboard cutout human characters do things, funny and engaging things, but the plot revolves around the change in Zen's circumstances. It is not a surprising story, but it is an enjoyable journey. The perspective of this non-human yet deeply-relatable god is both entertaining and unique. The culture of the planet Uxen is simultaneously familiar and yet unlike anything on Earth. In humanizing Zen, Smith makes us sympathize with the alien and even cheer his victory at the end. And indeed, though Iximi is initially disappointed with Zen's freedom, in freeing himself, we are told, he also frees the people of Uxen from their reliance on him, allowing their culture to grow beyond the stagnation it has fallen into by depending on Zen for everything.

The story, without chastising, critiques a culture's dependency on god figures and how much we ask of "god" when the solution often lies in our own hands. At the same time, there is a subtle condemnation of people who would take advantage of those considered to be 'other', as well as a hinted warning: in relying on others to take out our garbage or clean up after us, we may lose both the ability to do these things ourselves and the incentive to innovate new ways to handle these hated jobs. What happens when those we rely on, take advantage of, and take for granted decide, like Zen, that they've had enough?

Birthright

by April Smith

(Originally appeared in the August 1955 issue of *If*. It has never previously been republished in print.)

Cyril Kirk's first sight of the planet from the spaceship did nothing to abate the anger seething within him. He stared at it in disgust, glad there were no other passengers left to witness his arrival.

All during the long trip, he had felt their curious stares and excited whispers everywhere he passed, and he had felt a small wave of relief whenever a large batch of them had been unloaded on some planet along the way. None of them had come this far — which was hardly surprising, he thought; the last of them had been taken off two-thirds of the way to Nemar. He was very glad to see them go, though by that time they had stopped making their cautious, deferential attempts to draw him into conversation and elicit some clue about his mission and destination.

He had let them wonder. He knew that his aloofness was being taken as snobbishness, but he was past caring. They all recognized that he was a Planetary Administrator by the blazing gold insignia on the dark uniform, insignia calling for awe and respect all over the galaxy. They guessed that this was his first appointment, but the thing that really aroused their curiosity was the bitter, angry look that went with what they considered his arrogant reserve.

Since polite efforts at conversation by the braver or more confident among the company were met with icy monosyllables that cut off further attempts, they were left with a wide range of controversy. Some of them held, though they had never actually seen a Planetary Administrator before in the flesh, that all PA's were like this. They argued that the long, grueling years of study, the ascetic, disciplined life from childhood, and the constant pressure of competition, knowing that only a small percentage would finally make the grade, made them kind of inhuman by the time they finished. Besides, they were near-geniuses or they wouldn't have been selected in the first place—and everybody knows geniuses are sort of peculiar.

One of the bolder and more beautiful girls on board had been argued into making a carefully planned attempt to draw information out of him, and bets had been placed on the results. She was eager enough to try her hand at this rich prize, and her self-confidence was justified by a long trail of broken hearts in high places, but the attempt came to nothing. Kirk was aware of her efforts and aware that in another mood he would have appreciated her charm, but he felt too sick and miserable to respond.

Remembering her piquant, laughing face later in his cabin, Kirk thought morosely of the long train of girls he had known in the past. Many of them had been lovely—a fledgling PA was considered a highly desirable date, even though the chances were always that he wouldn't make it in the end. But Kirk had always been filled with an iron determination that he *was* going to make it in the end, and this meant no distractions. If he began to feel he might get really emotionally entangled with a girl, he stopped seeing her at once. He saw them seldom enough, anyway. The regulations of the PA Institute gave him a fair amount of free time, but the study requirements made the apparent freedom meaningless.

How hard he'd worked for the day he'd be wearing this uniform, he thought bitterly. How proud and happy he'd thought he'd feel wearing it! And now, instead, here he was, practically hiding in his cabin, hoping nobody would discover the name of his destination and guess the reason for the humiliated rage that was still coursing through him.

He'd gone over the interview with Carlin Ross a hundred times since the trip started, and he wasn't any nearer to making sense out of it than when he began...

He'd entered Ross's office for the interview in which he would be awarded his post, full of confidence and pride. The final examination results posted in the main lobby were headed by his name. He knew that, because of his good record and general popularity, he had been watched with special interest by the teachers and staff for some time; and he looked forward to being awarded a particularly desirable planet, in spite of its being his first post.

Technical ability and sound training in administration had long ago been decided upon as more important than practical experience, as mankind began to sicken of the bungling of political appointees. The far-flung planets that had been colonized or held an intelligent, humanoid population were so numerous that even an experienced Planetary Administrator could know very little about each one. Only someone brought up on a planet could have a detailed knowledge of it, and it was a basic premise of the Galactic Union that governors with a common upbringing and training on Terra were necessary to keep the varied parts of the empire from splitting off and becoming alienated from the rest.

Ross was one of the half-dozen men in the top echelon governing the galaxy and its warring components. His official title was Galactic Coordinator, and one of his minor duties was the supervision of the Institute of Training for Planetary Administration, which had been home to Kirk for so long. Although he was the Institute's official head, he was too busy to be seen in its halls more than rarely, but Kirk had had several brief talks with him and one long one. He had the feeling that Ross had a special interest in him, and this had added to his anticipation on the fatal day.

As he entered the room, Ross looked up, his blue eyes friendly and alert in the weathered, tanned face. "Hello, Kirk," he said. As always, the simple warmth of his smile threw Kirk off guard. It had never failed to surprise him the few times he had seen Ross. In this place of dedicated, serious men, of military crispness of speech, of stiffly erect carriage, Ross's relaxed body and quiet, open expression seemed startlingly out of place. Except for the alertness and intelligence of the eyes, he looked like a country farmer who had wandered in by mistake. Kirk, and his friends, had more than once wondered how such an anomaly had risen to the high position of Galactic Coordinator.

However, if his manner left you puzzled, it also made you feel surprisingly comfortable, and Kirk had felt relaxed and happy as Ross motioned him to a chair. Nothing prepared him for the shock that was to come.

He remembered the apparent casualness with which Ross had spoken. "I'm sending you to Nemar."

For a moment Kirk felt blank. The name did not register. His private speculations had centered on the question of whether he would be sent to a thriving, pleasant, habitable planet or to one of those whose bleak surface contained some newly discovered, highly valuable mineral and whose struggling colonists lived under pressurized domes. Either type could have held the chance to work up to the galactic eminence and power he had set his heart on. He had been over and over the list of planets that were due to receive new PA's (there was a rotational system of five years, with an additional five years made optional), and he had a private list of those which, as the star graduate of his class, he hoped he might draw. Nemar was not among them.

His face stayed blank for a minute as he searched his memory for the name, and as vague bits of information filtered through to him, his eyes widened in disbelief. "But, sir—" He fumbled for words. "That's on the very edge of the galaxy."

Ross's voice was quiet. "Yes, it's a long way."

"But there's nothing on it!"

Ross sounded a little amused. "There are some very nice people on it—the natives are of the same species as we are, though they look a little different. That means the air is breathable without aids. It's quite a pleasant planet."

"That's not what I mean, sir. I mean there's nothing of any value—no minerals, no artifacts, no valuable plant or animal products." He searched his memory for what little he could remember about Nemar from classes. He recalled that the planet had been discovered only forty years ago by a Survey ship that had gone off course far toward the outer rim of the galaxy. It had been incorporated into the Galactic Union because it was considered dangerous to leave any inhabited planet free of control; but it had not been considered a valuable addition. It was far off the established trade routes, and seemed to contain nothing worth the expense of transporting it. "The culture is very primitive, isn't it?" Kirk asked, half thinking aloud.

"It is so considered," Ross answered.

The reply struck Kirk as odd. A sudden hope filled him. Maybe something new had been discovered about the place, possibly something that only Ross and a few of the top command knew about. He threw a sharp glance at Ross's face, but it told him nothing. "I don't remember too much about the place from class," he ventured.

Ross rose, and with his incongruously quick, lazy grace strode to the filing cabinet along the wall, pulling out documents and pamphlets. He plumped them in a pile in front of Kirk. "Most of the factual information we have is in these. You can try the library, too, but I doubt if you'll find anything more." He added a book to the pile. "This covers their language. You'll have two months of intensive instruction in it before you go. You were always good in your language structure courses, so I doubt that you'll have any trouble with it. You'll have another two weeks to learn the stuff in these documents, and two more weeks to rest or do whatever you like before you leave." He resumed his chair. "You're luckier than some of the others. The boy who got Proserpine will have a stack of books up to there to absorb." He gestured toward the ceiling.

At the mention of Proserpine, Kirk's brown eyes darkened. Proserpine had been recently discovered, too, but that was all it had in common with Nemar. Its inhospitable surface held vast amounts of a highly valuable fuel ore, and it had been one of the places on his list. He wondered who was going there, his insides suddenly twisting with envy. He tried to keep his voice even. "I don't understand why I'm being sent to Nemar." He searched for words. After all, he couldn't exactly mention his graduating first and his record. "Is there something I don't know about? Has something valuable been discovered that hasn't been publicized, or—" He waited hopefully.

Ross's answer was flat. "No, there's nothing there that can be transported that's worth transporting."

Kirk felt despair surging through him, then suddenly changing to sharp anger. "I've worked hard. I have a good record. Why are you giving me this — this lemon? Why don't you give it to whoever graduated lowest, or better still to some older PA who bungled things somewhere, but not quite enough to be retired!" His face was burning with rage. Somewhere inside he felt shocked at himself for speaking to a Coordinator this way; at the same time he felt a violent urge to carry it farther and sock Ross in the nose. His body was shaking...

Remembering the scene now as he watched Nemar swing closer, Kirk felt the anger again, time hadn't dimmed it at all. Ross must have perceived his fury, but he had shown no signs of it. Looking as friendly as ever, he had told him mildly that he did not consider Nemar a "lemon", that he had excellent reasons for sending him there, but he preferred not to tell him what they were. He wanted him to discover them for himself after he arrived. The rest of the interview had concerned itself mainly with practical information, most of which Kirk had scarcely heard through his fog of emotion.

His endless speculations since then had gotten him nowhere. He had dredged out of his memory every incident that might reveal some trait for which he was being discreetly given a back seat. He recalled a roommate who had said he was going to become a living machine if he kept it up, and no machine had the right to have jurisdiction over people. But Jere had flunked out along the way, like most candidates who had an attitude like that. He went over the time he had been called to Ross's office and gently rebuked for working men under him on a project too hard. "I don't ask anything from them I don't ask of myself," he had protested.

"I know," Ross had answered, "and I respect that. But *you* work that hard from choice." Then he had nodded in dismissal.

Kirk had puzzled over these and other incidents, searching for a clue, but found nothing. All his probing in a more optimistic direction led to blind alleys also. The documents on Nemar, all the information he could dig up, confirmed Ross's statement that the planet held nothing of commercial value.

The planet, to judge by what he had read, was a pleasant place, apparently very pretty, with heavy vegetation and a warm, temperate climate, and the natives were hospitable and friendly. But all this held very little comfort for him and did little to assuage the sense of angry humiliation that had made him seek isolation from the other passengers.

He could see the planet more clearly now as the ship began to angle into an orbit, preparatory to sending out the smaller landing ship which would take him down. Hastily he reviewed in his mind once more the few facts he knew about the place, and shaped his tongue to the unfamiliar sounds of the native language. He fought down the feeling of humiliation, and straightened his shoulders. After all, to these people, he would be the most important person on the planet. If he was to be a big frog in a small puddle, he was still supreme administrator here, and he had no intention of letting them know his arrival signified a disgrace to him.

From the airlock of the landing ship, Kirk looked out on a cleared plain. In the foreground a group of natives were gathered to greet him, and a scattering of dark uniforms among them indicated the officials who would make up the Terran part of his staff. As the natives approached him, he noted the green-gold hair and the slightly greenish tinge to their skin, for which his studies had prepared him.

Nothing in his studies, however, had prepared him for the extraordinary grace and beauty of these people.

They were dressed, men and women alike, in a simple fold of bright-colored cloth circling their body from the waist and reaching a third of the way to their knees. Kirk noted, with a slight sense of shock, that the women wore nothing above the waist except for a strand of woven reeds, interlaced with shells and flowers, which fell loosely to their breasts. In these brief and primitive garments, the natives bore themselves with such imperious grace and assurance that for a moment Kirk felt as if his role had been abruptly reversed — as if instead of being the powerful representative of a great civilization to a backward people, he were the humble primitive waiting for their acceptance.

One of the older natives stepped forward from the rest, his palm outstretched, shoulder high, in greeting. "Welcome to Nemar," he said, his glance steady and gracious on Kirk's face.

Kirk recognized the words of the native language with surprise. The clear, musical quality of the native's speech made his own words, harsh and grating by comparison, sound like a different language, as he replied. "Thank you. I am very happy to be here."

As he spoke, he realized that the lie had for a moment felt almost like truth. For a moment he wondered if the planet's apparent primitiveness was deceptive and if its simplicity concealed a highly developed culture. But even as the hope surged through him, he remembered Ross's clear and definite statement to the contrary. Besides, there would be no point in keeping a thing like that secret from the rest of the galaxy, even if it could be done. Such a culture, moreover, would certainly have things of value to trade.

As these thoughts coursed through his mind, one of the Terrans stepped forward from the crowd. The insignia on his uniform were the same as his own, and he realized, with a surge of curiosity, that this must be his predecessor.

The man reached forward to shake his hand. "Hello. The name's Jerwyn." His tanned face was open and friendly, and reminded Kirk curiously of someone; he couldn't remember who. "Glad to see you."

I'll bet you are, Kirk thought: your gain, my loss. "Greetings from Terra," he replied, somewhat stiffly. "Cyril Kirk." He tried to keep his vague disapproval of Jerwyn's breezy informality out of his voice. It was hard to realize this man was also a Planetary Administrator. He seemed to have lost completely the look of authority that was the lifelong mark of the PA graduate.

After the various introductions and a short period of conversation, Kirk found himself seated beside Jerwyn in the small ground vehicle which was to take him to his headquarters. Jerwyn immediately resumed the standard Galactic-Terran language, which he had dropped during the introductions. "As soon as I show you around a bit, I'll be off on the landing ship you came in. I wonder how Terra will seem after all this time."

"Five years is a long time," Kirk ventured.

"Ten."

Kirk stared at him in astonishment. "You took the optional five years! Why in heaven would anyone—" He broke off suddenly. The question might be one Jerwyn would not care to answer. He threw him a speculative glance, wondering why he had been sent here and whether he, too, was bitter. Maybe a poor record, or something in his past he didn't care to go back to...? That didn't fit in his own case—but then there was no knowing what did fit in his own case. Jerwyn had an alert, perceptive look that indicated considerable intelligence, but still he somehow looked inadequate. Some quality an Administrator should have was lacking...dignity? drive?

Jerwyn's voice interrupted his thoughts. "Beautiful, isn't it?"

The groundcar had left the plain and was entering a heavily wooded section. For the first time, Kirk took a good look at his surroundings. Some of the trees and plants were very like those he had seen in parks at home. Still, there was a definitely alien feel to it all. The trees were low and wide and had peculiar contours, different from those of trees on Terra, and their flowering foliage came in odd sizes and colors. The sky wasn't quite the blue he was used to, and the shapes of the clouds were different. He noticed for the first time a heady, pungent perfume carried on the breeze, that was both pleasant and stimulating. It came, perhaps, from the wide-petaled flowers in oddly shimmering colors that clustered thickly everywhere.

"Yes, it's beautiful," he agreed, "but—" The feeling of despair and frustration welled up in him again. The warmth he sensed in Jerwyn made him suddenly long to blurt out the whole story. He controlled himself with difficulty, as he turned toward him. "It's pretty enough. It might make a good vacation resort if it weren't on the edge of nowhere." His pent-up emotion exploded as he spoke. "But five years in this hole! I'd feel a hell of a lot better if I were looking at some rocky, barren landscape with some mines on it—with *something* of value on it—with a name somebody'd heard of, where you could hope to get somewhere. I don't want to waste five years here!" He paused for breath, staring angrily at the lush landscape. "And for that matter, life on one of those planets where you live under domes, with a sealed-in atmosphere, is probably a lot more civilized and convenient than in this primitive jungle."

Jerwyn nodded slowly, an unspoken compassion in his face. "I know how you're feeling." He paused. "And it does seem pretty primitive here at first—no automatic precipitrons for cleaning your clothes, natural foods instead of synthetics, no aircars, no automatic dispensers for food or drinks or clothes; none of a hundred things you take for granted till you don't have them. But you get used to it. There are things to make up—" He broke off as the car began to descend into a valley. "Look!" His voice held an odd tone of affection. "There's your new home."

Kirk gazed downward at the settlement nested in the valley below them. He fished in his pocket for a magnascope to bring the view nearer and stared curiously, as the lens adjusted to the distance. He picked out groups of buildings, low units of some coarse, natural material, widely spaced. This was the largest city on the planet, he knew, but it seemed to be little more than a village. It was undoubtedly primitive—very primitive. Remembering the magnificent high buildings of Terra, he was filled with sudden homesickness for the speeding sidewalks crowded with people, the skylanes humming with aircars.

Turning the magnascope here and there, he kept his gaze trained on the town beneath him, studying it now in more detail. Slowly, some of his depression began to leave him, and he felt a strange sense of warmth begin to take its place. He stepped up the power of the glass till he could see the inhabitants walking in the streets. Like the natives who had met him at the landing ship, they walked with a beautiful, easy grace, a sumptuous ease that seemed somehow almost a rebuke of his own stiffly correct military posture. They gave an impression of combined leisure and vitality.

Gradually, as he watched, an odd feeling of nostalgia began to stir in him, an old, childish longing. He remembered suddenly a dream he had had years ago, in which he had run laughing through green meadows with a lovely girl.

He had fought against waking from it and returning to his desk piled high with books and his ascetically furnished room.

He blinked his eyes and put down the magnascope. "Rather attractive, in a way," he said grudgingly to Jerwyn. He settled back slowly into his seat.

"Just the same," he added, annoyed at himself for his sentimental lapse, "how have you managed to stand it all this time? I still can't figure how I came to get it in the neck like this." Abruptly, he plunged into the words he had been holding back, telling the whole story of his confusion to Jerwyn.

He rationalized to himself that perhaps Jerwyn could help him solve the mystery. At least he might tell him how he himself came to be sent to Nemar, without his having to ask directly; and this might give him a clue.

"I've been over the whole business a million times, trying to figure it out," he concluded. "Somebody with pull must have had it in for me. But who? And why? I never had any real run-ins with Ross. In fact, I'd always thought he liked me." He scowled. "Of course, he gives practically everybody that impression. Maybe he's just a professional glad-hander, though he certainly doesn't seem like it." He shook his head. "Maybe that's the secret of his success; I never could figure out how he got where he is. He certainly doesn't seem typical of the command. Oh, he's brilliant enough, but there's a quality about him I'd almost call — weak, I guess. Unsuitable for his post, anyway. He treats the janitor the same as — "

Kirk stopped abruptly. He suddenly had the answer to the question that had been nagging at the edge of his mind: it was Ross that Jerwyn reminded him of.

Trying to cover up his confusion, he went on rapidly, hoping Jerwyn would not notice. "Anyway, whatever his reasons were, he's played me a dirty trick, and if there's ever any way I can pay him back for it, I'll do it. I'll have five years to think about it. Me! The fair-haired boy of the Institute! On my way to the top!" His face flushed with resentment. "Sent to sweat out five years in this Godforsaken place with a bunch of savages hardly evolved out of the jungle!" He passed his hand over his forehead, wiping off sweat, feeling the full force of his pent-up anguish and rage flood through him.

Jerwyn spoke very quickly. "I felt pretty much the same way when I was sent here. But I feel differently now. I could try to explain. But I don't think it's a good idea. I don't think anyone could have explained to me. This is a place you've got to live in; you can't be told about it." He shifted in his seat as a small group of buildings came into view. "As for Ross — well, he was responsible for my being sent here, too, and I spent some time when I first came, thinking of ways to cut his body in little pieces and throw them in a garbage pulverizer — but I wouldn't waste my time if I were you. I know now he had his reasons." As he spoke the car pulled to a stop. "Well, here we are. This is where you'll be living and working."

Jerwyn stayed with Kirk while he was shown through various buildings. He found most of the office buildings full of bright murals and little watered patios, but lacking the simplest devices for working efficiency. He was introduced to various officials, Terran and Nemarian. Some of the latter, to his surprise, were women — a rare phenomenon for a primitive planet, he remembered from his classes.

By the time the touring was over and he had said goodbye to Jerwyn, he was too tired to do more than glance briefly at the quarters to which he was shown. Left alone in his rooms, he took a quick, awkward bath, too weary to feel more than a brief annoyance at the lack of automatic buttons for temperature controls, soaping, and drying, and fell exhausted on the low bed.

For a moment, as he woke, Kirk could not remember where he was. Drowsiness mingled with a sense of eeriness at the sound of long bird-calls unlike any on Terra and the unfamiliar rustling of leaves; the rays from the late afternoon sun seemed too crimson.

Then, as sleep fell from his eyes, he remembered. He glanced at the window above his bed from which the orange light filtered into the room and saw it was completely open to the outside air. Something would have to done about that, he thought grimly, or he'd never be able to sleep with an easy mind. There were always people, sooner or later, who hated you if you had power; or if they didn't hate you, they at least wanted you out of commission for one reason or another.

He sat up to take a better look at the room he had been too tired to investigate before. There were mats of woven reeds, and low carved chests, and flowers; the walls were clean and glimmering, and bare except for a single picture of two young native children. He got up and walked over to look at it more closely. A boy of about seven was holding his arm out to a girl, slightly younger, to help her on to the low, swaying branch on which he was sitting. The picture was full of sunshine and green leaves and happiness, and you could feel the trusting softness of her arms reaching up to him. An odd picture, Kirk thought. The children looked childlike enough, but the emotions looked adult.

As he looked at it, he heard a soft, swishing sound in the next room, and stiffened. There was no lock on the door, he noticed. Well, it was time to get up, anyway. He dressed hurriedly, trying to remember the layout of his rooms. Except for the bathroom, he recalled only one other room, a sort of arbored porch, one side completely open to the air, with a low table and some cooking equipment at one end.

As he opened the door, a faint whisk of something made of reeds went out of sight. A primitive broom, he thought, with a faint sense of relief. Some servant was tidying the house. He opened the door further — and stared.

A native girl was standing before him. She was extraordinarily lovely. The gold-green hair of her race rippled and flowed in waves over her bare back and shoulders down to the circlet of vermilion cloth girdling her thighs. The band of small shells that circled her throat was netted with wide orange and red flowers that half-hid, half-disclosed the firm naked breasts. The light brown, gold-flecked eyes beneath the gold-green eyebrows were soft; so was the tender mouth, rose-colored against the flawless skin, with its undertones of faint green. Her body, too, looked soft and yielding, but was borne with imperious grace that somehow dignified even the broom held loosely now in one delicate hand.

Kirk stared at this vision of beauty, taken by surprise, and found himself caught up in sudden desire. She was like something out of a dream. He tried to get hold of himself.

You're just not used to half-nude women, he told himself. You're used to girls in uniforms, crisp, businesslike uniforms. A wild suspicion caught at the edge of his mind. He didn't know anything about this planet, really — except that there was something he didn't know. Maybe they made a practice of diverting their rulers with beautiful women. She certainly didn't look like a servant. He smiled at the thought that came to him: this servant was the first indication of the luxury befitting a Planetary Administrator. The thought enabled him to gain control of himself again. He regained a semblance of his customary reserved look.

"Good afternoon," he said, in the native language.

She smiled and held out her hand.

He hesitated, then held out his own awkwardly. Did one shake hands with one's servants here? He wished he'd asked Jerwyn for more advice about protocol.

She took his hand and pressed it lightly for a moment. "I am Nanae." Her voice was low and musical. "I am going to clean and take care of your house."

She turned and with exquisite precision gestured toward the low table and cooking equipment at the end of the room. "I thought you would be waking soon. I have prepared some *jen* for you."

Jen? he thought. Oh, yes, a very light stimulant — the local variety of tea. He walked over to the low table and sat down, fighting the impulse to enter into conversation with her. He watched her as she poured the hot liquid into wide cups of polished gourd, her hair radiant about her shoulders. A stab of longing shot through him. The long years of training in the Institute paraded through his mind, the years of strict routine, hard work, ascetic, bare rooms, with women considered playthings that took too much time from needed study; the only beauty was the dream of power among the glittering stars.

Well, he wasn't going to give up and forget the dream, he told himself — and he wasn't going to be led astray by any pretty girls, particularly a maid. Hell, he thought suddenly, maybe Ross is testing me. Maybe he picked the worst planet in the whole damn galaxy to find out if I could do something with it. It's obvious if I can get this place on the trademaps, I can handle anything.

He looked speculatively at the girl as she pushed the cup toward him. He wondered how she came by her job. Did they hold beauty contests here for the honor of being cleaning woman in the PA's household? He realized he was feeling more cheerful. The *jen* and the soothing quietness of the girl's presence were doing him good. He felt a resurgence of his old energy and ambition that the interview with Ross had quelled for so long.

"Did you work for Jerwyn, too?" he asked. Yes, his voice was just right, courteous, but not too friendly, he thought.

"No, but I knew him." She looked at him with an odd smile. "He became one of our best dancers."

"Dancers!" Kirk stared at her in amazement. He started to open his mouth, then stopped. He'd better not ask any more questions till he'd had a chance to talk to some Terrans. Apparently, Jerwyn had gone native. Maybe it was his way of rebelling against being sent here in the first place — and he'd let himself go so far that he'd skipped his chance of reassignment at the end of the first five years, afraid of the problems of a new post after being a beachcomber for so long. That would account for the curious lack of deference he'd found in all these people. They were friendly enough, but they lacked proper respect for his position. You weren't supposed to be friendly to a PA; you were supposed to be humbly polite. He recalled the respect and awe he'd received on the ship.

As he finished his cup, he realized he was very hungry. He looked around instinctively for food. He had enough synthetics in his bags to do him for awhile, but he might as well make the plunge and start eating the native foods right away. No use coddling himself.

The girl noticed the look. "I didn't prepare food for you because dinner will be served in just a little while. We eat all together, down by the river. You will hear drums to announce when the meal is ready, and you get there by walking to the end of that path." She pointed a delicate finger at a small footpath winding by a few yards from where he sat.

Coming out of the little forest at the end of the path, Kirk paused to take in the scene. Between him and the river was a wild jumble of men and women, laughing and talking, children running and stumbling over small pet animals, piles of nuts and fruits and hot foods heaped together beside small fires. Some of the people sat on straw mats, but most, simply on the ground. There were neither tables nor chairs. To Kirk it looked like utter confusion.

With a sense of gratitude, he saw a tall, uniformed figure coming up to him, with a brisk, definite stride. The Terran's face was lined and firm, the kind of face Kirk was familiar with. The man with this face would be a man who stood for no nonsense, a man who was a little tough, but also fair and capable. He recognized him as he came closer.

"Hello, sir. I'm Matt Cortland, your second in command," he said brusquely. "I met you this afternoon, but you met so many people then it must have been just a blur of names and faces."

Kirk greeted him, feeling a sense of satisfaction that this man would be his chief assistant. He looked efficient; he should be able to help him learn the ropes and get a program of action started.

"No chairs," Cortland said laconically, as they walked toward the gathering. He chose a soft spot of lavender-tinted moss near a pile of hot food and sat down, cross-legged. Awkwardly, Kirk sat down beside him, folding his legs under him stiffly. "You can be served in your rooms, of course, if you like," Cortland went on, turning to him. "These people are very obliging. Very obliging." He reached for two of the leaf-wrapped, steaming objects, handing one to Kirk. "But you probably have a better chance of influencing them if you eat among them. If they can be influenced." He opened the leaf and bit into the yellow vegetable inside.

Kirk looked dubiously at the object in his hand. He hoped it wouldn't make him sick. Pushing back his sense of disgust, he bit into it carefully. The bland, sweetish flavor filled him with delightful surprise. It was rather like a mixture of sweet potato, carrot, and peach synthetics—but the texture and flavor were new and wonderful. Maybe civilization had lost something good when it gave up natural foods. Though, of course, their preparation was time-wasting and inefficient, he reminded himself; and swallowing synthetics required only a momentary break in your work when you were pressed for time. He looked up and found Cortland watching him.

"Pretty different from the food at home, eh?" He had slipped into the Terran language. "Good food and pretty girls." He gestured toward the graceful, half-nude women scattered along the mossy bank. "Everything for the lotus-eaters."

The phrase meant nothing to Kirk.

One of the girls came over to them with a large gourd full of fruit and nuts, and another on which she heaped hot foods from the piles on the ground as she passed. She placed them on the ground beside the two men.

"Yes, everything for the lotus-eaters," Cortland repeated. "Incidentally, I hope you're not under the impression that that girl is naked from the waist up."

Kirk looked at him questioningly.

"Oh, no. She's completely covered. They have taboos about naked breasts, just like we do." He laughed at Kirk's look of mystification. "You notice those strands of shells or woven reeds they wear around their necks?"

Kirk looked around. They all wore them.

"Well, that signifies they are dressed. If you ever see a native girl without one, she'll be terribly embarrassed." He stuck his hand out toward the bowl of hot food. "After you've been here long enough you'll think they're dressed, too."

He laughed, then looked more serious.

"I've been here a long time, getting nowhere," he said, in a different tone. "There are a lot of things that could be done here. I've spent a lot of time thinking about it. But Jerwyn —" He hesitated. "I hope *you* intend to make the name of the Galactic Union mean something here."

Kirk nodded, and Cortland went on. "Jerwyn tried when he first came. But after awhile he seemed to just give up. I couldn't do anything without him backing me, I don't have enough authority." He looked grim as he spoke. "And besides that, it takes more than one good man. Oh, the other GU men here are capable enough —" He glanced toward a group of Terrans sitting nearby. "They'll be over in a little while to speak to you, incidentally; I asked them to hold off for a little, while I briefed you a bit — no sense deluging you with new people while you're trying to eat."

"But to get back," he went on, "they're capable enough, or they were once, anyway, but none of them has the drive and brains it takes to push through a project to develop this planet. They've pretty well given up. Some of them like it here and some of them don't, but they've all stopped trying." A look of contempt crossed his face. "They go through the motions of doing some work to earn their salaries, knock off at noon, and spend their time lying around on the beaches with Nemarian girls. I've done what I could to keep a semblance of discipline, but it's uphill work."

Kirk looked at him steadily. "All that's going to be changed."

Cortland smiled. "Good." Their eyes met, with understanding.

148

"And I'm very happy to have a man of your caliber with me," Kirk said quietly.

Cortland gave him a long look. "Maybe you've got what it takes. Maybe you have." He nodded slowly. "I should have told you I don't entirely blame the men. This planet's a tough nut to crack." His voice was grim.

Kirk felt a vague uneasiness, but his look stayed determined. "We'll crack it."

"We've been here forty years, and we haven't made a dent. They're funny people, these Nemarians. They're really alien. I've been here fifteen years, and I don't understand them any better than when I came."

"That's quite a statement."

"They're very appealing. Naive. Childlike. The soul of courtesy — on the surface. But it's deceptive. And you could spend a lifetime trying to find out what's underneath."

A young boy of about twelve came up as he spoke, setting a large gourd full of steaming liquid down beside them with lithe grace, filling smaller cups from it as he did so. Cortland nodded at him, turning again to Kirk as the boy walked away. "Even their children aren't really childlike. Did you see his eyes — makes you damned uncomfortable."

As Kirk started to answer, drum-beats began to fill the air, first softly, then louder. Strange sounds from unfamiliar instruments began to mingle with them, and a clear, high instrument added a melody. The whole effect had an alien, discordant quality for Kirk, but as he listened further he grew intrigued and began to enjoy it; a mood — happy and romantic and energetic, all at once — came through to him from the music.

"The dancing's beginning," Cortland informed him.

Kirk saw young men and women rise by ones and twos and begin swaying and turning their bodies to the music. They all seemed to be doing different things, and yet somehow it made an integrated pattern. To his surprise older people and even young children gradually joined in, and managed not to look inappropriate, although the dance movements were rapid and strenuous.

He noticed a sweet, pungent odor filling his nostrils and realized it came from the steaming bowl beside them. He picked up one of the filled cups and tried it cautiously. It was delightful. He emptied it and poured another.

He felt Cortland's hand on his arm, and looked up to find him grinning at him. "Hey, take it easy with that stuff. That's fermented kara root — the local variety of booze. They can drink quarts of the stuff and be all right; I've never seen one of them really drunk. But you'd better not try it."

Kirk frowned. "Something different in our metabolism? I thought — "

"No, they're quite human," Cortland broke in. "And it's not a matter of immunity. I wondered about it for a long time—and got quite disgracefully drunk a couple of times, keeping up with them, before I figured it out." He sipped at his own cup. "No, the secret of their success is the dancing."

Kirk looked at the light, whirling figures, puzzled.

Cortland smiled at his bewilderment. "It's the exercise. It burns up the alcohol as fast as they drink it. When they're having a real feast, they dance and drink all night, till they collapse from pure exhaustion. They wake up feeling fine—not a sign of a hangover. Of course, tonight they'll only dance for a little while, so they'll only drink a little…"

"Sensible, aren't they?" The voice came out of the air behind them, sardonic, feminine. The language was Terran.

Kirk whirled and peered through the dusk, which was gathering rapidly. He saw a slightly amused pair of brown eyes, brunette hair, and a trim body dressed in chic good taste in expensive Terran clothes.

Cortland stood up. "Mrs. Sherrin…our new Planetary Administrator, Cyril Kirk."

She lowered herself to the ground, spreading out a small mat under her as she did so. "Jeannette, if you don't mind." She folded her legs under her carefully. "I don't mean to be disrespectful. But there's such a small number of us here, we need to be friends and stick together."

Cortland, who had been looking away for a moment turned to them. "If you'll excuse me, someone wants to talk to me." Kirk nodded.

"Did I meet your husband this afternoon?" he inquired politely, as Cortland strode off.

"No; I'm a widow."

"Oh, I'm sorry," he murmured.

"Don't be. Not for me, I mean. We'd been coming to a parting of the ways for a long time. But let's not talk about that. How do you like the dancing?"

He looked at the firelit figures, whirling in the growing dusk. "I don't know. I'm sort of overwhelmed by everything. It's all so new. I've heard so many confusing things—"

She nodded. "If you manage to make sense out of the Nemarians, you'll make history. It's better not to worry about it too much. Immerse yourself in their gay, happy life."

"What do you mean?"

She gave him a sharp look. "You'll find out what I mean. Didn't Cortland tell you?"

"What are you talking about?"

"Well, you might as well go in cold at that. Form your own conclusions as you go along. No use giving you prejudices before you start. Maybe you're the man who'll cut the Gordian knot. No use telling you it can't be done."

"What can't be done?"

"We'll all be rooting for you." She poured herself a drink and downed it quickly. "Great stuff, this. Makes you forget the petty annoyances of the garden-spot of the galaxy." She poured another. "To Nemar," she said, lifting it. "Now tell me about Terra. What's been happening back home?"

He could get nothing more out of her.

Kirk struggled to control his irritation as the last Nemarian on his list walked in, poised and self-confident, casually unconcerned about his lateness. Something would have to be done about their sloppiness and lack of discipline, but now wasn't the time. It wouldn't do to lose his temper at the first official meeting he called.

First he needed to stir some ambition in them, prod them out of their lethargy.

He looked around at the assembled members of his joint Terran-Nemarian staff. The Terran members were making an attempt to stand stiffly at attention, somewhat awkwardly as though they were out of practice. They threw rather disconcerted looks at his stern, impassive young face. The Nemarians stood casually erect or lounged against the wall.

Once more, he found himself troubled by a faint sense of incongruity. Something about these natives was not primitive. Without saying a word, just by standing and looking at him, they made him feel awkward and insecure.

He straightened his shoulders and tried to make his expression even more stern. He wished he looked older.

A sense of the power of his position overwhelmed him for a moment.

He glanced at the speech he'd prepared, then at the faces before him. Slowly he pushed it aside. Somehow he couldn't use those formal sentences with these people. Diplomatic phrases didn't sound right in Nemarian.

"Good morning," he said abruptly. "I won't waste time on preliminaries." He paused. "I've only been here a day, but so far I've seen very few signs of Terran influence—a more or less obsolete type of ground transportation, a few tools and household conveniences, some art objects. Very little else. I don't fully understand why conditions are so backward here on Nemar when it has been part of the Galactic Union for forty years."

The Terrans in the group stirred uneasily.

"The important thing, however, is that the situation be changed so that Nemar may be given the benefits of galactic culture."

He paused and looked around. The natives were listening courteously and looking slightly bored. The Terrans looked uneasy or embarrassed.

"What prevents this change," he went on, "is the fact that there is nothing of value to export." He leaned forward. "But I don't believe that this or any planet can possess nothing of value. It's simply a matter of finding it. It's a matter of looking into new places, with new techniques, or for new things. If a sufficiently thorough search is made, something will turn up." He tried to ignore the signs of restlessness in his audience.

"I'm going to organize research groups for this purpose immediately. Each of you will head a committee to investigate the possibilities in a particular field—fuels, plants, animal products, etc. You will bring the reports to me, and I will check them and indicate further directions of search."

He continued, outlining his plans in detail, stressing the great advantages to be gained, the wonderful things galactic culture had to offer them—the marvelous machines and labor-saving devices, the rich fabrics and jewels, the vidar entertainments, the whole fabulous technology of a great, advanced civilization. He spoke with enthusiasm, but as he continued, a growing sense of apprehension began to creep into his energetic, determined mood.

Something was wrong with their reactions.

He puzzled over it as he watched them file out of the room after he finished. The voice of one of his younger subordinates drifted back to him from the hall outside: "Made me homesick for good old Terra. I'd give a lot to see a good vidar-show right now..." Cortland pressed his arm lightly as he passed, nodding his approval of the proceedings.

One of the Terrans lingered a moment as the last of the group left. His expression was serious. "I'd like you to know that I'm all for you, sir, and I'm glad to see a man of your stature in the PA's office," he said nervously. "I hope we'll see some changes in the attitude of these Nemarians. I've never liked their attitude." He ran a hand through his sandy-colored hair. "They're funny people, sir. You've only been here a day, and nobody may have warned you yet. They're very courteous, but don't let it fool you. You're going to have trouble with them."

Kirk looked after him as he followed the others out, a sense of confusion and discouragement beginning to settle over him. He wandered slowly into the flowered patio adjoining the office.

The reaction of the Nemarian officials was the strangest. They had shown no open opposition. On the other hand, there had certainly been no cheering. Their attitude had been one of courteous interest, plus some quality he couldn't quite define. He searched for the right word...something almost like compassion, as if they were humoring a child's enthusiasm for a naive, impractical project.

He sat down by a clump of blue-green flowers. Maybe he was just nervous because of his inexperience, he thought. He'd had plenty of practice experience (supervised, of course), but it was a different matter managing an isolated planet, completely on his own. And he'd had the bad luck to come after a guy who'd apparently let discipline go to pieces. Maybe it was just the newness of the whole thing. Maybe —

But he knew better.

He had given them a good, efficient, well-organized plan of action. They should have been impressed — impressed and respectful. They should have been grateful he was plunging so enthusiastically into an effort to improve their situation. They should have been excited and hopeful.

There was something strange here, something he didn't understand.

He knew so little about Nemar.

The Terrans in the group had not reacted as they should have, either, he thought. Some of them had shown the sort of reaction he expected, but most of them had remained quiet, too quiet, with a peculiar, tolerant look. As if they knew something he didn't.

There was something disturbing about their whole manner. They were respectful and deferential, but not quite respectful enough. Their attitude was just a shade too casual. Something was wrong.

They even looked different, somehow, from the usual Terran on space duty. The dedicated look was gone and a softness had crept in.

Somehow, the planet had infected them.

The clear-eyed old Nemarian he'd been talking to had just turned away when she came up.

"Good evening. How do you like bird's eggs a la Nemar?" Jeannette pointed to the shells beside him.

"Hello. They're very good." He motioned her to sit down.

"The youngsters here gather them out of the trees. They make a sport of it." She reached for one from the pile near them and tapped it open. "Sentimental creatures — they always leave one or two so the mother bird won't be unhappy."

Kirk was trying to draw his eyes away from the young Nemarian mother in the group near him who was complacently nursing her baby in full view of everyone. Jeannette stared in the direction of his look.

"Oh, you'll get used to that soon enough."

He wondered if he would. They made a rather touching picture, though, he realized through his embarrassment. There was a lot of tenderness in the woman's gestures.

"They spoil their children rotten."

Kirk looked surprised. "The ones I've seen have been very courteous."

She shrugged. "Oh, they're polite enough. But just try and make them do something they don't want to! They're completely undisciplined—they're fed when they please, they sleep when they please, they do whatever they like. They have schools for them, but it's completely up to the children whether they want to go or not. The parents haven't a thing to say about it. No one ever lays a hand to them, no matter what they do."

"I haven't noticed any quarreling," he said, surprised at his own observation. It was true. He hadn't seen a sign of it, even between the children themselves, though they made enough noise yelling and romping.

"Oh, those tactics fit them perfectly for this society," she said indifferently. "The adults here are just like the children. Nobody ever does any work."

"But that's impossible. The food, the houses, the—"

"Well, I suppose I exaggerated. They do things they don't like once in awhile, if they want the end product enough. But mostly, if they can't make a big game of it, they don't do it. Tomorrow's nut-gathering day," she added irrelevantly.

"Nut-gathering day?"

"Yes. Everybody frolics off into the hills to pick nuts. Like a picnic. That's what I mean—if they didn't consider it a pleasure outing, the nuts could hit them on the head, and they'd never bother to pick them up." She cocked her head at him. "Want to go?"

"Go where? Nut-gathering, you mean?" He laughed. "No, thanks."

"Thought you might like to study the natives in their day-to-day activities, get the real local flavor. You might learn something, at that. Though I guess you'd have a rough time climbing the trees."

"I've had an hour a day at gymnastics for the past three years."

"Yes, you look in good shape." Her glance swept over him approvingly. "But gymnastics and those trees are two different things. The edible nuts grow on the tall trees, not the short ones, and they sway in the wind. The young men do most of the climbing. They're pretty wonderful physical specimens, I'll say that." She glanced at one of them near by, who was whispering in the ear of a Nemarian girl.

Kirk felt oddly annoyed. They were magnificent physical specimens, he thought. But then so were the women and children. He realized that he hadn't seen a sickly or weak-looking native since he arrived. Even the old people kept their magnificent posture, and managed to make age seem a matter of gathering wisdom instead of collecting infirmities. Weren't they ever sick, he wondered.

"The girls are lovely, too," he reminded her.

"Yes, but try to get near one of them," she flashed back. "They prefer their own." Her eyes narrowed. "They're pleasant people, but they're not pleasant to live with. It gets on your nerves after awhile."

"Why didn't you leave, Jeannette?"

"On the spaceship you came on?"

"Yes. There may not be another for five years."

"That's the big question," she said slowly. "I'm not sure I know the answer. I half intended to leave on the ship when it came. But when it came down to it, I didn't leave." She stared ahead of her. "Something about the place gets you. Maybe it's the life. Maybe you get used to lying around in the sun, and you feel kind of frightened at returning to all the hustle and bustle of Terra. And then, you keep waiting, hoping that—"

"Hoping what?"

For a moment, she looked defenseless and a little hurt. Then the cynical smile came back. "You don't even know what you're hoping for, really," she said lightly.

He knew she was evading him.

He lay in bed later, wondering what Jeannette could have meant, what could account for that brief hurt look.

She was an attractive girl, he thought idly. He wondered why he felt nothing for her, when the native girl aroused in him such an unreasonable longing. It would be a good deal more convenient to fall for Jeannette.

He couldn't afford to get mixed up with his maid.

Remembering her, he suddenly felt his body trembling.

All right, he told himself, so she's an ignorant, backward native on a planet nobody ever heard of. Practically a savage. And even here, she's just a maid, a cleaning woman. Nobody a Planetary Administrator could think about getting mixed up with. But how do they turn them out like that?

How do they turn them out like that, he thought—every movement fluid, every position graceful, every gesture exquisite? How does this nonentity of a planet turn out a girl with the kind of walk the video-stars back home practice and work years to approach? With a voice with that indescribable music and precision? With a flawless skin, radiant hair, a serenity and self-confidence that would make the greatest beauties on Terra envious? With a quiet, careless pride that made him, the new ruler of her planet, awkward and insecure in the presence of his own servant?

Jeannette had been jealous, he realized suddenly. She was jealous of these girls, of their grace, of their radiance. Her cynicism covered a bitter envy.

For a long time he lay there, trying to sleep, haunted by Nanae's luminous eyes.

He started working the next morning.

There was no use putting it off, he thought. Nemar seemed to act like a drug, gradually depriving you of your drive and ambition. He wasn't going to give it a chance to let its poison seep into him.

He flung himself into his duties as Planetary Administrator with a grim determination. He struggled to organize the affairs of the planet on a more efficient basis. He introduced new methods and techniques. He worked tirelessly, relentlessly, hardly noticing their passage as one day followed another. And every moment he could spare, he devoted to the project for finding something of value to export.

He was going to put this planet on the map. He didn't know how yet, but he was going to do it.

He was going to turn his misfortune into a triumph.

Every hint of a possibility was followed up with eagerness. Every lead, every clue, was the subject of exhaustive study and investigation. His days were a succession of guarded hopes and disappointments, of surges of optimism and long stretches of discouragement. He pushed his wearied body into greater and greater efforts, working unflaggingly through the day and most of the night, spurred by the anger that still burned in him.

The natives, he knew, looked at the light burning late into the night and thought he was a little crazy. He gave up eating with them. It was too easy, there by the river, to drift into staying later and later, drinking their hot wine, chatting, watching the dancing. It was too hard to resist the temptation of midnight swimming later with the young men and women at the nearby beach, with revels and bonfires on the lavender sands afterward.

At the end of two weeks, he sat on his bed, taking stock of what he had accomplished.

It was very little.

And he was very tired.

The tiredness was familiar. It was just like school all over again, he thought, the same long exhausting hours of driving oneself relentlessly. He wondered when he'd be able to relax. He didn't dare relax now. When he had a lead, a definite hope of some kind, he could begin to let up. But not till then. It would be too easy to give up and let go altogether, go the way Jerwyn had gone.

He was beginning to understand why Jerwyn had given up.

He was beginning to understand a lot of things — the odd, cryptic remarks he had heard about the natives when he first arrived, the mixed admiration and exasperation they seemed to arouse.

He remembered a man named Gandhi from ancient Indian history.

The Nemarians could have given Gandhi lessons.

Working with them was like working with an invisible wall of resistance that weakened here and strengthened there, gave in unexpectedly at one place and resisted implacably at another.

At times his plans were praised; then they were put into effect with an efficiency that astonished him. At other times they were criticized, in a casual, friendly manner that enraged him. Then they were not put into effect at all. When he insisted on obedience, the natives reacted with an attitude of patient tolerance, and did nothing. Most of the time, his orders were received indifferently and carried out with an agonizing slowness.

He pushed and prodded them. He reasoned with them. He shouted at them.

He reaped nothing but frustration.

They didn't hate him. He knew that. He had never seen a trace of malice in their expressions. People smiled at him when he passed, and children came up to tug at his hand and ask him to come to visit their house. There was none of the stony hatred here he knew existed in many places for the all-powerful Galactic Union.

They simply seemed to lack all appreciation of the importance of his position.

Yet they knew, he thought. They knew he had what amounted to almost unlimited power over their planet. They knew a space-fleet that had burned life off the face of entire planets lay at his disposal. They knew he could crush any rebellion instantly.

But, of course, they weren't rebelling, he thought. They weren't even openly uncooperative. There it was again: they weren't even unfriendly; they deluged him with constant invitations.

They knew of his power, but they acted as if it didn't exist.

And he wasn't sure they weren't going to win with him, as they had with Jerwyn. The Galactic Union did not look with approval on any call for aid except in a military crisis; such a request was in effect an affidavit of failure. Besides, he didn't want to complain. He didn't want to set himself against them. He was working for them, not just for himself.

He sighed and began to get ready for bed.

Primitive people had always fought progress and change. They had always clung to old, outworn methods. But there was more to it than that, he thought. Primitive people were usually full of superstitious fear of change, but the Nemarians were not afraid. You couldn't think of them as fearful. They knew the danger—they knew the strength and power that faced them—but they were not afraid. They didn't even "handle with care".

Where did their courage come from?

Or was it just blind stupidity, he thought, a refusal to look facts in the face, to admit that they were the helpless, backward subjects of an immensely more powerful and more advanced civilization?

He pulled off a shoe absently, and he thought of all the documents and reports he had read about Nemar. Ross had given them to him, and he had searched in them for a clue to help him understand why Ross was sending him here. He had read and reread them, and they had told him little more than Ross himself about Nemar.

There was something peculiar about all those documents, he thought, something odd about the way they were written. They described an undeveloped planet without valuable resources or any kind of technology, in no way out of the ordinary. But between the lines was something that said this planet was out of the ordinary, in spite of the apparent facts. There was the unavoidable feeling that something was left unsaid.

What were they trying to hide? Why hadn't they let him know what he was in for?

Terrans had been coming for forty years. In forty years, they must have learned something. They must have found out something about what made these people the way they were, and about how to deal with them. There should have been warnings and suggestions and at least, if nothing else, descriptions of methods that had been tried and failed. It should all have been there, out in the open; it should have been down in black and white: this is the situation, so far as we know it; these are the problems.

Instead, there had been only routine description, and veiled hints and allusions.

He hadn't been here long, he thought. There was a lot to learn here yet. The other Terrans, the ones who had been here a long time, knew something he didn't know. He could tell from their faces, from their attitude toward him. Cortland didn't know, or he would have told him, and some of the others didn't either, but most of them did. They knew something, but whether it was pleasant or unpleasant knowledge, he couldn't tell. Whatever it was, it affected them. They neglected their work, and they had a different look from the Terrans back home.

Jerwyn had known, and he hadn't told him. He'd said he'd have to live here to find out.

He lay down and stretched out wearily on the bed.

Well, the answers here exist, he thought. Somehow, when he had all the pieces, the jigsaw would have to fit together and make a coherent picture.

Maybe he was looking in the wrong direction.

But he didn't know where to look.

He thought of the day he had just been through, remembering incident after incident when he had had all he could do to keep his temper under control. Annoyance welled up in him again, as he recalled the series of frustrations, the useless arguments.

His mind was still revolving in an upheaval of confusion and anger as he fell asleep.

It was barely past dawn when he awoke. He tried to fall asleep again and failed. Giving up, he dressed and wandered into the other room and the garden beyond. He felt the early morning coolness slipping over his shoulders like a garment, and a sense of the futility of all his struggling filled him. He felt a sudden longing to rest, bask in the sun, live as the natives did in sunny, amiable unconcern.

He stiffened, annoyed at himself. That would mean giving up everything he had worked so hard for all his life, ending up as a lazy failure. He felt a surge of anger inside him toward something he could hardly name.

As he stood there, he saw two Nemarian children, a boy and a girl about five years old, emerge from the trees and begin to pick the shimmering flowers in the garden. Irritation rose hotly in him. He knew that it was out of proportion, built out of a hundred frustrating incidents, but he found he didn't want to control it. He wanted to lash out at somebody.

"Stop stealing my flowers!" he yelled. He was surprised at the harshness of his own voice.

The children did not start fearfully or run, as he expected. They turned and stared at him in an unconcerned manner. "You can't steal flowers," the boy said matter-of-factly. "They don't belong to anybody." He looked at Kirk questioningly. "You didn't plant them, did you?"

Kirk stared at him, speechless.

The boy went on, his tone slightly indignant. "Anyway, it's very rude of you to speak to us like that!"

"They are quite right," an angry voice cut in. Kirk whirled around to find Nanae standing beside him, a basket in her hand. Her hair, radiant in the sunlight, was caught back from her face with a green ribbon, and the brown, gold-flecked eyes, for once, were not soft, but sparkling with anger. "These are my sister's children," she said icily. "They help me gather flowers for your table. Do you think just because they are young you have the right to treat them without respect?"

Staring at her angry face, Kirk felt his own anger ebbing. Into his mind a forgotten incident flashed back from his childhood. Through a door left ajar in a neighboring apartment he had seen a ripe purple fruit imported from a newly discovered planet, and had taken it, curious to find out what unsynthetic food might taste like. He had been discovered, and angrily whipped and locked in his room. He remembered wiping away the tears, alone in his room, smarting with humiliation, and vowing he would show them, he would show them all; he would grow up to be so powerful he could have anything he wanted, and everybody would be afraid of him.

He looked now at Nanae, who had put an arm around each of the children, cradling them to her. His anger left him completely. Remembering the hurt child he had once been, he found himself longing for the touch of softness and kindness that had never come to him, wishing that even now for a moment he could take the children's place—lay his head against her breast, and feel her fold him in and brush her hand through his hair. He felt something melting inside of him. He could feel the lines of his face softening as he looked at them.

The words stuck, but he forced them out. "I'm sorry."

"It's all right," said the boy.

Leaning down, Kirk put an arm tentatively around each of the children, half-surprised at himself for the gesture. As he felt their small bodies relax against his, it seemed as though some deep inner tension began to flow out of him. He straightened up to find Nanae's glance on him surprisingly warm, almost tender. The approval in her eyes filled him with an unfamiliar kind of happiness.

"You mean Ross spent five years here!" Kirk stared in amazement at Cortland, sitting beside him.

The older officer turned toward him, shifting his position on the grassy ledge to which they had climbed for a look at the surrounding countryside. "Yes, that's right. Ross was straight out of the Institute then, had an A-1 record, and this place had just been discovered. They thought then it might have all sorts of valuable minerals and things. It seemed like a great chance." He shrugged. "As it turned out, of course, there was nothing, but nobody could have known then."

"They know now," Kirk said shortly. He sat looking over the valleys beneath them, silent for a moment. It was discouraging to learn Ross had been here and had not turned up anything: Ross was capable, whatever else he might be, and it would take luck as well as work to succeed where he had failed. And his luck didn't seem to be working out too well, he thought, unhappily.

But this might throw some new light on why he'd been sent here. Maybe Ross's reason for sending the Institute's star pupil had been one he could never have guessed at the time — a gesture of sentimentality. Maybe he wanted to help these people with whom he had spent his first years as an Administrator. Maybe he wanted to make up for his own failure to help lift their living standards.

He turned toward the other man. "Cortland, you say you've done a lot of traveling here. How about the rest of the planet? Are any of the other villages more advanced; are the people any different?"

Cortland laughed shortly. "Thinking of hiring yourself a new native staff? Your impatience about worn out bucking this one? Can't say I blame you, but it's no go. All these villages are the same. One outfit's as bad as the next. Oh, they go in for different things — one will go all out for sculptures, one will be great on weaving, and another one maybe will grow a special kind of fruit. But the people are all alike — all equally charming and equally impossible. All sweet and friendly on the surface and stubborn as mules underneath. All acting like they know something they're not talking about, like they've got some secret hidden behind those clear, guileless eyes of theirs, some source of strength that makes them able to tell us to go to hell — figuratively, of course — when they don't like our orders." He leaned forward, intently. "I'd give a lot to find out what makes them tick." A look of insecurity, almost of anxiety filled his eyes.

A sudden gust of wind blew a flurry of leaves against Kirk's face. He brushed them away, feeling chilled.

Cortland blinked his eyes, and his face resumed its customary firm look. "But to get back to your question — this village here is supposed to be a center of government. When the Nemarians have to decide on anything that affects the whole planet, the Council in this village does it. The Council has nothing to do with the Galactic Union set-up, of course. It's strictly local, was here before GU discovered this place. You probably studied up on it before you came here."

Kirk nodded. Every planet with an indigenous population had its own political set-up. It was GU policy not to interfere with them, unless their interests clashed in some way.

Cortland went on. "Anyone who likes being in on that sort of thing packs up and emigrates to this village. I don't know whether you've noticed, but these people are pretty casual about moving from one town to another. Anyway, when your would-be politician gets here, the people take him in and watch him awhile, and then, if they like him all right, he's put on the Council. What a system! The truth is, most of the Nemarians consider political work something of a nuisance and would just as soon somebody else did it. They don't care for power the way we do. They look on it as just a heavy responsibility and a burden."

Kirk shifted his leg uncomfortably, feeling a bit self-conscious.

"By the way," Cortland added casually, "how are you getting on with that girl?"

"What girl?"

"That beautiful creature who keeps house for you."

"Nanae?"

"Yes, Nanae. The beauty of the village, the girl who cooks breakfast for you, the head of the Council—"

"What did you say? What was that about the Council?"

"She's head of the Council. Didn't you know?"

"How can she be? She's a maid, she—"

"They don't have maids here. She's being neighborly. And they have sort of a "power corrupts" philosophy here. If you're in a position of authority, you're sort of expected to go out and do humble tasks for people once in awhile, so you won't get to feeling above them. These people like to keep everyone on the same low—"

"But head of the Council!" Kirk broke in. "She's just a young girl!"

"So what? You're just a young man."

"But—"

"Sorry for the levity. But they let women do everything here. They've got equality of the sexes, old man. They—"

"We'd better be starting back," Kirk broke in. He rose to his feet.

He walked silently down the hill beside Cortland, his head whirling.

When they reached the village, he left Cortland as quickly as he could and hurried in the direction of his house, incoherent thoughts tumbling over each other in his mind. His face burned as he remembered his condescension, the way he had fought his desire for her by holding her off with curt remarks, indicating with raised eyebrows that he wished no personal conversation. He thought of the occasional glint of amusement he had seen breaking through her serene courtesy.

Why had she kept coming, he wondered.

He saw, with a start, that he was nearly to his house, and he realized he had been hoping Nanae would be there. He had to talk to her, though he had no idea what he would say. As he drew closer, he saw a flicker of motion inside the porch.

He walked forward quietly, and then stood a moment watching her, silently. She had her back to him and was sweeping, as she had been that first time he saw her. Her thighs were wrapped in soft, violet cloth, and a cascade of violet flowers jeweled the lovely hair which rippled and swirled down her back and shoulders. Not a wasted motion, he thought, not a gesture that isn't beautiful. He wondered why he had ever felt sweeping a floor was a menial task. She moved like a great dancer.

She turned as he watched and saw him. "Hello." She smiled, and he felt himself tremble a little.

"I just heard about you—about your being head of the Council," he blurted out. "I want to apologize; I didn't know, I—"

"What difference does it make?" She looked genuinely puzzled.

"I thought you were a maid, a...a sort of person who waits on other people, on Terra," he tried to explain. "I didn't know you were just doing this to be kind. I've been very rude. I—I hardly know what to say..."

Her eyes widened. "Do you treat people who clean your houses on Terra one way and officials another? You are funny, you Terrans."

"Yes, I guess we are funny." He searched for words. "This is the first time I've really talked to you, isn't it?"

She smiled. "We've just been people in the same room." She spoke gently. "I've seen you were unhappy and confused under that proud manner. I wanted to help, but you weren't ready to let anyone help."

"Why did you keep coming?" He waited anxiously for her answer.

"I liked you." Her glance was half-tender and a little amused. "And I knew you wanted me here, even though you tried not to show it." She paused. "There was another reason, too."

"What was it?"

"You know Marlin Ross lived here once?" He nodded. "Well, there was a note from him on the spaceship you came on. It was addressed to my father, asking him to take care of you. He and Ross were good friends. But my father is dead now, and so the letter was given to me."

"And so you've been taking care of me."

"Yes."

"But I'm sure he didn't mean it literally—taking care of my house and fixing my food and—"

"No, of course not. He just meant to take care of you, give you what you needed. But you needed this. You needed to be waited on a little."

"I guess I did." He could find nothing adequate to say. "Thank you."

There was a moment of silence.

She put aside the broom, which was still poised in one hand. "Let me make you some *jen*. You look tired."

"Thank you." Kirk sat down, with a deep sigh, and leaned back, watching her precise, exquisite movements, as she prepared the hot liquid. He found himself longing to touch her, to reach out and feel the soft, supple flesh, the rippling hair. The sight of her beautiful, firm breasts moving as she worked tortured him. The low necklace that signified they were covered didn't work very well for him, he thought. The flowers twined into it kept falling aside as she bent and turned, tantalizing him more. He pulled his eyes away, and forced himself to think of other things.

She had been very kind, he realized.

She hadn't made him feel like a fool.

He stood waiting for the last of the staff to assemble, letting the feel of triumph course through his body. He felt heady, exultant, a little drunk with joy. This was his moment. This made it all worthwhile—the long hours, the sleepless nights, the relentless work, the struggle. They would see. They would see he hadn't been driving himself and them for nothing.

He stared down for a moment at the piece of ore which he had brought to show them. It contained unpolished zenites.

Nemar possessed zenites, the fabulous gems valued all over the galaxy for their shimmering, glowing beauty of changing color. Infinitely more precious and rare than diamonds, they served often as a galactic medium of exchange, where weight was important. A handful of them could be worth the whole cargo of a trading ship.

He was not surprised that no one had found the ore deposits before. They were the products of immense and peculiar pressures and no appreciable amount of the ore was ever found except very deep underground. He was very glad now he had specialized in geology and mineralogy instead of social structure and alien psychology. Otherwise, the geologic reports he had received of the area would have seemed perfectly routine and ordinary. The nagging feeling that there was something a little unusual about the soil analysis would never have come into consciousness as a definite, tremulous hunch.

He could have sent Cortland or one of the others out there with the tools and instruments to dig and make test after test, searching several feet under the surface for the elusive end-trail of a lode. But he had wanted to go himself. He had packed and prepared for the two-day trip, steeling himself against the disappointment he was almost sure to receive.

He looked at the faces of his staff members, all present now, thinking of that first meeting with them and the peculiar reception his plans had received. Now it would be different; now everything he had asked of them was justified.

Drawing a long breath, he began to tell them what had happened.

As he went on, his fiery enthusiasm began to waver. His voice boomed too loudly in the quiet room. Once or twice his words faltered, as he glanced at the dispassionate face of a native. As he finished, he looked around, a sense of dismay and fear creeping into his feeling of triumph.

They had listened too quietly. Only Cortland and a few other Terrans had shown any indication of the excitement and jubilation he expected. The others seemed unimpressed and undisturbed. With a sinking feeling in the pit of his stomach, he called for discussion.

There was a pause. Finally, one of the older Nemarians spoke. "This is a very important matter. If these mines are put into operation, it will affect the lives of everyone on Nemar. I must ask that you give us a little time to think over the implications."

He spoke courteously, but Kirk knew the request would have to be respected. He wanted to shout at them, to ask them to understand this wonderful thing that had happened, to tell them they were going to be rich! But this was the way they did things, and this was the way it would have to be done. He pushed down the impatience burning in him. "Will a day do?"

The Nemarian hesitated a moment, then nodded. "Very well. A day should be enough."

Kirk watched them file out a few minutes later. He wondered where his sense of elation had gone.

Apprehension filled him again as he watched the staff assemble the next morning. The faces of the Nemarian members increased his discomfort. Why didn't they look happier, more excited? Why should they look at him with that unspoken sympathy in their eyes. He was afraid to hear what they had to say.

The native who had spoken the day before moved forward a little. "We're very sorry," he said gently. Kirk felt his heart sinking. "We realize that you have worked very hard in what you consider to be our interests. We hoped you would come up with something more acceptable than these mines. But we cannot put the plans for mining these gems of yours into operation. We are very sorry," he said again, "but the Council has voted against it."

"The Council!" Kirk stared at him. He fought to control his voice. "You know perfectly well that the power of my command is supreme over any local councils of whatever nature." He stiffened. "But that isn't the point. I guess I haven't made things clear to you somehow. These gems — which you refer to as if they were a child's baubles—can make this insignificant planet a power in the galaxy. They can make the name of Nemar respected throughout the whole Galactic Union. You can trade them." He spoke each word slowly and carefully as if he were explaining to a child. "I'm not having expensive machinery constructed and sending you down hundreds of feet into the ground so that your women can *wear* these jewels. They're extremely pretty, but you probably feel the flowers the girls pluck and put in their hair do just as well for ornaments, and perhaps you're right."

He paused, trying to hold on to his temper. "It will be dark and dusty and uncomfortable down in those mines, as I told you yesterday when you asked about it. It will be hard work, and I know you're not fond of hard work." He could not keep the sarcasm out of his voice. "But I assure you, it will be worth it. A really good specimen of one of these little *gems* (he underlined the word) can buy half the cargo of a spaceship. These jewels can make it worthwhile for the great trading ships to swarm through space out to this isolated fragment of the cosmos. You can acquire the technologies of other planets with them. The evolution of this planet can be speeded up a dozen times. You can become of importance in the scheme of things, leave this backward, primitive way of life behind you."

As he paused for breath, one of the Nemarians spoke quietly. "We don't want to push ahead that fast." He looked at Kirk serenely. "We are interested in improving conditions here, of course. We want to acquire things that will make our lives more pleasant and luxurious. Some day we wish to become a highly developed society, technologically. We wish growth and change— but only very slowly, very carefully. We want to be very, very sure we do not bring in pain when we bring in new pleasures. We need to study each new change to see what it might mean." He paused. "In this case, it took very little study. This mining project would mean the young men would be put to backbreaking labor in underground, unhealthy conditions. There might be circumstances which could justify such a thing. But not for jewels which are intrinsically worthless."

"Worthless! I just told you—"

"I mean they are not valuable in themselves. You can make cheap, synthetic jewels that are almost as beautiful, can't you?"

"Yes, of course, but—"

"So they are only valuable because they are rare, because you *call* them valuable, because they show the people who buy them have enough money to buy them. Wearing them is really a way of saying, I'm rich, to everyone who sees you." He shrugged. "We don't care about that sort of thing here."

Kirk clenched his fists in frustration. Maybe he should have specialized in alien psychology. He made another try. "I know you don't. That's not the point. The point is that you can trade them for other things, for—"

The older native who had announced the Council decision broke in again. "As you said, the mining is very hard, disagreeable work. We feel that when you begin to do disagreeable things for an end that is not valuable in itself, you are beginning to tread a dangerous path. There is no telling where it will end. One such situation leads to another. We might end up cooped up in a room all day, shut away from the sun and air, turning bolts on an assembly line to make machines, as we have heard often happens on Terra." He looked slightly shocked at the picture. "Being surrounded by technical conveniences isn't worth that." He looked at Kirk patiently, as though this should be self-evident. "On Terra and on most of the other planets we have had word of, people seem to spend their time making all kinds of things that have no value in themselves, because they can be sold or traded. Other people spend their time trying to persuade people to buy these useless things. Still other people spend all day making records of how many of these things have been sold. No! This path is not for us." He shook his head. "We don't know how it came about that all these people spend their time at these unpleasant, useless things. They can't have wanted it that way. No human being could want to spend his time doing silly, pointless things. How could you believe in yourself? How could you walk proudly? How could you explain it to your children? We must be careful not to make the mistake of taking the first step in that direction."

Kirk felt hopelessly confused. The reasoning was all wrong, but how could he explain it to them?

He began slowly, from another angle...

He stood there for a long time after they had left, trying to control his rage. He had tried everything he could think of. He had argued, reasoned, pleaded with them. He had raged at them, threatened them. Nothing had worked.

The threats had not disturbed them.

He thought of sending out an emergency beam for help. But what would he say when the ship arrived: put these people under martial law—force them to work—it's for their own good? He'd like to see if they could do it, he thought. He'd be betting they couldn't.

He paced up and down, clenching his fists.

He could have all the council members jailed, he thought. Only there weren't any jails on Nemar.

Resentment burned in him. They'd let him work and struggle and slave day and night—for this. He swung his fist into the wall suddenly, with all his might. The pain stung, but he felt a little better.

He looked at the bruised hand, wondering what to do. He was too restless to go home and stay by himself, burning up with unspent rage; and he certainly couldn't go and sit among the natives, listening to them chatter and laugh.

He decided to take a walk.

He heard a rustle of leaves after he had gone a little way and saw a pair of feminine legs through the underbrush. He tried to turn aside. He didn't feel like talking to Jeannette now.

But she had already seen him. "Hello, there," she said, pushing aside a branch from where she was sitting. "Are you taking a walk, too? Thought you were always sticking to the old grindstone this time of day."

"Hello, Jeannette."

"Sit down and rest for a minute. I need some company."

He hesitated, then sat down reluctantly.

"You don't look too cheerful," she said, looking at him. "Something eating you?"

"Just this place," he said wearily. "And the people."

"Yes, it gets you after a while, doesn't it? It's pretty hard to take."

He leaned against a tree and tried to relax.

"It's hard to live with," she went on, "the constant sense of inferiority..."

He wondered if he had heard her correctly. "What did you say?"

"I said, it's hard to live with."

"No, no. I meant the last part."

"The constant sense of inferiority. Is something the ma—"

"What are you talking about?"

"I'm talking about the Nemarians, naturally."

"You surely don't consider them superior to us!" he said incredulously.

"Let's not fool ourselves," she said. "There isn't one of them that isn't superior to every Terran here."

He stared at her.

"Of course, we do fool ourselves. I've been doing it a long time. Or trying to, anyway. But I've been sitting here thinking. Among other things, about why I didn't leave on that ship you came on, as I'd planned."

"Why didn't you?" he asked.

"The same reason nobody else did, but Jerwyn; and he had to."

"Plenty of them don't like it here," he said. "There's plenty of griping."

"Not really," she said. "It's not really griping. It's just a way of making yourself feel better. Only the ones who haven't been here too long do it, and one or two others who are real old-line die-hards, like your Mr. Cortland.

"Why didn't you leave?"

"Because this is a good deal, of course. The climate's lovely; the scenery's beautiful; life is sort of a perpetual pleasure outing. The only trouble is, you're always on the fringes. You're the kid from across the tracks."

"I don't understand."

"That wasn't the right phrase, because that implies snobbishness, and they're not snobbish. But they don't quite accept you. They let you hang around; they let you play with them. But you're not really one of them."

"Why on earth should you want to be one of them! They're just a bunch of ignorant primitives, while we come from the highest center of culture civilization has ever attained."

"Yes, yes, I know all that. We're very good at pushing buttons and keeping in the right traffic lanes. But let's look the facts in the face. I've been sitting here making myself look the facts in the face. Have you ever seen one of them act mean?"

"Well, not mean exactly, but—"

"No, you haven't. They can get plenty angry, but they don't get mean. There's a difference."

He said nothing.

"Have you ever seen a child here tear the wings off an insect?" She went on, not waiting for his reply. "No, you haven't. And you won't. Have you ever seen a native with a hard, cruel face? No, again. Have you ever seen one that wasn't gentle with children?"

"I guess not. I never thought about it."

She turned to him with an odd tremulousness in her face, replacing her usual cynical look and slightly raised eyebrows. "They love their children here. They really love them." She looked at him. "They don't *say* they love them and then hit them and humiliate them because they accidentally break the vase Aunt Matilda gave the family for Christmas. Their child's happiness means more to them than any vase, than any material object. They never humiliate their children. That's why they grow up to walk like kings and queens.

"They grow up being loved," she said. "They all love each other. And it isn't because they try. They don't try to be good and nice and love their fellow-men, like we do. It's just something that flows out of them. They're full of warmth inside, and it flows out.

"And something else—" she went on. "Have you ever caught one in a lie?"

"No, but that doesn't mean—"

"People like your Mr. Cortland think they're sly and deceptive because they're always courteous, and still you can't push them around. But he's wrong. They're courteous because they're sorry for us, not because they're afraid of us."

"Sorry for us?"

"Yes, sorry for us. They're sorry for us because we don't know how to enjoy life, because we worry about all sorts of things that don't matter, and knock ourselves out working, and need other people to reassure us of our own worth. Because we have bad tempers and awkward bodies, and we don't have that warmth inside of us flowing out toward other people.

"Even toward us," she said. "They're kind to us. They're tolerant. They want us to be happy. And they do accept us eventually. If we stay here enough years. If we change. Maybe not quite as one of them, but almost. Sometimes they even marry us."

Kirk shook his head, trying to clear it. "I can't think. I feel confused, I—"

"Still thinking about our great technological achievements? We're pretty cocky about them, aren't we? We come here all set to spread enlightenment among the savages." She shrugged. "They're not impressed with our magic machines. They're not selling their planet for a handful of beads. They took a good look at us and decided to try to keep what they had."

She looked at him steadily. "Personally, I've decided I can do without the vidar-shows. I'm going to stay and try to make the grade here. I'm going to work at becoming a better human being. I'm tired of being flippant and smart and sophisticated. I'd like to be happy." She paused. "Maybe a Nemarian will even fall in love with me eventually and marry me."

"You want to marry one of them!"

"You catch on fast." She blinked. "Sorry. That's not a very good beginning. It's going to take awhile to shake that flippancy." She caught his eyes. "Wouldn't you like to marry Nanae?"

He didn't answer.

She smiled oddly. "Yes, I'd like to marry one of them and have children like theirs." She hesitated. "I said once, they spoil their children rotten. I guess they do in a way, but the children turn out fine. We Terrans just aren't used to children with a sense of their rights. These children overwhelm me." She lowered her eyes. "You know how flippant I am—when I try it in their presence I feel terribly stupid. They make me aware of every affectation; their eyes are so clear—like a deer's—I feel like a fool." She looked at him tremulously, defensively. "Anyway, I said that about their being spoiled, out of envy. When I first saw how their mothers held them—all that tenderness, all that love, all that warmth—I envied them with a terrible bitterness. It wasn't that I had bad parents. Just ordinary ones, trying to do their best and all that."

"Why do you keep talking about children all the time? After all, it's the adults who run things."

"The children are the adults of the future. It's the way they're brought up that makes these people what they are. You and I — all of us from Terra — we've been brought up on a limited, scientifically regimented, controlled amount of love. These natives have something we'll never have. We've got to work and strive for what comes as naturally to them as breathing."

As she spoke, Kirk suddenly remembered the close-packed faces of Terrans speeding by in the opposite direction on the moving sidewalks at home — tense faces, hard faces, resigned faces, sad faces, timid faces, worried faces. Maybe one in fifty serene and self-confident, maybe one in a hundred vibrantly, joyously alive. Maybe. Probably not that many.

He thought of the faces of the Nemarians.

Jeannette was still talking. "They are what human beings should be," she said slowly. "Somehow they've kept their birthright — the ability to be full of the joy of living whenever they're not in real trouble or sorrow, the ability to be happy just because they're alive. I haven't understood these people because I didn't want to understand them. I didn't want to see that they were better than I am. They're very simple, really; it's we who are complicated and devious."

"Why hasn't anybody ever heard of this place?" Kirk asked.

"It's isolated," she said, "and people don't leave here, once they've seen what's here. They don't write too much, either, because by the time the spaceship arrives again, they understand. They cooperate with the authorities, who are trying to keep this place as much of a secret as possible. Publicize it, and within ten years it would be swarming with wealthy businessmen on vacation and jaded neurotics trying to get away from it all. The Nemarians would be lost in the shuffle."

She was still a moment. "My husband came here to get away from it all. He heard rumors of this place a long way off and traced them. I didn't want to come. I liked cities and night-clubs; I liked being surrounded by amiable, promiscuous men. He dragged me here against my will. Now he's dead, and I'm caught up in his dreams. These people are irresistible; they call out to something basic and deep in you, and you respond to it whether you want to or not. You can't leave this place — unless you have to. Like you will."

Kirk stood up abruptly. "Jeannette, do you mind? I feel terribly confused. A lot has happened to me today. I want to walk alone awhile and think things out."

She nodded, with a sudden look of compassion.

He walked away from her slowly, turning half unconsciously in the direction of his house. His mind was a swirl of confusion. He tried to think. He needed to get it all straightened out.

The sense of inferiority, she'd said, the constant sense of inferiority. Let's not fool ourselves, she'd said. There isn't one of them that isn't superior to every Terran here.

And he'd just sat there, stupefied, not denying it.

Because once it was spoken, put into words, it had a certain rightness. A certain obviousness. He'd known it all the time.

He hadn't let himself know it, though. He'd struggled against it, choking it back when it started seeping up from his unconscious. He'd worked so hard and kept himself so busy and exhausted he didn't have time to think. He'd thought so hard about other things he didn't have time to think about the truth.

He'd arrived here looking for the answer to a mystery. Thinking maybe the planet had a secret value, hoping maybe it held an explosive or new weapon that was classified as Super Top Secret, wondering if maybe it weren't really primitive.

And nobody could have told him: it does have a secret value — secret because you're too blind to see it. Nobody could have told him; these people are more advanced than you are. Because advanced meant machines. Advanced didn't mean happy, loving, graceful, courageous, honest.

They couldn't have told him with words if he couldn't see it with his eyes — if he couldn't see that the glowing faces of the natives held a secret worth learning.

The only secret that really mattered.

How to be happy.

Nanae was there waiting when he reached the house, as though she had been expecting him.

She looked at him silently, then smiled. "You're not angry?"

"Angry?"

"About the Council decision."

"Oh — oh, I was. I'm all mixed up now. I've been doing some thinking."

She looked at him intently, then nodded slowly. "Do you know why you were sent here?" she asked.

"I'm just beginning to get a glimmering of it."

"Did you know we are the only planet yet discovered whose people have never known war?"

"No, I didn't know."

"Ross came to Nemar when the Galactic Union first discovered it. He didn't find any of the things he was looking for, but he did discover something else, a way of life." She paused. "Have you ever gone over his record?"

"No."

"You should, sometime. He's done a great deal of good." She looked at him steadily, her eyes clear and soft. "He keeps sending the very best of the Institute graduates here, hoping they'll study our society and work out some theories about what makes us the way we are. He hopes some of the happiness here can be transplanted.

"We don't know why we're the way we are. We don't even know how it's possible to be any other way, and we don't understand why anyone should be willing to fight wars, or why they should lie or hit their children or make long speeches that don't say anything."

Kirk was silent.

"We're inside the problem," she said. "We can't see ourselves from the outside."

Kirk spoke very slowly, thinking it out. "You mean, Ross sent me here to study you, to try to find out what factors are involved in —"

"Yes. He sent you here to learn."

He was quiet, digesting that.

"One day you'll be in Ross's place," she said.

He accepted the words quietly, knowing it was true.

Yesterday, that would have seemed like the most desirable thing in the universe, the height of happiness.

It seemed like a long time ago.

It meant nothing now but a heavy burden.

He sat thinking of Nanae after she had gone, of how he had longed to put his arms around her and draw her to him, kiss the soft mouth, run his hands through the long, glowing strands of hair.

He'd have to work first, work at changing himself, becoming the kind of person she could love. She would love differently and more deeply than the girls he had known. She would love with a passion and tenderness they'd never be capable of. That kind of love would have to be earned.

He wondered whether she'd be willing to go to Terra with him.

He got up and moved toward the bedroom. Tomorrow was going to be a busy day—changing things, making apologies. Feasting. Dancing. Going midnight swimming.

He realized suddenly that he was very happy.

Afterword by Janice L. Newman

I wasn't sure, when I started reading, whether I would like "Birthright". After all, the idea of a 'primitive civilization' unlocking some great truth that we from supposedly more 'advanced' cultures are blind to is a hoary cliché. The conceit that a so-called simpler life as a hunter-gatherer is *necessarily* superior to the technological sophistication and high standard of living we enjoy today seems patently ridiculous to me.

Thus, I was pleasantly surprised that this was not at all the basis of "Birthright".

The alien society in "Birthright" is not primitive. They do not eschew technological advances. They are not Luddites. They merely refuse to participate in or partake of anything that will cause anyone to suffer. In some ways, it is the ultimate in personal responsibility. We are told not to buy from companies that abuse their workers. The Nemarians take this to its ultimate extreme.

How does such a moral imperative come to be? It develops naturally in a society founded upon universal mutual respect. A place where children are not punished, but are gently guided (as modern science now suggests is more productive). A place where no one is above any other. A place where all people, regardless of gender, are truly equal.

I'm sure that many who read "Birthright" found it unbearably naive. Yet it holds up surprisingly well under closer consideration. The world of Nemar is a utopia, but it is clear that Ross, and later Cyril Kirk, recognize that its way of life is not scalable to the sprawling, space-faring group they represent. The broader society from whence they came has, like our own, built itself up on human suffering and changing on a grand scale simply isn't possible. At the same time, Ross sent his best, brightest, and most adaptable students to Nemar specifically in the hope that they will be able to bring something back from it. Not treasure, but culture.

From a modern perspective, by which I mean an early 21st century perspective, a fascinating progressivism underlies the entire premise of Nemar's society. Cyril Kirk arrives on the planet as a white man who is used to being respected, listened to, and deferred to. Initially, he interprets the Nemarians' refusal to behave in a cowed or deferential manner as a lack of respect. It takes a change of perspective for him to understand that his position, his gender, his intelligence, and the color of his skin (and, in a modern context, his sexuality, gender-presentation and the fact that he is able-bodied) do not carry any weight with the Nemarians. They do not put him above them, and he finds this bewildering and insulting until he begins to grasp — with a woman's help — that the Nemarians are treating him as a true equal. All of the privilege he was born with means nothing on Nemar.

Heady stuff, especially when one considers that it was first published in 1955!

Furthermore, rather than reacting violently or angrily to his sudden loss of privilege, Kirk realizes that he wants to strive to become more like the Nemarians. As we navigate the difficulties of living in a world where people are increasingly demanding respect and recognition despite being outside of what is considered the 'normal' or 'default' for humanity, it behooves us to remember Cyril Kirk and his revelation, even if he comes from a story written over 65 years ago. How many of us could accept the loss of privilege with such grace?

Normally this is where I would tell you a little about April Smith: who she was, where she came from, and what we know of her background. Unfortunately, even using all the modern tools at our disposal, we have been unable to discover anything about her. We do not know when she was born or when she died. We do not know what influenced her to write "Birthright". Indeed, we do not even know if she was a woman! (Though it would be surprising if she weren't, simply because it was far, far more common for women to adopt male pseudonyms when publishing SF than the reverse.)

Her situation is not unique. She joins many other women of whom we have little to no knowledge beyond a name on a table of contents, sometimes even for women who wrote several stories. Even when we do know who a woman was, it is often only in the context of male partners or friends. For example, everything we know of Thelma D. Hamm, another author in this anthology, comes by way of mentions of her alongside her husband. The two of them were often mentioned together — but as of this writing there are almost no bios for her, only for him.

All we know about 'April Smith', if that was indeed her name, we must extrapolate from 'Birthright'. We can guess that she believed in universal equality. We can project that she must have had an unusually progressive viewpoint during the post-WWII period when the USA was leaning very conservative. We can imagine that she had hope for humanity, despite its flaws.

In the end, her words must stand alone. Indeed, we are lucky even to have that much of her, and can only be grateful to have had the opportunity to re-discover this beautiful, bittersweet story.

The Piece Thing

by **Carol Emshwiller**

(Originally appeared in the May 1966 issue of *Science Fiction Quarterly*. It was reprinted once, in a hardcover-only edition, in 2011.)

"MOTHER, Mother. Please. What is the word? Where is the thread? Send, send, loud and strong to me. I must come home."

I soared high and veered to the right, then I turned around quickly and went back, faster and farther. Then I slowed and turned left.

"Mother, Mother. I cannot hear you. I've lost the thread. Send out to me. Please, Mother."

I spiraled to the ground, then; a spark went out when I touched it. I stopped and rested on a red stone. I was very quiet. I listened and listened, but there was no sending sound.

"Mother!"

Up, I told myself; try higher. Perhaps she is there, sending you in to her along with the others. I left the rock and flew up very high until it got cold and it was hard to keep going.

Then, up high, I relaxed and floated on a ridge of cold gases.

"Mother, one is gone. It is I. I am lost and I cannot hear you any more. Please. Send me in to you; I want to come home with the others as I always do."

The drifting gas took me sideways. I watched and rested as we passed over a mountain far below.

I must try hard, I thought. I'm nothing without Mother, and I must try hard to find her. I left the lazy gases then and went higher, because that was the hardest way to go, and I knew it would be hard. Up I went until there was nothing but cold emptiness.

It was hard. It was the hardest thing I had ever done, but I kept on. "Mother, one is gone and it is I. Oh, it's so *hard* to find you."

I went on and on for a long time. Sometimes I got tired and drifted with forces of nothingness that pulled me. And while I drifted I sometimes thought, "What am I?" for I was nothing without Mother. Then, when I had rested and drifted a little I went on as fast as I could. And every interval and every pulse, I sent out a call for Mother.

I went on. A long time passed; I grew thin and small until I began to be afraid I would be gone altogether. So I turned on my back to rest and save myself; I drifted then, with the unseen forces for a long time, not even calling out anymore.

At first there were three forces, but gradually two got weaker until there was just one great force. I lay still and let it pull me, for I was small and nearly gone. It pulled me until at last there was no longer just nothingness, and I drifted with another gas and found a new warmth. This revived me some, and I was able to send again a few calls; but still I only drifted. Draughts pulled me down, and I saw that there was land far below, and many things — things that were familiar and things, too, that I'd never seen before.

I waited and watched and moved with the currents. I was weak but sometimes I sent out to Mother. "I have seen many things," I called. "I want to tell you. You will like hearing of them. Please call me in. I miss you and I miss the others," but I never got an answer.

Still I drifted, worn out, confused and discouraged — so discouraged sometimes that I went long times without sending out. And often I thought, "Who am I?" and "What am I?"

Then I passed over a large forest and many lakes and rocky ground. I drifted lower on the breeze and there was a rock, warmed by the sun; it reminded me of long ago before these hard, hard times, so I swooped down with what little strength I had. A spark went up when I touched it, and then I lay out flat on it, warm and feeling better than I had for a long time.

I didn't send. I was discouraged still, but I listened — and after a time, I heard a sending far away. Was it Mother? It had to be.

"Mother, here I am. Come for me. At last I've found you, but I am weak from searching. Come take me to you. Renew me. I need you so much."

I called loudly with all my last energy, but there was no answer. Just more sending and sending. It came closer, and after a while I heard the thoughts. They were confused and spoke of things I didn't know. It didn't sound like Mother.

"The old thing's tickin' fast, all right," I heard. "There's something in these rocks, I'll bet. This is my big chance; I can feel it. This is it. Listen to the thing tick. It's got a beautiful case of the jitters. Whew, it's hot! I'll stop and have a drink to celebrate the find."

The thoughts stopped moving closer, but still they were very close now. There was the thought of thirst and the thought of burning liquid—hot, yet cool at the same time. Then, "That's better, much better. Come on, ticker, let's find where this load is."

And then I saw it.

"Oh, Mother, it sends but it cannot be you. Can it?"

It came closer and it smelled, hot and bitter. I didn't have the strength to rise. I had called out so hard.

"Then the thing said, "Hell," and then "Hell," again, and then, "What the hell is this?" It came down close to me—very close—and bitter, damp air came from a hole in it and blew upon me. If I was stronger I would leave.

"Maybe I've had a drop too much," it said.

Then it walked all the way around me, and closer and farther away. "Damn," it thought. "I never did see anything like it before. Radioactive. Say, it might be worth something even if it ain't a uranium lode. Somebody'd pay good money for somethin' like this—scientists or somebody." It leaned close and pushed at me a little bit with a stick.

"Mother," I whispered, sending lightly.

"Huh?"

It received me. "Mother?" I asked.

"Say, what is this?" The hot breath retreated somewhat.

"Are you Mother?" I didn't think it was, but I wanted to make very sure before I gave up.

"Is that you?" the thing asked, now speaking in a whisper. "Is that you, callin' inside my head?"

"I call, I send to you. I search for Mother."

The creature backed off then. "Get out," it shouted. "Get out of my head; I don't like it." It pulled out a small black metal thing and pointed it at me. "What are you, anyway?"

"I cannot answer unless I can send to you. Do you want an answer?"

"O.K., but watch out. Don't you move; I've got ya covered."

"I'm too tired to move," I said, "and I could not harm you even if I wished. I'm helpless without Mother."

The creature came a little closer again, but not as close as before.

"I don't know what I am," I said. "I don't know and I would like to know. Tell me what I am."

The thing took another step closer. "If *you* don't know then *nobody* does," it said. "Where did you come from anyway? Dropped from a flying saucer I suppose. Damn, I *am* drunk; I don't believe in them things."

"I come from Mother."

"Ha! Don't we all?" The creature came quite close again.

"I'm looking for her. I've traveled a long way through the cold void to find her, but I can't find her. She never answers me. I call and call."

"You *did* come from out there, then." *The thing's valuable*, the creature thought. *It's worth more than uranium, any day.*

"I'm just a piece," I went on; "I'm not a whole. I'm nothing without Mother. Mother is the whole and I'm just a piece. What shall I do?"

"I'll look after you," the creature said, then it thought, *I'll look after you damn well – in fact till I see the scientist. It'll cost them something to get hold of you, too.* "You're helpless without Mother, eh? Well then, come to Papa."

Then, after a moment's wait, there were sharp prongs that bit into my sides. I was lifted a moment and then dumped into a metal box and the lid shut tight against the breezes and the blue sky. "There you are," the creature said, "nice and snug. Don't you worry none. I'll look after you from now on."

"It's very hot in here," I told it.

"I'm hot, too," it said. "It's a hot day; we're *all* hot, so cut out complaining."

"Mother, Mother, I need you," I called as loud as I could.

"Stop yappin' for your mother; she ain't here. She ain't on this earth, in fact. You just remember that. She ain't here, and I'd be mighty surprised if she was. Now shut up and stop botherin' me; I'm going to look after you from now on, whether you like it or not."

I kept quiet then, but it was so hot in the box. And the bouncing. It was a harsh way of moving this creature had—a harsh and bumpy way. Not like Mother. I wanted to send again. We had moved a ways now; perhaps she could hear me from here. But the creature didn't want any more sending. He said Mother wasn't here. I didn't believe him, not really. Mother was somewhere and I would find her sometime. I would send and send. But I didn't send now.

It got hotter and hotter; I was getting small again, and I began to be afraid I might go completely, so finally I did call out. "I'm going," I said. "I'm too hot. I shrivel. Help me."

"Don't think I don't feel exactly the same way," the creature said, "but I guess it's about time for a break. I could use one too. Lord, it *is* hot!"

The bumpy movement stopped, and that was some relief. The creature thought, drank, again, and I could almost feel it when it took a long, long drink. It felt good to it. Then it opened the box where I was, and something splashed in and covered me with dampness.

"Here," it said, "this'll do you good. Make you forget your troubles."

It burned and it prickled. "It hurts," I cried.

"Of course it hurts the first time down. You gotta get used to it. Keep quiet and don't be a crybaby."

"Ouch, ouch."

"I said shut up. From now on you speak when you're spoken to, and stop cluttering up my mind."

So I suffered and didn't say anything as we bounced along again; after a while the burning got a little better, though the itching was just as bad — if not worse. Soon I felt myself changing, somehow. I wondered what it was, and I wished Mother was near and could tell me and comfort me. I felt so peculiar; I knew something strange and significant was happening to me, but I didn't know what.

After a while the itching stopped a bit and the changes seemed to slow; then I listened to the creature's sending to itself. "Bet this thing's important," it thought. "I'll go to town right away, tomorrow first thing. I could sure use the dough. I might even get a thousand dollars. That's what I'll hold out for, I guess."

It walked a while just looking at the rocks and trees, and then it thought, "Whiskey's runnin' out. I could go on a real binge in town tomorrow night. That's what I'll do; I'll get in a real good one when I sell this thing. I won't come to for a couple of days." Then it walked faster and thought happy thoughts.

Soon, by its thoughts, I knew we were coming to where it lived, and that the bouncing would stop. I felt glad about that.

Then we did stop and it got cooler — for the creature especially, for we were in some sort of a shelter that kept out some of the heat. Still, inside the box, it was stuffy and the heat was slower in leaving it.

"May I come out now, please?" I asked the creature. "It is stuffy here in the box and still hot."

"I should say not," it answered. "I don't want to take any chances that you'll skip out on me; you're too valuable. You're a real museum piece and I'm going to hang on to you till I see some cold cash. That box is where you'll stay till then, so you might as well make yourself comfortable. And stop jumpin' into my mind all the time. It bothers me. I don't like it. Shut up from now on or you'll really get yourself heated up, on the stove too."

So I was quiet and just listened, and the creature thought, *food*, and went about fixing itself some.

I was changing fast again. All my top and round ridges had stopped itching and now had lost all feeling. This frightened me and I yearned for Mother. I needed her reassurance and comforting—and most of all her explanation of what this was all about. And I wondered what I was and what I was becoming.

I lay and waited a long time, frightened about myself; after a while, I felt my whole top cracking into little pieces. I couldn't resist sending out, then. "I'm falling apart," I cried. "Mother, Mother."

But no one answered—not even the creature. Then I listened to see what the creature was doing and if it was lying down—not sending any more, and not listening any more, either. It was just silent nothingness inside.

I dared to send out a few more loud calls for Mother, then. The creature didn't hear them and they didn't seem to disturb it; but I got no answer from Mother, either, so I stopped and lay quiet, feeling the changes coming in myself.

After a little while longer, my cracking top broke up into hundreds of tiny pieces. Loveable little pieces, I felt, every one of them. They belonged to me; I had made them and they no longer frightened me.

What darlings, I thought, and I swelled with pride. Cool juices filled me and I swelled and swelled and suddenly I felt a hunger a new kind of hunger I'd never had. Hunger for food…organic food. Then I seemed to split underneath and I had mouths—many of them—that opened and shut.

The little pieces stirred about me. They were so small yet, so weak and tiny. "Wake up," I told them softly; "wake up, darlings. We must find food."

I changed still, and parts grew out and over and inside. And I swelled more; but thought I was bigger, I was meager. I needed more substance. I was hungry.

I swelled till I touched the top of the box. I pressed against it and it popped open.

"Come, little ones, wake and move. I need you, every one. I need you now."

They came awake slowly. They cuddled close to me; they climbed on top of me and down my sides, and some of the strongest raised themselves a bit, testing their powers.

"That's right, fly. Try it when you are strong enough. Farther and farther, but not too far. Keep the thread; don't get lost. I need you all."

And they practiced and grew stronger. "Now," I said, "fly out and tell me about the creature, those that are strong and dried out." And they flew out and they sent back. "Yes!"

I raised myself out of the box then, and down to the floor. I was heavy as I'd never been before, round and heavy, and I needed substance. "I'm glad it is this creature," I said to the little ones. "It put me in a hot box and told me not to send. I don't like it and I'm very hungry."

I came to where the creature was lying. I could raise myself still, though I was heavy, and I had a foot now to help. I came down on it and started to feed. It was so good.

Then it woke suddenly, sending out a big noise. It clawed at me and even ripped me in my soft places; but I was feeding and getting substance fast, and I repaired myself with the new juices as it tore. I grew bigger and stronger every moment. Its noise grew very loud, then, and it tore at me harder and harder; but I was quite big. I fed as fast as I could, and soon the noise lessened and stopped; and soon after that there was nothing left to sip anymore at all.

I was still not big, but I was bigger. I almost feared I wouldn't be able to get out the opening of the shelter, but I did squeeze through it.

"Come, darlings," I called, "we must find more creatures like that one. We'll go to that place it thought of. Town, it said. Fly out and find it and tell me things. But keep the thread; don't go too far. I need you all for I must eat more and grow more…lots more, and you must find the food."

I looked down at myself then, as I started away, and I saw that I was beautiful. I saw my reds and blues, and the shimmering green, and the white parts inside. How contented I felt, how calm. I no longer wanted to send to Mother. I no longer had questions.

I knew exactly what I was.

Afterword by Natalie Devitt

Originally published in *Science Fiction Quarterly* in 1956, the same year *Invasion of the Body Snatchers* was released in theaters, "The Piece Thing" is a different kind of alien invasion story, one with a heart, you might say.

Like a number of Carol's stories, "The Piece Thing" is written as a first-person narrative, a viewpoint she enjoyed writing from for the challenge. In this story's case, it helps to create a compelling character arc. "The Piece Thing" takes on an alien perspective, but also a familiar one.

The alien begins the story as a child, separated from its parent for the first time and just beginning to learn about the world around it. The alien ends as a mother, willing to do anything to feed its children. It's a more sympathetic character than the cruel and greedy human it encounters, and we find ourselves in the uncomfortable position of rooting for a creature that will not hesitate to kill and eat any human in its path. Like most good horror, there is a powerful element of "if—only"—in this case, if only the alien had encountered a different human, perhaps a kinder one, or at least a smarter one. What might a telepathic alien and a sympathetic human have accomplished? Instead, ignorance and cupidity rule the day, and the human is the agent of his own demise. It's not hard to extend the metaphor, especially in an era where people knew that at any moment a seemingly-capricious government could decide to bring the end to humanity. While the story can be absolutely heartbreaking to read at certain points, what I admire about it, and about Carol's work in general, is how concise her writing is. Not a single word is wasted.

Born in 1921 in Ann Arbor, Michigan, Carol had a writing career that spanned decades and genres. She was often referred to as a poet, fabulist and magic realist. Growing up in the Great Lakes State and then in France, Carol served in the Red Cross during World War II. She graduated from the University of Michigan in 1949 and studied art at École des Beaux-Art in Paris as a Fulbright scholar. Carol enrolled in a drawing class, where she met her future husband, artist and filmmaker Ed Emshwiller, with whom she had three children. Carol also served as Ed's muse for the women portrayed in his artworks for countless SF magazines and paperbacks.

Despite having a father who was at one point employed as an English professor, Carol struggled with writing in school, due in large part to her poor spelling. So turned off was she, that she did not start writing professionally until she was in her early 30s. She credited all of the SF writers she and Ed befriended for sparking her interest in the genre. Beginning in the mid-1950s, her stories started appearing in the pages of SF magazines (*Piece* is her fifth SF sale) — and later, in literary and feminist magazines. She went on to be associated with the progressive "New Wave" SF of the 1960s, a movement with a name inspired by the French New Wave.

Surprisingly, Carol didn't publish a novel-length work until 1990, when she released *Carmen Dog*, which was followed by more long works of narrative fiction, including the Philip K. Dick Award-winning book *The Mount* (2002). Collections of Emshwiller's short stories include *Joy In Our Cause* (1975), *Verging on the Pertinent* (1989), the World Fantasy award winning collection *The Start of the End of It All* (1990), *Report to the Men's Club and Other Stories* (2002), *I Live with You* (2005), and *The Collected Stories of Carol Emshwiller* Vol. 1 (2011), *In the Time of War & Master of the Road to Nowhere and Other Tales of the Fantastic* (2011), and *The Collected Stories of Carol Emshwiller Vol. 2* (2016).

After moving to New York in the early 1980s, she spent years teaching writing at New York University's School of Continuing Education, until she retired from teaching in 2003. When she was not in New York, she could often be found in the Sierra Nevada Mountains, a location that influenced the settings of her westerns, *Ledoyt* (1995) and *Leaping Man Hill* (1999).

She passed away in 2019, at the age of 97, but not before receiving some of the genre's greatest awards: the ACCENT/ ASCENT fiction prize, the Pushcart Prize, the Nebula Award, the Fantasy Award for Life Achievement, and the World Fantasy Award for Lifetime Achievement.

News for Dr. Richardson
by Miriam Allen deFord

(This nonfiction piece originally appeared in the May 1956 issue of *The Magazine of Fantasy and Science Fiction*, in response to "The Day After We Land on Mars" by Dr. Robert S Richardson, from the May 28, 1955 issue of *Saturday Review*. It has never been republished before now.)

I am going to tell Dr. Robert S. Richardson a secret.

Women are not walking sex organs.

They are human beings. They are people, just like men.

"I feel that the men stationed on a planet," says Dr. Richardson, "should be openly accompanied by women to relieve the sexual tensions that develop among healthy normal males."

I couldn't agree with him more—if he would end that sentence at the word "women." There is not the slightest doubt that the unprecedented conditions that will exist in a scientific "occupation force" on Mars or any other extraterrestrial body will mean some reshuffling and modification of the sex mores (outmoded anyway, and more often neglected than followed—ask Dr. Kinsey) which obtain on earth, or at least in Western society, today.

But what makes Dr. Richardson think that (a) only males undergo sexual tensions, or that (b) the recommended way to "relieve the sexual tensions" of his Martian outpost would be to import a sort of spaceborne bagnio for its members?

To anyone not blinded by subconscious male arrogance, it would occur that the best solution to an indubitable problem would be to approximate, as closely as the situation will admit, the culture in which the advance guard on Mars had been reared from infancy. In other words, that group of scientific and technological workers which will first colonize Mars or any other planet should be selected without any criteria except those of health, adaptability, education, and technical ability, so as to form a community as like as possible to the community from which the colonists came.

I do not take it that Dr. Richardson contemplates practicing discrimination in his Martian personnel as to race, nationality, or political or religious belief. But apparently it has never entered his mind that there should also be no discrimination as to sex.

Is there any reason why women should not be as eligible as men to become part of that personnel?

It is true that (largely because of the discouragements and obstacles set in their path by people with Dr. Richardson's implicit viewpoint) fewer women than men do turn to the physical sciences as a career. But even so there are plenty of young women, healthy and temperamentally suited to the rigors of extraterrestrial life, who have been trained as physicists, chemists, astronomers, engineers, and in all the needed professional disciplines, down to multitudes of laboratory and technical assistants. If such an opportunity were offered them as the great adventure Dr. Richardson outlines, numbers of them would be eager to participate in it. (And please let me emphasize that I am not suggesting recruiting women merely for the minor posts; every position from highest to lowest should be open to the best-qualified applicant. The kind of man who would be reluctant to serve under a woman superior is not the kind of man who would be able to undergo the other social frictions of those years of isolation.)

Physically, indeed, women would be better suited than men as Martian pioneers. As Dr. Ashley Montagu and others have abundantly proved, they have greater endurance, more latent strength, more resistance to disease. To quote Montagu, "The fact is that the female is constitutionally stronger than the male and only muscularly less powerful; she has greater stamina and lives longer." Muscular superiority will not be one of the desiderata on Mars, where gravity is light and, besides, machines will do all the heavy work.

The notion that women are inherently more emotional and excitable than men is a hoary myth that belongs back in the days of 18th century "vapors" and Victorian swoonings. Actually, the convention that induces men to repress every indication of emotion makes neurosis more prevalent among them than among women.

The other moss-grown legend that women don't get on with other women, can't cooperate for the common good, has been exploded long ago except in the minds of a few unrealistic wishful thinkers. It is true only of women — and men — who have nothing better to occupy their time and energy than personalities, not of working, useful persons of either sex. I can assure you, incidentally, that there is much less bickering and backhand knifing in conventions of feminine organizations than in those of masculine: I know; I've reported plenty of both.

Women associate on a basis of equality with men in college classes, in business, on juries, on conducted tours, on committees, in voting booths: why not in the personnel of the first Martian expedition?

Moreover, opening the Martian working lists to women as well as to men will mean that not all those sent to Mars will have to be unmarried; like tends to like, and many couples with the same or similar professional qualifications can be sent together. Whether any children should be born on Mars of these married couples on the staff is another question, to be decided by the planners; probably strict birth control would have to be enforced. But this is a separate problem irrelevant to the argument — and in any case would arise just as much with respect to that superbrothel Dr. Richardson envisions.

Undoubtedly, however, the vast majority of the colonists, both men and women, *will* be unmarried. Previous marriage, to a person not also selected for the group, would have to constitute a bar to inclusion in the personnel, for one could hardly ask a wife (or husband) to wait alone on earth for so long. But with a bisexual instead of a monosexual staff of pioneer observers, investigators, and technicians, nature would inevitably take its course among the unmarried colonists — just as it does in any mixed group on this planet. To be sure, as I said above, there would still have to be some modification of our conventional sex customs; couples united under the unique conditions of the Martian project might or might not wish to continue their association when they returned to earth.

I can anticipate Dr. Richardson's first reaction to this substitute for his plan. "Think of the rivalries, the jealousies, the enmities, the perpetual turmoil, the feuds and hatreds and killings," he will say. "Science will be forgotten while men battle over women and women over men."

But why? Right here on Terra we have nothing but mixed groups of men and women, in every community. And of course we do have rivalries and jealousies and all the rest, right down to suicide and murder.

But that isn't the normal or usual course of affairs. Most people manage to go through their lives without such upsetting experiences. And this will be a group deliberately winnowed for temperamental stability, and with its primary interest in intellectual pursuits. Among the several hundred on Mars, there will be lots of room for sexual selection. Perhaps there *will* be some of the pioneers, both men and women, who will never find a sexual partner, or will lose the one they found. (There will also be some who prefer celibacy or who are simply not concerned with life outside their work.) But so there are here on earth; and both society and the people affected survive. Life does not give all its most precious gifts to everybody, and the deprived, if they are healthy beings, usually live through their deprivations without serious damage to their psyches.

Besides, what would prevent similar tensions and disturbances between Dr. Richardson's young men and the "nice girls" shipped in to console them — whether each girl is to be allotted to a selected man, or the entire group is to serve the community indiscriminately (a point Dr. Richardson doesn't make plain)? H. Chandler Davis has summed it up succinctly: "Men do fight over women, but I deny that they fight nastier over women who are respected."

Of course I can think of one reason why Dr. Richardson would prefer the "nice girls" to a bisexual working force. Presumably the concubines would be chosen, among other attributes, for charm and beauty; and there is no guarantee that because a woman is young, healthy, temperamentally suitable, and a darned good physicist or engineer she will also be pretty — whatever the standard of prettiness may be by the time we get to Mars. But if only pretty girls ever got married or had love affairs, this would be a 75% celibate culture right here and now!

It is pretty disheartening, after all these years, to discover how many otherwise enlightened and progressive-minded men still retain in their subconscious this throwback attitude toward half of humanity, which relegates women to the position of possessions, of ancillary adjuncts to men — what Simone de Beauvoir calls "the second sex": creatures who, in David Graham Phillips' sarcastic phrase, are formed only "to minister satisfyingly to the physical and sentimental needs of men."

To quote Mr. Davis again, in Dr. Richardson's prospectus "the men are to go to Mars to do science and the women are to go there to be used by the men." There is implied in the very blandness of such a proposal a deep-rooted contempt for women which may shock its possessor when it is brought out into the open.

Some 30-odd years ago Mathilde and Mathias Vaerting wrote a book called *The Dominant Sex*. They posited a sort of pendulum-swing throughout history between patriarchal and matriarchal systems, and their thesis was that most of the so-called masculine mental and emotional characteristics are really those of the dominant sex, whichever it may be at the time, most of the so-called feminine those of the subordinate sex. What they advocated was stopping the pendulum at the middle of its swing, thus achieving a culture based on sexual equality and partnership.

More recent research has invalidated a good deal of their evidential historical material, but the general thesis still holds. We in the Western world today are gradually emerging from a long period of male-centered civilization, and approaching what the Vaertings would have considered the middle of the pendulum swing. There are even signs, especially in this country (*e.g.,* Momism), that we are beginning to tend toward a female-centered culture instead. Both extremes are equally undesirable. The times of greatest advance in human progress are those when neither sex is subservient to the other.

Dr. Richardson thinks "space travel may force us to adopt a more realistic attitude toward sex than that which prevails at present." Granted and amen. But then he goes on to propose an expedient which he himself acknowledges is taken from the mores of a savage tribe. The people who form the first Martian expedition are hardly likely to be Masai. But neither will they be people from the New Stone Age or the Feudal Period or from any other primitive era. They will be people born and bred in the 20th century (or the 21st), with all that that implies.

The completely naive assumptions in Dr. Richardson's article are a holdover from those centuries when man was the sun and woman the planet revolving about him; when profound contempt for women was masked in "chivalry," when women were called "the sex," and a woman's sole functions in life were to stand in the background and feed and serve and solace and satisfy her man, to cheer and encourage and admire slavishly the master who owned her and provided her with economic support, and to produce sons to carry on the tradition and—unavoidably and not too acceptably—daughters to serve similarly the sons of other women.

Unfortunately, heredity does not work that way. Every woman inherits her father's genes as well as her mother's, just as every man inherits his mother's genes as well as his father's. So eventually the pendulum swings. Mankind is one of the many species in which there is a minimum distinction between the sexes, outside of the obvious sexual characteristics. Human beings are neither angler fish, in which the tiny male is a parasite on the female, nor birds of paradise, in which the dull little female scarcely seems of the same genus as her gorgeous mate. They are closest to those many animals which feed, forage, hunt, and carry on all the non-sexual as well as the sexual activities of life together, on an equal footing.

There is one very simple way to test the deepest convictions of anyone on any subject—not the convictions he thinks he holds, but those buried where only a psychoanalyst could uncover them. That is to turn his theses inside out, and let him look at them then.

Let us suppose that Dr. Richardson's proposals were reversed. Let us suppose that he had suggested that several hundred young women scientists be sent to Mars, and that "to relieve their sexual tensions" shiploads of "nice boys" be sent to serve them.

The mere thought of such a reversal would undoubtedly horrify him.

Well, that's the way both women and men emancipated from his atavistic prejudices feel about his extraterrestrial bordello.

Afterword by Kerrie Dougherty

I'm ashamed to say that I had never heard of Miriam Allen deFord before being asked to write this afterword. But the taste of her talent provided by her "tartly eloquent" rebuttal of Dr. R.S. Richardson's "The Day After We Land on Mars" has left me eager to search out more of her work.

Born in 1888, deFord described herself as a "born feminist". She was a suffragist, a social and political activist, a promoter of birth control, a fervent anti-Fascist, and a Humanist (a signatory to the second Humanist Manifesto). As an author, her early output included articles and pamphlets for the causes she embraced, as well as twelve volumes in the Little Blue Book series of educational and how-to titles. A dedicated Fortean, she carried out some investigations on Fort's behalf that earned her a mention in his book *Lo!* (1931). DeFord began writing mystery stories in the 1940s before turning her talents to science fiction in the early 1950s. Successful in both genres, she continued writing mysteries, true crime, and science fiction until her passing in 1975.

The Dr. Richardson, for whom deFord's article was "news", was Mt. Wilson Observatory astronomer Dr. Robert Shirley Richardson, author of a number of books and popular articles on astronomy, and scientific advisor on the films *Destination Moon* and *When Worlds Collide*. Richardson was also a science-fiction writing contemporary of deFord's, using the pseudonym Phi(l)lip Latham.

Originally published in the *Saturday Review* (May 28, 1955), Richardson's article *The Day After We Land on Mars* was republished in a slightly expanded form in the December 1955 issue of *The Magazine of Fantasy & Science Fiction* (*F&SF*). While much of the article was based on realistic speculation about the many issues that would need to be considered in establishing a base on Mars, it generated controversy for what the author called its "shocking" suggestion that Western sexual mores would need to be modified for space exploration, and that "nice girls" should be sent to Mars to "relieve the sexual tensions" of the all-male crew of the first Martian outpost. Richardson's original article can be found online (https://wrs03.tripod.com/55.html) and I recommend reading it to gain a deeper understanding of deFord's counter arguments.

In the age of the Kinsey Reports, when frank discussion about sex was considered *de rigueur*, very few readers of *F&SF* seem to have taken issue with the idea that space exploration might require, or even precipitate, a change in Western sexual mores. What roused their ire was that Richardson's only suggestion for assuaging male sexual frustration on a long duration space mission was the creation of, as deFord puts it, a "spaceborne bagnio".

DeFord's article was one of two responses to the Richardson piece appearing in the May 1956 *F&SF* under the blanket title *Of Mars and Men*. Poul Anderson's *Nice Girls on Mars* offers a "male perspective" rebuttal to Richardson's suggestion, while deFord's article presents a feminist perspective on Richardson's male-centred assumptions—although editor Anthony Boucher coyly attempts to deflect criticism from those readers who might feel threatened by a "feminist" viewpoint by describing the article as putting forward "...not [a] feminist, but merely human point of view".

While not forgetting the cultural context of the period in which it was written, reading Richardson's article made my blood boil. It's therefore not surprising that a long-time feminist activist like Miriam deFord was equally incensed by its casual assumption that women could, and should, be treated as sex objects servicing intrepid space explorers, rather than equal participants in space activities. She marshals her counter-arguments, demonstrating how a mixed crew would obviate the sexual tension issues, using the best evidence available to her at the time. One can only wish that she had revisited this article in the early 1960s and reinforced her case for the equality of women in space exploration with the results of the Lovelace Clinic tests, which subjected a group of female pilots (popularly known today as the Mercury 13) to the same physical and psychological tests that were used in the selection of NASA's first group of astronauts. They passed with flying colours, their results exceeding those of the male astronauts in some instances.

The first female space traveller, Valentina Tereshkova, made it into orbit in 1963, some seven years after deFord's "News for Dr Richardson" (and only a little more than two years after the first man in space), but it was another twenty years before Western cultural attitudes to female roles changed sufficiently for women to become permanent members of NASA's astronaut corps. Within this decade the first women will land on the Moon and hopefully by the mid-2030s we'll see women as participants in the first mission to Mars. It will have taken about 80 years, but Miriam deFord's vision of mixed crews on long duration space missions, working, living and loving on an equal footing will finally become inevitable reality.

Woman's Work

by **Garen Drussaï**

(Originally appeared in the August 1956 issue of *The Magazine of Fantasy and Science Fiction*. It has been reprinted twice in English: In 1980 and 1992.)

Sheila sat instantly up in bed, her eyes wide awake and startled. The alarm on her wrist was giving off small electric shocks. *Someone was coming up the walk!* She turned it off quickly and looked at the clock.

Only ten minutes after four. It was still dark outside. She sighed wearily as she thought of the difficult task that lay before her in these next few minutes.

Hal's voice whispered tensely from beside her. "Is it time yet?"

"Yes," she answered. "They seem to come earlier each day." She slipped out of bed and hurriedly put on a robe. Then she turned on a small light and carefully picked up a number of gadgets from her night table, putting them into the outsize pockets of her robe.

Hal twisted anxiously in the bed as he watched her preparations. "Are you sure you've got enough this time?" he finally asked. "We just can't go on this way. We've got to lick them!"

Sheila bent over Hal tenderly and kissed him. "Don't worry, darling. This is my job. I'll do my best." She straightened up, grimly, as the door bell rang.

As she opened the front door the shocking brightness of sunshine flooded her face. She blinked rapidly to accustom her eyes to the brilliance of it. Then, in a moment, she saw him. He was quite young and nice-looking. What a shame, she thought bitterly, that they had to be enemies.

He was doing calisthenics on the front lawn, his jumping belt taking him yards up at a time. She watched him almost hypnotically, her head going up and down, up and down, up—frantically she sought a button concealed on the door jamb and pressed it. Instantly the gravity control started working and the young man, his jumping belt now useless, took it off and came toward her.

"Good — *good* — good morning!" He beamed at her. "Isn't this a wonderful day? Look at all this lovely sunshine." He extended his arms in a sweeping gesture. "And all for you — you lucky lady!"

A slight smile turned up the corners of Sheila's mouth. She'd show him, she thought. She'd prick his Sunshine Bubble right now. She pressed another button on the door — and immediately the sun was blotted out and pre-dawn night surrounded them.

"Aha!" The young man scarcely seemed surprised. "You have your little jokes. Well, now that you've had some fun outwitting me, suppose you let me give you a little gift. Just as a friendly token from my company to you."

He held a small box out to her as she twisted a dial set into the door handle. Suddenly a heavy downpour descended all around the front door. Sheila couldn't help herself. She burst into laughter at his dismay. Then before she realized it, he was inside the door…and she couldn't stop laughing. He had squirted some laugh powder at her.

That's when the young man started his sales pitch. She didn't know what he was selling. Even if she signed for it, she still wouldn't know until it was delivered. Not when she was under the influence of a laugh drug. Then she thought of Hal lying there in the bedroom — trusting her to do her best. With superhuman effort she took a pill from her pocket and gulped it down between laughs. In a few moments the laughs subsided, and tears started streaming down her face.

The salesman was game. Sheila had to admit that. He kept talking, and his head started to shake affirmatively and positively — up and down, up and down. But Sheila, still crying, wasn't going to be taken in again by that hypnotic procedure. She slipped one of the gadgets on the back of her neck and set it to vibrating, and then soon she was shaking her head too — but negatively, from side to side.

She thought of her warm, comfortable bed and wished she was back in it. Suddenly she was — or thought she was, anyway. He was supporting her on a pneumatic float! Making her forget what she must do. Lulling her into a state of acceptance… This would never do. Hal wouldn't forgive her if she let him down. They just couldn't afford to buy one more thing.

She rushed over to the wall and, wiping the tears from her eyes so she could see, activated the Simulator. Then, instead of seeming to rest on a pneumatic couch, she felt the sharp ridges of a rocky ledge pressing into her flesh. She didn't care. The discomfort of it mattered little if she could win.

Sheila turned and looked at him. He was still talking away, as bright and animated as ever, still with, no doubt, a few tricks up his sleeve. Now, she thought, now while I still can, I'll give him all I've got! She slipped plugs into her ears, a rather difficult operation when her head was still shaking from side to side. Then in one quick sweep she flipped the playback switch on the tape recorder, letting loose a deafening mixture of the sound of babies wailing and dogs barking.

The salesman stopped talking, and Sheila knew he was about to get his noise deadener out of his pocket. With a cry of battle on her lips, she slapped an oxygen mask on her teary face and let loose a stench bomb of so powerful and hideous an odor that the young man stopped, completely frozen. Finally, with a howl of anguish and frustration, he ran out into the chilly dawn.

Oh! How wonderful Sheila felt. The taste of triumph was sweet and delicious. She hastily deactivated all the gadgets (though it would be a few minutes before the effects wore off), then she purified the stench of the room, and suddenly feeling unbearably tired, she stumbled back into the bedroom.

Hal, still in bed, looked searchingly at her. She laughed — as well as she could with tears still running down her cheeks, head shaking from side to side, and the sharp rocks still digging into her.

"We won! Hal, we won!" she cried out, and collapsed on the bed.

Suddenly Sheila sat up, a shocked look on her face. "Hal," she said accusingly, "why are you still in bed? Do you realize it's four-thirty? I'm up and at my work by four o'clock. How do you expect me to make ends meet if you're not out working?"

Hal smiled at her, and stretched leisurely as he stood up.

"Don't worry, dear. I'm not loafing. I just got a terrific idea this morning. I'm going to let the other guys soften up my prospects at four and five in the morning." He stood looking down at her, a kind of dreamy, gloating look on his face.

"Then, when I give my pitch about six o'clock — just after they've been through a couple of *displays* — and just before they've had time for their morning coffee... Sheila, my love, they'll be pushovers!"

"Oh Hal," she said, "how wonderful you are!"

He walked to the bathroom, and then turned, just at the door.

"Now you watch out, Sheila. Watch out for those six-o'clock-pitches. Don't *you* fall for them!"

She looked numbly after him, thinking of the hours ahead till she could escape to the shops and shows that made up her day. Then she straightened up determinedly.

After all, this was woman's work.

The alarm on her wrist was giving off small electric shocks. *Someone was coming up the walk!*

Afterword by Laura Brodian Freas Beraha

"A man can work from sun to sun, But a woman's work is never done."
— Jean Little, *Orphan at My Door: The Home Child Diary of Victoria Cope*

In Drussaï's story of a dystopian future, civilization thrives on extreme competitive salesmanship. It is the wife's job to keep the wolf from the door. Just an extrapolation of the division of labor for most couples back in the 1950s. Even to this day, many times it's the wife who takes the multitudes of spam calls and either extinguishes the connection or, just for fun, tries to humiliate the caller who had the nerve to try an astonishingly transparent scam. All the while, her husband looks on, nodding in amusement. Did you catch the ironic twist at the end of this story? If not you might wish to take a second glance at it.

A graduate of the University of California Los Angeles, Drussaï was born in the Bronx, New York, to immigrant parents from Austria-Hungary. Although they were fluent in English, the family spoke Yiddish at home. Her influences were motion pictures and classic literature, her view of writing decidedly romantic rather than formulaic.

Mrs. Drussaï was best known for her galactic suburban style, set from the point of view of the housewife in domestic settings. Her science fiction stories were published in the mid nineteen fifties, her mentor being *The Magazine of Fantasy and Science Fiction* editor and writer Anthony Boucher. She also wrote mystery novels, along with several short stories; her "Why Don't You Answer, Theodore" was published in 1979 in *Mike Shayne Mystery Magazine* in May 1970. The Los Angeles Times published a profile of her in 1977.

She remained a Californian for most of her adult life, mostly in the northern California city of Santa Rosa, where she passed away in 2009 at the age of 93—just one of the many women authors who briefly dipped her toes in the genre, making a brief but indelible imprint on the silver age of science fiction.

Poor Little Saturday
by Madeleine L'Engle

(Originally appeared in the October 1956 issue of *Fantastic Universe*. It was most recently reprinted in 2012.)

The witch woman lived in a deserted, boarded-up plantation house, and nobody knew about her but me. Nobody in the nosy little town in south Georgia where I lived when I was a boy knew that if you walked down the dusty main street to where the post office ended it and then turned left and followed that road a piece until you got to the rusty iron gates of the drive to the plantation house, you could find goings-on would make your eyes pop out. It was just luck that I found out. Or maybe it wasn't luck at all. Maybe the witch woman wanted me to find out because of Alexandra. But now I wish I hadn't, because the witch woman and Alexandra are gone forever and it's much worse than if I'd never known them.

Nobody'd lived in the plantation house since the Civil War when Colonel Londermaine was killed and Alexandra Londermaine, his beautiful young wife, hung herself on the chandelier in the ballroom. A while before I was born some northerners bought it, but after a few years they stopped coming and people said it was because the house was haunted. Every few years a gang of boys or men would set out to explore the house but nobody ever found anything, and it was so well boarded up it was hard to force an entrance, so by and by the town lost interest in it. No one climbed the wall and wandered around the grounds except me.

I used to go there often during the summer because I had bad spells of malaria when sometimes I couldn't bear to lie on the iron bedstead in my room with the flies buzzing around my face, or out on the hammock on the porch with the screams and laughter of the other kids as they played torturing my ears. My aching head made it impossible for me to read, and I would drag myself down the road, scuffling my bare, sun-burned toes in the dust, wearing

197

the tattered straw hat that was supposed to protect me from the heat of the sun, shivering and sweating by turns. Sometimes it would seem hours before I got to the iron gates near which the brick wall was lowest. Often I would have to lie panting on the tall, prickly grass for minutes until I gathered strength to scale the wall and drop down on the other side.

But once inside the grounds it seemed cooler. One funny thing about my chills was that I didn't seem to shiver nearly as much when I could keep cool as I did at home where even the walls and the floors, if you touched them, were hot. The grounds were filled with live oaks that had grown up unchecked everywhere and afforded an almost continuous green shade. The ground was covered with ferns that were soft and cool to lie on, and when I flung myself down on my back and looked up, the roof of leaves was so thick that sometimes I couldn't see the sky at all. The sun that managed to filter through lost its bright, pitiless glare and came in soft yellow shafts that didn't burn you when they touched you.

One afternoon, a scorcher early in September, which is usually our hottest month (and by then you're fagged out by the heat, anyhow), I set out for the plantation. The heat lay coiled and shimmering on the road. When you looked at anything through it, it was like looking through a defective pane of glass. The dirt road was so hot that it burned even through my calloused feet, and as I walked clouds of dust rose in front of me and mixed with the shimmying of the heat. I thought I'd never make the plantation. Sweat was running into my eyes, but it was cold sweat, and I was shivering so that my teeth chattered as I walked. When I managed finally to fling myself down on my soft green bed of ferns inside the grounds, I was seized with one of the worst chills I'd ever had in spite of the fact that my mother had given me an extra dose of quinine that morning and some 666 Malaria Medicine to boot. I shut my eyes tight and clutched the ferns with my hands and teeth to wait until the chill had passed, when I heard a soft voice call:

"Boy."

I thought at first I was delirious, because sometimes I got light-headed when my bad attacks came on; only then I remembered that when I was delirious I didn't know it; all the strange things I saw and heard seemed perfectly natural. So when the voice said, "Boy," again, as soft and clear as the mockingbird at sunrise, I opened my eyes.

Kneeling near me on the ferns was a girl. She must have been about a year younger than I. I was almost sixteen so I guess she was fourteen or fifteen. She was dressed in a blue and white gingham dress; her face was very pale, but the kind of paleness that's supposed to be, not the sickly pale kind that was like mine showing even under the tan. Her eyes were big and very blue. Her hair was dark brown and she wore it parted in the middle in two heavy braids that were swinging in front of her shoulders as she peered into my face.

"You don't feel well, do you?" she asked. There was no trace of concern or worry in her voice. Just scientific interest.

I shook my head. "No," I whispered, almost afraid that if I talked she would vanish, because I had never seen anyone here before, and I thought that maybe I was dying because I felt so awful, and I thought maybe that gave me the power to see the ghost. But the girl in blue and white checked gingham seemed, as I watched her, to be good flesh and blood.

"You'd better come with me," she said. "She'll make you all right."

"Who's she?"

"Oh—just Her," she said.

My chill had begun to recede by then, so when she got up off her knees, I scrambled up, too. When she stood up her dress showed a white ruffled petticoat underneath it, and bits of green moss had left patterns on her knees and I didn't think that would happen to the knees of a ghost, so I followed her as she led the way toward the house. She did not go up the sagging, half-rotted steps that led to the veranda, about whose white pillars wisteria vines climbed in wild profusion, but went around to the side of the house where there were slanting doors to a cellar. The sun and rain had long since blistered and washed off the paint, but the doors looked clean and were free of the bits of bark from the eucalyptus tree that leaned nearby and that had dropped its bits of dusty peel on either side; so I knew that these cellar stairs must frequently be used.

The girl opened the cellar doors. "You go down first," she said. I went down the cellar steps, which were stone and cool against my bare feet. As she followed me she closed the cellar doors after her and as I reached the bottom of the stairs we were in pitch darkness. I began to be very frightened until her soft voice came out of the black.

"Boy, where are you?"

"Right here."

"You'd better take my hand. You might stumble."

We reached out and found each other's hands in the darkness. Her fingers were long and cool and they closed firmly around mine. She moved with authority as though she knew her way with the familiarity born of custom.

"Poor Sat's all in the dark," she said, "but he likes it that way. He likes to sleep for weeks at a time. Sometimes he snores awfully. Sat, darling!" she called gently. A soft, bubbly, blowing sound came in answer, and she laughed happily. "Oh, Sat, you are sweet!" she said, and the bubbly sound came again.

Then the girl pulled at my hand and we came out into a huge and dusty kitch-en. Iron skillets, pots, and pans were still hanging on either side of the huge stove, and there was a rolling pin and a bowl of flour on the marble-topped table in the middle of the room. The girl took a lighted candle off the shelf.

"I'm going to make cookies," she said as she saw me looking at the flour and the rolling pin. She slipped her hand out of mine. "Come along." She be-gan to walk more rapidly. We left the kitchen, crossed the hall, went through the dining room, its old mahogany table thick with dust, although sheets cov-ered the pictures on the walls. Then we went into the ballroom. The mirrors lining the walls were spotted and discolored; against one wall was a single delicate gold chair, its seat cushioned with pale rose and silver woven silk; it seemed extraordinarily well preserved. From the ceiling hung the huge chan-delier from which Alexandra Londermaine had hung herself, its prisms catch-ing and breaking up into a hundred colors the flickering of the candle and the few shafts of light that managed to slide in through the boarded-up win-dows. As we crossed the ballroom, the girl began to dance by herself, grace-fully, lightly, so that her full, blue and white checked gingham skirts flew out around her. She looked at herself with pleasure in the old mirrors as she danced, the candle flaring and guttering in her right hand.

"You've stopped shaking. Now what will I tell Her?" she said as we start-ed to climb the broad mahogany staircase. It was very dark so she took my hand again, and before we had reached the top of the stairs I obliged her by being seized by another chill. She felt my trembling fingers with satisfaction. "Oh, you've started again. That's good." She slid open one of the huge double doors at the head of the stairs.

As I looked in to what once must have been Colonel Londermaine's study, I thought that surely what I saw was a scene in a dream or a vision in delirium. Seated at the huge table in the center of the room was the most extraordinary woman I had ever seen. I felt that she must be very beautiful, although she would never have fulfilled any of the standards of beauty set by our town. Even though she was seated, I felt that she must be immensely tall. Piled up on the table in front of her were several huge volumes, and her finger was mark-ing the place in the open one in front of her, but she was not reading. She was leaning back in the carved chair, her head resting against a piece of blue and gold embroidered silk that was flung across the chair back, one hand gently stroking a fawn that lay sleeping in her lap. Her eyes were closed and some-how I couldn't imagine what color they would be. It wouldn't have surprised me if they had been shining amber or the deep purple of her velvet robe. She had a great quantity of hair, the color of mahogany in firelight, which was cut quite short and seemed to be blown wildly about her head like flame. Under her closed eyes were deep shadows, and lines of pain were about her mouth. Otherwise there were no marks of age on her face but I would not have been surprised to learn that she was any age in the world—a hundred or twenty-five. Her mouth was large and mobile, and she was singing something in a deep, rich voice. Two cats, one black, one white, were coiled up, each on a book, and as we opened the doors a leopard stood up quietly beside her but did not snarl or move. It simply stood there and waited, watching us.

The girl nudged me and held her finger to her lips to warn me to be quiet, but I would not have spoken—could not, anyhow, my teeth were chattering so from my chill, which I had completely forgotten, so fascinated was I by this woman sitting back with her head against the embroidered silk, soft, deep sounds coming out of her throat. At last these sounds resolved themselves into words, and we listened to her as she sang. The cats slept indifferently, but the leopard listened, too:

> *I sit high in my ivory tower,*
> *The heavy curtains drawn.*
> *I've many a strange and lustrous flower,*
> *A leopard and a fawn*
>
> *Together sleeping by my chair*
> *And strange birds softly winging,*
> *And ever pleasant to my ear*
> *Twelve maidens' voices singing.*
>
> *Here is my magic maps' array,*
> *My mystic circle's flame.*
> *With symbol's art He lets me play,*
> *The unknown my domain,*
>
> *And as I sit here in my dream*
> *I see myself awake,*
> *Hearing a torn and bloody scream,*
> *Feeling my castle shake...*

Her song wasn't finished but she opened her eyes and looked at us. Now that his mistress knew we were here, the leopard seemed ready to spring and devour me at one gulp, but she put her hand on his sapphire-studded collar to restrain him.

"Well, Alexandra," she said, "whom have we here?"

The girl, who still held my hand in her long, cool fingers, answered, "It's a boy."

"So I see. Where did you find him?"

The voice sent shivers up and down my spine.

"In the fern bed. He was shaking. See? He's shaking now. Is he having a fit?" Alexandra's voice was filled with pleased interest.

"Come here, boy," the woman said.

As I didn't move, Alexandra gave me a push, and I advanced slowly. As I came near, the woman pulled one of the leopard's ears gently, saying, "Lie down, Thammuz." The beast obeyed, flinging itself at her feet. She held her hand out to me as I approached the table, If Alexandra's fingers felt firm and cool, hers had the strength of the ocean and the coolness of jade. She looked at me for a long time and I saw that her eyes were deep blue, much bluer than Alexandra's, so dark as to be almost black. When she spoke again her voice was warm and tender: "You're burning up with fever. One of the malaria bugs?" I nodded. "Well, we'll fix that for you."

When she stood and put the sleeping fawn down by the leopard, she was not as tall as I had expected her to be; nevertheless she gave an impression of great height. Several of the bookshelves in one corner were emptied of books and filled with various shaped bottles and retorts. Nearby was a large skeleton. There was an acid-stained washbasin, too; that whole section of the room looked like part of a chemist's or physicist's laboratory. She selected from among the bottles a small, amber-colored one and poured a drop of the liquid it contained into a glass of water. As the drop hit the water, there was a loud hiss and clouds of dense smoke arose. When they had drifted away, she handed the glass to me and said, "Drink. Drink, my boy!"

My hand was trembling so that I could scarcely hold the glass. Seeing this, she took it from me and held it to my lips.

"What is it?" I asked.

"Drink it," she said, pressing the rim of the glass against my teeth. On the first swallow I started to choke and would have pushed the stuff away, but she forced the rest of the burning liquid down my throat. My whole body felt on fire. I felt flame flickering in every vein, and the room and everything in it swirled around. When I had regained my equilibrium to a certain extent, I managed to gasp out again, "What is it?"

She smiled and answered,

> "Nine peacocks' hearts, four bats' tongues,
> A pinch of moon dust, and a hummingbird's lungs."

Then I asked a question I would never have dared ask if it hadn't been that I was still half drunk from the potion I had swallowed. "Are you a witch?"

She smiled again and answered, "I make it my profession."

Since she hadn't struck me down with a flash of lightning, I went on. "Do you ride a broomstick?"

This time she laughed. "I can when I like."

"Is it—is it very hard?"

"Rather like a bucking bronco at first, but I've always been a good horse-woman, and now I can manage very nicely. I've finally progressed to side-saddle, though I still feel safer astride. I always rode my horse astride. Still, the best witches ride sidesaddle, so... Now run along home. Alexandra has lessons to study and I must work. Can you hold your tongue or must I make you forget?"

"I can hold my tongue."

She looked at me and her eyes burnt into me like the potion she had given me to drink, "Yes, I think you can," she said. "Come back tomorrow if you like. Thammuz will show you out."

The leopard rose and led the way to the door. As I hesitated, unwilling to tear myself away, it came back and pulled gently but firmly on my trouser leg.

"Good-bye, boy," the witch woman said. "And you won't have any more chills and fever."

"Good-bye," I answered. I didn't say thank you. I didn't say good-bye to Alexandra. I followed the leopard out.

She let me come every day. I think she must have been lonely. After all, I was the only thing there with a life apart from hers. And in the long run the only reason I have had a life of my own is because of her. I am as much a creation of the witch woman's as Thammuz the leopard was, or the two cats, Ashtaroth and Orus. (It wasn't until many years after the last day I saw the witch woman that I learned that those were the names of the fallen angels.)

She did cure my malaria, too. My parents and the townspeople thought that I had outgrown it. I grew angry when they talked about it so lightly and wanted to tell them that it was the witch woman, but I knew that if ever I breathed a word about her I would be eternally damned. Mama thought we should write a testimonial letter to the 666 Malaria Medicine people, and may-be they'd send us a couple of dollars.

Alexandra and I became very good friends. She was a strange, aloof crea-ture. She liked me to watch her while she danced alone in the ballroom or played on an imaginary harp—though sometimes I fancied I could hear the music. One day she took me into the drawing room and uncovered a por-trait that was hung between two of the long, boarded-up windows. Then she stepped back and held her candle high so as to throw the best light on the picture. It might have been a picture of Alexandra herself, or Alexandra as she might be in five years.

"That's my mother," she said. "Alexandra Londermaine."

As far as I knew from the tales that went about town, Alexandra Londermaine had given birth to only one child, and that stillborn, before she had hung herself on the chandelier in the ballroom—and anyhow, any child of hers would have been this Alexandra's mother or grandmother. But I didn't say anything, because when Alexandra got angry she became ferocious like one of the cats and was given to leaping on me, scratching and biting. I looked at the portrait long and silently.

"You see, she has on a ring like mine," Alexandra said, holding out her left hand, on the fourth finger of which was the most beautiful sapphire and diamond ring I had ever seen—or rather, that I could ever have imagined, for it was a ring apart from any owned by even the most wealthy of the townsfolk. Then I realized that Alexandra had brought me in here and unveiled the portrait simply that she might show me the ring to better advantage, for she had never worn a ring before.

"Where did you get it?"

"Oh, She got it for me last night."

"Alexandra," I asked suddenly, "how long have you been here?"

"Oh, awhile."

"But how long?"

"Oh, I don't remember."

"But you must remember."

"I don't. I just came—like Poor Sat."

"Who's Poor Sat?" I asked, thinking for the first time of whoever it was that had made the gentle bubbly noises at Alexandra the day she found me in the fern bed.

"Why, we've never shown you Sat, have we!" she exclaimed. "I'm sure it's all right, but we'd better ask Her first."

So we went to the witch woman's room and knocked. Thammuz pulled the door open with his strong teeth and the witch woman looked up from some sort of experiment she was making with test tubes and retorts. The fawn, as usual, lay sleeping near her feet. "Well?" she said.

"Is it all right if I take him to see Poor Little Saturday?" Alexandra asked her.

"Yes, I suppose so," she answered. "But no teasing." And she turned her back to us and bent again over her test tubes as Thammuz nosed us out of the room.

We went down to the cellar. Alexandra lit a lamp and took me back to the corner farthest from the doors, where there was a stall. In the stall was a two-humped camel. I couldn't help laughing as I looked at him because he grinned at Alexandra so foolishly, displaying all his huge buck teeth and blowing bubbles through them.

"She said we weren't to tease him," Alexandra said severely, rubbing her cheek against the preposterous splotchy hair that seemed to be coming out, leaving bald pink spots of skin on his long nose.

"But what—" I started.

"She rides him sometimes." Alexandra held out her hand while he nuzzled against it, scratching his rubbery lips against the diamond and sapphire of her ring. "Mostly She talks to him. She says he is very wise. He goes up to Her room sometimes and they talk and talk. I can't understand a word they say. She says it's Hindustani and Arabic. Sometimes I can remember little bits of it, like: *iderow, sorcabatcha*, and *anna bibed bech*. She says I can learn to speak with them when I finish learning French and Greek."

Poor Little Saturday was rolling his eyes in delight as Alexandra scratched behind his ears. "Why is he called Poor Little Saturday?" I asked.

Alexandra spoke with a ring of pride in her voice. "I named him. She let me."

"But why did you name him that?"

"Because he came last winter on the Saturday that was the shortest day of the year, and it rained all day so it got light later and dark earlier than it would have if it had been nice, so it really didn't have as much of itself as it should, and I felt so sorry for it I thought maybe it would feel better if we named him after it... She thought it was a nice name!" She turned on me suddenly.

"Oh, it is! It's a fine name!" I said quickly, smiling to myself as I realized how much greater was this compassion of Alexandra's for a day than any she might have for a human being. "How did She get him?" I asked.

"Oh, he just came."

"What do you mean?"

"She wanted him so he came. From the desert."

"He *walked!*"

"Yes. And swam part of the way. She met him at the beach and flew him here on the broomstick. You should have seen him. He was still all wet and looked so funny. She gave him hot coffee with things in it."

"What things?"

"Oh, just things."

Then the witch woman's voice came from behind us. "Well, children?"

It was the first time I had seen her out of her room. Thammuz was at her right heel, the fawn at her left. The cats, Ashtaroth and Orus, had evidently stayed upstairs. "Would you like to ride Saturday?" she asked me.

Speechless, I nodded. She put her hand against the wall and a portion of it slid down into the earth so that Poor Little Saturday was free to go out. "She's sweet, isn't she?" the witch woman asked me, looking affectionately at the strange, bumpy-kneed, splay-footed creature. "Her grandmother was very good to me in Egypt once. Besides, I love camel's milk."

"But Alexandra said she was a he!" I exclaimed.

"Alexandra's the kind of woman to whom all animals are he except cats, and all cats are she. As a matter of fact, Ashtaroth and Orus are she, but it wouldn't make any difference to Alexandra if they weren't. Go on out, Saturday. Come on!"

Saturday backed out, bumping her bulging knees and ankles against her stall, and stood under a live oak tree. "Down," the witch woman said. Saturday leered at me and didn't move. "Down, *sorcabatcha!*" the witch woman commanded, and Saturday obediently got down on her knees. I clambered up onto her, and before I had managed to get at all settled she rose with such a jerky motion that I knocked my chin against her front hump and nearly bit my tongue off. Round and round Saturday danced while I clung wildly to her front hump and the witch woman and Alexandra rolled on the ground with laughter. I felt as though I were on a very unseaworthy vessel on the high seas, and it wasn't long before I felt violently seasick as Saturday pranced among the live oak trees, sneezing delicately.

At last the witch woman called out, "Enough!" and Saturday stopped in her traces, nearly throwing me, and knelt laboriously. "It was mean to tease you," the witch woman said, pulling my nose gently. "You may come sit in my room with me for a while if you like."

There was nothing I liked better than to sit in the witch woman's room and to watch her while she studied from her books, worked out strange-looking mathematical problems, argued with the zodiac, or conducted complicated experiments with her test tubes and retorts, sometimes filling the room with sulphurous odors or flooding it with red or blue light. Only once was I afraid of her, and that was when she danced with the skeleton in the corner. She had the room flooded with a strange red glow, and I almost thought I could see the flesh covering the bones of the skeleton as they danced together like lovers. I think she had forgotten that I was sitting there, half hidden in the wing chair, because when they had finished dancing and the skeleton stood in the corner again, his bones shining and polished, devoid of any living trappings, she stood with her forehead against one of the deep red velvet curtains that covered the boarded-up windows and tears streamed down her cheeks. Then she went back to her test tubes and worked feverishly. She never alluded to the incident and neither did I.

As winter drew on she let me spend more and more time in the room. Once I gathered up courage enough to ask her about herself, but I got precious little satisfaction.

"Well, then, are you maybe one of the northerners who bought the place?"

"Let's leave it at that, boy. We'll say that's who I am. Did you know that my skeleton was old Colonel Londermaine? Not so old, as a matter of fact; he was only thirty-seven when he was killed at the battle of Bunker Hill — or am I getting him confused with his great-grandfather, Rudolph Londermaine? Anyhow he was only thirty-seven, and a fine figure of a man, and Alexandra only thirty when she hung herself for love of him on the chandelier in the ballroom. Did you know that the fat man with the red mustache has been trying to cheat your father? His cow will give sour milk for seven days. Run along now and talk to Alexandra. She's lonely."

When the winter had turned to spring and the camellias and azaleas and Cape Jessamine had given way to the more lush blooms of early May, I kissed Alexandra for the first time, very clumsily. The next evening when I managed to get away from the chores at home and hurried out to the plantation, she gave me her sapphire and diamond ring, which she had strung for me on a narrow bit of turquoise satin.

"It will keep us both safe," she said, "if you wear it always. And then when we're older we can get married and you can give it back to me. Only you mustn't let anyone see it, ever, ever, or She'd be very angry."

I was afraid to take the ring but when I demurred Alexandra grew furious and started kicking and biting and I had to give in.

Summer was almost over before my father discovered the ring hanging about my neck. I fought like a witch boy to keep him from pulling out the narrow ribbon and seeing the ring, and indeed the ring seemed to give me added strength, and I had grown, in any case, much stronger during the winter than I had ever been in my life. But my father was still stronger than I, and he pulled it out. He looked at it in dead silence for a moment and then the storm broke. That was the famous Londermaine ring that had disappeared the night Alexandra Londermaine hung herself. That ring was worth a fortune. Where had I got it?

No one believed me when I said I had found it in the grounds near the house — I chose the grounds because I didn't want anybody to think I had been in the house or indeed that I was able to get in. I don't know why they didn't believe me; it still seems quite logical to me that I might have found it buried among the ferns.

It had been a long, dull year, and the men of the town were all bored. They took me and forced me to swallow quantities of corn liquor until I didn't know what I was saying or doing. When they had finished with me, I didn't even manage to reach home before I was violently sick and then I was in my mother's arms and she was weeping over me. It was morning before I was able to slip away to the plantation house. I ran pounding up the mahogany stairs to the witch woman's room and opened the heavy sliding doors without knocking. She stood in the center of the room in her purple robe, her arms around Alexandra, who was weeping bitterly. Overnight the room had completely changed. The skeleton of Colonel Londermaine was gone, and books filled the shelves in the corner of the room that had been her laboratory. Cobwebs were everywhere, and broken glass lay on the floor; dust was inches thick on her worktable. There was no sign of Thammuz, Ashtaroth or Orus, or the fawn, but four birds were flying about her, beating their wings against her hair.

She did not look at me or in any way acknowledge my presence. Her arm about Alexandra, she led her out of the room and to the drawing room where the portrait hung. The birds followed, flying around and around them. Alexandra had stopped weeping now. Her face was very proud and pale, and if she saw me miserably trailing behind them she gave no notice. When the witch woman stood in front of the portrait the sheet fell from it. She raised her arm; there was a great cloud of smoke; the smell of sulphur filled my nostrils, and when the smoke was gone, Alexandra was gone, too. Only the portrait was there, the fourth finger of the left hand now bearing no ring. The witch woman raised her hand again and the sheet lifted itself up and covered the portrait. Then she went, with the birds, slowly back to what had once been her room, and still I tailed after, frightened as I had never been before in my life, or have been since.

She stood without moving in the center of the room for a long time. At last she turned and spoke to me.

"Well, boy, where is the ring?"

"They have it."

"They made you drunk, didn't they?"

"Yes."

"I was afraid something like this would happen when I gave Alexandra the ring. But it doesn't matter… I'm tired…" She drew her hand wearily across her forehead.

"Did I—did I tell them everything?"

"You did."

"I—I didn't know."

"I know you didn't know, boy."

"Do you hate me now?"

"No, boy, I don't hate you."

"Do you have to go away?"

"Yes."

I bowed my head, "I'm so sorry..."

She smiled slightly. "The sands of time...cities crumble and rise and will crumble again and breath dies down and blows once more..."

The birds flew madly about her head, pulling at her hair, calling into her ears. Downstairs we could hear a loud pounding, and then the crack of boards being pulled away from a window.

"Go, boy," she said to me. I stood rooted, motionless, unable to move. "Go!" she commanded, giving me a mighty push so that I stumbled out of the room. They were waiting for me by the cellar doors and caught me as I climbed out. I had to stand there and watch when they came out with her. But it wasn't the witch woman, my witch woman. It was *their* idea of a witch woman, someone thousands of years old, a disheveled old creature in rusty black, with long wisps of gray hair, a hooked nose, and four wiry black hairs springing out of the mole on her chin. Behind her flew the four birds, and suddenly they went up, up, into the sky, directly in the path of the sun until they were lost in its burning glare.

Two of the men stood holding her tightly, although she wasn't struggling but standing there, very quiet, while the others searched the house, searched it in vain. Then as a group of them went down into the cellar I remembered, and by a flicker of the old light in the witch woman's eyes I could see that she remembered, too. Poor Little Saturday had been forgotten. Out she came, prancing absurdly up the cellar steps, her rubbery lips stretched back over her gigantic teeth, her eyes bulging with terror. When she saw the witch woman, her lord and master, held captive by two dirty, insensitive men, she let out a shriek and began to kick and lunge wildly, biting, screaming with the blood-curdling, heart-rending screams that only a camel can make. One of the men fell to the ground, holding a leg in which the bone had snapped from one of Saturday's kicks. The others scattered in terror, leaving the witch woman standing on the veranda supporting herself by clinging to one of the huge wisteria vines that curled around the columns. Saturday clambered up onto the veranda and knelt while she flung herself between the two humps. Then off they ran, Saturday still screaming, her knees knocking together, the ground shaking as she pounded along. Down from the sun plummeted the four birds and flew after them.

Up and down I danced, waving my arms, shouting wildly until Saturday and the witch woman and the birds were lost in a cloud of dust, while the man with the broken leg lay moaning on the ground beside me.

Afterword by Erica Friedman

If I were to ask you about a story you thought evocative, it is likely that you would reach for one that had resonated deeply with you when you read it. You would likely tell me of how you could still smell that smell, or remember the heat of the sun on your face on days like that. We call that feeling nostalgia.

When we turn towards speculative literature, we find ourselves imagining sensations we have never had or, in the case of science fiction, smells we will never smell and suns we will never feel. That phenomenon of creating these new sensations that we've never experienced, but somehow have felt, is called imagination.

What word can we use, then, for the feeling Madeleine L'Engle's "Poor Little Saturday" evokes in us? The time and place are not that long ago, and not that far away—we might be able to reach into our own childhoods for those feelings—but the setting is as alien, as fantastic as a distant planet. And while we might have had that—or some other similar—childhood, *these* experiences are not ones we could have had.

L'Engle's writing evokes nostalgic feelings for imaginary places and imaginary feelings for nostalgic places. Clearly we need a new word: Nostalginary

Although L'Engle was herself born in New York City, this story draws on years after her family had moved to Jacksonville, Florida, to be near her ill grandmother. Transferred from school to school, frequently at boarding schools where her creativity did not translate to good grades, she escaped into writing her fiction, as so many of us have escaped into reading it.

The world surrounding "Poor Little Saturday" in 1956 was as uncertain as ours is now. The time and place and sensations invoked in this story are the more personal experiences of a young person unsure if they have a future at all. No matter what portal of experience opens up in a story, *that* is surely something we can all resonate to. We may not have had *this* experience, but the smell of grass and warmth of the sun and feelings of fear and love and wonder always evoke our own similar experiences.

L'Engle's ability to tie all of these threads of experience and emotion together in a short story and still make it epic is exactly what has given generations of readers nostalginary experiences.

Written 6 years before *A Wrinkle in Time*, "Poor Little Saturday" has much of L'Engle's brand of magical realism that continues to enthrall readers today. And yet, just a few years after writing this story, L'Engle was ready to quit writing, her first novel having been rejected more than 30 times before being picked up for publication. But, of course, *Wrinkle* won her the Newberry Award in 1962...

...and the rest is history.

The Red Wagon
by Jane Roberts

(Originally appeared in the December 1956 issue of *The Magazine of Fantasy and Science Fiction*. It has been reprinted twice: in 1958 and 1975.)

Phillip lay in Peter's body, snuggled up with the teddy bear in the farthest corner of the bed. He lay muttering to himself in the darkness, urging Peter's baby tongue to enunciate words that he would not speak for years to come.

But Peter shivered and opened his eyes. He glanced about his room fearfully, only letting his head protrude from the warm covers. Then he relaxed. Everything was the same as before. He could make out the shape of the straight chair by his bed, the outline of the white enameled bureau, the box of toys in the corner.

Still, something woke him up. He wiggled about uncomfortably wondering if he was scared enough to go into his parents' room. Still considering, he sat up cautiously.

"For God's sake, go back to sleep," Phillip said.

Peter froze. He was only five years old but he knew that voices shouldn't speak without people. Still, it was a grown-up order, and children had to obey grownups. He thought about it for a second, then lay back down and closed his eyes.

But no one had said anything about obeying a grown-up voice with no one around. He waited, then opened his eyes slyly, one at a time. A voice can't spank, he reasoned, but he moved cautiously, just in case.

"Will you go to sleep?" Phillip groaned. He didn't want to frighten the boy, but nights *were* the only time he had to himself.

Peter cringed. The voice sounded awfully near. He looked around wildly — there just wasn't anyone. Trembling, he lay back in the darkness. Could it be a bogy-man? His heart jumped at the thought. No, he'd been a good boy all day yesterday, at least he thought he had. Still...

"Are you a bogy-man?" he whispered.

"No, I'm not a bogy-man," Phillip muttered, annoyed at the turn of events.

"Well, who are you then?"

Phillip sighed. A question and answer session with a child at this hour of the night! "I'm just...just Phillip," he said. "Now go to sleep."

Peter's tensed muscles relaxed just a bit. It was Somebody, then, he thought, relieved. But the voice sounded so very near. Suddenly he sat straight up in bed. Mommie says I talk in my sleep, he thought, I wonder...

"Phillip who?" Peter asked the question quickly, then slammed both hands down hard on his mouth.

"*Mumph*!"

Phillip cursed and sputtered, noticing the sudden action too late. But Peter giggled. Here he was scared and it was himself all along. He touched his lips wonderingly. It was like having a playmate inside.

He looked about the room again, this time more confidently. Yes. Everything was the same. Except for the bed, he thought, feeling funny again. It wasn't too long ago that the crib had been taken away. A crib! He'd had enough children to know what they were for! — There. He'd thought something crazy again. If Mommie knew, he would get a spanking.

Peter sucked his lip. It was *so* true, he brooded. He'd had two children by Jeannie. Frowning, he shook his head. That was silly. Girls were sissies, everyone knew that. He thought back. Well, what had he meant, then? he wondered. But Phillip pulled the thought away from him in panic. Peter's eyes finally began to close. Only babies played with girls, he thought sleepily. Everyone knew that.

Phillip sighed. The boy was asleep at last. He waited a moment to make sure, then stimulated the optic nerve and stared through Peter's eyes at the quiet child's room. My god, he'd win this time. He'd win no matter what.

He was a nice boy, Phillip mused, this boy he had become. But that was beside the point. It's not that I mind being a child, he told himself for the hundredth time, it's just that I want to retain awareness of myself. Suddenly the thought of Peter filled him with loathing. It was so ridiculous to let a child's mentality supersede his own experienced mind.

And how ironical — he could think with his mind unimpaired, and had to speak with the high-pitched, stuttering voice of a five-year-old. And frightening! More than once Phillip had caught himself thinking in the boy's limited vocabulary. That, he knew, was the first danger signal, the first hint of vanishing identity.

He stared defiantly at the silent room, at the toy box and the teddy bear.

This time, he told them, this time things will be different! I'm aware of the pit-falls now, and I'll guard myself carefully. This time, he told them, there will be no steady deterioration of mv memories, no insidious infiltration of the child's personality. *Do you hear me?* he whispered. *This time you won't have a chance!*

But it was morning. Peter woke up and ran to the window. It was sunny. He would get out his old cart. He would even let Loren play, if Mommie didn't find out. She said Loren told lies.

"Loren tells lies, Loren tells lies." Chanting merrily, he found his socks and tried to put them on.

"Must you act like such an idiot?" The words were out before Phillip could stop himself. He had to stop this sort of thing, he thought. The boy would be a nervous wreck.

Peter dropped his socks. There. He'd heard it again. Idiot. Idiot. He ran into his parents' room, forgetting his shoes and socks.

"Mama," he demanded, "What's an idiot?"

"An idiot is a dumb boy and you are a dumb boy for waking me up at six o'clock in the morning. Go to bed."

Peter held his ground until his mother's slim finger pointed to the door. She's a beauty all right, Phillip thought.

"You're a beauty," Peter said, with sudden inspiration.

His mother's eyes widened and she laughed. "Where did you ever pick that up?" she asked. "You're as bad as your father." But Peter grinned because he knew his mother was pleased. He kissed her and tiptoed to the door, closing it softly behind him.

Phillip smiled to himself; but remembering his own problems, he immediately grew sober, realizing again that he had to find a way to keep his own thoughts away from Peter. He sighed, frightened at the irascibility of his own mood. Twice that week he had grown so horrified at the antics he was forced to endure that he had overwhelmed Peter completely, thrown aside the toys in rage, and sent the teddy bear flying across the room. The tantrum alarmed him all the more because he was aware of the danger of such childishness.

The thread of thought broken for the moment, he watched Peter lift out his assortment of trains from the toy box. He noticed with perverse satisfaction the slight tremble in the boy's hand as he lifted the last car to the small track, and forced the childish face into an adult grimace.

If Peter was too young to understand, at least he was also too young to explain matters to his parents, Phillip thought, recalling the boy's last attempt to tell them.

"Mommie," Peter had said, "I'm a big boy, really."

And his mother smiled, brushed back the hair from his forehead. "Of course you are, darling." And Peter had felt such relief because he thought she understood.

But this isn't getting me anywhere. Phillip clenched his fists. *If only I had someone to talk to, some place to write my own ideas*—He stopped suddenly, amazed at the simplicity of the plan that spontaneously made itself clear. And late that night, while Peter slept, Phillip wrote the first entry of the journal that he hoped would preserve his sanity.

April 8—I have finally decided to keep a journal. Although I had thought of the idea before, the obstacles to its fulfillment seemed to render it impractical. Everything considered, however, I feel that the invaluable fruits of such an action more than justify any possible exposure, especially since I have taken steps which render such an event unlikely. And already I feel so much better. It seems so good to use my vocabulary again, to speak, even on paper, in the older accustomed manner.

I do not believe there is any doubt that this manuscript will one day be acclaimed as the only testament of the first human being who proved the disputed theory of reincarnation. Peter and I shall be famous!

Meet it is I set it down, as the tormented Dane justly observes. One must have documentary evidence to confound the materialistic skeptics and the credulous followers of narrow superstitious dogmas, to demonstrate to them what such a man as I can achieve in the way of proof.

For I know too well how all knowledge of past existences is forgotten in the process of new growth, as the old personality merges with the new.

In that—what shall one call it? that time? that space? that life?—in that which exists between existences, I have been aware that I have briefly conquered this law of forgetfulness. I have managed, by severe determination, to maintain my knowledge and memory at the beginning of each succeeding incarnation…but even I have been so irresistibly drawn to my new personality that by the age of four or five I have forgotten all else.

This time, however, I shall triumph; and the world shall know to whom it owes this vindication of the despised truth.

Immediately on discovering my rebirth as Peter, I set up a plan of action which is designed to assure continued awareness of my self. This plan consists in fighting my own inertia, imposing my will upon Peter's, and refusing, yes refusing, to let his interests touch my own at all. In other words I shall maintain distinct separateness. My enthusiasm for this plan knows no bounds.

The mechanics involved in writing the journal are fairly simple. (I must remember to include all, so that any suspicion of fraud in the future is impossible.) I bide my time until Peter is asleep, then, operating the muscles of his body much as one would manipulate the metal mechanism of a robot, I proceed with due caution to the other side of the room, turn on the small night light and begin work. The toy box serves me as a table. Peter's height makes any other piece of furniture inaccessible. It may surprise you that the boy does not waken, but I have found that while he is sleeping, my control over him is quite complete.

I decided, very cleverly, to write with lemon juice. The script disappears immediately, as you know, and should the parents ever enter the room, they would merely think the boy had walked in his sleep. Is it any wonder I am jubilant over my little plan?

April 9 — You have no idea of the problems that confront one in such a position as mine! I must have an audience, someone I can talk to, or I fear for my sanity. The journal is a help, but without any verbal communication I fear I will grow to doubt my own existence. My words here evaporate as quickly as I write them till I imagine that I only dream. And I must do something with Peter. *He must be aware of me as a person!* I exercise my memory daily to further compliment my own ego, but there is *just no one to talk to.*

April 11 — Without bragging, I must say that sometimes my ingenuity seems boundless. I hit on a most marvelous plan today — I have become Peter's imaginary companion. I talk to him regularly now, and his parents merely suppose that the boy has fallen prey to one of those amusing childish foibles of which one frequently hears. Indeed, it is not unusual for children to conjure up such imagined playmates. Note for thought: have others, also, discovered the true nature of things, and hit upon this very same plan? If so, what was their fate?

April 13 — I spent all afternoon playing with trains — of all things. Since trains never interested me — except for a slight curiosity with their wheels — I was in no danger; still it was not a good idea. Peter can be a most annoying little monster, however. He insisted on visiting some of his playmates today, a venture of which I strongly disapproved. I cannot, at this time, risk any unwarranted outside influence, and an argument ensued until he finally agreed to stay home in return for my promise to play trains. You can imagine my pique.

April 19 — It is hard to find time to write now — Peter keeps me so busy. His father took us to the lake today, and my mind was alive with nostalgic memories of similar incidents in past lives. But my struggle is so fatiguing, and there was something in father's voice that aroused in me the deepest panic! There is a small incident that frightened me considerably:

I must have said something earlier in the day to startle Peter, for his mind was worried. It was while we stood by the lake that he looked up at his father and asked him if his name was really Peter. His father, amused at the earnestness of the boy's face, laughed and assured him that such was the case. My heart sank within me. Here, for the first time, Peter began to get a hint that he and I were one, and the father, by his jesting manner, made Peter feel that it was ridiculous to suppose he was anyone else—but that he was Peter and Peter alone.

But the worst part is that I myself was almost convinced, if only for a brief moment! It was then that I heard in my mind the same reasonable tone of countless other parents who had made me forget. This sort of insidiousness must be guarded against. It is not to be borne! *I shall forget nothing.*

April 20—Father has promised—Peter's father, I mean, has promised the boy a new cart for his birthday and Peter is already annoying me with demands that I pull it for him when it arrives! Can you imagine a more ludicrous situation—a man of my learning involved in pulling a child's wagon around the block! The results of such foolhardiness could be disastrous were I so inclined—which, I assure you, I am not. The fact is, I am resolved to use the greatest caution when the cart arrives, since the smallest pull in my character toward such things can be dangerous—and as a child I was always fascinated by wheeled toys. It seems that a set of child's books would be a more appropriate gift for the boy in any case.

April 22—Peter grows impatient to visit his playmates, and with such fine weather setting in, I am afraid I shall have to give in. I dislike the prospect of spending hours at a time with a group of youngsters, but I fear even more the impending birthday party and the presentation of the wagon. Peter will be six, however, and this also adds to the burden of my thoughts, since I have never maintained control this long before. I consider this an achievement...and I find myself filled with doubts.

April 29—Do you know, I forgot the journal completely? My days have been so fully spent that at night I am too exhausted to do anything but sleep. Tonight, however, after tossing restlessly and falling into an uneasy slumber, I awoke suddenly, bathed in a cold sweat. Peter was dreaming—or rather *I had become Peter* and my mind had been dreaming *Peter's dream.* Imagine my terror! In the dream I was playing happily in front of the house with Peter's new wagon. I wrenched myself away from the image, and rushed to the journal. After writing I feel somewhat more calm.

May 10—Today Mommie took us to the circus, and I was unaccountably excited by the carnival atmosphere, the carousels, the many-costumed populace. In fact, I was quite thrilled by the unusual activity. I imagine that the event reminded me of other such amusements in other lives, though at the present I can think of none. My struggle takes so much of my energy that I find that many details quite escape me.

May 22 — Yesterday we didn't do nothing. I mean — Yesterday we didn't do anything. *Why, oh why am I so weary?* Why is it so difficult to construct a simple sentence? I think I need rest.

May 28 — I forgot the jornel intierly. But its spring and we got so much to do. Theres a bunch of us that play and I stay up later cause it dont get dark so soon. And I tell the kids about the wagen Im gona get.

May 29 — God help me! I just read my last entry and the terror that filled me as I realized its significance was almost too much to bear. I might never have realized what had happened had my mood not been so black this evening that I felt an overwhelming desire to seek relief by reading some of the words that I myself had written. My hand trembled as I held the paper up to the light, and then to see those tragic words leap up at me… Perhaps the crisis is past now. I shall take the greatest care from now on. And I will reread each entry.

June 3 — Peter continually nags me to find out if he really will get a new wagon. Finally in anger I told him that I hoped he never got one, and that if he did, I never wanted to see it. He immediately burst into tears. Perhaps I was too severe, but this foolish toy has gained some evil significance for me and I think of it only with dread. Peter's thoughts are filled with nothing else and I turn my own mind away only by the strongest exercise of my will power.

June 7 — It was intolerably warm today. We played outside with no sweaters. I mean Peter did.

June 10 — Odd that I resented Peter's getting a wagon. Actually I have always been partial to them myself, and look forward to his receiving it.

June 13 — I am so weery. Sometimes I am chased by doubts but I read over what I wrote and don't see anything wrong. What is it I have forgot?

June 14 — My birthday is soon. I should be glad. I will be six. Wrong. Peter will. I am afraid. Maybe cause so many grownups will come. They chase boys with wagens.

June 16 — The party is day after tomorro. I don't want to go. Mommie says I have to. I do so want to go.

June 17 — I'm dreaming I guess cause Im riting and I cant yet. I can print tho. I print my name good but its hard to make letters. I didn't want to get out of bed but something made me. I got back but it made me get up agin. I heer somebody cry but I don't see nobody. My hands is tired.

J$_U$Ne 18 — — I goT *a* ReD wageN. It is ReD. peTeR

Afterword by Kathryn Heffner

Jane Roberts is perhaps best remembered as a spirit channeler and populariser of new age mysticism. Yet, before contacting the spirit entity known as 'Seth' and publishing 16 titles (selling over 7.5 million books!) in her series on ESP, Roberts began her career writing short fiction and poetry. Awarded a writing scholarship to Skidmore College, Roberts published her prose in small poetry presses before trying her hand at science fiction. In the summer of 1956, she was the first woman who was invited to the Milford Writer's Conference, organized by SF giants Damon Knight, James Blish, and Judith Merril. Only a handful of months later, Roberts submitted her short story 'The Red Wagon' to *The Magazine of Fantasy and Science Fiction*.

The 'Red Wagon' explores the dilemmas of dual and dissimilar consciousness within a young child, in a way adapting the science fiction trope of the hyper-intelligent being—but in this case, the brain is at odds with itself! Throughout the short story, the rationality of the elder Phillip confronts the emotionalism and sentimentality of the young Peter. Roberts works to explore the nature of the psyche through the supernatural and scientific, as we watch Phillip lose all agency to the strong consciousness of the child.

Fundamental to the story is its epistolary presentation. While Peter sleeps at night, Phillip uses a journal to document his experiences sharing consciousness with the child. As the adult Phillip recoils from his inability to intellectualize while inhabiting Peter the child, he also experiences cognitive decline. These journal entries document Phillip's dwindling agency, as the child Peter's simple fascinations with the world overtake Phillip's adult observations. The story's conclusion, with the last journal entry a misspelled and grammatically incorrect sentence, provides an eerie climax. Is Phillip gone? Has his personality fused with Peter's? The end is thought-provokingly ambiguous and bittersweet.

Just three years after the publication of 'The Red Wagon', *The Magazine of Fantasy and Science Fiction* published another story in a format similar to the one Jane Roberts pioneered. Most adults today remember reading 'Flowers for Algernon', with its poignant story of Charlie Gordon's cognitive rise and fall.

Resonances with Robert's work appear in both style and theme, the most dramatic similarity being the way the story ends: Charlie Gordon's final progress report is a few sentences riddled with spelling and grammatical errors, suggesting that he has returned to the mental capacity at which he began.

Although Roberts' story depicts a decline while Keyes' story is about the rise and decline of a man's mind, the device used in both—journal entries contrasting eloquent thoughts against imperfect and childish constructions—is notably similar. Keyes' story may have refined the stylistic technique, but Roberts' piece is the inarguable predecessor, and perhaps even provided inspiration for Keyes' seminal work.

Channeling of a spirit, indeed!

The Queer Ones
by Leigh Brackett

(Originally appeared in the March 1957 issue of *Venture*. It was reprinted in in a hardcover-only edition in 2011; before that, it was most recently reprinted in 1986.)

I ran down Buckhorn Mountain in the cloud and rain, carrying the boy in my arms. The green lightning flashed among the trees. Buckhorn is no stranger to lightning, but this was different. It did not come from the clouds, and there was no thunder with it. It ran low, searching the thickets, the brush-choked gullies, the wet hollows full of brambles and poison ivy. Thick green hungry snakes looking for something. Looking for me.

Looking for the boy who had started it all.

He peered up at me, clinging like a lemur to my coat as I went headlong down the slope. His eyes were copper-colored. They had seen a lot for all the two-and-a-half years they had been open on this world. They were frightened now, not just vaguely as you might expect from a child his age, but intelligently. And in his curiously sweet shrill voice he asked:

"Why mus' they kill us?"

"Never mind," I said, and ran and ran, and the green lightning hunted us down the mountainside.

It was Doc Callendar, the County Health Officer, who got me in on the whole thing. I am Hank Temple, owner, editor, feature writer, legman, and general roustabout of the *Newhale News*, serving Newhale and the rural and mountain areas around it. Doc Callendar, Sheriff Ed Betts and I are old friends, and we work together, helping out where we can. So one hot morning in July my phone rang and it was Doc, sounding kind of dazed.

"Hank?" he said. "I'm at the hospital. Would you want to take a run up here for a minute?"

"Who's hurt?"

"Nobody. Just thought something might interest you."

Doc was being cagey because anything you say over the phone in Newhale is public property. But even so the tone of his voice put prickles between my shoulder blades. It didn't sound like Doc at all

"Sure," I said. "Right away."

Newhale is the county seat, a small town, and a high town. It lies in an upland hollow of the Appalachians, a little clutter of old red brick buildings with porches on thin wooden pillars, and frame houses ranging from new white to weathered silver-gray, centered around the dumpy courthouse. A very noisy stream bisects the town. The tannery and the feed-mill are its chief industries, with some mining nearby. The high-line comes down a neat cut on Tunkhannock Ridge to the east and goes away up a neat cut on Goat Hill to the west. Over all towers the rough impressive hump of Buckhorn Mountain, green on the ridges, shadowed blue in the folds, wrapped more often than not in a mist of cloud.

There is not much money nor any great fame to be made in Newhale, but there are other reasons for living here. The girl I wanted to marry couldn't quite see them, and it's hard to explain to a woman why you would rather have six pages of small-town newspaper that belong to you than the whole of the *New York Times* if you only work for it. I gave up trying, and she went off to marry a gray flannel suit, and every time I unlimber my fishing rod or my deer rifle I'm happy for her.

The hospital is larger than you might expect, since it serves a big part of the county. Sitting on a spur of Goat Hill well away from the tannery, it's an old building with a couple of new wings tacked on. I found Doc Callendar in his office, with Bossert. Bossert is the resident doctor, a young guy who knows more, in the old phrase, than a jackass could haul downhill. This morning he looked as though he wasn't sure of his own name.

"Yesterday," Doc said, "one of the Tate girls brought her kid in, a little boy. I wasn't here, I was out testing those wells up by Pinecrest. But I've seen him before. He's a stand-out, a real handsome youngster."

"Precocious," said Jim Bossert nervously. "Very precocious for his age. Physically, too. Coordination and musculature well developed. And his coloring—"

"What about it?" I asked.

"Odd. I don't know. I noticed it, and then forgot it. The kid looked as though he'd been through a meat-grinder. His mother said the other kids had ganged up and beaten him, and he hadn't been right for several days, so she reckoned she'd better bring him in. She's not much more than nineteen herself. I took some X-rays—"

Bossert picked up a couple of pictures from the desk and shoved them at me. His hands shook, making the stiff films rattle together.

"I didn't want to trust myself on these. I waited until Callendar could check them, too."

I held the pictures up and looked at them. They showed a small, frail bony structure and the usual shadowy outline of internal organs. It wasn't until I had looked at them for several minutes that I began to realize there was something peculiar about them. There seemed to be too few ribs, the articulation of the joints looked queer even to my layman's eyes, and the organs themselves were a hopeless jumble.

"Some of the innards," said Doc, "we can't figure out at all. There are organs we've never seen nor heard of before."

"Yet the child seems normal and perfectly healthy," said Bossert. "Remarkably so. From the beating he'd taken he should have had serious injuries. He was just sore. His body must be as flexible and tough as spring steel."

I put the X-rays back on the desk. "Isn't there quite a large literature on medical anomalies?"

"Oh, yes," said Doc. "Double hearts, upside-down stomachs, extra arms, legs, heads—almost any distortion or variation you can think of. But not like this." He leaned over and tapped his finger emphatically on the films. "This isn't a distortion of anything. This is *different*. And that's not all."

He pushed a microscope slide toward me.

"That's the capper, Hank. Blood sample. Jim tried to type it. I tried to type it. We couldn't. There isn't any such type."

I stared at them. Their faces were flushed, their eyes were bright, they quivered with excitement, and suddenly it got to me too.

"Wait a minute," I said. "Are you trying to tell me—"

"We've got something here," said Doc Callendar. "Something—" He shook his head. I could see the dreams in it. I could see Callendar standing ten feet tall on a pedestal of medical journals. I could see him on podiums addressing audiences of breathless men, and the same dreams were in Bossert's eyes.

I had my own. The *Newhale News* suddenly a famous name on the wire-services, and one Henry Temple bowing with modest dignity as he accepted the Pulitzer Prize for journalism.

"Big," said Bossert softly. "The boy is more than a freak. He's something new. A mutation. Almost a new species. The blood-type alone—"

Something occurred to me and I cut him short. "Listen," I said. "Listen, are you sure you didn't make a mistake or something? How could the boy's blood be so different from his mother's?" I hunted for the word. "Incompatibility. He'd never have been born."

"Nevertheless," said Doc Callendar mildly, "he was born. And nevertheless, there is no such blood-type. We've run tests backward and forward, together and independently. Kindly allow us to know what we're talking about, Hank. The boy's blood obviously must have been compatible with his mother's. Possibly it's a more advanced Type O, universally compatible. This is only one of the many things we have to study and evaluate."

He picked up the X-ray films again and looked at them, with an expression of holy ecstasy in his eyes.

I lighted another cigarette. My hands were shaking now, like theirs. I leaned forward.

"Okay," I said. "What's the first thing we do?"

Doc's station wagon, with COUNTY HEALTH SERVICE painted on its side, slewed and snorted around the turns of the steep dirt road. Jim Bossert had had to stay at the hospital, but I was sitting beside Doc, hunched forward in a sweat of impatience. The road ran up around the shoulder of Tunkhannock Ridge. We had thick dark woods on our right going up, and thick dark woods on our left going down. Buckhorn hung in the north like a curtain across the sky.

"We'll have to be careful," Doc was saying. "I know these people pretty well. If they get the idea we're trying to pull something, we'll never get another look at the kid."

"You handle it," I said. "And by the way, nobody's mentioned the boy's father. Doesn't he have one?"

"Do you know the Tate girls?"

"No. I've been through Possum Creek all right, but through it is all."

"You must have gone fast," said Doc, grinning. "The answer is physiologically yes, legally are you kidding?" He shifted into second, taking it easy over a place where the road was washed and gullied. "They're not a bad bunch of girls at that, though," he added reflectively. "I kind of like them. Couple of them are downright married."

We bucketed on through the hot green shadows, the great centers of civilization like Newhale forgotten in the distance behind us, and finally in a remote pocket just under Tunkhannock's crest we came upon a few lean spry cattle, and then the settlement of Possum Creek.

There were four ancient houses straggled out along the side of the stream. One of them said GENERAL STORE and had a gas pump in front of it. Two old men sat on the step.

Doc kept on going. "The Tates," he said, straight-faced, "live out a little from the center of town."

Two more turns of the road, which was now only a double-rutted track, brought us to a rural mailbox which said TATE. The house behind it was pretty well run down, but there was glass in most of the windows and only half the bricks were gone from the chimney. The clapboards were sort of a rusty brown, patched up with odds and ends of tarpaper. A woman was washing clothes in an old galvanized tub set on a stand in the side yard. There was a television aerial tied on cockeyed to the gable of the house. There was a sow with a litter in a pen right handy to the door, and a little way at the back was a barn with the ridge-pole swayed like an old horse. A tarpaper shack and a battered house-trailer were visible among the trees — probably the homes of the married daughters. An ancient man sat in an ancient rocking chair on the porch and peered at us, and an ancient dog beside him rose up heavily and barked.

I've known quite a lot of families like the Tates. They scratch out enough corn for their pigs and their still-houses, and enough garden for themselves. The young men make most of their money as guides during hunting season, and the old men make theirs selling moonshine. They have electricity now, and they can afford radios and even television sets. City folks call them lazy and shiftless. Actually, they find the simple life so pleasant that they hate to let hard work spoil their enjoyment of it.

Doc drove his station wagon into the yard and stopped. Instantly there was an explosion of dogs and children and people.

"There he is," Doc said to me, under cover of the whooping and woofing and the banging of screen doors. "The skinny little chap with the red hair. There, just coming down the steps."

I looked over and saw the boy.

He was an odd one, all right. The rest of the Tate tribe all had straight hair ranging from light brown to honey-blond. His was close and curly to his head and I saw what Jim Bossert had meant about his coloring. The red had undertones of something else in it. One would almost, in that glare of sunlight, have said silver. The Tates had blue eyes. His were copper-colored. The Tates were fair and sunburned, and so was he, but there was a different quality of fairness to his skin, a different shading to the tan.

He was a little boy. The Tate children were rangy and big boned. He moved among them lightly, a gazelle among young goats, with a totally unchildlike grace and sureness. His head was narrow, with a very high arch to the skull. His eyes were grave, precociously wise. Only in the mouth was there genuine childishness, soft and shy.

We got out of the car. The kids — a dozen of them, give or take a couple — all stopped as though on a signal and began to study their bare feet. The woman came from the washtub, wiping her hands on her skirt. Several others came out of the house.

The little boy remained at the foot of the steps. His hand was now in the hand of a buxom girl. Judging by Bossert's description, this would be his mother. Not much over nineteen, handsome, big-breasted, full-hipped. She was dressed in tight jeans and a boy's shirt, her bare feet stuck into sandals, and a hank of yellow hair hung down her back.

Doc spoke to them all, introducing me as a friend from town. They were courteous, but reserved. "I want to talk to Sally," he said, and we moved closer to the steps. I tried not to look at the boy lest the glitter in my eye give me away. Doc was being so casual and hearty it hurt. I could feel a curious little prickle run over my skin as I got close to the child.

It was partly excitement, partly the feeling that here was a being different from myself, another species. There was a dark bruise on the child's forehead, and I remembered that the others had beaten him. Was this *otherness* at the bottom of their resentment? Did they sense it without the need for blood samples and X-rays?

Mutant. A strange word. A stranger thing to come upon here in these friendly familiar hills. The child stared at me, and the July sun turned cold on my back.

Doc spoke to Sally, and she smiled. She had an honest, friendly smile. Her mouth was wide and full, frankly sensuous but without coquetry. She had big blue eyes, and her sunburned cheeks were flushed with health, and she looked as uncomplicated and warmly attractive as a summer meadow. I wondered what strange freak of genetics had made her the fountainhead of a totally new race.

Doc said, "Is this the little boy you brought in to the hospital?"

"Yes," she said. "But he's better now."

Doc bent over and spoke to the boy. "Well," he said. "And what's your name, young man?"

"Name's Billy," he answered, in a grave sweet treble that had a sound in it of bells being rung far off. "Billy Tate."

The woman who had come from the washtub said with unconcealed dislike, "He ain't no Tate, whatever he might be."

She had been introduced as Mrs. Tate, and was obviously the mother and grandmother of this numerous brood. She had lost most of her teeth and her gray-blonde hair stood out around her head in an untidy brush. Doc ignored her.

"How do you do, Billy Tate," he said. "And where did you get that pretty red hair?"

"From his daddy," said Mrs. Tate sharply. "Same place he got his sneaky-footed ways and them yellow eyes like a bad hound. I tell you, Doctor, if you see a man looks just like that child, you tell him to come back and get what belongs to him!"

A corny but perfectly fitting counterpoint to her words, thunder crashed on Buckhorn's cloudy crest, like the ominous laughter of a god.

Sally reached down suddenly and caught up the boy into her arms…

The thunder quivered and died on the hot air. I stared at Doc and he stared at me, and Sally Tate screamed at her mother.

"You keep your dirty mouth off my baby!"

"That ain't no way to talk to Maw," said one of the older girls. "And anyway, she's right."

"Oh," said Sally. "You think so, do you?" She turned to Doc, her cheeks all white now and her eyes blazing. "They set their young ones on my baby, Doctor, and you know why? They're jealous. They're just sick to their stomachs with it, because they all got big hunkety kids that can't do nothin' but eat, and big hunkety men that treat them like they was no better'n brood sows."

She had reached her peak of fury so quickly that it was obvious this row had been going on for a long while, probably ever since the child was born.

Possibly even before, judging by what she said then.

"Jealous," she said to her sisters, showing her teeth. "Every last one of you was dancing up and down to catch his eye, but it was me he took to the hayloft. *Me*. And if he ever comes back he can have me again, for as often and as long as he wants me. And I won't hear no ill of him nor the baby!"

I heard all this. I understood it. But not with all, or even most of my mind. That was busy with another thing, a thing it didn't want to grapple with at all and kept shying away from, only to be driven back shivering.

Doc put it into words.

"You mean," he said, to no one in particular, "the boy looks just like his father?"

"Spit an' image," said Sally fondly, kissing the red curls that had that queer glint of silver in them. "Sure would like to see that man again, I don't care what they say. Doctor, I tell you, he was beautiful."

"Handsome is as handsome does," said Mrs. Tate. "He was no good, and I knew it the minute I saw —"

"Why, Maw," said Mr. Tate, "he had you eating out of his hand, with them nicey ways of his." He turned to Doc Callendar, laughing. "She'd a' gone off to the hayloft with him herself if he'd asked her, and that's a fact. Ain't it, Harry?"

Harry said it was, and they all laughed.

Mrs. Tate said furiously, "It'd become you men better to do something about getting some support for that brat from its father, instead of making fool jokes in front of strangers."

"Seems like, when you bring it up," said Mr. Tate, "it would become us all not to wash our dirty linen for people who aren't rightly concerned." He said courteously to Doc, "Reckon you had a reason for coming here. Is there something I can do?"

"Well—" said Doc uncertainly, and looked at the boy. "Just like his father, you say."

And if that is so, I thought, *how can he be a mutant? A mutant is something new, something different, alien from the parent stem. If he is the spit an' image outside, then build and coloring bred true. And if build and coloring bred true, probably blood-type and internal organs —*

Thunder boomed again on Buckhorn Mountain. And I thought, *Well, and so his father is a mutant, too.*

But Doc said, "Who was this man, Sally? I know just about everybody in these hills, but I never saw anyone to answer that description."

"His name was Bill," she said, "just like the boy's. His other name was Jones. Or he said it was."

"He lied," said Mrs. Tate. "Wasn't Jones no more than mine is. We found that out."

"How did he happen to come here?" asked Doc. "Where did he say he was from?"

"He come here," Mrs. Tate said, "driving a truck for some appliance store, Grover's I think it was, in Newhale. Said the place was just new and was making a survey of teevees around here, and offering free service on them up to five dollars, just for goodwill. So I let him look at ours, and he fussed with it for almost an hour, and didn't charge me a cent. Worked real good afterward, too. That would 'a been the end of it, I guess, only Sally was under his feet all the time and he took a shine to her. Kept coming back, and coming back, and you see what happened."

I said, "There isn't any Grover's store in Newhale. There never has been."

"We found that out," said Mrs. Tate. "When we knew the baby was coming we tried to find Mr. Jones, but it seems he'd told us a big pack of lies."

"He told me," Sally said dreamily, "where he come from."

Doc said eagerly, "Where?"

Twisting her mouth to shape the unfamiliar sounds, Sally said, "Hryl-liannu."

Doc's eyes opened wide. "Where the hell is that?"

"Ain't no place," said Mrs. Tate. "Even the schoolteacher couldn't find it in the atlas. It's only another of his lies."

But Sally murmured again, "Hrylliannu. Way he said it, it sounded like the most beautiful place in the world."

The stormcloud over Buckhorn was spreading out. Its edges dimmed the sun. Lightning flicked and flared and the thunder rolled. I said, "Could I take a look at your television?"

"Why," said Mrs. Tate, "I guess so. But don't you disturb it, now. Whatever else he done, he fixed that teevee good."

"I won't disturb it," I said. I went up the sagging steps past the old man and the fat old dog. I went into the cluttered living room, where the springs were coming out of the sofa and there was no rug on the floor, and six kids apparently slept in the old brass bed in the corner. The television set was maybe four years old, but it was the best and biggest made that year. It formed a sort of shrine at one end of the room, with a piece of red cloth laid over its top.

I took the back off and looked in. I don't know what I expected to see. It just seemed odd to me that a man would go to all the trouble of faking up a truck and tinkering with television sets for nothing. And apparently he hadn't. What I did see I didn't understand, but even to my inexpert eye it was obvious that Mr. Jones had done something quite peculiar to the wiring inside.

A totally unfamiliar component roosted on the side of the case, a little gadget not much bigger than my two thumbnails.

I replaced the back and turned the set on. As Mrs. Tate said, it worked real good. Better than it had any business to. I got a peculiar hunch that Mr. Jones had planned it that way, so that no other serviceman would have to be called. I got the hunch that that component was important somehow to Mr. Jones.

I wondered how many other such components he had put in television sets in this area, and what they were for.

I turned off the set and went outside. Doc was still talking to Sally.

"...some further tests he wants to make," I heard him say. "I can take you and Billy back right now..."

Sally looked doubtful and was about to speak. But the decision was made for her. The boy cried out wildly, "No! No!" With the frantic strength of a young animal he twisted out of his mother's arms, dropped to the ground, and sped away into the brush so swiftly that nobody had a chance even to grab for him.

Sally smiled. "All them shiny machines and the funny smells frightened him," she said. "He don't want to go back. Isn't anything wrong with him, is there? The other doctor said he was all right."

"No," said Doc reluctantly. "Just something about the X-rays he wanted to check on. It could be important for the future. Tell you what, Sally. You talk to the boy, and I'll come back in a day or two."

"Well," she said. "All right."

Doc hesitated, and then said, "Would you want me to speak to the sheriff about finding this man? If that's his child he should pay something for its support."

A wistful look came into her eyes. "I always thought maybe if he knew about the baby —"

Mrs. Tate didn't give her time to finish. "Yes, indeed," she said. "You speak to the sheriff. Time somebody did something about this, 'fore that brat's a man grown himself."

"Well," said Doc, "we can try."

He gave a last baffled glance at the woods where the boy had disappeared, and then we said goodbye and got into the station wagon and drove away. The sky was dark overhead now, and the air was heavy with the smell of rain.

"What do you think?" I said finally.

Doc shook his head. "I'm damned if I know. Apparently the external characteristics bred true. If the others did —"

"Then the father must be a mutant too. We just push it back one generation."

"That's the simplest explanation," Doc said.

"Is there any other?"

Doc didn't answer that. We passed through Possum Creek, and it began to rain.

"What about the television set?" he asked.

I told him. "But you'd have to have Jud or one of the boys from Newhale Appliance look at it, to say what it was."

"It smells," said Doc. "It stinks, right out loud."

The bolt of lightning came so quickly and hit so close that I wasn't conscious of anything but a great flare of livid green. Doc yelled. The station wagon slewed on the road that now had a thin film of mud over it, and I saw trees rushing at us, their tops bent by a sudden wind so that they seemed to be literally leaping forward. There was no thunder. I remembered that, I don't know why.

The station wagon tipped over and hit the trees. There was a crash. The door flew open and I fell out through a wet whipping tangle of branches and on down to the steep-tilted ground below. I kept on falling, right down the slope, until a gully pocket caught and held me. I lay there dazed, staring up at the station wagon that now hung over my head. I saw Doc's legs come out of it, out the open door. He was all right. He was letting himself down to the ground. And then the lightning came again.

It swallowed the station wagon and the trees and Doc in a ball of green fire, and when it went away the trees were scorched and the paint was blistered on the wrecked car, and Doc was rolling over and over down the slope, very slowly, as if he was tired and did not want to hurry.

He came to rest not three feet away from me. His hair and his clothes were smoldering, but he wasn't worrying about it. He wasn't worrying about anything, any more. And for the second time there had not been any thunder, close at hand where the lightning was.

The rain came down on Doc in heavy sheets, and put the smoldering fire out.

Jim Bossert had just come from posting Doc Callendar's body. For the first time I found myself almost liking him, he looked so sick and beat-out. I pushed the bottle toward him, and he drank out of it and then lighted a cigarette and just sat there shaking.

"It was lightning," he said. "No doubt at all."

Ed Betts, the sheriff, said, "Hank still insists there was something screwy about it."

Bossert shook his head at me. "Lightning."

"Or a heavy electric charge," I said. "That comes to the same thing, doesn't it?"

"But you saw it hit, Hank."

"Twice," I said. "Twice."

We were in Bossert's office at the hospital. It was late in the afternoon, getting on for supper time. I reached for the bottle again, and Ed said quietly,

"Lightning does do that, you know. In spite of the old saying."

"The first time, it missed," I said. "Just. Second time it didn't. If I hadn't been thrown clear I'd be dead too. And there wasn't any thunder."

"You were dazed," Bossert said. "The first shock stunned you."

"It was green," I said.

"Fireballs often are."

"But not lightning."

"Atmospheric freak." Ed turned to Jim Bossert. "Give him something and send him home."

Bossert nodded and got up, but I said, "No. I've got to write up a piece on Doc for tomorrow's paper. See you."

I didn't want to talk any more. I went out and got my car and drove back to town. I felt funny. Hollow, cold, with a veil over my brain so I couldn't see anything clearly or think about anything clearly.

I stopped at the store and bought another bottle to see me through the night, and a feeling of cold evil was in me, and I thought of green, silent lightning, and little gimcracks that didn't belong in a television set, and the grave wise face of a child who was not quite human. The face wavered and became the face of a man. A man from Hrylliannu.

I drove home, to the old house where nobody lives now but me. I wrote my story about Doc, and when I was through it was dark and the bottle was nearly empty. I went to bed.

I dreamed Doc Callendar called me on the phone and said, "I've found him but you'll have to hurry." And I said, "But you're dead. Don't call me, Doc, please don't." But the phone kept ringing and ringing, and after a while I woke part way up and it really was ringing. It was two-forty-nine A.M.

It was Ed Betts. "Fire up at the hospital, Hank. I thought you'd want to know. The south wing. Gotta go now."

He hung up and I began to put clothes on the leaden dummy that was me. The south wing, I thought, and sirens went whooping up Goat Hill. The south wing. That's where X-ray is. That's where the pictures of the boy's insides are on file.

What a curious coincidence, I thought.

I drove after the sirens up Goat Hill, through the clear cool night with half a moon shining silver on the ridges, and Buckhorn standing calm and serene against the stars, thinking the lofty thoughts that seem to be reserved for mountains.

The south wing of the hospital burned brightly, a very pretty orange color against the night.

I pulled off the road and parked well below the center of activity and started to walk the rest of the way. Patients were being evacuated from the main building. People ran with things in their hands. Firemen yelled and wrestled with hoses and streams of water arced over the flames. I didn't think they were going to save the south wing. I thought they would be doing well to save the hospital.

Another unit of the fire department came hooting and clanging up the road behind me. I stepped off the shoulder and as I did so I looked down to be sure of my footing. A flicker of movement on the slope about ten feet below caught my eye. Dimly, in the reflected glow of the fire, I saw the girl.

She was slim and light as a gazelle, treading her furtive way among the trees. Her hair was short and curled close to her head. In that light it was merely dark, but I knew it would be red in the sunshine, with glints of silver in it. She saw me or heard me, and she stopped for a second or two, startled, looking up. Her eyes shone like two coppery sparks, as the eyes of an animal shine, weird in the pale oval of her face. Then she turned and ran.

I went after her. She ran fast, and I was in lousy shape. But I was thinking about Doc.

I caught her.

It was dark all around us under the trees, but the firelight and the moonlight shone together into the clearing where we were. She didn't struggle or fight me. She turned around kind of light and stiff to face me, holding herself away from me as much as she could with my hands gripping her arms.

"What do you want with me?" she said, in a breathless little voice. It was accented, and sweet as a bird's. "Let me go."

I said, "What relation are you to the boy?"

That startled her. I saw her eyes widen, and then she turned her head and looked toward the darkness under the trees. "Please let me go," she said, and I thought that some new fear had come to her.

I shook her, feeling her small arms under my hands, wanting to break them, wanting to torture her because of Doc. "How was Doc killed?" I asked her. "Tell me. Who did it, and how?"

She stared at me. "Doc?" she repeated. "I do not understand." Now she began to struggle. "Let me go! You hurt me."

"The green lightning," I said. "A man was killed by it this morning. My friend. I want to know about it."

"Killed?" she whispered. "Oh, no. No one has been killed."

"And you set that fire in the hospital, didn't you? Why? Why were those films such a threat to you? Who are you? Where—"

"Hush," she said. "Listen."

I listened. There were sounds, soft and stealthy, moving up the slope toward us.

"They're looking for me," she whispered. "Please let me go. I don't know about your friend, and the fire was—necessary. I don't want anyone hurt, and if they find you like this—"

I dragged her back into the shadows underneath the trees. There was a huge old maple there with a gnarly trunk. We stood behind it, and now I had my arm around her waist and her head pressed back against my shoulder, and my right hand over her mouth.

"Where do you come from?" I asked her, with my mouth close to her ear. "Where is Hrylliannu?"

Her body stiffened. It was a nice body, very much like the boy's in some ways, delicately made but strong, and with superb coordination. In other ways it was not like the boy's at all. I was thinking of her as an enemy, but it was impossible not to think of her as a woman, too.

She said, her voice muffled under my hand, "Where did you hear that name?"

"Never mind," I said. "Just answer me."

She wouldn't.

"Where do you live now? Somewhere near here?"

She only strained to get away.

"All right," I said. "We'll go now. Back up to the hospital. The sheriff wants to see you."

I started to drag her away up the hill, and then two men came into the light of the clearing.

One was slender and curly-headed in that particular way I was beginning to know. He looked pleasantly excited, pleasantly stimulated, as though by a game in which he found enjoyment. His eyes picked up the fitful glow of the fire and shone eerily, as the girl's had.

The other man was a perfectly ordinary type. He was dark and heavy-set and tall, and his khaki pants sagged under his belly. His face was neither excited nor pleasant. It was obvious that to him this was no game. He carried a heavy automatic, and I thought he was perfectly prepared to use it.

I was afraid of him.

"...to send a dame, anyway," he was saying.

"That's your prejudice speaking," said the curly-haired man. "She was the only one to send." He gestured toward the flames. "How can you doubt it?"

"She's been caught."

"Not Vadi." He began to call softly. "Vadi? Vadi!"

The girl's lips moved under my hand. I bent to hear, and she said in the faint ghost of a whisper:

"If you want to live, let me go to them."

The big dark man said grimly, "She's been caught. We'd better do something about it, and do it quick."

He started across the clearing.

The girl's lips shaped one word. "Please!"

The dark man came with his big gun, and the curly-headed one came a little behind him, walking as a stalking cat walks, soft and springy on its toes. If I dragged the girl away they would hear me. If I stayed where I was, they would walk right onto me. Either way, I thought, I would pretty surely go to join Doc on the cold marble.

I let the girl go.

She ran out toward them. I stood stark and frozen behind the maple tree, waiting for her to turn and say the word that would betray me.

She didn't turn, and she didn't say the word. The curly-headed man put his arms around her and they talked rapidly for perhaps half a minute, and I heard her tell the dark man that she had only waited to be sure they would not be able to put the fire out too soon. Then all three turned and went quickly away among the dark trees.

I stayed where I was for a minute, breathing hard, trying to think. Then I went hunting for the sheriff.

By the time I found Ed Betts, of course, it was already too late. But he sent a car out anyway. They didn't find a trace of anyone on the road who answered the descriptions I gave.

Ed looked at me closely in the light of the dying fire, which they had finally succeeded in bringing under control. "Don't get sore at me now, Hank," he said. "But are you real sure you saw these people?"

"I'm sure," I said. I could still, if I shut my eyes and thought about it, *feel* the girl's body in my arms. "Her name was Vadi. Now I want to talk to Croft."

Croft was the Fire Marshal. I watched the boys pouring water on what was left of the south wing, which was nothing more than a pile of hot embers with some pieces of wall standing near it. Jim Bossert joined us, looking exhausted and grimy. He was too tired even to curse. He just wailed a little about the loss of all his fine X-ray equipment, and all his records.

"I met the girl who did it," I said. "Ed doesn't believe me."

"Girl?" said Bossert, staring.

"Girl. Apparently an expert at this sort of thing." I wondered what the curly-haired man was to her. "Was anybody hurt?"

"By the grace of God," said Bossert, "no."

"How did it start?"

"I don't know. All of a sudden I woke up and every window in the south wing was spouting flame like a volcano."

I glanced at Ed, who shrugged. "Could have been a short in that high-voltage equipment."

Bossert said, "What kind of a girl? A lunatic?"

"Another one like the boy. There was a man with her, maybe the boy's father, I don't know. The third one was just a man. Mean looking bastard with a gun. She said the fire was necessary."

"All this, just to get rid of some films?"

"It must be important to them," I said. "They already killed Doc. They tried to kill me. What's a fire?"

Ed Betts swore, his face twisted between unbelief and worry. Then Croft came up. Ed asked him, "What started the fire?"

Croft shook his head. "Too early to tell yet. Have to wait till things cool down. But I'll lay you any odds you like it was started by chemicals."

"Deliberately?"

"Could be," said Croft, and went away again.

I looked at the sky. It was almost dawn, that beautiful bleak time when the sky is neither dark nor light and the mountains are cut from black cardboard, without perspective. I said, "I'm going up to the Tates'. I'm worried about the boy."

"All right," said Ed quickly, "I'll go with you. In my car. We'll stop in town and pick up Jud. I want him to see that teevee."

"The hell with Jud," I said. "I'm in a hurry." And suddenly I was. Suddenly I was terribly afraid for that grave-faced child who was obviously the unwitting key to some secret that was important enough to justify arson and murder to those who wanted to keep it.

Ed hung right behind me. He practically shoved me into his car. It had COUNTY SHERIFF painted on its door, and I thought of Doc's station wagon with its COUNTY HEALTH SERVICE, and it seemed like a poor omen but there was nothing I could do about it.

There was nothing I could do about stopping for Jud Spofford, either. Ed went in and routed him out of bed, taking the car keys with him. I sat smoking and looking up at Tunkhannock Ridge, watching it brighten to gold at the crest as the sun came up.

Finally Jud came out grumbling and climbed in the back seat, a tall lanky young fellow in a blue coverall with *Newhale Electric Appliance Co.* embroidered in red on the pocket. His little wife watched from the doorway, holding her pink wrapper together.

We went away up Tunkhannock Ridge. There was still a black smudge of smoke above the hospital on Goat Hill. The sky over Buckhorn Mountain was clear and bright.

Sally Tate and her boy were already gone.

Mrs. Tate told us about it, while we sat on the lumpy sofa in the living room and the fat old dog watched us through the screen door, growling. Sally's sisters, or some of them at least, were in the kitchen listening.

"Never was so surprised at anything in my life," said Mrs. Tate. "Pa had just gone out to the barn with Harry and J. P. — them's the two oldest girls' husbands, you know. I and the girls was washing up after breakfast, and I heard this car drive in. Sure enough it was him. I went out on the stoop — "

"What kind of a car?" asked Ed.

"Same panel truck he was driving before, only the name was painted out. Kind of a dirty blue all over. 'Well,' I says, 'I never expected to see *your* face around here again!', I says, and he says — "

Boiled down to reasonable length, the man had said that he had always intended to come back for Sally, and that if he had known about the boy he would have come much sooner. He had been away, he said, on business, and had only just got back and heard about Sally bringing the child in to the hospital, and knew that it must be his.

He had gone up to the house, and Sally had come running out into his arms, her face all shining. Then they went in together to see the boy, and Bill Jones had fondled him and called him Son, and the boy had watched him sleepily and without affection.

"They talked together for a while, private," said Mrs. Tate, "and then Sally come and said he was going to take her away and marry her and make the boy legal, and would I help her pack. And I did, and they went away together, the three of 'em. Sally didn't know when she'd be back."

She shook her head, smoothing her hair with knotted fingers. "I just don't know," she said. "I just don't know."

"What?" I asked her. "Was there something wrong?" I knew there was, but I wanted to hear what she had to say.

"Nothing you could lay your hand to," she said. "And Sally was so happy. She was just fit to burst. And he *was* real pleasant, real polite to me and Pa. We asked him about all them lies he told, and he said they wasn't lies at all. He said the man he was working for did plan to open a store in Newhale, but then he got sick and the plan fell through. He said his name was Bill Jones, and showed us some cards and things to prove it. And he said Sally just misunderstood the name of the place he come from because he give it the old Spanish pronunciation."

"What did he say it was really?" Ed asked, and she looked surprised.

"Now I think of it, I guess he didn't say."

"Well, where's he going to live, with Sally?"

"He isn't settled yet. He's got two or three prospects, different places. She was so happy," said Mrs. Tate, "and I ought to be too, 'cause Lord knows I've wished often enough he would come back and get that pesky brat of his, and Sally too if she was minded. But I ain't. I ain't happy at all, and I don't know why."

"Natural reaction," said Ed Betts heartily. "You miss your daughter, and probably the boy too, more than you know."

"I've had daughters married before. It was something about this man. Something—" Mrs. Tate hesitated a long time, searching for a word. "Queer," she said at last. "Wrong. I couldn't tell you what. Like the boy, only more so. The boy has Sally in him. This one—" She made a gesture with her hands. "Oh, well, I expect I'm just looking for trouble."

"I expect so, Mrs. Tate," said Ed, "but you be sure and get in touch with me if you don't hear from Sally in a reasonable time. And now I'd like this young man to look at your teevee."

Jud, who had been sitting stiff and uncomfortable during the talking, jumped up and practically ran to the set. Mrs. Tate started to protest, but Ed said firmly, "This may be important, Mrs. Tate. Jud's a good serviceman, he won't upset anything."

"I hope not," she said. "It does run real good."

Jud turned it on and watched it for a minute. "It sure does," he said. "And in this location, too."

He took the back off and looked inside. After a minute he let go a long low whistle.

"What is it?" said Ed, going closer.

"Damnedest thing," said Jud. "Look at that wiring. He's loused up the circuits, all right — and there's a couple tubes in there like I never saw before." He was getting excited. "I'd have to tear the whole thing down to see what he's really done, but somehow he's boosted the power and the sensitivity way up. The guy must be a wizard."

Mrs. Tate said loudly, "You ain't tearing anything down, young man. You just leave it like it is."

I said, "What about that dingus on the side?"

"Frankly," said Jud, "that stops me. It's got a wire to it, but it don't seem to hitch up anywhere in the set." He turned the set off and began to poke gently around. "See here, this little hairline wire that comes down and bypasses the whole chassis? It cuts in here on the live line, so it draws power whether the set's on or not. But I don't see how it can have anything to do with the set operating."

"Well, take it out," said Ed. "We'll take it down to the shop and see whether we can make anything of it."

"Okay," said Jud, ignoring Mrs. Tate's cry of protest. He reached in and for the first time actually touched the enigmatic little unit, feeling for what held it to the side of the case.

There was a sharp pop and a small bright flare, and Jud leaped back with a howl. He put his scorched fingers in his mouth and his eyes watered. Mrs. Tate cried, "Now, you've done it, you've ruined my teevee!" There was a smell of burning on the air. The girls came running out of the kitchen and the old dog barked and clawed the screen.

One of the girls said, "What happened?"

"I don't know," Jud said. "The goddamned thing just popped like a bomb when I touched it."

There was a drift of something gray — ash or dust — and that was all. Even the hairline wire was consumed.

"It looks," I said, "as though Mr. Jones didn't want anybody else to look over his technological achievements."

Ed grunted. He looked puzzled and irresolute. "Hurt the set any?" he asked.

"Dunno," said Jud, and turned it on.

It ran as perfectly as before.

"Well," said Mrs. Tate, "thank goodness."

"Yeah," said Ed. "I guess that's all, then. What do you say, Hank? We might as well go."

I said we might as well. We climbed back into Ed's car and started—the second time for me—back down Tunkhannock Ridge.

Jud was still sucking his fingers. He wondered out loud if the funny-looking tubes in the set would explode the same way if you touched them, and I said probably. Ed didn't say anything. He was frowning deeply. I asked him what he thought about it.

"I'm trying to figure the angle," he said. "This Bill Jones. What does he get out of it? What does he *make?* On the television gag, I mean. People usually want to get paid for work like that."

Jud offered the opinion that the man was a nut. "One of these crazy guys like in the movies, always inventing things that make trouble. But I sure would like to know what he done to that set."

"Well," said Ed, "I can't see what more we can do. He did come back for the girl, and apart from that he hasn't broken any laws."

"Hasn't he?" I said, looking out the window. We were coming to the place where Doc had died. There was no sign of a storm today. Everything was bright, serene, peaceful. But I could feel the cold feeling of being watched. Someone, somewhere, knew me. He watched where I went and what I did, and decided whether or not to send the green lightning to slay me.

It was a revelation, like the moments you have as a young child when you become acutely conscious of God. I began to shake. I wanted to crawl down in the back seat and hide. Instead I sat where I was and tried to keep the naked terror from showing too much. And I watched the sky. And nothing happened.

Ed Betts didn't mention it, but he began to drive faster and faster until I thought we weren't going to need any green lightning. He didn't slow down until we hit the valley. I think he would have been glad to get rid of me, but he had to haul me all the way back up Coat Hill to get my car. When he did let me off, he said gruffly,

"I'm not going to listen to you again till you've had a good twelve hours' sleep. And I need some myself. So long."

I went home, but I didn't sleep. Not right away. I told my assistant and right-hand man, Joe Streckfoos, that the paper was all his today, and then I got on the phone. I drove the local exchange crazy, but by about five o'clock that afternoon I had the information I wanted.

I had started with a map of the area on my desk. Not just Newhale, but the whole area, with Buckhorn Mountain roughly at the center and showing the hills and valleys around its northern periphery. By five o'clock the map showed a series of red pencil dots. If you connected them together with a line they formed a sprawling, irregular, but unbroken circle drawn around Buckhorn, never exceeding a certain number of miles in distance from the peak.

Every pencil dot represented a television set that had within the last three years been serviced by a red-haired man — for free.

I looked at the map for a long time, and then I went out in the yard and looked up at Buckhorn. It seemed to me to stand very high, higher than I remembered. From flank to crest the green unbroken forest covered it. In the winter time men hunted there for bear and deer, and I knew there were a few hunting lodges, hardly more than shacks, on its lower slopes. These were not used in summer, and apart from the hunters no one ever bothered to climb those almost perpendicular sides, hanging onto the trees as onto a ladder, up to the fog and storm that plagued the summit.

There were clouds there now. It almost seemed that Buckhorn pulled them down over his head like a cowl, until the gray trailing edges hid him almost to his feet. I shivered and went inside and shut the door. I cleaned my automatic and put in a full clip. I made a sandwich and drank the last couple of drinks in last night's bottle. I laid out my boots and my rough-country pants and a khaki shirt. I set the alarm. It was still broad daylight. I went to bed.

The alarm woke me at eleven-thirty. I did not turn on any lamps. I don't know why, except that I still had that naked feeling of being watched. Light enough came to me anyhow from the intermittent sulfurous flares in the sky. There was a low mutter of thunder in the west. I put the automatic in a shoulder holster under my shirt, not to hide it but because it was out of the way there. When I was dressed I went downstairs and out the back door, heading for the garage.

It was quiet, the way a little town can be quiet at night. I could hear the stream going over the stones, and the million little songs of the crickets, the peepers, and the frogs were almost stridently loud.

Then they began to stop. The frogs first, in the marshy places beside the creek. Then the crickets and the peepers. I stopped too, in the black dark beside a clump of rhododendrons my mother used to be almost tiresomely proud of. My skin turned cold and the hair bristled on the back of my neck and I heard soft padding footsteps and softer breathing on the heavy air.

Two people had waded the creek and come up into my yard.

There was a flare and a grumble in the sky and I saw them close by, standing on the grass, looking up at the unlighted house.

One of them was the girl Vadi, and she carried something in her hands. The other was the heavy-set dark man with the gun.

"It's okay," he told her. "He's sleeping. Get busy."

I slid the automatic into my palm and opened my mouth to speak, and then I heard her say:

"You won't give him a chance to get out?"

Her tone said she knew the answer to that one before she asked it. But he said with furious sarcasm:

"Why certainly, and then you can call the sheriff and explain why you burned the house down. And the hospital. Christ. I told Arnek you weren't to be trusted." He gave her a rough shove. "Get with it."

Vadi walked five careful paces away from him. Then very swiftly she threw away, in two different directions, whatever it was she carried. I heard the two things fall, rustling among grass and branches where it might take hours to find them even by daylight. She spun around. "Now," she said in a harsh defiant voice, "what are you going to do?"

There was a moment of absolute silence, so full of murder that the far-off lightning seemed feeble by comparison. Then he said:

"All right, let's get out of here."

She moved to join him, and he waited until she was quite close to him. Then he hit her. She made a small bleating sound and fell down. He started to kick her, and then I jumped out and hit him over the ear with the flat of the automatic. It was his turn to fall down.

Vadi got up on her hands and knees. She stared at me, sobbing a little with rage and pain. Blood was running from the corner of her mouth. I took the man's gun and threw it far off and it splashed in the creek. Then I got down beside the girl.

"Here," I said. "Have my handkerchief."

She took it and held it to her mouth. "You were outside here all the time," she said. She sounded almost angry.

"It just happened that way. I still owe you thanks for my life. And my house. Though you weren't so tender about the hospital."

"There was no one to be killed there. I made sure. A building one can always rebuild, but a life is different."

She looked at the unconscious man. Her eyes burned with that catlike brilliance in the lightning flares.

"I could kill him," she said, "with pleasure."

"Who is he?"

"My brother's partner." She glanced toward Buckhorn and the light went out of her eyes. Her head became bowed.

"Your brother sent you to kill me?"

"He didn't say —"

"But you knew."

"When Marlin came with me I knew."

She had begun to tremble.

"Do you make a career of arson?"

"Arson? Oh. The setting of fires. No. I am a chemist. And I wish I —"

She caught herself fiercely and would not finish.

I said, "Those things are listening devices, then."

She had to ask me what I meant. Her mind was busy with some thorny darkness of its own.

"The little gadgets your brother put in the television sets," I said. "I figured that's what they were when I saw how they were placed. A string of sentry posts all around the center of operations, little ears to catch every word of gossip, because if any of the local people get suspicious they're bound to talk about it and so give warning. He heard my calls this afternoon, didn't he? That's why he sent you. And he heard Doc and me at the Tates'. That's why —"

Moving with that uncanny swiftness of hers, she rose and ran away from me. It was like before. She ran fast, and I ran after her. She went splashing through the shallow stream and the water flew back against me, wetting my face, spattering my clothes. On the far bank I caught her, as I had before. But this time she fought me.

"Let me go," she said, and beat her hands against me. "Do you know what I've done for you? I've asked for the knife for myself. Let me go, you clumsy fool —"

I held her tighter. Her soft curls pressed against my cheek. Her body strove against me, and it was not soft but excitingly strong.

" — before I regret it," she said, and I kissed her.

It was strange, what happened then.

I've kissed girls who didn't want to be kissed, and I've kissed girls who didn't like me particularly. I've kissed a couple of the touch-me-not kind who shrink from any sort of physical contact. I've had my face slapped. But I never had a girl *withdraw* from me the way she did.

It was like something closing, folding up, shutting every avenue of contact, and yet she never moved. In fact she had stopped moving entirely. She just stood with my arms around her and my lips on hers, and a kind of a coldness came out of her, a rejection so total I couldn't even get mad. I was shocked, and very much puzzled, but you can't get mad at a thing that isn't personal. This was too deep for that. And suddenly I thought of the boy.

"A different breed," I said. "Worlds apart. Is that it?"

"Yes," she said quietly. "Worlds apart."

And the coldness spread through me. I stood on the bank of the stream in the warm night, the bank where I had stood ten thousand times before, boy and man, and saw the strange shining of her eyes, and I was more than cold, I was afraid. I stepped back away from her, still holding her but in a different way.

"It wasn't like this," I said, "between your brother and Sally Tate."

The girl-thing said, "My brother Arnek is a corrupt man."

"Vadi," I said. "Where is Hrylliannu?"

The girl-thing looked past my shoulder and said, "Marlin is running away."

I looked too, and it was so. The big man's head was harder than I had thought. He had got up, and I saw him blundering rapidly away along the side of my house, heading for the street.

"Well," I said, "he's gone now. You must have come in a car, didn't you?" She nodded.

"Good," I said. "It won't be challenged as soon as mine. We'll take it."

"Where are you going?" she asked, catching her breath sharply.

"Where I was going when you stopped me. Up Buckhorn."

"Oh no," she said. "No, you can't, you mustn't." She was human again, and afraid. "I saved your life, isn't that enough for you? You'll never live to climb Buckhorn and neither will I if —"

"Did Sally and the boy live to climb it?" I asked her, and she hung her head and nodded. "Then you'll see to it that we do."

"But tonight!" she said in a panic. "Not tonight!"

"What's so special about tonight?" She didn't answer, and I shook her. "What's going on up there?"

She didn't answer that, either. She said with sudden fierceness, "All right, then, come on. Climb Buckhorn and see. And when you're dying, remember that I tried to stop you."

She didn't speak again. She led me without protest to the car parked on the dirt road. It was a panel truck. By day it would have been a dirty blue.

"He's going to kill them, isn't he?" I said. "He killed Doc. You admit he wants to kill me. What's going to save Sally and the child?"

"You torture me," she said. "This is a world of torture. Go on. Go on, and get it done."

I started the panel truck. Like the television set, it worked better than it had any business to. It fled with uncanny strength and swiftness over the dirt roads toward Buckhorn, soft-sprung as a cloud, silent as a dream.

"It's a pity," I said. "Your brother has considerable genius."

She laughed. A bitter laugh. "He couldn't pass his second year of technical training. That's why he's here."

She looked at Buckhorn as though she hated the mountain, and Buckhorn, invisible behind a curtain of storm, answered her look with a sullen curse, spoken in thunder.

I stopped at the last gas station on the road and honked the owner out of bed and told him to call Sheriff Betts and tell him where I'd gone. I didn't dare do it myself for fear Vadi would get away from me. The man was very resentful about being waked up. I hoped he would not take out his resentment by forgetting to call.

"You're pretty close to Buckhorn," I told him. "The neck you save may be your own."

I left him to ponder that, racing on toward the dark mountain in that damned queer car that made me feel like a character in one of my own bad dreams, with the girl beside me—the damned queer girl who was not quite human.

The road dropped behind us. We began to climb the knees of the mountain. Vadi told me where to turn, and the road became a track, and the track ended in the thick woods beside a rickety little lodge the size of a piano-box, with a garage behind it. The garage only looked rickety. The headlights showed up new and sturdy timbers on the inside.

I cut the motor and the lights and reached for the handbrake. Vadi must have been set on a hair-trigger waiting for that moment. I heard her move and there was a snap as though she had pulled something from a clip underneath the dashboard. The door on her side banged open.

I shouted to her to stop and sprang out of the truck to catch her. But she was already out of the garage, and she was waiting for me. Just as I came through the door there was a bolt of lightning, bright green, small and close at hand. I saw it coming. I saw her dimly in the backflash and knew that in some way she had made the lightning with a thing she held in her hand. Then it hit me and that was all.

When I came to I was all alone and the rain was falling on me just the way it had on Doc...

But I wasn't dead.

I crawled around and finally managed to get up, feeling heavy and disjointed. My legs and arms flopped around as though the coordinating controls had been burned out. I stood inside the garage out of the rain, rubbing my numb joints and thinking.

All the steam had gone out of me. I didn't want to climb Buckhorn Mountain any more. It looked awfully black up there, and awfully lonesome, and God alone knew what was going on under the veil of cloud and storm that hid it.

The lightning flashes — real sky-made lightning — showed me the dripping trees going right up into nothing, with the wind thrashing them, and then the following thunder cracked my eardrums. The rain hissed, and I thought, it's crazy for one man to go up there alone.

Then I thought about Sally Tate and the little red-headed kid, and I thought how Ed Betts might already be up there somewhere, plowing his way through the woods looking for me. I didn't know how long I'd been out.

I made sure I still had my gun, and I did have. I wished I had a drink, but that was hopeless. So I started out. I didn't go straight up the mountain. I figured the girl would have had time to find her brother and give him warning, and that he might be looking for me to come that way. I angled off to the east, where I remembered a ravine that might give me some cover. I'd been up Buckhorn before, but only by daylight, with snow on the ground and a couple of friends with me, and not looking for anything more sinister than a bear.

I climbed the steep flank of the mountain, leaning almost into it, worming and floundering and pulling my way between the trees. The rain fell and soaked me. The thunder was a monstrous presence, and the lightning was a great torch that somebody kept tossing back and forth so that sometimes you could see every vein of every leaf on the tree you were fighting with, and sometimes it was so dark that you knew the sun and stars hadn't been invented yet. I lost the ravine. I only knew I was still going up. There wasn't any doubt about that. After a while the rain slacked off and almost stopped.

In an interval between crashes of thunder I heard voices.

They were thin and far away. I tried to place them, and when I thought I had them pegged I started toward them. The steep pitch of the ground fell away into a dizzying downslope and I was almost running into a sort of long shallow trough, thickly wooded, its bottom hidden from any view at all except one directly overhead. And there were lights in it, or at least a light.

I slowed down and went more carefully, hoping the storm would cover any noise I made.

The voices went on, and now I could hear another sound, the scrinch and screek of metal rubbing on metal.

I was on the clearing before I knew it. And it wasn't a clearing at all really, just one of those natural open places where the soil is too thin to support trees and runs to brush instead. It wasn't much more than ten feet across. Almost beside me were a couple of tents so cleverly hidden among the trees that you practically had to fall on them, as I did, to find them at all.

From one of them came the sleepy sobbing of a child.

In the small clearing Vadi and Arnek were watching a jointed metal mast build itself up out of a pit in the ground. The top of it was already out of sight in the cloud but it was obviously taller than the trees. The lamp was on the ground beside the pit.

The faces of Vadi and her brother were both angry, both set and obstinate. Perhaps it was their mutual fury that made them seem less human, or more unhuman, than ever, the odd bone-structure of cheek and jaw accentuated, the whole head elongated, the silver-red hair fairly bristling, the copper-colored eyes glinting with that unpleasantly catlike brilliance in the light. They had been quarreling, and they still were, but not in English. Arnek had a look like a rattlesnake.

Vadi, I thought, was frightened. She kept glancing at the tents, and in a minute the big man, Marlin, came out of one of them. He was pressing a small bandage on the side of his head, over his ear. He looked tired and wet and foul-tempered, as though he had not had an easy time getting back to base.

He started right in on Vadi, cursing her because of what she had done.

Arnek said in English, "I didn't ask her to come here, and I'm sending her home tonight."

"That's great," Marlin said. "That's a big help. We'll have to move our base anyway now."

"Maybe not," said Arnek defiantly. He watched the slim mast stretching up and up with a soft screeking of its joints.

"You're a fool," said Marlin, in a tone of cold and bitter contempt. "You started this mess, Arnek. You had to play around with that girl and make a kid to give the show away. Then you pull that half-cocked trick with those guys in the station wagon and you can't even do that right. You kill the one but not the other. And then *she* louses up the only chance we got left. You know how much money we're going to lose? You know how long it'll take us to find a location half as good as this? You know what I ought to do?"

Arnek's voice was sharp, but a shade uncertain. "Oh, stop bitching and get onto those scanners. All we need is another hour and then they can whistle. And there are plenty of mountains."

"Are there," said Marlin, and looked again at Vadi. "And how long do you think she'll keep her mouth shut at *your* end?"

He turned and walked back into the tent. Arnek looked uncertainly at Vadi and then fixed his attention on the mast again. Vadi's face was the color of chalk. She started once toward the tent and Arnek caught her roughly and spoke to her in whatever language they used, and she stopped.

I slid around the back of the tents to the one Marlin was in. There was a humming and whining inside. I got down on my hands and knees and crawled carefully over the wet grass between the tents, toward the front. The mast apparently made its last joint because it stopped and Arnek said something to Vadi and they bent over what seemed to be a sunken control box in the ground. I took my chance and whipped in through the tent flap.

I didn't have long to look around. The space inside was crammed with what seemed to be electronic equipment. Marlin was sitting hunched up on a stool in front of a big panel with a dozen or so little screens on it like miniature television monitors. The screens, I just had time to see, showed an assortment of views of Buckhorn and the surrounding areas, and Marlin was apparently, by remote control, rotating one by one the distant receivers that sent the images to the screens. They must have been remarkably tight-beamed, because they were not much disturbed by static. I knew now how the eye of God had watched Doc and me on Tunkhannock Ridge.

I didn't know yet how the lightning-bolts were hurled, but I was pretty sure Ed Betts would get one if his car showed up on a scanner screen, and who would be the wiser? Poor Ed hit by lightning just like old Doc, and weren't the storms something fierce this summer?

Marlin turned around and saw it wasn't Arnek. He moved faster than I would have thought possible. He scooped up the light stool he was sitting on and threw it at me, leaping sideways himself in a continuation of the same movement. In the second in which I was getting my head out of the way of the stool he pulled a gun. He had had a spare, just as he must have had a car stashed somewhere in or near the town.

He did not quite have time to fire. I shot him twice through the body. He dropped but I didn't know if he was dead. I kicked the gun out of his hand and jumped to stand flat against the canvas wall beside the front flap, not pressing against it. The canvas was light-proof, and the small lamps over the control panels did not throw shadows.

Arnek did not come in.

After a second or two I got nervous. I could hear him shouting "Marlin! Marlin!" I ran into the narrow space behind the banks of equipment, being extremely careful how I touched anything. I did not see any power leads. It dawned on me that all this stuff had come up out of a pit in the ground like the mast and that the generator must be down there below. The floor wasn't canvas at all, but some dark gray material to which the equipment was bolted.

I got my knife out and started to slit the canvas at the back. And suddenly the inside of the tent was full of green fire. It sparked off every metal thing and jarred the gun out of my hand. It nearly knocked me out again. But I was shielded by the equipment from the full force of the shock. It flicked off again almost at once. I got the canvas cut and squirmed through it and then I put three or four shots at random into the back of the equipment just for luck.

Then I raced around the front and caught Arnek just as he was deciding not to enter the tent after all.

He had a weapon in his hand like the one Vadi had used on me. I said, "Drop it," and he hesitated, looking evil and upset. "Drop it!" I told him again, and he dropped it. "Now stand away," I said. "Walk out toward your sister, real slow, one step at a time."

He walked, and I picked up the weapon.

"Good," I said. "Now we can all relax." And I called Sally Tate, telling her it was safe to come out now.

All this time since I was where I could see her Vadi had stood with one hand over her mouth, looking up into the mist.

Sally Tate came out of the other tent. She was carrying the boy, and both their faces were pale and puffy-eyed and streaked with tears.

"It's all right now," I said. "You can go—" I was going to say "home," and then there was a sound in the sky that was not wind or thunder, that was hardly a sound at all, but more of a great sigh. The air pressed down on me and the grass was flattened as by a down-driven wind and all the branches of the trees bowed. The mist rolled, boiled, was rent, torn apart, scattered.

Something had come to rest against the top of the mast.

Arnek turned and ran to Vadi and I did not stop him. I moved closer to Sally Tate, standing with her mouth open and her eyes big and staring.

The mast began to contract downward, bringing the thing with it.

I suppose I knew then what the thing was. I just didn't want to admit it. It was cylindrical and slender, about fifty feet long, with neither wings nor jets. I watched it come slowly and gracefully down, attached by its needle-sharp nose to the magnetic grapple on top of the mast. The mast acted as automatic guide and stabilizer, dropping the ship into a slot between the trees as neatly as you would drop a slice of bread into the slot of a toaster.

And all the time the bitter breath of fear was blowing on me and little things were falling into place in my mind and I realized that I had known the answer for some time and had simply refused to see it.

A port opened in the side of the ship. And as though that was the final symbolic trigger I needed, I got the full impact of what I was seeing. Suddenly the friendly protecting sky seemed to have been torn open above me as the veiling cloud was torn, and through the rent the whole Outside poured in upon me, the black freezing spaces of the galaxy, the blaze and strangeness of a billion billion suns. I shrank beneath that vastness. I was nothing, nobody, an infinitesimal fleck in a cosmos too huge to be borne. The stars had come too close. I wanted to get down and howl and grovel like a dog.

No wonder Arnek and Vadi and the boy were queer. They were not mutants — they were not even that Earthly. They came from another world.

A little ladder had extended itself downward from the port. A man came briskly to the ground and spoke to Arnek. He resembled Arnek except that he was dressed in a single close-fitting garment of some dark stuff. Arnek pointed to me, speaking rapidly. The man turned and looked at me, his body expressing alarm. I felt childish and silly standing there with my little gun. Lone man of Earth at an incredible Thermopylae, saying, "You shall not land."

All the time Arnek and the stranger had been talking there had been other activities around the ship. A hatch in the stern had opened and now from both hatches people began to come out helter-skelter as though haste was the chief necessity. There were men and women both. They all looked human. Slightly odd, a little queer perhaps, but human. They were different types, different colors, sizes, and builds, but they all fitted in somewhere pretty close to Earthly types. They all looked a little excited, a little scared, considerably bewildered by the place in which they found themselves. Some of the women were crying. There were maybe twenty people in all.

I understood then exactly what Arnek and Marlin had been up to and it seemed so grotesquely familiar and prosaic that I began to laugh.

"Wetbacks," I said aloud. "That's what you're doing, smuggling aliens."

Aliens. Yes indeed.

It did not seem so funny when I thought about it.

The stranger turned around and shouted an order. The men and women stopped, some of them still on the ladders. More voices shouted. Then those on the ladders were shoved aside and eight men in uniform jumped out, with weapons in their hands.

Sally Tate let go one wild wavering shriek. The child fell out of her arms. He sat on the wet ground with the wind knocked out of him so he couldn't cry, blinking in shocked dismay. Sally tottered. Her big strong healthy body was sunken and collapsed, every muscle slack. She turned and made a staggering lunge for the tent and fell partly in through the doorway, crawled the rest of the way like a hurt dog going under a porch, and lay there with the flap pulled over her head.

I didn't blame her. I don't even know what obscure force kept me from joining her.

Of the eight men, five were not human. Two of them not even remotely.

I can't describe them. I can't remember what they looked like, not clearly.

Let's be honest. I don't *want* to remember.

I suppose if you were used to things like that all your life it would be different. You wouldn't think anything about it.

I was not used to things like that. I knew that I never would be, not if we ourselves achieved space-flight tomorrow. I'm too old, too set in the familiar pattern of existence that has never been broken for man since the beginning. Perhaps others are more resilient. They're welcome to it.

I picked up the boy and ran.

It came on again to rain. I ran down Buckhorn Mountain, carrying the boy in my arms. And the green lightning came after us, hunting us along the precipitous slope.

The boy had got his breath back. He asked me why we had to die. I said never mind, and kept on running.

I fell with him and rolled to the bottom of a deep gully. We were shaken. We lay in the dripping brush looking up at the lightning lancing across the night above us. After a while it stopped. I picked him up again and crept silently along the gully and onto the slope below.

And nearly got shot by Ed Betts and a scratch posse, picking their cautious way up the mountainside.

One of the men took the child out of my arms. I hung onto Ed and said inanely, "They're landing a load of wetbacks."

"Up there?"

"They've got a ship," I told him. "They're aliens, Ed. Real aliens."

I began to laugh again. I didn't want to. It just seemed such a hellishly clever play on words that I couldn't help it.

Fire bloomed suddenly in the night above us. A second later the noise of the explosion reached us.

I stopped laughing. "They must be destroying their installations. Pulling out. Marlin said they'd have to. Christ. And Sally is still up there."

I ran back up the mountain, clambering bearlike through the trees. The others followed.

There was one more explosion. Then I came back to the edge of the clearing. Ed was close behind me. I don't think any of the others were really close enough to see. There was a lot of smoke. The tents were gone. Smoking trees were slowly toppling in around the edges of a big raw crater in the ground.

There was no trace of the instruments that had been in the tents.

The ship was still there. The crew, human and unhuman, were shoving the last of the passengers back into the ship. There was an altercation going on beside the forward port.

Vadi had her arm around Sally Tate. She was obviously trying to get her aboard. I thought I understood then why Sally and the boy were still alive. Probably Vadi had been insisting that her brother send them along where they wouldn't be any danger to him, and he hadn't quite had the nerve to cross her. He was looking uncertain now, and it was the officer who was making the refusal. Sally herself seemed to be in a stupor.

Vadi thrust past the officer and led Sally toward the ladder. And Sally went, willingly. I like to remember that, now, when she's gone.

I think—I hope—that Sally's all right out there. She was younger and simpler than I, she could adapt. I think she loved Bill Jones—Arnek—enough to leave her child, leave her family, leave her world, and still be happy near him.

Ed and I started to run across the clearing. Ed had not said a word. But his face was something to look at.

They saw us coming but they didn't bother to shoot at us. They seemed in a tremendous hurry. Vadi screamed something, and I was sure it was in English and a warning to me, but I couldn't understand it. Then she was gone inside the ship and so were Arnek and Sally and the officer and crewmen, and the ladders went up and the ports shut.

The mooring mast began to rise and so did the ship, and the trees were bent with the force of its rising.

I knew then what the warning was.

I grabbed Ed bodily and hauled him back. The ship didn't have to be very high. Only above the trees. I hauled him as far as blind instinct told me I could go and then I yelled, "Get down! Get down!" to everybody within earshot and made frantic motions. It all took possibly thirty seconds. Ed understood and we flopped and hugged the ground.

The mast blew.

Dirt, rocks, pieces of tree rained down around us. The shock wave pounded our ears. A few moments later, derisive and powerful, a long thin whistling scream tore upward across the sky, and faded, and was gone.

We got up after a while and collected the muddy and startled posse and went to look at what was left of the clearing. There was nothing. Sally Tate was gone as though she had never existed. There was no shred of anything left to prove that what Ed and I had seen was real.

We made up a story, about a big helicopter and an alien racket. It wasn't too good a story, but it was better than the truth. Afterward, when we were calmer, Ed and I tried to figure it out for ourselves. How it was done, I mean, and why.

The "how" was easy enough, given the necessary technology. Pick a remote but not too inconveniently isolated spot, like the top of Buckhorn Mountain. Set up your secret installation—a simple one, so compact and carefully hidden that hunters could walk right over it and never guess it was there when it was not in use. On nights when conditions are right—that is to say, when the possibility of being observed is nearest to zero—run your cargo in and land it. We figured that the ship we saw wasn't big enough to transport that many people very far. We figured it was a landing-craft, ferrying the passengers down from a much bigger mothership way beyond the sky.

A star-ship. It sounded ridiculous when you said it. But we had seen the members of the crew. It is generally acknowledged by nearly everybody now that there is no intelligent life of any terrestrial sort on the other planets of our own system. So they had to come from farther out.

Why? That was a tougher one to solve. We could only guess at it.

"There must be a hell of a big civilization out there," said Ed, "to build the ships and travel in them. They obviously know we're here."

Uneasy thought.

"Why haven't they spoken to us?" he wondered. "Let us in on it too."

"I suppose," I said, "they're waiting for us to develop space-flight on our own. Maybe it's a kind of test you have to pass to get in on their civilization. Or maybe they figure we're so backward they don't want to have anything to do with us, all our wars and all. Or both. Pick your own reason."

"Okay," said Ed. "But why dump their people on us like that? And how come Marlin, one of our own people, was in on it?"

"There *are* Earthmen who'll do anything for money," I said. "Like Marlin. It'd not be too hard to contact men like him, use them as local agents."

"As for why they dump their people on us," I went on, "it probably isn't legal, where they came from. Remember what Marlin said about Vadi? *How long will she keep her mouth shut at your end?* My guess is her brother was a failure at home and got into a dirty racket, and she was trying to get him out of it. There must be other worlds like Earth, too, or the racket wouldn't be financially sound. Not enough volume."

"But the wetbacks," Ed said. "Were they failures, too? People who couldn't compete in the kind of a society they must have? And how the hell many do you suppose they've run in on us already?"

I've wondered about that myself. How many aliens have Marlin, and probably others like him, taken off the star-boats and dressed and instructed and furnished with false papers, in return doubtless for all the valuables the poor devils had? How many of the people you see around you every day, the anonymous people that just look a little odd somehow, the people about whom you think briefly that they don't even look human — the queer ones you notice and then forget — how many of them *aren't* human at all in the sense that we understand that word?

Like the boy.

Sally Tate's family obviously didn't want him back. So I had myself appointed his legal guardian, and we get on fine together. He's a bright kid. His father may have been a failure in his own world, but on ours the half-bred child has an I.Q. that would frighten you. He's also a good youngster. I think he takes after his aunt.

I've thought of getting married since then, just to make a better home for the boy, and to fill up a void in my own life I'm beginning to feel. But I haven't quite done it yet. I keep thinking maybe Vadi will come back some day, walking with swift grace down the side of Buckhorn Mountain. I do not think it is likely, but I can't quite put it out of my mind. I remember the cold revulsion that there was between us, and then I wonder if that feeling would go on, or whether you couldn't get used to that idea of differentness in time.

The trouble is, I guess, that Vadi kind of spoiled me for the general run of women.

I wonder what her life is like in Hrylliannu, and where it is. Sometimes on the bitter frosty nights when the sky is diamond-clear and the Milky Way glitters like the mouth of hell across it, I look up at the stars and wonder which one is hers. And old Buckhorn sits black and silent in the north, and the deep wounds on his shoulder are healing into grassy scars. He says nothing. Even the thunder now has a hollow sound. It is merely thunder.

But, as Arnek said, there are plenty of mountains.

Afterword by Cora Buhlert

Do we even need to rediscover Leigh Brackett? After all, she is one of only two women writers (the other is C.L. Moore) from the golden age of science fiction who are well-remembered today, often labelled as "outliers" even though they weren't.

Leigh Douglas Brackett (1915 – 1978) is a genre legend. She burst onto the scene in 1940 and quickly carved out a niche for herself, penning adventures on far-flung worlds for pulp magazines like *Planet Stories* and *Startling Stories*. At the time, her action-packed tales were often dismissed as pure escapism, unlike the more serious science fiction John W. Campbell (with whom Leigh Brackett and her husband Edmond Hamilton famously did not get along) published over in *Astounding*.

Thus, it's often overlooked that Leigh Brackett's early science fiction adventures are also highly critical of capitalism, colonialism and imperialism. Leigh Brackett's heroes and heroines are outsiders, drifters, rebels and petty criminals who live on the margins of society. Several of them, including her most famous creation, the interplanetary outlaw Eric John Stark, are also people of colour, at a time when the genre was still chalk-white.

In the 1940s, Leigh Brackett was dubbed "the Queen of Space Opera", but she was so much more than that. In addition to science fiction, Leigh Brackett also wrote hardboiled crime fiction. When director Howard Hawks chanced to read her 1944 crime novel *No Good from a Corpse*, he recruited her to write the screenplay for the 1946 noir classic *The Big Sleep* — in collaboration with none other than William Faulkner. This led to a decades-long screenwriting career, which includes such classics as *Rio Bravo* (1959), *Hatari!* (1962), *El Dorado* (1967) and *The Long Goodbye* (1973). Leigh Brackett even wrote an early draft of the screenplay for *The Empire Strikes Back*, which is only fitting, since *Star Wars* borrowed heavily from the sword and planet stories Brackett wrote in the 1940s.

The screenplay for *The Empire Strike Back* also won Brackett a highly deserved posthumous Hugo Award. Sadly, Hugo glory eluded her during her lifetime, though Brackett was the first woman ever nominated for a Hugo

Award, for the post-apocalyptic novel *The Long Tomorrow* in 1956. But it would take until 2020 for Brackett's work from the 1940s to win not one but two Retro Hugos for her 1944 novel *Shadow Over Mars* and an essay about "The Science Fiction Field."

But even if we think we know everything there is to know about Leigh Brackett, there are still stories by her that are little known and have rarely been reprinted. First published in the March 1957 issue of the short-lived magazine *Venture Science Fiction*, "The Queer Ones" has only had a handful of reprints, most of them more than forty years ago.

By 1957, it was increasingly becoming clear that the habitable solar system, in which most of Leigh Brackett's stories of the 1940s had been set, did not exist. And so "The Queer Ones" takes place not on Venus or Mars, but right here on good old Earth, though Brackett's gift for atmospheric descriptions makes the Appalachian backwoods feel as menacing and alien as the deserts of Mars.

As happens so often with Brackett's stories, the protagonists, whether human or not, are outsiders. And as in many of her stories, Leigh Brackett shows a lot of sympathy for those dismissed or derided by society, such as unwed mother Sally Tate, her son Billy, and their sprawling rural family.

Leigh Brackett also makes use of her mystery writing skills, because "The Queer Ones" reads like a hardboiled crime tale, and it's easy to imagine Humphrey Bogart playing the first person narrator, small town newspaperman Hank Temple. Only the mystery to be solved is not earthly in nature.

"The Queer Ones" is very much a story of its time. It draws on the UFO sighting craze of the 1950s and on Cold War fears of infiltration by aliens, but these aliens are alien in the most literal sense of the word.

Leigh Brackett's tendency to tackle social issues of the day in her science fiction is also on display, because these aliens are not evil Communist stand-ins come to invade Earth, but illegal immigrants looking for a better life. Even the title — which feels so very old-fashioned to us today — can be seen as a reference to the Immigration and Nationality Act of 1952, since homosexuality and other "perverse" acts were explicitly listed among several criteria for denying visas to potential immigrants.

"The Queer Ones" may not be as flashy as Leigh Brackett's better known tales of adventures on Mars and Venus, but it is an excellent story and highly deserving of rediscovery.

The Canvas Pyramid
by **Jane Roberts**

(Originally appeared in the March 1957 issue of *The Magazine of Fantasy and Science Fiction*. It has only been republished once, in 1958.)

The town was flat. The sun baked men's bones into hard loaves and their skin was crusty and dry. The men's huts leaned wearily, one against the other, and the odor of okra and pork sunk deep into the cracks and crevices, the dusty bedclothes, the timber and soul of the huts themselves.

This was the town and its people. And each hut was one room with a creaky bed, a bureau, an ancient sink, stove-grimy pinups of movie stars, calendars, saints. And there were children with rickets, birth-dirty; tired women with tongueless eyes; forsaken men who sat listless and unwondering.

Tiny hovel heaps; these houses crowded one upon the other beside the dusty dirt road; backward and age-spent, this town only fifty miles from glittering Daytona, tourists and neon hotels. Only once or twice, now and then, did a visitor arrive, startling the town, walking gingerly from a shining auto up to a ramshackle step or porch.

Only itinerant salesmen, gaudy with false amiability, flashing a "Brother, I'm your friend" smile. And it was impolite to offend, a sacrilege not to please, and so they nodded, the dusty men, the unwondering women, they nodded and signed, paid down payments on appliances, insurance policies, gadgets that they knew would somehow never arrive.

And the children stood and stared long after the stranger had passed from sight. Reverently they watched even the cloud of dust that enclosed the miraculous machine, but they were silent for they knew no words to express their wonder, and their elders had never known.

But they knew he was no salesman, that very night that the shining black limousine pulled up way out at the edge of town. It stopped a moment, a night-black beetle. The lights flashed on. Three men sprang out, wire-thin, supple as weeds.

They stood silently for a moment in the darkness, and then with the head-lights glimmering they moved quickly, delicately as insects, back and forth from car to field. Ropes writhed in dirt and stone, hammers pounded, and a weary monstrosity of canvas settled down with heaves and groans.

And in the morning the tent waited; waited to be filled with the earth-weary, time-worn women; the ricket-ridden, lost-eyed children; the men who sat sullenly in the black-mouthed doorways. And so they knew, the people, as they squatted on mattresses littered with refuse, they knew when they saw the flapping canvas pyramid that this was no ordinary salesman with whom they had to deal.

They wondered what he wanted, here in the weary, scrubby-poor town, with his limousine and his tent, his curving-smile mouth and spinach-green eyes. They wondered what he wanted, he and the two men that followed and watched and listened closely when he spoke.

And Brother Michael smiled and picked his teeth. He daubed perfume on his frayed coat lapel and gazed with hopeful speculation at the distance between the tent and town. He had parked not too close, and yet not too far away, and this involved a subtle psychological distinction, in that his very position made him part, and yet not part, and was a token of welcome but not familiarity.

And if his suit was store-bought, somewhat elegant, still it claimed a slight, calculated shabbiness about the lapel, and each morning with infinite caution Brother Michael dusted his shiny black oxfords with a film of dust. And his manner? That, too, was a study in subtle variations, each calculated to give a definite effect. It was dignified, definitely the bearing of a leader, and yet touched with a hint of humility and even, when the occasion warranted, self-depreciation.

He was tall and dark, a considerable asset, rather stockily built, and his carefully waved black hair fell in a practiced tumble over his wide forehead. The spinach-green eyes beneath could smile with disarming frankness, or in an instant glow with the fire of diabolical inspiration.

In fact, from the waist up, Brother Michael was altogether pleased with his appearance. It was only the legs, undeniably long and regrettably knock-kneed, that caused him undue concern. It looked, on initial examination, as if God had intended the self-styled Brother to be all legs, and only at the last moment fashioned the rest of the torso with the material still left unused.

So early that morning Brother Michael sent his two Brothers of the Inner Temple to meet and size up the population of the town. Only then did he extract a portable icebox from his car, a bottle from his small black bag, and sitting back, enjoy all by himself the cooling draughts of rye on the rocks.

He picked his teeth, unconsciously shoved the deep wave on his forehead into place, and surveyed with satisfaction the scene his eyes devoured. For it was the beginning of the orange season, the most auspicious time. The smell of pork was strong and empty pop bottles littered door jambs and window sills.

It was easy to tell about these small Florida towns, even before the tent was erected and the first testimony made in the name of the Lord. It was a simple method. When there were pop bottles the season was good and people had money; when it was bad the people drank water.

Brother Michael sighed, finished off his drink, and entered the tent through the back flap. The dankness inside pushed at his neck and shoulders and his nostrils quivered at the heavy scent of bodies that had hidden in the folds. Someday he would have a church. Then at least the odor of one congregation could escape through open windows before the next arrived.

Still there was work to be done, and he unsnapped a small section of canvas that opened only peephole size, and taking out a pair of binoculars, he stared with glittering eyes toward the town.

Brother Larry was just approaching the first hut. He was also tall, but very lean, with a youthful white face and wilted corn-silk hair. He knocked on the door, then turned and stared with studied abstraction at the street about him. When he finally looked up to see a thin, straight-mouthed woman standing before him, Brother Larry seemed at first to be taken by surprise, as if it were the last thing he could think of, to be standing there and caught off guard.

"Oh," he said, stammering, and his long arms made a helpless gesture at his sides. Good, Brother Michael thought, watching. But still a trifle too self-conscious, too mute. He'd told Larry a million times that the arms shouldn't just *dangle*, they should *speak*. They should convey, in one gesture, your overwhelming sorrow at the necessity of disturbing the good woman of the house.

Still, youthful earnestness was conveyed by each muscle of Larry's body. It bent forward almost in half at the waist, and the hands, sprouting out at the end of the narrow arms, seemed to beg for admittance.

Brother Michael grinned with satisfaction. The woman was smiling hesitantly. Larry took a step backward, stumbled, and whoosh, he was inside. That step backward always took them off guard. They opened the door in sudden alarm, and all at once you were in. It was the best possible technique, and Brother Michael laughed. He'd sold a lot of encyclopedias that way.

He put the binoculars away, not needing them to know what was going on inside. Brother Larry would stubbornly refuse the offer of the one available chair as if acknowledging that he was unworthy of such fine attention.

Instead, shoving his unruly hair backward with a boyish gesture, he would suddenly plop down on the floor, ignore the dirt and litter and smile disarmingly at the grimy, astonished children.

"Boy, it's just good to sit down," and then, "I hate to bother you-all, but could I have a glass of wata?" —and all in perfect southern accent, though Brother Larry was born and raised in Northern Ohio.

And the battle was won. This small gesture, this insignificant request immediately put the woman at ease, and more, it seemed to indebt Brother Larry to her own hospitality. And Larry, when he had drunk deeply, would smile.

"Matter of fact," he'd say, "I'm here with Brother Michael," and he would lower his voice and bow his head. "But I was just so thirsty" (frank, now) "that I just had to get in outa that ole heat.

"What? Well, I really shouldn't be telling you this, but since you-all been so nice to me and all—well, Brother Michael, he received a message from God for all the poor folk.

"I know just what you mean, it was hard for me to believe at first. But once I heard! Oh, Sister, the spirit of God is sweet, and He gave me forgiveness and healed my soul.

"Yes, matter a fact, he will be at the tent. I shouldn't be telling you this, but he might, he just very well might receive a vision from God this very night! I'd better be gitting on, now. Remember, though, don't you tell anyone now.

"But just imagine, Brother Michael can tell the poor how to get rich, and not just spirit-wise either, but rich in good hard cash.

"Well, thank you again Miss... Oh, it's Mrs. I sure am sorry. I just naturally thought them young boys was your brothers. Well goodby, Sister. The Lord be with you."

Brother Michael waited and finally picked up the binoculars. Larry had had plenty of time to give the pitch and be back by now. Then he scowled. Larry was halfway to the tent; he was whistling, and a cigarette dangled from his thin lips. He looked toward Brother Michael and waved jauntily, and Mike cursed. A million times, a million times he'd told that damn fool to preserve that boyish routine until he was safely inside. Lord almighty, even suckers had eyes. It didn't pay to underestimate them.

Still Larry had done well and soon the town would be buzzing with the legend ready-made of Brother Michael's holiness and the message he had received from God. He motioned to John and Larry and ducked inside the tent. Nobody would get a glimpse of him until the proper time, and by then Sue would have time to do her stuff.

"*Sister* Sue," John said, laughing.

Brother Michael picked his teeth. "She'd better remember to take off her rouge and nail polish this time," he warned.

John colored; his wide rabbit face wrinkled and screwed itself up in anxious puckers. He was fat but neat, kindly and obedient as a pet. Now, though, his face darkened, and his wide, light eyes looked peeved.

"Aw, she's all right, Mike. She only forgot once. There ain't nobody that can work 'em up like Sue."

Mike smiled suddenly, forgivingly, and patted John on the shoulder. "OK. Just check her over first to make sure."

They sat, the three of them in the late afternoon, way out behind the tent where no one could see. Larry went out to the car to get smokes, and when he returned his eyes were worried.

"Mike, some jerk's coming up the road the other way." He stopped for breath and took a swig of rye. "Looks like a cut-in. He's all dressed in robes."

Mike looked up quickly. "Better'n mine?"

"Yeah."

Mike thought a moment, then sent John to the trunk. "My best black suit," he ordered. "No use trying to overawe him with robes, then." And to Larry, "Look like he's got dough?"

Larry put his glass down, looking bewildered. Direct questioning always made him sweat.

"Well?"

"Material of his robes looked good, what I could see." Larry wrinkled his forehead and started chewing on a piece of grass. "Seems like he'd be riding if he had dough."

But John was back, and quickly Mike put on the elegantly plain black suit and white tunic. With one hand he smoothed down the wave in his hair, and with the other he pressed his eyelids shut. The two other men, also changing, were reverently silent. Finally Brother Michael opened his eyes. Gone was the irresolution and indecision. Calm, powerful, assured, the black eyes stared outward with divine benevolence.

The bottles were shoved in a hastily dug hole, the cigarette stubs hidden, and the three men advanced side by side to the front of the tent. Brother Michael wore his plain suit as if it were a bishop's robe. Serene dignity radiated outward from his being, and yet his bowed head proclaimed his humility, his awareness that he was but a lowly emissary of the Lord.

Nevertheless his eyes, beneath the half-closed lids, were restless. He tilted his head backward, lifted it up in an attitude of prayer, and through his slit lids surveyed from head to toe the stranger who was almost upon them. And he didn't like it one bit. Even before the other spoke, Mike knew he had been in business a long time. His makeup was flawless. His composure and stance gave the appearance of frightening authenticity, and for a moment Brother Michael felt a touch of undeniable fear.

Suppose, suppose, he thought, this man was actually a man of God. Often he'd had nightmares in which he met, for the first time, a sincere priest or minister, an authentic preacher who would, at one glance, strip away his own hypocrisy and studied holiness. In his particular line of business this was admittedly unlikely, but now cold sweat beaded his folded palms.

But then he pulled himself together. What real man of God could afford robes like this boy was wearing? No bona fide preacher was that well off. With startling rapidity his mind searched for a way to cut himself in; and he wondered, at the same time, what this joker was doing way out here if he had a good racket of his own.

The men came together cautiously. Brother Michael opened his eyes half-way, folded his hands again, and took a step forward.

"Good afternoon, Brother, welcome in the name of the Lord."

The stranger bowed, inclined his head toward Brother Michael and ignored Brothers Larry and John who stood uneasily, scowling beneath sanctimonious smiles.

"Blessings in the name of the Lord."

Brother Michael groaned inwardly. This boy must really have a good gimmick, he thought. The white gown was spotless, even the hem was untouched by the dust of the road. Showmanship like that came high. He let his face shine in an expansive smile of welcome.

"Did you wish to speak to me, Brother, concerning the business of the Lord?"

The stranger's full, fleshy lips moved only slightly, and his hollow eyes glimmered beneath heavy white brows. He looked, Mike thought, like an Inquisition monk, every line of his face set in disapproving, severe lines, an alien to humor.

"Could we speak privately, without the aid of your two blessed assistants in the Lord? In all humility," he said, "the business I have in mind is of the most private nature and secrecy is essential."

Brother Michael smiled, resisting an impulse to tell the stranger to go to hell. The other's college English annoyed him, and more than that, there was his studied appearance of legitimacy, and a sober, almost sinister fanaticism in his manner that made Brother Michael more uneasy than he would admit. But beneath this, there was something Mike couldn't put his finger on — something terrifyingly familiar in the other's appearance, and he felt that the stranger was watching him so closely that it almost seemed he was picking up some significant clues from Mike's own mind.

Still, he looked well-heeled, and Mike tilted his head, closed his eyes and considered. Then, nodding gently, he held up one hand to the others as if in blessing. The gesture meant, stick around and listen outside.

Brothers Larry and John returned the gesture, bowed slightly, and walked slowly and with dignity toward the town. They would circle and return. Brother Michael smiled.

"You don't believe in the second immersion?" he asked, his eyes narrowing at the other's reply. It was a loaded question and the stranger had given the wrong answer, at least for the South. Suddenly Mike felt more relaxed. Obviously the other had no connections down here. There wasn't anything to worry about.

So he spread his legs apart more comfortably and leaned backward. "What did you have in mind, Brother?" But the expression on the stranger's face did not soften or relax at Mike's easier tone, and the pasty white skin retained its loose, solemn folds. Mike's face hardened for a moment before he let his wide black eyes recapture their silent fervor.

"Surely," he probed, "you didn't travel here merely to make the acquaintance of a poor brother in the Lord?" And the other's attention snapped taut. His lips opened in a silent, humorless smile that broadened the heavy triangle of his nose.

"I am interested in bringing more souls to the true light." He eyed Brother Michael severely and Mike rocked back slightly on his heels.

"Of course, of course, Brother, aren't we all? We all try our best," he muttered, glancing off in the distance to show that the time of business was at hand.

"I'll come to the point, then. I've worked up a new method of conversion that I should like to try."

Brother Michael let a tinge of youthful bewilderment touch his eyes. "A new method?" he asked. "Surely the old, proven ways are best." And as he spoke, something inside Mike turned over. Something warned him to say no. Without finding out what it was, or what was in it for him. To refuse quickly so that he would not be tempted. The man repelled him, yet he still felt drawn by that indefinable sense of familiarity.

He made up his mind and his face was a study in gratitude and regret. "I'm terribly sorry, terribly. But even in the Brotherhood of the Lord we have our weaknesses, and I admit that in the matter of conversion I am somewhat old-fashioned." He brushed back a lock of hair and let his hands dangle helplessly at his sides.

"To tell the truth, I'm flattered, flattered that you should like to work here, but after all"—he lowered his voice—"who are we to dabble with the tried methods of conversion?"

The stranger watched Brother Michael intently as he listened, then bowed his head. "We all obey the will of the Lord," he replied sonorously. "Still, my parishioners are well blessed with material possessions, and I am prepared to offer five hundred dollars for the privilege of experimenting this evening."

$500... Mike shook his head and picked his teeth. For that much money he could like anyone. He leaned forward cautiously. "A thousand."

The stranger smiled sorrowfully. "I'm afraid that my offer must stand. Surely a humble follower of the Lord does not require more." Mike smiled. He wondered if the stranger knew that he would never have touched the deal if he had gone all the way on price. A deal for a thousand would have a catch in it somewhere.

But he felt uncomfortable under the other's scrutiny again and looked up. "What do you want me to do?"

Even then there was no hint of eagerness in the stranger's face. "Hardly anything," he said. "When you have prepared the people for their...their..."

"Testimonials," Mike said, lifting his eyebrow.

"Yes. When you have prepared them, merely end up with the words, '*The Lord is a great white bird.*' I'll take over from there."

Brother Michael smiled and coughed politely, and the other man withdrew two hundred-dollar bills from his gown. "The rest after the ceremony," he said, not looking at the money, acting as if it were not there at all...

The people's faces that night were apathetic, passive, yet something within them waited to be kindled. Sister Sue, in a long, dark dress, stood swaying before them, her black hair flowing and her dark eyes shining from a pale white face.

> "*Glory, glory, glory to the Lord,*
> *Glory, glory, glory to the Lord,*
> *Glory, glory, glory to the good Lord Jesus.*
> *Hallelujah, Hallelujah, Hallelujah!*
> *Down you sinners,*
> *Hide your heads, weep with shame,*
> *Wash your hearts with the blood of the Lamb,*
> *Blood of the Lamb, Blood of the Lamb,*
> *Blood of the Good Lord, Jesus...*"

And the weary-eyed women and the hungry, lean men beat their breasts and sobbed, and lowered their heads and listened to the voice of the messenger of God. Sister Sue motioned to Brother Michael that her job was done, the people were prepared and waiting and suddenly she stopped yelling and the heads raised and Brother Michael stood before them.

His face was contorted with sorrow and his voice so soft that every ear strained to hear his words.

"Oh sinners, sinners! Oh, sinners, how you have wounded the Good Lord Jesus. How you have sinned against Him, thrust a million nails into His still burning flesh.

"Adulterers, hypocrites," his voice boomed, "do you think He knows you not? He knows well that you sin in private and in darkness and behind closed doors. His vengeance seeks you out. In very truth His justice should cut you down, here and now, while you think yourselves hidden in the multitude.

"But the Lord, ah, the Lord is merciful. He... He... *Wait!* Wait. I hear Him! I hear the Lord! He's near, very near. Feel His wings hover about you. He's here, I tell you, here!"

The crowd shivered, trembled, their eyes glued to the figure before them. And suddenly Brother Michael screamed, covered his face with his robe. "Oh Jesus, Master, speak to me!" He was on his knees, collapsed before the Lord, and Brother John, on cue, began to speak in tongues.

"Forgive me, oh Lord," someone wailed, and the women began to yell.

"Oh, Lord, Lord." Brother Michael screamed and everyone waited in ecstasy. "Oh the Lord is like a great white bird, His wings beateth me down," and suddenly, between Brother Michael and the congregation stood a third figure, the figure of the stranger. And Mike grew cold. What was it, what, and he racked his brain.

What was it that made the stranger's appearance so terribly familiar? But he stopped thinking as the voice ripped through the tent:

"FOLLOW ME, FOLLOW ME INTO THE VERY STRONGHOLD OF THE LORD. FOLLOW ME INTO HIS TEMPLE. THE LORD HAS SPOKEN. FOLLOW ME, OH YE SINNERS, INTO THE HEART OF THE MERCIFUL LORD."

And his voice was no voice Mike had ever heard before, and his face was no face that had ever looked upon the earth before. And Brother Michael covered up his head and followed, sobbing, rushing blindly with the others, and the weight of his own guilt dragged down upon him.

The temple rose, shimmering, outside in the darkness, and rays of love radiated outward from its glowing interior. Even then, even then Mike was vaguely aware that nothing had been in that spot before, only brown grasses and insects, scrubby stumps of trees.

He stumbled, fell. Waves of exultation drove him onward until the goal was almost in sight. "Wait, wait," he called to the others, tripping over his white gown, but they rushed on and passed him by.

But what was he doing? What? "Stop, stop," a voice within him cried, but stumbling, his body still rushed on. "Stop, stop," the voice called, and brought his legs to a sudden halt. "Pull yourself together," he screamed, and bit his arm till the blood came and his temples pounded.

"Don't fall for it. It's a gimmick," he ordered, and he closed his mind and eyes from the shimmering temple and his heart from the waves of love. Immediately a chasm of loneliness opened up inside his mind, a feeling of banishment, the sudden knowledge that all his quests would be in vain. He shook his head, sobbing, suddenly knowing this to be the final trick of the charlatan, calculated to drive him crazy, to send him running to the temple. To the temple that was not a temple.

Sweat iced his palms. Resolutely he blanked his mind, and suddenly everything swept into focus. He saw the people, whose reason he had helped destroy. He saw them dash past, and with horrible clarity he glimpsed for the last time the stranger's face before it disappeared inside.

And he knew, when he saw the face, why the man had seemed familiar. Why the stranger had watched him so closely when he talked. Because the figure of the charlatan was composed down to the last detail from the image of Mike as he had always wanted to be. The white hair instead of black — the broad cheekbones — the straight legs, the built-in appearance of authenticity.

"God," Mike yelled and he meant it. The man — was it a man? — had formed himself according to the picture already existing in his own mind. Why? What was he, really? And Mike looked up to the temple. Not a temple, but a ship. And a ship that earth would not know for years to come.

Mike started forward but Larry went running by, and Mike lunged out, grabbed him. "Let me go, let me go," Larry yelled, and Mike gave him a right to the jaw and sat, panting, holding him down.

But he caught a new movement out of the corner of his eye, and he knocked Larry out and left him lying on the ground. The ship was moving! The people! Where was that bastard taking the people? He groaned and started running. He had betrayed his own kind to a…a pied piper from some other where. He was the judas goat — the judas *man*…

He got closer and as he did the ship started spinning. It sent him reeling to the ground.

The night was deathly quiet. The moon shone on the flapping canvas pyramid, the empty pop bottles, the crowded huts. Mike walked over to Larry and helped him up. They stood together staring at the silence. Mike reached into the pocket of his gown. Inside he felt the extra bills, and he knew how much was there.

Afterword by Lorelei Esther

"The Canvas Pyramid" was Roberts' third published short story. Though her science fiction marked a divergence from the poetry that characterized the beginning of her career, her stories, and "The Canvas Pyramid" in particular, still contain literary prose and stirring imagery that are clearly written from the soul. "The Canvas Pyramid" is also a prime example of Roberts' skill at blending spiritualism into the science fiction genre, a common thread amongst many of her early pieces. One can detect some of the otherworldly themes of Jane Roberts' later works, but this story is much more reminiscent of her early life and style. "The Canvas Pyramid" is both the epitome of Jane Roberts' pre-Seth awakening, as well as an entertaining and thought-provoking read — a stunning experience that leaves the reader reeling with questions embedded with implicit answers.

Born in the midst of the Great Depression in 1929, Roberts was raised in extreme poverty by her grandparents and abusive mother. Her experiences growing up in a poor family clearly influence some of the most striking descriptions in the story. From the leaning, pork-smelling huts, to the pop bottles in the windows, Roberts' imagery contains a depth on the level of John Steinbeck's *The Grapes of Wrath*.

For 18 months of her early adolescence, Roberts lived in a Roman Catholic orphanage, and religion became a major factor in her life. "The Canvas Pyramid" revolves around religion, though in an unusually pessimistic light: rather than portraying a hopeful belief system, Christianity is yet another "too good to be true" product for con-men and con-things alike to shop to poor, helpless masses. If there is a God in the universe of "The Canvas Pyramid", He's certainly not anywhere near the small Florida town where it takes place. Such a spiteful take on religion is unusual for the time, and it possibly describes Roberts' personal view of the subject, as well as the freedom the science fiction pages granted her to express that opinion.

I think the most interesting aspect of the story is that there is no hero. The people of the town, victims all, flock mindlessly to their fate like gullible sheep. Brother Michael (or 'Mike' as he increasingly sees himself) is charismatic as the viewpoint character, but is as much a villain as any con-man. As for the other preacher, while his motives are unknown, he inspires a peculiar, un-heroic dread. The grayness of each character's morality, and the ambiguity of who's to blame, aids beautifully in Roberts' allegorical social commentary.

Overall, "The Canvas Pyramid" is an expertly crafted collection of Roberts' experiences and views, with a spectacular dash of the paranormal. It is everything one could want from a science fiction story.

We Move on Turning Stone
by Leah Bodine Drake

(Originally appeared in the April 1957 issue of *The Magazine of Fantasy and Science Fiction*. It has never been republished before now.)

We move on turning stone
Through the dark-bright of space,
Lighted by lonely sun
And the moon's known face.

We turn up every stone
Hoping to find some bright-
Ness in the dark. Alone
We seek an unknown light.

Darkly we turn our face
To suns and moons unknown;
We seek through lonely space
For brightness not in stone.

Lonely in unknown space,
Hopeful of dark or bright,
We seek in every face,
We turn towards any light.

Afterword by Erica L. Frank

Leah Bodine Drake wrote macabre and fantastic poetry through the thirties, forties, and fifties; she died of cancer in 1964, just a month short of her sixtieth birthday. She won several poetry awards, which were published in mainstream magazines as well as science fiction and horror venues.

Most of her poetry focused on supernatural themes: Ghosts, witches, the fae; nightmares and death; man's foolishness in the face of otherworldly powers. More were published by *Weird Tales* or in Arkham House collections than in science fiction magazines, but *The Magazine of Fantasy and Science Fiction* published several of her later poems.

"We Move on Turning Stone" is a departure from her normal writing habits. Many of her poems are about the dangers of encounters with mythic creatures; only a few touch on the wonder and yearning that makes us seek out those risks. *Turn, stone, bright, lone*: these are repeated in every verse. Drake brings us a vision of space travel imagined not as conquest or colonization, but as a search for beauty and comfort.

Moonshine
by Ruth M. Goldsmith

(Originally appeared in the June 1957 issue of *The Magazine of Fantasy and Science Fiction*. It has only been republished once, in 1958.)

The day Ocie Powell's still blew up it brought down two ducks headed back north and an Ix ship that had been gliding low. Only the ducks were lucky enough to drop out of sight for good and miss the rest of the confusion.

For a time Ocie and his partners, Lee Oliver and Ranse Hawkins, lay where they landed in a clump of palmettos. Under the circumstances it was pleasant to rest there, even necessary. They'd found the cooking-off hot and tiring and tedious and had offered these findings to each other as reasons for sampling the run—until they got against giving reasons. Then they'd just kept on sampling. When they opened their eyes now the twisted pine branches above revolved around them. When they closed their eyes they revolved around themselves.

But the Ixians, grassy-green, four-legged, and two-headed, climbed out of their ship and set out determinedly to locate the disturbance that had brought them down.

The three men waited, patiently and peaceably, for the world to right itself, until the sound of tramping feet bothered them into raising their heads. The site had been chosen with an eye to the view. On a clear day and with normal vision they could see far across the level ground with its meager scattering of tall, straight-trunked pines—far enough in every direction to give them plenty of time to leave in case someone they didn't feel like welcoming was coming.

They saw the Ixians some distance away, spread out fanwise and moving toward them. The Florida sun sparkled sharply off the approaching figures, and the three looked around for their flat-topped cowboy hats and pulled them low over their eyes.

"Looks like the sheriff's done bought hisself some uniforms," Ocie said.

"Man, they sure are *bright*," Lee said. "They must've raised the fines to pay for that outfit."

"We'd better be getting out of here," Ocie said.

Spanish moss hung still on the branches, and mash dripped slowly down, as they studied the possibility. It meant getting up and going over to the truck, starting it up—which might be difficult because it was an aging and ailing machine—and then bouncing over the open ground until they came to the road. It was an energetic measure.

On the other hand, as Ranse Hawkins finally decided it, "We stay still, maybe they won't find us."

The feet tramped steadily nearer. Ocie found the funnel on the ground near him and, holding it to his eyes like a telescope, peeked out once through the palmetto fans and spotted the antennae on top of the green heads. "Walkie-talkie," he whispered disgustedly, shoving the funnel in his pocket. "That ain't hardly playing fair."

The antennae bent and pointed at where the men were hidden, and quivered at each other. The feet trudged a little more and stopped. The three could hear better than they could see and they knew that they'd been ringed in.

They got up sheepishly, hands in the air.

"Howdy, Sheriff," they said pleasantly, swaying slightly toward the newcomers.

The delicate antennae swayed silently back at them.

It was a little interplanetary misunderstanding: a sheriff, like everyone else, and perhaps most especially a sheriff, ought to be friendly enough to speak when he's spoken to, but the Ixians couldn't communicate except by their antennae. Otherwise, they might right now be receiving honors for concluding a successful expedition.

Having waved a cordial "How do you do?" with their antennae, they started moving off in the direction from which they'd come, back toward their ship, convinced that they could not pursue this investigation further and would have to mark the spot on their maps as a place to be avoided.

Ocie and Lee and Ranse moved with them, hands still in the air, but rapidly losing their peaceableness and patience. It was an odd procession. The Ixians, puzzled but still trudging, were zipping messages back and forth at the head, while the three men brought up a somewhat threshing tail—Ocie plump and looking plumper because he always stuffed things in his pockets, the other two long and lean and a little springy at the knees. The men were preoccupied with the affront of not having their greeting returned; and with their heads down to keep out the glare, they didn't even notice they were at the rear.

The sight of the grounded spaceship rubbed salt into their wounded feelings. "Wasting the taxpayers' money on newfangled swamp-buggies," Lee complained indignantly, "instead of spending it paving the roads."

"That's what comes of putting the wrong men in office," Ocie said. He'd been about to climb in the hatch, but he swung around abruptly. He was so mad he threw the first thing that came to hand—the funnel—against the side of the ship and didn't even notice how the antennae recoiled from the sharp sound.

"Sheriff," he said slowly, "there ain't *me,* nor nobody else in my family, ever going to vote for *you* again."

Darkness engulfed them inside the ship, and the only sound was of their own heavy breathing. It was a place where anyone who was going to have misgivings would have them, and Lee said, "I ain't so sure that was the sheriff. Looked a little different somehow."

"If they were federal men they should have said so," Ocie said, still hot under the collar. "By God, I'm going to ask them. They ain't got no right not to talk to me." He started up, but the ship lurched and it was too late then for doubt to rescue anybody. They blacked out as the ship took off.

A boxlike room with metal walls and no windows, a single door with grillwork, dim light over all—that was what the three saw when they came to. They raised themselves carefully to sitting positions and reached for the makings of cigarettes.

"'Tain't the county jail," Ocie said, authoritatively.

"It's some place," Ranse said, trying to hold the little cigarette paper steady in his hand, "that makes tobacco act like them Mexican jumping beans."

"Must be a federal prison," Lee said.

Ocie twisted the end of his cigarette slowly. "They can't put us in no federal prison—not without a fair trial, they can't." But the words were quiet; there was no strength left for fiery indignation.

It was at this moment that an Ixian appeared at the grillwork door. Silently and soberly they looked at it and saw a green creature with two heads and four legs and something sprouting from the top of the heads. A set of retractable arms reached out to grasp the grill as the creature pressed close to get a good look.

"Foreigners," Ocie said, over a dry throat.

"Enemies of the United States," Ranse concluded.

They'd been captured, that much they remembered. Usually they weren't. Among other reasons, they set up stills to show their spirit; they knew of the days when, it was said, every self-respecting man had a still, and by tradition they resented being told what to do or what not to do.

It was spirit that made them open their throats now, as they sat with their backs to the wall, and cut loose with the rebel yell; but it was fright that made their yell so fiendishly shrill.

There was nowhere for the shrieks to go except out the door, and there stood the green creature who couldn't talk, couldn't hear, except by means of his sensitive antennae.

The antennae recoiled, then started a long slow slide down the Ixian's foreheads. He fell away from the door and groped back to his companions. Hospitalized and nourished, he'd regain his faculties, but the wound was serious enough to put the green creatures on a split stick. Their instructions on leaving Ix had run more or less: Think. Think. Think. Establish satellite to revolve around earth, concealed from detection. Gather information by instrument from satellite and by trips to earth — analyze, correlate. Avoid provoking incident but take specimens when possible without arousing suspicion. Think. Think. Think.

They'd followed their instructions to the letter because obedience was second nature to them. It had happened that one of the ships sent out to explore had been accidentally brought to earth, and that some of the inhabitants had climbed aboard very willingly and accompanied them back to the base. As researchers they were inordinately pleased with the specimens; and with the inborn stubbornness of researchers, they didn't intend to be pried loose easily from the chance of gaining information from them. But the specimens had suddenly turned dangerous enough to put the whole undertaking in jeopardy.

They sent an urgent query back to Ix, asking what to do with the specimens, and decided that while waiting for an answer they would treat them with the great courtesy and respect due to the best thinkers, the greatest honor that could be accorded on Ix.

By the time two more of the Ixians had suffered the loss of antennae, due to the rebel yell, they divined that these particular thinkers didn't like to do their thinking in a small locked room.

So the door of the cell swung open and Ocie, Lee, and Ranse settled their cowboy hats on their heads in a manner that spoke of grim determination, and walked out as though they had holsters at the hip. The Ixians bowed respectfully as they came.

"Looks like the googies is trying to be friendly," Ocie said. They'd taken to calling their captors the googies because of the sound the padded feet of the Ixians made when they walked — like walking in shoes full of water. But the sudden friendliness didn't turn their heads and they countered it by just touching their hands to the big brims of their hats; their eyes stayed watch-ful.

With pride gleaming through their deference, the Ixians showed them the large laboratory where they weighed, measured, analyzed, and recorded in-formation about earth and its life. It didn't interest their newest specimens at all. They had no reason to recognize the results of the studies and looked with suspicion even at such simple things as the Ixian equivalents of Bunsen burn-ers and calculators.

The gardens were better. The plants grew in something like soil and were irrigated by what might be water. The googies offered them food and they ate and found it filling. "This ain't bad," Ocie said. He was partial to sweets and starches and he was eating something that tasted awfully sweet, though it looked like eggplant, and something that looked like wheat but tasted like corn.

"I'd rather have me a dish of okra or turnip greens or black-eye peas," Lee said.

"There's a plenty, anyway," Ranse said. "We won't go hungry."

The food did lull them though, and made the shock of their next discovery that much worse. Urged persistently toward the scanner, they finally made out enough to realize that that was earth way down there. Then someone let out a low whistle that made the googies step back apprehensively.

Ocie pointed to the far-off earth and pointed to himself and the others and made motions of flying by flapping his arms. Relieved and happy, uncompre-hending, the googies waved their antennae wildly in return.

"Looks like we're going to have to *fight* our way out of here," Ocie said.

"We fight our way out of here" — Ranse shook his head — "and we're in for a right smart *drop!*"

The three returned to their cell by preference. They studied all around their problem but couldn't come up with a way of getting back to earth.

"It never rains but it pours," Ocie said, searching his pockets. "Getting treed by a bunch of foreigners and now I don't know where my tobacco is at." He brought something out of his pocket but it wasn't tobacco. It was yeast, and then the plan came together, just naturally.

"Eggplant sweet as sugar," Lee said.

"Something that tastes like corn must *be* like corn," Ocie said.

"Plenty of equipment in that place where they work," Ranse said, getting up and pushing his hat back to a jaunty angle.

The Ixians were pleased to see their specimens making use of their facilities and settling down to study. They came over to watch whenever they could spare a minute from their own work, and admired the extremely careful attention the three gave to their operations. They felt a sort of dry-as-dust affinity for the experimenters, and hoped to learn a great deal.

They did. The result of the studies wasn't good but it was whisky — clear, scalding, and with powerful effect on the googies. "Why, they got a skinful," Ocie remarked in astonishment, "just from dipping their sprouts in the stuff."

And considerably later, Ranse said wearily, "I never seen anyone get such a *long* jag from just such a little."

Picture the poor Ixians, precision workers of the cosmos, who always measured by the finest lines of the instrument, always calculated to more places than was necessary, always checked and rechecked results like little victims of compulsive behavior complexes — picture the Ixians, freed for the first time from the burden of being exact!

They sent Ix a report that earth was the most amazing thing they'd ever seen; that it doubled itself and bounced in its orbit; that it defied description; and, finally, that they couldn't bear to *think* about it. The ships that were supposed to go to earth would sometimes go there and sometimes just race each other through space like hot-rods.

Anxious queries ticked in from Ix. but all these were torn from the machine without being read, folded into miniature spaceships, and sent sailing. For the three master distillers the Ixians felt nothing but good will sprinkled with prankish affection, slapping them on the back with their antennae and tugging their big hats down over their eyes whenever they came near. So Ocie and the others forgot about trying to talk to them and stayed in their cell as much as possible.

"Well," Ocie said by way of consolation, "it was a good run, anyway."

"Yep," Lee said, "and it sure was nice not having to watch for the sheriff while we was cooking-off."

"It sure was," Ranse said slowly, and by then the plan had come together, just naturally.

"You can talk googie better than us," Lee said to Ocie. "You got more padding, so you can listen to them better. You can talk them into taking you down and bringing you back. It ain't as though they was losing us for good."

The understanding of the googies had expanded amazingly. They landed Ocie near the wreckage of the still and he signaled for them to wait, and drove off to town in the truck.

It was while he was in the store buying twenty cases of fruit jars that he had the bad luck to run into the sheriff. "Howdy, Ocie," the sheriff said.

"That's a powerful lot of fruit jars for a single man to be buying."

"It sure enough is, Sheriff," Ocie said. "And I'll swear, that's just what I told my friend when he asked me to get them for him. But he's courting this widow woman and he's just got a notion that if he takes around these fruit jars, and some fruits and vegetables for her to put up in them, she'll just naturally ask him around to help eat them."

"I'm real glad to hear that, Ocie," the sheriff said. "Real glad. I'd sure hate to come along, just doing my duty, and find you using them jars for something illegal."

"If I was you I wouldn't waste no time looking, Sheriff," Ocie advised him honestly, "'cause you ain't likely to find me."

All the same, when Ocie went back on the satellite and told of the meeting, the three agreed they'd better delay the first delivery to earth while the sheriff had time to hunt and not find.

When they were finally ready to go, another batch was ready for cooking off. They instructed the googies in the intricate process and left three of them to tend to it. But they didn't realize what a fine time the googies were having being irresponsible for a change.

The Ixians landed them on earth again with their load and they transferred the fruit jars full of whisky from the ship to the truck and covered them with a tarpaulin. Lee and Ranse sat in the cab with Ocie, and the happy Ixians sat on the load and on the tailgate, swinging their legs. They liked the feeling of the cool dark air flowing by their antennae, and the unpredictable bouncing of the truck made the green creatures merry. They laughed at the way foliage and phone poles rushed into the beam of the right headlight and then vanished. There were things on earth they never knew existed.

The three Ixians left on the satellite suspected they were missing a lot of fun and took off to join the others. The fire under the cooker was left to itself.

A Highway Patrol car parked at an intersection signaled the truck to stop. "Your left headlight is out," the trooper said, coming up to them.

"Officer," Ocie said, "I'm aiming to get that fixed soon's I get to town."

"Let's see your license," the trooper said sternly, playing his flashlight into the cab of the truck.

Ocie started searching his pockets. "I got it right here somewhere," he said.

The trooper took a step to the rear and played his flashlight over the back of the truck. The Ixians sparkled and shone in the beam. All those heads and legs were green, glittering, and unnerving. But the Ixians saw only a man and they were full of good will toward men. Antennae whipped out to slap him on the back; arms reached out and pulled his big-brimmed trooper's hat down snugly over his eyes.

Ocie accelerated and took the next turnoff back the way they'd come.

There was a mysterious flash in the sky that night that some people are still wondering and talking about. But the three guessed what had happened when they found the googies who'd been left to tend the cooking-off waiting by the other ships.

"The still must have blowed up," Lee said.

"It must have blowed the whole place up with it," Ocie said, "and that's a pity 'cause that was a right nice spot. We ain't likely to find as pretty a one again soon."

"Maybe they can piece it together again," Ranse said, "afterwards. Right now, we got to get this stuff hid."

"We bury it under the road," Ocie said. "The law'll never think of looking for it there."

They'd only started to dig up the dirt road when the sound of approaching feet stopped them.

But it wasn't the Highway Patrol, nor the sheriff and his deputies, nor agents of the State Beverage Department or the Federal Alcohol Tax Unit. For the first time in Ixian history a police force had been sent out to bring back an expedition.

The police bowed slightly and began a rapid quizzing of the renegades with their antennae. Sobering, the googies answered falteringly; and sobered, they waved their antennae sadly toward their friends and took off obediently with their police.

The three returned to their digging.

"They'll probably just get fines, maybe suspended," Ocie said, trying not to feel so bad.

The sound of the shovels was all that was heard for a while; then Ocie said, "I ain't ordinarily a drinking man, but it'd be a shame to bury *all* these jars, after what we been through."

Afterword by Alyssa Winans

Stories of first encounters have long appeared in both science fiction writing and mainstream media, to the extent that it may feel like all the stones have been overturned. Ruth M. Goldsmith's *Moonshine* shows us an approach that still feels fresh and charming despite all the first encounter tales that came after its first publishing in 1956.

Moonshine is one of only two published works by Goldsmith, and online searches reveal little further information about any works that may have gone unpublished. In light of the lack of information about her writing exploits, we can perhaps infer just two things about Goldsmith. One is that she cared deeply for both her parents and books, as she left most of her estate to the Mystic & Noank Library that served her Connecticut hometown. The second is that she had a sense of humor.

Goldsmith builds her story, *Moonshine*, on layers of mistaken identity, cultural misunderstandings, and a hefty helping of good-natured mischief. Readers get to enjoy two wildly different groups brought together by a somewhat unconventional abduction, as well as the age-old bonding activity of home distilling.

At first, it seems hard to glean much depth from such clueless parties, but they exhibit moments of cleverness when Goldsmith has her seemingly simple characters reveal that they have opinions on taxation, are always on the lookout for strategic opportunities, and sometimes have to write reports to their higher ups on a distant homeworld, just like the rest of us non-moonshiners and non-googies occasionally might. We can understand the simple joy the Ixians feel when they're experiencing a truck ride for the first time, or discovering the feeling of camaraderie with someone across a language barrier. In this way, we find serious moments of common ground and relatability within Goldsmith's comedy, just as the aliens and humans find a connection within the story.

It takes a deft hand to weave a tale with so many misunderstandings while keeping it from tipping from charm into frustration, and Goldsmith manages to walk the line the whole way through. The story is fairly short, and I found myself wondering what shenanigans Ocie and his crew might get up to after. What would the reprimanded Ixians tell their comrades about their wondrous time inspecting the Earth and its strange, brilliant minds?

The fact that we only have two stories from Goldsmith is a shame, but just as her beloved local library was the beneficiary of her legacy, so did she bequeath all of us another sort of estate: a refreshing jaunt of story that leaves us wanting more.

The Wines of Earth

by Margaret St. Clair

(Originally appeared in the September 1957 issue of *The Magazine of Fantasy and Science Fiction*. It was most recently reprinted in 1985.)

Joe da Valora grew wine in the Napa Valley. The growing of premium wine is never especially profitable in California, and Joe could have made considerably more money if he had raised soybeans or planted his acreage in prunes. The paperwork involved in his occupation was a nightmare to him; he filled out tax and license forms for state and federal governments until he had moments of feeling his soul was made out in triplicate, and he worked hard in the fields too. His son used to ask him why he didn't go into something easier. Sometimes he wondered himself.

But lovers of the vine, like all lovers, are stubborn and unreasonable men. And, as with other lovers, their unreasonableness has its compensations. Joe da Valora got a good deal of satisfaction from the knowledge that he made some of the best Zinfandel in California (the Pinot Noir, his first love, he had had to abandon as not coming to its full excellence in his particular part of the Napa Valley). He vintaged the best of his wine carefully, slaved over the vinification to bring out the wine's full freshness and fruitiness, and had once sold an entire year's product to one of the "big business" wineries, rather than bottling it himself, because he thought it had a faint but objectionable "hot" taste.

Joe da Valora lived alone. His wife was dead, and his son had married a girl who didn't like the country. Often they came to see him on Sundays, and they bought him expensive gifts at Christmas time. Still, his evenings were apt to be long. If he sometimes drank a little too much of his own product, so that he went to bed with the edges of things a bit blurred, it did him no harm. Dry red table wine is a wholesome beverage, and he was never any the worse for it in the morning. On the nights when things needed blurring, he was careful not to touch the vintaged Zinfandel. It was too good a wine to waste on things that had to be blurred.

Early in December, when the vintage was over and the new wine was quietly doing the last of its fermentation in the storage containers, he awoke to the steady drumming of rain on his roof. Well. He'd get caught up on his bookkeeping. He hoped the rain wouldn't be too hard. Eight of his acres were on a hillside, and after every rain he had to do some reterracing.

About eleven, when he was adding up a long column of figures, he felt a sort of soundless jarring in the air. He couldn't tell whether it was real, or whether he had imagined it. Probably the latter. His hearing wasn't any too good these days. He shook his head to clear it, and poured himself a glass of the unvintaged Zinfandel.

After lunch the rain stopped and the sky grew bright. He finished his noon-time glass of wine and started out for a breath of air. As he left the house he realized that he was just a little, little tipsy. Well, that wasn't such a bad way for a vintner to be. He'd go up to the hillside acres and see how they did.

There had been very little soil washing, he saw, inspecting the hillside. The reterracing would be at a minimum. In fact, most of the soil removal he was doing himself, on the soles of his boots. He straightened up, feeling pleased.

Ahead of him on the slope four young people were standing, two men and two girls.

Da Valora felt a twinge of annoyance and alarm. What were they doing here? A vineyard out of leaf isn't attractive, and the hillside was well back from the road. He'd never had any trouble with vandals, only with deer. If these people tramped around on the wet earth, they'd break the terracing down.

As he got within speaking distance of them, one of the girls stepped forward. She had hair of an extraordinary copper-gold, and vivid, intensely turquoise eyes. (The other girl had black hair, and the two men were dark blonds.) Something about the group puzzled da Valora, and then he located it. They were all dressed exactly alike.

"Hello," the girl said.

"Hello," da Valora answered. Now that he was near to them, his anxiety about the vines had left him. It was as if their mere proximity — and he was to experience this effect during all the hours they spent with him — as if their mere proximity both stimulated and soothed his intellect, so that cares and pettinesses dropped away from him, and he moved in a larger air. He seemed to apprehend whatever they said directly, in a deeper way than words are usually apprehended, and with a wonderful naturalness.

"Hello," the girl repeated. "We've come from" — somehow the word escaped

Joe's hearing—"to see the vines."

"Well, now," said Joe, pleased, "have you seen enough of them? This planting is Zinfandel. If you have, we might go through the winery. And then we might sample a little wine."

Yes, they would like to. They would all like that.

They moved beside him in a group, walking lightly and not picking up any of the wet earth on their feet. As they walked along they told him about themselves. They were winegrowers themselves, the four of them, though they seemed so young, in a sort of loose partnership, and they were making a winegrowers' tour of—of—

Again Joe's hearing failed him. But he had the fancy that there would never be any conflict of will among the four of them. Their tastes and wishes would blend like four harmonious voices, the women's high and clear, the men's richer and more deep. Yet it seemed to him that the copper-haired girl was regarded with a certain deference by her companions, and he thought, wisely, that he knew the reason. It was what he had so often told his wife—that when a lady really likes wine, when she really has a palate for it, nobody can beat her judgment. So the others respected her.

He showed them through the winery without shame, without pride. If there were bigger wineries than his in the Napa Valley, there were smaller ones too. And he knew he made good wine.

Back in the house he got out a bottle of his vintaged Zinfandel, the best Zinfandel he had ever made, for them. It wasn't only that they were fellow growers, he also wanted to please them. It was the '51.

As he poured the dark, fragrant stuff into their glasses he said, "What did you say the name of your firm was? Where did you say you were from?"

"It isn't exactly a firm," the dark-haired girl said, laughing. "And you wouldn't know the name of our home star."

Star? Star? Joe da Valora's hand shook so that he dribbled wine outside the glass. But what else had he expected? Hadn't he known from the moment he had seen them standing on the hillside? Of course they were from another star.

"And you're making a tour...?" he asked, putting down the bottle carefully.

"Of the nearer galaxy. We have only a few hours to devote to earth."

They drank. Joe da Valora wasn't surprised when only one of the men, the darker blond, praised the wine with much vigor. No doubt they'd tasted better. He wasn't hurt; they'd never want to hurt him—or at least not much hurt.

Yet as he looked at the four of them sitting around his dining table—so young, so wise, so kind—he was fired with a sudden honorable ambition. If they were only going to be here a few hours, then it was up to him, since nobody else could do it—it was up to him to champion the wines of Earth.

"Have you been to France?" he asked.

"France?" the dark-haired girl answered.

"Wait," he told them, "wait. I'll be back." He went clattering down the cellar stairs.

In the cellar, he hesitated. He had a few bottles of the best Pinot Noir grown in the Napa Valley; and that meant—nobody could question it—the best Pinot Noir grown in California. But which year should he bring? The '43 was the better balanced, feminine, regal, round, and delicate. The '42 was a greater wine, but its inherent imbalance and its age had made it arrive at the state that winemakers call fragile. One bottle of it would be glorious, the next vapid, passé and flat.

In the end, he settled on the '42. He'd take his chances. Just before he left the cellar, he picked up another bottle and carried it up with him. It was something his son had given him a couple of years ago; he'd been saving it for some great occasion. After all, he was championing the wines of *Earth*.

He opened the '42 anxiously. It was too bad he hadn't known about their coming earlier. The burgundy would have benefited by longer contact with the air. But the first whiff of the wine's great nose reassured him; this bottle was going to be all right.

He got clean glasses, the biggest he had, and poured an inch of the wine into them. He watched wordlessly as they took the wine into their mouths, swished it around on their palates, and chewed it, after the fashion of wine-tasters everywhere. The girl with the copper hair kept swirling her glass and inhaling the wine's perfume. He waited tensely for what she would say.

At last she spoke. "Very sound. Very good."

Joe da Valora felt a pang of disappointment whose intensity astonished him. He looked at the girl searchingly. Her face was sad. But she was honest. "Very sound, very good," was all that she could say.

Well, he still had an arrow left in his quiver. Even if it wasn't a California arrow. His hands were trembling as he drew the cork out of the bottle of Romanée-Conti '47 his son had given him. (Where had Harold got it? The wine, da Valora understood, was rare even in France. But the appellation of origin was in order. Harold must have paid a lot for it.)

More glasses. The magnificent perfume of the wine rose to his nose like a promise. Surely this…

There was a long silence. The girl with the dark hair finished her wine and held out her glass for more. At last the other girl said, "A fine wine. Yes, a fine wine."

For a moment Joe da Valora felt he hated her. Her, and the others. Who were these insolent young strangers, to come to Earth, drink the flower, the cream, the very pearl, of Earth's vintages, and dismiss them with so slight a compliment? Joe had been drinking wine all his life. In the hierarchy of fine wines, the Zinfandel he made was a petty princeling; the Pinot '42 was a great lord; but the wine he had just given them to drink was the sovereign, unquestioned emperor. He didn't think it would be possible to grow a better wine on earth.

The girl with the copper-gold hair got up from the table. "Come to our ship," she said. "Please. We want you to taste the wine we make."

Still a little angry, Joe went with them. The sun was still well up, but the sky was getting overcast. It would rain again before night.

The ship was in a hollow behind the hillside vineyard. It was a big silver sphere, flattened at the bottom, that hovered a few feet above the rows of vines. The copper-haired girl took his hand, touched a stud at her belt, and they rose smoothly through the flattened bottom into a sort of foyer. The others followed them.

The ship's interior made little impression on Joe da Valora. He sat down on a chair of some sort and waited while the copper-haired girl went into a pantry and came back with a bottle.

"Our best wine," she said, holding it out for him to see.

The container itself was smaller and squatter than an Earth bottle. From it she poured a wine that was almost brownish. He was impressed by its body even in the glass.

He swirled the wine glass. It seemed to him he smelled violets and hazelnuts, and some other perfume, rich and delicate, whose name he didn't know. He could have been satisfied for a half hour, only inhaling the wine's perfume. At last he sipped at it.

"Oh," he said when he had swished it in his mouth, let it bathe his palate, and slowly trickle down his throat. "Oh."

"We don't make much of it," she said, pouring more into his glass. "The grapes are so hard to grow."

"Thank you," he said. "Now I see why you said, 'A fine wine.'"

"Yes. We're sorry, dear Earth man."

"Don't be sorry," he said, smiling. He felt no sting of inferiority, no shame for Earth. The distance was too great. You couldn't expect Earth vines to grow the wine of paradise.

They were all drinking now, taking the wine in tiny sips, so he saw how precious it was to them. But first one and then the other of them would fill his glass.

The wine was making him bold. He licked his lips, and said, "Cuttings? Could you…give me cuttings? I'd take them to, to the University. To Davis." Even as he spoke he knew how hopeless the words were.

The darker blond man shook his head. "They wouldn't grow on Earth."

The bottle was empty. Once or twice one of the four had gone to a machine and touched buttons and punched tapes on it. He knew they must be getting ready to go.

"Goodby," he said. "Thank you." He held out his hand to them in leave-taking. But all of them, the men too, kissed him lightly and lovingly on the cheek.

"Goodby, dear human man," the girl with the copper hair said. "Goodby, goodby."

He left the ship. He stood at a distance and watched it lift lightly and effortlessly to the height of the trees. There was a pause, while the ship hovered and he wondered anxiously if something had gone wrong. Then the ship descended a few feet and the copper-haired girl jumped lightly out of it. She came running toward him, one of the small, squat bottles in her hand. She held it out to him.

"I can't take it—" he said.

"Oh, yes. You must. We want you to have it." She thrust it into his hands.

She ran back to the ship. It rose again, shimmered, and was gone.

Joe da Valora looked at where the ship had been. The gods had come and gone. Was this how Dionysus had come to the Greeks? Divine, bearing a cargo that was divine? Now that they were gone, he realized how much in love with them he had been.

At last he drew a long sigh. He was where he had always been. His life would go on as it always had. Taxes, licenses, a mountain of paperwork, bad weather, public indifference, the attacks of local-optionists—all would be as it had been. But he had the bottle of wine they had given him. He knew there would never, in all his foreseeable life (he was sixty-five), be an event happy enough to warrant his opening it. But they had given him one of their last three bottles.

He was smiling as he went back to the house.

Afterword by T. D. Cloud

Though this book is full of fantastic SF authors forgotten by the large scope of history, it seems that Margaret St. Clair's contributions to literature as a whole are particularly underrated. St. Clair played jump rope with the boundaries separating genres during her prolific writing career in a way that few authors could. "The Wines of Earth" provides a wonderful example of her myriad interests, combining them all in ways that I scarcely find in fiction today, much less back then. St. Clair was a student of mythology as well as a vocal proponent of feminism, Wicca, and even nudism! It's her love of folklore and myths that come to the forefront in the tale of Joe Da Valora's encounter with extraterrestrial vintners and make it, in my opinion, a worthy addition to the strange mishmash of a genre St. Clair practically made for herself.

The story begins as many do: with an everyman living a life we all can relate to. We accompany Joe (and I feel we must call him by his first name; we can't help but know him by the end of the first page) as his eyes are opened to the vastness of the universe and his small place in it. By the very sweat of his brow and calluses on his hands, we know that he has worked hard for his achievements, the crowning example of which is a Zinfandel so sublime that it must be saved for only the most special of occasions. To a man who has dedicated his life to the humble task of bringing forth beauty from the earth, this wine is the pinnacle of what he knows himself capable of producing.

In much the way I imagine humanity must have felt when Prometheus brought fire to mankind, it is only when we're made cognizant of our limitations that we can truly appreciate when we are offered more. The discovery of a group of space travelers eager to sample his wine encourages Joe to bring out his best, but the finest wine Earth can elicit earn nothing more than a quiet, polite response from beings who are accustomed to growing and making far superior vintages. Our man Joe has the privilege of sampling that wine himself, and is even gifted one of the last three bottles of it before the god-aliens take their leave. Joe sees them off as a changed man, and we, the reader, close the book changed as well.

What's so compelling about St. Clair's "The Wines of Earth" isn't that it's a scifi story that merges wine with alien encounters—it's that it manages to link this story with the wide canon of mythologized tales of gods meeting man, both leaving a little changed from the experience. For a science fiction story about wine and the people who make it—terrestrial and otherwise—it's surprisingly impactful, and I, for one, certainly wish I could have a glass, too.

About the Authors

Dr. Lisa Yaszek ("Games" by Katherine MacLean)

Regents Professor of Science Fiction Studies, at Georgia Tech's School of Literature, Media and Communication, Dr. Lisa Yaszek is one of the foremost scholars on science fiction (and women's participation therein). She literally wrote the book on women in science fiction (*Galactic Suburbia: Recovering Women's Science Fiction*, available from Ohio State University Press) and she edits the *The Future is Female* (Library of America) women's science fiction anthology series.

Andi Dukleth ("Captive Audience" by Anne Warren Griffith)

Inveterate reporter and comic book artist, Andi Dukleth is no stranger to mass media! In addition to being a journalist for several San Diego news outlets, she also has published her art in a number of books, most recently the *Accidental Aliens* anthology series.

Erica Frank ("Gallie's House" by Thelma D. Hamm and "We Move on Turning Stone" by Leah Bodine Drake)

Perhaps best known as the Archivist and frequent writer for the Hugo-Nominated Galactic Journey (galacticjourney.org), Erica Frank offers three decades of experience in the publishing and sf fandom fields, possessed of an encyclopedic knowledge of the contributions of women in the speculative genre over the past century.

Jessica Dickinson Goodman ("The First Day of Spring" by Mari Wolf)

Ms. Dickinson Goodman is a science fiction writer, technologist, and activist in the San Francisco Bay Area. She is currently helping review Star Trek episodes for Galactic Journey, with a focus on history, politics, women, and power. When she's not writing, she can be found recruiting queer volunteers for her community garden, gossiping in Arabic with her friends in the Middle East, and solo-camping across the mountain West.

Christine Sandquist ("The Agony of the Leaves" by Evelyn E. Smith)

Moderator for Reddit's Fantasy subform, assistant to Hugo winner Mary Robinette Kowal, and publicist for Journey Press, Christine Sandquist is one of the vital hubs of modern science fiction fandom. She has also taken an informal crash course in classic women's science fiction, making her uniquely equipped to straddle both eras!

Marie Vibbert ("Two-bit Oracle" by Doris Pitkin Buck)

Marie Vibbert is one of the titans of modern science fiction. Some 50 of her stories have appeared in magazines big and small, along with 20 poems (she was nominated for the Rhysling in 2015). Her first full length novel, *Galactic Hellcats* (Vernacular Books) was released in 2021 to rave reviews.

Cat Rambo ("Change the Sky" by Idris Seabright)

Twice President of the Science Fiction Writers of America, Nebula nominee in 2012, and published in virtually every notable SF mag, Cat Rambo is yet still on an upward trajectory. Their latest book, *You Sexy Thing* (Starscape), just came out Nov. 2021 and had already been dubbed "a thoroughly entertaining sci-fi romp."

Gwyn Conaway ("Miss Quatro" by Alice Eleanor Jones)

Member of Costume Designers Guild Local 892, Gwyn Conaway is considered an authority on the intersection between clothing and social psychology. Look for her science fiction romance series (under the byline "Etta Pierce") as well as her fashion articles for Galactic Journey!

Robin Rose Graves ("The Princess and the Physicist" by Evelyn E. Smith)

Founder of the sf booktube channel: "The Book Wormhole", Robin Rose Graves has published a number of sf short stories and poetry. She is currently hard at work on her first novel, and in her free time, she writes about the original *Star Trek* at Galactic Journey.

Janice L. Newman ("Birthright" by April Smith)

By trade, Janice L. Newman is an author, fusing romance with virtually every speculative genre, from hard science fiction to modern fantasy to fairy tales. Her first book, *At First Contact: Three Stories of Nontraditional Love* (Journey Press), was released Nov. 30, 2021. She is also the editor for Galactic Journey.

Natalie Devitt ("The Piece Thing" by Carol Emshwiller)

We are happy to welcome back Natalie Devitt, a film school graduate with wide knowledge of sci-fi and horror. An accomplished teacher at the high school level, she also covered *The Twilight Zone*, Seasons 4 and 5, as well as all of *The Outer Limits* TV shows for Galactic Journey.

Kerrie Dougherty ("Of Mars and Men: News for Dr. Richardson" by Miriam Allen deFord)

There are few who would be as qualified to cover deFord's scathing rebuttal to Dr. Richardson than Kerrie Dougherty. Recently awarded the Order of Australia for her work in space history, she is the author of a number of scholarly and popular books, articles and blog posts on space history and heritage and space education. She is also the co-author of three Star Wars guidebooks and the *Doctor Who Visual Dictionary*.

Dr. Laura Brodian Freas Beraha ("Woman's Work" by Garen Drussaï)
Laura Brodian Freas Beraha is closely acquainted with the genre, having worked with (and been married to) illustrator legend Frank Kelly Freas. But she is a star in her own right: an author, a pianist, singer with a Doctorate of Music Education. She today teaches dancing in the style of Jane Austen's *Pride & Prejudice*.

Erica Friedman ("Poor Little Saturday" by Madeleine L'Engle)
Erica Friedman is a bonafide cultural icon, perhaps *the* authority in the Western Hemisphere on *yuri* (lesbian relationships) in anime and manga. Her *By Your Side: The First 100 Years of Yuri Anime and Manga* (Journey Press), coming out mid-2022, will be a landmark in the field. She also runs Okazu (okazu.yuricon.com), "The world's oldest and most comprehensive blog on lesbian-themed Japanese cartoons, comics and related media."

Kathryn Heffner ("The Red Wagon" by Jane Roberts)
Currently working toward her PhD in science fiction history at the University of Kent in England, Kathryn Heffner has literally made science fiction fandom her life's work. In her spare time, she has been a librarian and a university engagement ambassador.

Cora Buhlert ("The Queer Ones" by Leigh Brackett)
Several time Hugo nominee for her fan writings Cora Buhlert is also a prolific author. Pegasus Pulp Press publishes her works in a number of genres: from hard-boiled pulp to sword and sandal to science fiction parody. She is also the West German correspondent for Galactic Journey, covering movies, books, and most recently, the terrific *Raumpatrouille Orion* (*Space Patrol Orion*).

Lorelei Esther ("The Canvas Pyramid" by Jane Roberts)
Can anyone be more of a rising star than 17-year old Lorelei Esther? Valedictorian, illustrator for *The Kitra Saga*, comic book artist, writer, singer/songwriter, and much more, she is already setting the world afire. Look for her

art under the lorelei.esther byline on Instagram, and her frequent articles on science fiction topics at Galactic Journey!

Alyssa Winans ("Moonshine" by Ruth M. Goldsmith)

Artist Alyssa Winans has made her mark in the science fiction world with her wonderful book covers, securing the Hugo nomination for best professional artist in both 2020 and 2021. She is also known for her illustrations and game art, clients including Harmonix, FableVision, Tor Books, Tor.com Publishing, Hodder & Stoughton, Cricket Magazine, and the Warner Animation Group. She is currently on the Google Doodle team!

T. D. Cloud ("The Wines of Earth" by Idris Seabright)

Illustrator, graphic designer, and speculative author T. D. Cloud is perhaps best known for the historical knowledge she infuses into her romantic book series. When she's not prodigiously producing novels, she can be found staffing various museums and libraries, applying her knowledge of the past for the general public.

~

The lifeblood of every author is audience feedback. Please consider leaving a review (of whatever length) on Amazon, GoodReads, or your favorite platform.

About the Publisher

Founded in 2019 by Galactic Journey's Gideon Marcus, **Journey Press** publishes the best science fiction, current and classic, with an emphasis on the unusual and the diverse. We also partner with other small presses to offer exciting titles we know you'll like!

Also available from Journey Press:

Rediscovery Vol 1
Science Fiction by Women: 1958-1963

Fourteen selections of the best science fiction of the Silver Age, written by the unsung women authors of yesteryear and introduced by today's rising stars. Curated by the team that produces the Hugo-nominated Galactic Journey.

Join us and rediscover these lost treasures.

I Want the Stars by Tom Purdom
A Timeless Classic

Fleeing a utopian Earth, searching for meaning, Jenorden and his friends take to the stars to save a helpless race from merciless telepathic aliens.

Hugo Finalist Tom Purdom's *I Want the Stars* is one of the first science fiction novels to star a person of color protagonist.

Sibyl Sue Blue by Rosel George Brown
The *Original* Woman Space Detective

Who she is: Sibyl Sue Blue, single mom, undercover detective, and damn good at her job.
What she wants: to solve the mysterious benzale murders, prevent more teenage deaths, and maybe find her long-lost husband.
How she'll get it: seduce a millionaire, catch a ride on his spaceship, and crack the case at the edge of the known galaxy.

CPSIA information can be obtained
at www.ICGtesting.com
Printed in the USA
LVHW031044200322
713908LV00006B/906